The Du Lac Prophecy

Book 4 of The Du Lac Chronicles

Mary Anne Yarde

This novel is entirely a work of fiction. The names, characters and incidents portrayed in it are the work of the author's imagination. Any resemblance to actual persons, living or dead, events or localities is entirely coincidence.

The Du Lac Prophecy has a recommended reading age of 16+

Copyright © 2018 Mary Anne Yarde

Cover Design by BespokeBookCovers.com

ISBN-13: 978-1-7177-4355-8

All rights reserved. No part of this book may be reproduced or transmitted in any form or by any means, electronic, mechanical, photocopying, recording or otherwise without the prior permission of the author.

Scripture quotations taken from

The Holy Bible, New International Version (Anglicised edition)

Copyright © 1979, 1984, 2011 by Biblica (formally International Bible Society).

Used by permission of Hodder & Stoughton Publishers, an Hachette UK company

All rights reserved

'NIV' is a registered trademark of Biblica (formally International Bible Society)

UK trademark number 1448790

The Du Lac Prophecy is written in British English.

Also by Mary Anne Yarde

The Du Lac Chronicles series

The Du Lac Chronicles
The Pitchfork Rebellion (Novella)
The Du Lac Devil
The Du Lac Princess
The Du Lac Prophecy

Place names in the early 6th Century

The Kingdom of Cerniw — Cornwall, England
Trevena — Tintagel, Cornwall, England
Goon Brenn — Bodmin Moor, Cornwall, England

The Kingdom of Dumnonia — Devon, England

The Kingdom of Wessex — Hampshire / Wiltshire / Somerset, England
Hantescire — Hampshire, England

The Isle of Avalon — Glastonbury, Somerset, England
Glastingberie Abbey — Glastonbury Abbey, Somerset, England
We Are Weary All Hill — Wearyall Hill, Glastonbury, Somerset, England

Aquae Sulis — Bath, England

Londinium — London, England

The Foreigners Land — Wales
The Kingdom of Dyfed — Pembrokeshire, Wales

"Do not suppose that I have come to bring peace to the earth. I did not come to bring peace, but a sword."

Matthew 10:34

Chapter 1

Spring AD 501. Benwick Castle. The Kingdom of Brittany.

They said that death was the wages of sin. They also said that eternal life was a gift from God. You die, but once. And then you live forever.

The horses came to a skidding halt. One of the unfortunate animals fell to his knees in exhaustion, his chest heaving, his breath forever broken. But instead of compassion, he received only the sting of a whip and an unforgiving hand as the pull of the reins forced the bit in his mouth to grind against his teeth and cut his gentle lips. But the man who held the horse's life in his hands cared not for the animal's suffering. Instead, he continued to tighten the reins until the poor horse's head was turned towards his heaving stomach at such an ungodly angle that it made breathing almost impossible. The horse who stood next to this poor pathetic beast tripped over the pole that was between them and almost fell over as the coupling rein, which ran from his bit to the draft rein of the horse that was down, dragged against his mouth. He tried to keep his balance, but to do so he had to put one trembling hoof on his fallen stablemate's shoulder.

"Get up," the man who held the reins yelled. He then brought the whip down again and again. Both horses jumped and the one that was standing tried desperately to get away from the whip. The coupling rein gave way and then snapped. The horse that stood, shied and then reared, his ears back and the whites of his eyes showing his fear.

The horse on the ground, so loyal, so desperate to please, tried to scramble back to his feet, but the whip that bloodied his body showed no signs of mercy. The horse screamed in agony, willing this torment to end. The sound was piercing and utterly heartbreaking for the grooms who could do nothing but watch the horror unfold in front of their eyes. The weight of the whip's blows kept the horse from rising and in the end, the horse concluded that it would be better to lie down and die than to get up and live. Abbot Daniel was contemplating the same thing. He coughed, spitting out dirt and blood and bits of broken teeth.

Abbot Daniel, a kindly man who followed the teachings of Jesus to the letter, stood accused of helping a convicted demon worshiper escape justice just before her planned execution by fire. He had, of course, denied the charges. If they had instead asked him if he had helped a woman, who was innocent of the crimes she had been charged with, escape an unjust and cruel death, then that would have been a different matter altogether. But they didn't ask him that.

Mordred Pendragon, with the Church of Rome's consent, had decided to take matters into his own hands and force a confession. Mordred had at first threatened, explaining in detail what he would do to the Abbot if he did not cooperate. But Abbot Daniel had just looked the other way and thought of how the chief priests and the teachers of the law had tried to force a confession from Jesus. Jesus had stood firm and so would he. In anger, Mordred had tied him to the chariot, and then with a heavy hand, he had whipped the two beautiful bay horses into a gallop. Abbot Daniel had lost his footing almost immediately, unable to keep up with the speed of the horses. And then it was just a case of remembering to breathe while he was dragged along the unforgiving earth with as much sympathy as a sack of mouldy grain. His right arm had soon dislocated from its socket, and it wasn't long before the left arm followed. The pain was unimaginable. It was like being torn apart limb by limb.

"Don't just stand there, get me another pair of horses," Mordred demanded, laying his whip one more time upon the horse's bloodied carcass. "I have not finished with him yet."

Abbot Daniel coughed as he tried to clear his throat once again. He wished someone would offer him water to wash away the blood in his mouth, even wine vinegar would not have been unwelcomed, but none was forthcoming. No one even glanced his way. It was as if he didn't exist. He took a moment to catch his breath and then rolled on to his back with difficulty. He had felt his left leg break when Mordred had steered his chariot around an old oak. His leg had hit the tree trunk with an almighty wallop, and he had screamed with the pain of it, but he might as well of stayed silent for no one, apart from God, heard his cry. The pain was unbearable now, and he prayed for strength to get through this trial.

The sun, at that moment, decided to peek out from behind a cloud. Abbot Daniel felt the warmth on his battered face and, with it, he felt God's presence. But then a man's shadow fell over him, blocking out the sun and the sky, but not God. No man could ever take God away from him.

"How's the leg?" Mordred asked, at the same time he stamped upon the shattered bone.

Abbot Daniel screamed, but Mordred just laughed.

"That is enough," Bastian, the general of King Philippe's army, stated with abhorrence as he too came to stand over the Abbot. "You may be able to get away with things like this in Rome, but in Brittany, we tend to stay away from the barbaric."

"Save your sermon, *Cousin,* for I do not want to hear it. The Church and the King asked me to loosen the Abbot's tongue, and that is what I have done. I promise you — I will have a confession from him within the hour."

While these two great men argued, Abbot Daniel closed his eyes and prayed. But he did not pray for himself. There was no point praying for a lost cause. He knew he would die, for he had foreseen his death in a dream and yet he did not fear it. His death would make way for another. And he prayed for that other, for young Sampson would need all the help from God he could get. Sampson would become a beacon of light in the dark days that were sure to follow this one. Abbot Daniel wished that he could see his once student come into his glory, but that was not to be. The Abbot's thoughts then turned to the woman he had helped to escape. He prayed that she would reach her destination safely. He prayed that she would overcome her terrible suffering and live a long and happy life with the man she loved. If she didn't, then his sacrifice was for naught.

Mordred and Bastian's conversation became more heated. But the Abbot didn't notice as he lost himself in familiar prayers that pushed his pain aside and brought him comfort. It was only when Mordred spat into his face that he remembered where he was, but he did not open his eyes. Let him spit, let him do his worst, for he would endure everything that Mordred could think to throw at him.

Abbot Daniel knew in his heart that he had done the right thing. He took comfort in the words of Peter, *"For it is better, if it is God's will, to suffer for doing good than for doing evil."* Lady Amandine had been falsely accused and he could not, he would not, let them burn her. How could he stand in front of his congregation, how could he stand in front of God, if he did not take a stand against such atrocities? But that did not mean he wanted to admit to the crime, for there were others who also helped her escape.

The man who had planned Lady Amandine's escape was a ghost. He was supposed to be dead. Abbot Daniel had been shocked to see Merton du Lac standing in the Chapter House very much alive. Merton had got down on his knees and begged for the Abbot to save the woman that he loved. Abbot Daniel had felt overwhelmed, and he had taken a seat and looked at Merton with disbelief.

"How?" He had uttered the word with confusion as he looked upon Merton's scarred face and broken body. Merton had been publicly tortured when Philippe took the throne from Merton's brother. No man could survive the abuse he had endured. Everyone had thought he had died. There had even been a body in the dungeons. Everyone had assumed it was Merton's.

"Me," Sampson had said as he came out of the shadows.

Abbot Daniel had shaken his head in wonder and smiled. He should have known. If a miracle were needed, then you could always count on Brother Sampson to deliver.

"I am not in agreement with this foolishness," Brother Sampson had stated, getting straight to the point. "We cannot go against the Church. The Church has condemned her and so must we. I am sorry, but I will not risk my life for Lady Amandine."

Abbot Daniel would never forget the look on Merton's face when he heard Sampson's words. Merton looked as if all remaining hope had been cruelly snatched from him. He was like a drowning man who asked only for a rope to be thrown, but instead, was told to learn how to swim and then left to drown.

"Please," Merton had begged with tears in his eyes. "Don't let them kill her. Please…"

"You are asking us to risk our lives," Sampson had answered Merton sharply as if he was reprimanding him. "Are our lives less worthy than hers?"

"We are servants of God," Abbot Daniel had replied with a frown. This wasn't the man he knew. He had never known Brother Sampson to put his own welfare above others before. "You forget, Brother Sampson, what our purpose is in this life." Abbot Daniel had risen to his feet and crossed to where the monk stood. "We are here to serve. We are here to be a voice for the weak and the oppressed. We are here to help those who are chained in the dark to see the light." He had placed his hand on the young monk's shoulder and looked into his face. "You are trembling? What is it that has made you so afraid?"

Brother Sampson had shook his head, and for a moment it looked as if he would not speak. "I cannot feel God here," Sampson had finally admitted. His face had showed not only shame at such a confession, but also fear. "There is too much pain, too much sorrow. He has gone from this kingdom. I cannot stand it. All I can feel is despair. I cannot protect anyone here. I have never felt so powerless."

Abbot Daniel had let go of the monk and he had taken a step back, although his eyes had not wavered from Sampson's face.

"God isn't with you?" Merton had asked, his voice sounded brittle, and Abbot Daniel had turned to look at him. "But God is always with you. That's why—"

"That is why you wanted me to come. I know that is why. But that is what I have been trying to tell you," Sampson had stated. "It started on the road to Cerniw, I felt his guidance slip from my grasp, and I felt myself becoming something I am not. I became judgemental. I saw faults whereas before I always looked for the good in people. When I stayed in that pagan woman's house for the night, I felt as if God were sand and no matter how hard I tried to hold onto him he just kept slipping through my fingers. And then on the boat as we made our way here, it was as if the farther we travelled away from Briton, the farther God was from me. I fear God is trying to warn us. I fear that God does not want us to rescue Lady Amandine."

"You cannot think to let them burn her?" Merton's voice had been barely above a whisper. "You saved my life—"

"That is true," Sampson had interrupted. "I saved your life, but only because God told me to. God has said nothing to me about Lady Amandine. He does not want this. That is why God is not with me. I am blind without his guidance. It is like going into battle without any weapons. Only a fool would do such a thing. You wouldn't do such a thing—"

"I went into battle without any weapons," Merton had contradicted. "The day Philippe did this to me. I took on an army."

"But you were fearless," Sampson had stated. "And you were reckless. You were The Devil."

"The Devil was the name others gave me. It didn't make me fearless." Merton had scoffed. "No man is fearless. I was terrified. But I did what I had to do. I fought because my brother needed me. Amandine needed me. And now I need you. I cannot live without her. I will not live without her. If she dies, I die."

"What sentimental nonsense you speak. As if I would let you die," Sampson had stated with surprising passion. "Lady Amandine's path does not run alongside yours. It is God's will that she dies."

"God's will?" Merton had asked with a quiet rage. "Have you ever stopped to ask yourself whether it is *God's* will or *man's* will? Or maybe it is *your* will. I, for one, do not believe that it is God's — so do not blame him for your shortcomings. I am not going to let them kill her. I cannot."

"Neither am I," Abbot Daniel had agreed. "Brother Sampson, Lady Amandine does not deserve to die on a pyre. If you want my opinion, I do not think anyone does. Death by fire is nothing more than a spectacle for the evil pleasures of man.

"I will help you save her, Merton. She is going to be so overjoyed when she discovers that you are alive. She never forsook you. Not once. Not in her heart. No matter what they did to her. No matter what they said. No matter what *I* said, for that matter. My predecessor made her speak words of condemnation, but I could see in her eyes that she did not mean what she said. Merton, you lost your way, and I can see your scars and I witnessed your abuse, but it is Amandine who has ultimately paid for your mistakes."

"Alan has told me of what she has endured," Merton had replied as a lone tear slid down his scarred cheek. "You call yourselves men of God, but I cannot recall in any of the teachings of Jesus the part where he sanctioned abuse. What your predecessor did to her…"

Merton had shaken his head in disbelief.

"The late Abbot was a wolf in sheep's clothing. He did not worship God. He worshipped himself as well as gold and false idols. Tell me, what do you propose?" Abbot Daniel had asked, his gaze not wavering from Merton's scarred face.

"I was told you are going to give her religious counsel before they come…" Merton had coughed to clear the lump that had formed in his throat. "…before they come for her. I thought if Sampson were to dress up as Sister Mary Elizabeth—"

"FOR THE LAST TIME, I AM NOT DRESSING UP AS A NUN," Sampson had exploded with rage. "Can you see now, Daniel, why I am against it?"

For a moment Abbot Daniel had been lost for words, for never had he seen Sampson lose his temper before. "You are asking us to lie?" Abbot Daniel had finally addressed Merton "What you ask, we cannot do."

"You cannot lie?" Merton had scoffed as he looked at Sampson.

Abbot Daniel had followed Merton's gaze. He saw Sampson's face heat in embarrassment, and he had wondered at it.

"But you are more than happy to acquit the guilty and condemn the innocent?" Merton had asked, looking back into the Abbot's face as he did so. "Does that not make you all liars? And here I was thinking God detests a lying tongue? I was accused of being a demon — one of Satan's own — and you stood by and did nothing while Philippe tortured me. I am like this because of your silence. Do you really think that is what God wanted? If he did, would he have not told you to leave me alone to die?" he had turned his attention back to Sampson. "Amandine is no demon worshipper, unless you think her love for me, a mortal man — a man that God asked you to save — makes her so. It was bad enough that you did nothing while I was being beaten, but to stand by and watch as Amandine is burnt to death…" Merton had choked on these words, and he had taken a long moment to compose himself. "Do you really think that God will judge you for wearing a woman's clothing?"

"It is written," Sampson had stated.

"So it must be true. I think God will judge you more by your inactions. Unless, of course, you want her to die—"

"Of course we do not want her to die," Sampson had argued. "But what you ask of us is impossible. The laws of God are laws for a reason. I know I lied to you about the severity of the injury to your back, but I did so for your own good, for you were not well enough to hear the truth—"

"You told me I was cursed," Merton had reminded him, his voice scathing.

"Sampson?" The Abbot had questioned in shock. "You lied?"

"The Church has condemned her. We are part of that Church, we cannot go against their judgement," Sampson had stated, ignoring the Abbot's question.

"The Church's judgement?" Merton had spat out the words. "You are such a bunch of hypocrites. You only follow the teaching of Jesus when it pleases you."

"The Church is the Church. The Church is God's will. Amandine must die because it is God's will," Sampson had stated.

"Then your God is no better than the Devil."

"How dare you speak so IN GOD'S HOLY HOUSE. GET OUT," Sampson had raised his voice until he was screaming the words. He had wiped the spittle from his mouth with the back of his hand and pointed towards the door. "I AM DONE WITH YOU AND YOUR VILE PRESENCE. BE GONE FROM MY SIGHT. I WISH NOW THAT I HAD LET YOU DIE…" Sampson, realising what he had said, had stopped speaking abruptly, and he had stared at Merton with undisguised shock. "I didn't…I didn't mean that. I'm…I don't wish that…"

"Jesus who was everything that was good, would not have allowed another to take his place on the cross," Abbot Daniel had said. "Instead, he sacrificed himself so that all sinners would find forgiveness."

"I would gladly take her place, if that is what you are asking," Merton had answered.

"No, that is not what I am asking. That is not what I am asking at all. Jesus never turned anybody away if they were in need. He cared nothing for rank or occupation. He was not interested in past deeds. Innocence was not a prerequisite. Think of all those people that he set free from the burden of their sins by offering something as simple as unconditional love. It breaks my heart when I think of all he suffered because of us," the Abbot had shook his head as he spoke. "Jesus showed us the right way to live. And yet here we are. Still debating about right and wrong. Brother Sampson, I don't know about you, but I do not preach from the pulpit about forgiveness and mercy only to ignore my sermon when I step out of the church. I speak what is in my heart and what I truly believe. I do not preach the doctrine of Rome if I do not agree with their words. You called us hypocrites, Merton, but I can assure you I am not. And as for God abandoning you," he had turned his attention back to Sampson. "I believe that is utter nonsense. God is with you, my son. He has not left you. But you are so afraid of your own demise that you would turn away from him and then have the audacity to pretend that it is *he* who has turned away from you. God turns away from no one. He never shuts the door in anyone's face. Never."

"Then why can't I feel him?" Sampson had asked, his voice breaking with emotion.

"Because you are dragging your feet when God is trying to hurry you along. You are acting like a reluctant toddler who no longer wants to walk and is instead raising his arms and demanding to be carried. God, like any caring parent, has bent down and picked you up and yet you are still complaining that your feet hurt. Think on this, if God did not want us to save Lady Amandine, then he would not have spared Merton in the first place. I cannot command you to help Merton rescue Amandine, but I will do everything in my power to liberate her, even if that means I have to dress up as a nun myself because I truly believe that is what God wants and Amandine is, I think we all agree, innocent."

"If you are caught, you could die?" A tear had trickled down Sampson's face as he spoke these words. "You are too important to the people of Brittany to risk your life for one insignificant soul. I am too important—"

"You are too important? Was *Jesus* too important?" Abbot Daniel had smiled at the confusion in Sampson's face. "When in doubt, ask yourself this, what would Jesus do? Would he condone burning an innocent woman? No. I do not believe he would. He would have done everything in his power to free her. But he is not here, so it falls to us to act as he would. God is watching us, Brother Sampson. He will forgive us of this small indiscretion, and if he does not, then I will say I coerced you. Your soul will always be safe, for it is in my keeping."

***

Abbot Daniel did not regret his choice. How could he refuse such a desperate plea, even though he knew what it would mean for him? He would never forget Merton begging him to help save the woman he loved... Never. No wonder Amandine had been so stubborn in her refusal to denounce Merton as the Devil. It all made sense now. She was as willing to die for him as he was for her. How brave they both were to risk falling in love when everything and everyone was against them. He fleetingly wished that he had felt a love such as theirs. But now was not the time for regrets. Now was the time to make sure his mouth remained closed so that he would take the names of those involved in Amandine's rescue to the grave. It was for the best that he lied — he was sure God would understand. He *knew* God would understand. Not that his lies mattered. Mordred wasn't interested in the truth, anyway.

"The King says to bring him," King Philippe's Herald stated, with a look of disgust on his face that he did nothing to conceal.

Mordred swore and threw the whip at the Abbot. He did not take kindly to his sport being interrupted.

"It must be your lucky day," Mordred growled as he pulled out a vicious-looking knife and cut the rope that attached the Abbot to the chariot. "But don't worry, I haven't finished with you yet. We can come out to play again later..." Mordred grinned and then he made his way back to the castle, whistling merrily to himself as he did so. The servants scattered, like a flock of frightened sheep, as he approached them, before regathering to whisper to each other. Whereas the Breton soldiers, who had witnessed the event, looked on with both fear and contempt.

As soon as Mordred was out of sight the grooms rushed to the horses, they did not speak, but their faces told everything as they tried to calm the beast that was still alive. They unstrapped him from the chariot and led him away, although one groom stayed behind and he sat down at the dead horse's head and openly wept. A good horse had died this day and for what? To appease a madman's temper? Surely that was in itself a crime?

Two soldiers helped the Abbot to his feet. He cried out as he tried to take his weight on his broken leg. He felt lightheaded and dizzy. The world came in and out of focus. It was like living in a dream. A nightmare. Abbot Daniel would have collapsed back onto the unforgiving earth if the soldiers had not held him so tightly. They kept him on his feet and, for that, he was grateful.

"Drink, drink," Bastian encouraged as he held his wine skin to the Abbot's lips.

No wine vinegar for him. The weak ale trickled down his parched throat and chased the dirt and the blood away.

"I am so sorry," Bastian said. "I had no idea this was where it would…" he left the rest unsaid, for what could he say in the sight of such cruelty. He was as responsible for Amandine's escape as the Abbot, but it was the Abbot that was taking the beating for them all.

"I will kill him, I swear it," one of the soldiers, who was holding the Abbot up, promised under his breath. For everyone liked Abbot Daniel. He was a good man. Everyone said so. No one believed that he had committed the crime he stood accused of. This was a mockery of justice and the law. "How dare he do this to you. I will kill him. I will find a way—"

"No," the Abbot insisted weakly. "Do not think to avenge me. Mordred is my cross to bear. I do not need any help to carry him. Do not risk your life for me, I do not ask you to, and I do not want you to. For Christ taught us forgiveness. I had forgiven Mordred even before he had thought to beat me…"

"You are too generous," the soldier stated. "Far too generous."

"I will not stay here," the other soldier said, his voice, like his comrade's, filled with emotion. "I'll not be a part of this, and I will not take orders from that butcher."

"Shh, my child," the Abbot soothed, although his voice shook with pain and fear. For although he was not afraid of death, he did fear how he would die. He saw a pyre in his immediate future for Mordred had promised, and he wasn't the sort of man to go back on his words. "The prophecy has not yet come to pass. You must stay and see this through to the end."

"The dragon is here. The dragon is on the throne," Bastian replied, shaking his head at the cruelty of fate and how it destroyed good men while rewarding the bad. He knew the men he commanded were threatening mutiny and if he did not contain them, then he too would find himself tied to a chariot, but everything these two soldiers had said was the truth. Bastian had made a mistake. He knew that. He had chosen the wrong side. He should have stood with the du Lacs and refused to be seduced by the whispered words of a pretender. If only he had stayed loyal, then none of this would have happened. But it was too late for regrets. Much too late.

"Philippe is not the dragon," Abbot Daniel contradicted. "Mordred is. And besides, the prophecy does not end with the coming of the dragon. Don't you understand? It concludes with the death of it." The Abbot began to cough again, and Bastian once more held the wineskin to his mouth.

"If Mordred is the dragon, then there will be no death. No end. Many have tried to take his life, but he still lives," Bastian said when the Abbot finished drinking.

"There is always an end. Keep the faith. Truth always conquers lies. Love always conquers hate," Abbot Daniel spoke with years of wisdom.

"Not always," Bastian stated grimly. "Not always…"

Chapter 2

King Philippe of Brittany looked upon the nobles who had gathered in his Great Hall to hear Abbot Daniel confess his sins. The nobles reminded him of a flock of red kites, who were waiting with beady black eyes to peck clean the bones of a good and godly man. They knew not what compassion was. They looked only to what his death would mean to them. And how they could gain financially from his demise. Jesus had been right. The rich would never make it to Heaven.

His gaze lingered on Lord Madec and Lord Prigent. He should have sentenced them to death weeks ago. They were troublemakers. They were traitors. Instead, he had given them, what he had hoped, enough rope to hang themselves. But no matter how much rope he threw their way, they somehow managed to elude death.

Lord Madec, sensing that he was being observed, turned to look at the King. He bowed his head, somewhat mockingly, and turned back to his conversation. Lord Madec laughed at something Lord Prigent said, and everyone turned to look at them. Philippe longed to speak out and ask Lord Madec what he and Lord Prigent found so amusing, but he feared that if he did, he would not like the answer. No man liked being made a fool of, and Philippe was no exception.

Mordred walked into the Hall, still whistling, and everyone fell silent. Mordred was splattered with blood, which made his presence more foreboding than usual. If death could take on a form, Philippe fancied that it would come in the disguise of Mordred Pendragon.

How he hated him. How he feared him.

"Did he confess?" Archbishop Verus asked with eager eyes.

Philippe felt a cold knot of panic settle in his chest as he waited for Mordred to speak. He gave a quick prayer to God that Abbot Daniel had not only kept his nerve but, more importantly, kept his mouth shut.

Mordred sat himself down at a table and pulled out his knife. He looked scathingly at a bowl of fruit that had been placed on the table, and then with a swiftness of hand he stabbed an apple. "Not yet," he said, and he bit into the apple. "But I promise you," he spoke as he chewed, "it will not be long. He will confess."

Philippe stopped himself from sighing his relief. The Abbot was a stronger man than he had first thought.

"He cannot confess to a crime he did not commit," Brother Jagu stated, stepping towards the throne. "Sire, I beg you in the name of our Lord Jesus, let our Abbot go free. He is innocent of the crimes he stands accused of."

"Hold your tongue, Brother Jagu. Mordred will decide if the Abbot is guilty or not. Your opinion has not been asked for, and your words are not welcomed. Go back to the monastery and await me there," Archbishop Verus ordered with a sneer.

"Sire, please," Brother Jagu begged, ignoring the Archbishop.

"He will confess," Mordred said again. "If I were you, I would put as much distance between the Abbot and yourself as possible. Your defence of him is admirable, but it is unnecessary. He is a traitor."

"Not until proven guilty," Brother Jagu insisted. "Sire—"

"I told you to go back to the monastery," Archbishop Verus stated, his voice like ice. "If you think to disobey me, it will end very badly for you."

Brother Jagu shook his head ever so slightly, his eyes beseeching Philippe's for assistance.

Philippe's expression did not alter. He could do nothing for the Abbot, and it would go against him if he dared to stand with the monk.

"Go back to the monastery. I will send word once we have Abbot Daniel's confession," Philippe promised. He wished he could say what was truly in his heart, but he could not. The Abbot's life was already forfeit, and there was nothing he could do to change the outcome.

"But he has done nothing wrong," Brother Jagu persisted.

"He is a traitor and will die as such," Lord Madec stated with mockery.

"He interfered with justice," Lord Prigent agreed.

"Burn him," cried another and soon others took up the call until it became a chant.

"Please, please. Do not condemn until we have gathered all the evidence," Brother Jagu pleaded.

"I saw him," another noble shouted. "I saw him jump from a window. I alerted the soldiers. He is guilty."

"You saw him jump from a window?" Brother Jagu asked with a hint of mockery. "You saw the Abbot jump from a window? Abbot Daniel is an old man, long gone are his days of jumping from windows. Your eyes deceived you."

"I know what I saw. It was the Abbot. He took justice into his own hands. He must be punished."

"I saw him too," Lord Madec stated. "He was holding the hand of Lady Amandine as if she were his lover. I saw them running for the harbour."

You lying bastard, Philippe thought, but he did not say anything as he watched this nightmare play out in front of him as if it were an elaborate story made up by a bard.

"A false witness will not go unpunished, and whoever pours out lies will not go free," Brother Jagu quoted the sacred book, but his words did nothing to curb the tongues of the nobles.

"I saw him fornicating with her," Lord Prigent added with a hint of malice.

"He is evil."

"He is a liar."

"I saw him too, running with a woman and then they fell upon the grass like a pair of animals."

"I saw him as well, with his habit around his waist."

"Burn him."

"You shall not give false testimony against your neighbour," Brother Jagu cried with desperation, but still the accusations kept coming, and nothing he could say would stop them.

"He will be found guilty even if he isn't…" Brother Jagu's words tapered off as he realised the truth. He looked at Philippe and shook his head in disbelief.

"For the last time, go back to the monastery," Archbishop Verus stated between his teeth. "I will deal with you later."

"He is innocent of the crimes he stands accused of," Brother Jagu stated. "Nothing you say will ever convince me otherwise. He is being used as a scape-goat—"

"I said get out," Archbishop Verus yelled.

"With their mouths the godless destroy their neighbours," Brother Jagu stated with an air of disbelieving horror at the events that were unfolding before him. "Never forget that *the cruel bring ruin on themselves."* He lowered his head so no one would see the tears that he cried.

The nobles were not at all perturbed by his words, and they heckled him as he made his way out of the Hall.

Brother Jagu paused when he reached the door, and Philippe wondered if the monk was going to turn around and say more. But he didn't. He opened the door and carried on walking.

With the monk's departure, the nobles became even more vocal in their condemnation, and their stories about the Abbot became even more fantastical. In a matter of minutes, the Abbot was convicted by acclamation. It mattered not what the Abbot said in his defence. The vote had been cast. Who needed a confession anyway?

***

The Great Hall of Benwick Castle fell silent as the Abbot was brought forward. Weak with exhaustion and pain the Abbot raised his head slowly and looked at the King. Their eyes connected for the fleetest of seconds and then the Abbot lowered his gaze.

Philippe looked back with shock and horror, but he quickly schooled his features to one of indifference. Best not to let anyone see that he cared.

The soldiers lowered the Abbot onto the reed-covered floor with care, although the Abbot still cried out in pain as they did so. The soldiers then took a reluctant step back and left their dearly loved Abbot to his fate, for there was nothing else that they could do except to pray to God that the King would be generous.

Philippe took a moment to compose himself, and as he did so he looked into the faces of his nobles. He saw in their expressions triumph, gloating, ridicule, hatred, greed, and pleasure. He saw all of this and more. And no wonder. The Abbot had been a champion of the common man, and the rich never liked being slighted. There were only a handful of nobles that looked disturbed by what they were witnessing. But no one dared to voice their disgust at the Abbot's treatment. There were too many soldiers from Rome in this Hall to risk losing their tongue, or their lives because they dared to have an opinion that differed from Mordred's. Like them, Philippe too erred on the side of caution. He had no idea where all these Roman soldiers came from. They had not been here at the start of the day, but they were certainly here now and in a far greater number than he was comfortable with. The red of their uniforms was quite a contrast to the blue that the Breton soldiers wore. He dared not think what their presence meant. But he felt a cold shiver travel down his spine all the same.

With reluctance, Philippe stood up and crossed to where the Abbot sat in a growing pool of his own blood. He certainly was a wretched sight to behold, and Philippe blinked back tears. The Abbot had been a friend and now look where their friendship had led. It broke his heart to look upon the Abbot, just like it had broken his heart when he had signed Amandine's death warrant. Being a king wasn't easy, he had never been under any illusion that it would be, but no one had ever told him it would be this hard either. No one had told him about the many sacrifices he would have to make. Or how his decisions would affect the people that he cared about. He had been so naive. Seeing only power, riches, and respect. He had been such a fool. Such an arrogant, ignorant, young fool. He knew now that he was far too young to wear a crown that didn't fit — that would never fit.

Philippe was very conscious that all eyes were upon him. It was an uncomfortable sensation. It was as if he was the one being judged and not the Abbot. He tried to shake off such a notion. He was the king and therefore beyond suspicion, although he sensed that the next few moments of his life would be scrutinized and gossiped about for many moons to come. He wanted to turn around and shout at his nobles and ask them that if they thought they could do better then, by all means, take the throne. He didn't want it anymore. He just wanted things to go back to how they were. A fanciful dream for a man who, on the face of it, had got everything he had ever wanted.

"Tell me the truth, and I will spare your life," Philippe heard himself promise as he looked down at the Abbot. He was surprised that his voice sounded normal. It was even a little condescending. He was becoming good at not displaying his true feelings. He was becoming good at playing the game of kingship and power. How he hated himself for that.

The promise he made to the Abbot was an empty one. Nothing could save the Abbot's life now. Nothing. Blood continued to pour from the Abbot's many wounds. It was only a matter of time. Mordred had done his worst. The Abbot would be dead by sunset if not before. He had lost too much blood to survive for long.

Philippe wished he could look away, he wished that he did not have to witness Abbot Daniel's fall from grace, but someone had to take the blame for such utter incompetence. Better the Abbot than him.

Amandine du Lac had escaped justice just moments before her execution, and no one knew how she had done it. She had been in a locked chamber, and there had been two heavily armed soldiers guarding the door. Amandine had been in her room when Abbot Daniel and Sister Mary Elizabeth had entered to listen to her last confession. But between them leaving, and the soldiers opening the door to escort her to her death, Amandine had escaped. Some wild rumours were flying around the court about how she had managed it. It was said that the Devil had rescued her. Being so much in the Devil's favour was why she was going to be burnt on the pyre in the first place. Fire would burn the Devil out of her — that was what the wise men from the Church of Rome said. They were doing her a good deed by ordering her execution to be carried out in such a way. She should have been grateful. She should have welcomed the verdict. She should have been pleased and accepted her fate with dignity. But she was a du Lac. They should have known she wouldn't go to the grave quietly. The du Lacs never did.

Philippe would have been more than happy to run with this theory. But it was not to be, for Mordred would not allow it. Like a hunting dog with his nose to the ground, Mordred picked up the scent and gathered the evidence. He presented it with much ceremony a mere two hours after Amandine had escaped. He had stated in no uncertain terms that the soldiers who guarded her door, the Abbot, and the Sister, had collaborated to rescue Lady Amandine from justice. The Abbot had pretended outrage at being thus accused and he, like the soldiers, vehemently denied any hand in her escape. But then they would. No one goes to the stake pleading their guilt. As for Sister Mary Elizabeth, there was no sign of her. Philippe was not surprised although he did not show it. How can you find someone who was never there in the first place?

When the alarm bell had rung, and a voice had cried, *"The prisoner's escaped. The prisoner's escaped."* Philippe had risen from his throne in apparent amazement, and like everyone else, he ran outside. He had immediately summoned his horse and his knights.

With Mordred and his knights by his side, they had galloped out of the castle. The peasantry was still making their way down to the beach to witness Amandine's death, and some of them had not moved fast enough when the horses had stampeded towards them. Philippe had tried to pull his horse up, for it was not in his nature to murder indiscriminately, but Mordred had no such care. What did it matter if a couple of peasants died under the hooves of a hundred knights? They bred like rabbits anyway. They were very easy to replace.

"MERCENARIES! SIRE! MERCENARIES!" a soldier had yelled as he staggered towards them. He was holding his arm at a very peculiar angle, and the front of his tunic was dripping blood. "Mercenaries," he cried again as he fell to his knees. "Saxon mercenaries," the man muttered with despair. Mordred had kicked his horse on and rode over the soldier who had shown such courage, and had endured such hardship, to deliver his message.

Philippe had kicked his horse on too, although he had glanced back briefly at the dead soldier. And, not for the first time, he wondered what had made Mordred so devoid of compassion and decency.

When they stormed the harbour, they had all pulled their horses up short and stared in disbelief at the carnage before them. A few of the horses had whinnied with terror, and all of them had fidgeted on their feet, for they smelt blood in the air. Philippe had cursed softly under his breath. Those who had been ordered to guard the harbour were dead. Two gulls tugged unmercifully at a man's innards that had spilled out of his body, and another was pecking out the eyes of the so recently departed. Above them more gulls and other such opportunist flew, calling to each other about the feast down below.

Philippe had to fight back the bile as he looked upon the carnage. It was a sickening sight to behold and one he had not expected.

"Why did no one ring the warning bell?" Philippe asked, trying to distract himself from the sight before him, but he answered his own question when he turned his horse towards the harbour master's house. There in the doorway lay a soldier. An arrow was protruding from his back. The warning bell was just out of his reach.

The bastards who had attacked the harbour were not ordinary mercenaries — any fool could see that. The mercenaries had lost only one of their comrades compared to the many Breton soldiers who had guarded the harbour. There must have been a hundred Saxons to reap such devastation.

In a characteristic fit of rage, Mordred had beheaded the dead Saxon. He held his head up for all to see and then he threw it into the sea. The head bobbed on the current for just a moment before it sunk into the inky darkness to become food for the fish.

"To the boats," Mordred had yelled. At the same time, he had pointed at a boat that was sailing towards the horizon.

Philippe had turned to look at the boat, shielding his eyes with his hand against the glare of the sun. That was the boat Amandine was on. Philippe would bet money on it. They had come for her. Merton's men. They had come. He silently prayed for those on her boat to row faster because, despite the slaughter of his men, he had no wish to see Amandine burn on a pyre. No wish at all…

As much as he prayed Amandine would escape he had to agree when Mordred had commanded the soldiers to bring Amandine back. Alive preferably. She could not be burnt alive on a pyre if she were dead. But whoever it was who had rescued Amandine had thought of everything. They had taken the oars. Every last one of them. The boats were useless. Philippe had to fake a cough to cover up his laugh. If he didn't know better, he would say Merton du Lac had planned this escape. It had his signature to it. But that was impossible — Merton was dead. Philippe tried his best not to think of Merton. He had never thought himself capable of the things he had done to Merton that day. But he had wanted the crown of Brittany so very much. He should have listened to those who said Merton's men would one day have their revenge. He should have heeded the warning. Merton's men had come seeking vengeance, and by the looks of it, they had it.

Chapter 3

Abbot Daniel's breathing was becoming more erratic. This kind and gentle man was practically naked, so torn were his clothes. He was also covered in blood from head to foot. The Abbot could not look more wretched, but he was far from defeated. And Philippe secretly applauded the monk's bravery while he cringed at his own cowardliness. Philippe knew how Amandine had escaped her chamber. He knew. He had allowed it to happen because he was in love with her. And the Abbot knew that he knew. The Abbot's silence was all that was keeping Philippe on his throne, for if the truth were out then Mordred Pendragon would kill him — that is if the Church did not get there first.

The sound of a knife being scraped along a whetstone captured Philippe's attention, and his gaze sought Mordred's. Mordred glowered back and continued to sharpen his blade, the sound was threatening. Menacing. Philippe was the first to look away, and he felt like a submissive dog. Damn the man. But Mordred was the Kingmaker. He had helped Philippe topple his cousin, Budic Du Lac, from the throne of Brittany. If it were not for Mordred, Philippe would still be fawning over that incompetent bastard. How he wished he still were.

He took a chance and glanced back into Mordred's face. Mordred's eyes shone with anger, but also a perverse sort of pleasure. It was almost as if Mordred had wanted this to happen. It was almost as if he had planned it.

"Another circuit with the horses should loosen his tongue," Mordred stated, the blood of his Roman ancestors still pumping through his veins. Philippe feared that it would take more than one death to satisfy Mordred's bloodlust this day.

"Another circuit would silence his tongue forever," Philippe disagreed, but then he realised that maybe he was too hasty in dismissing Mordred's suggestion. Dead men were not known for sharing secrets. But Abbot Daniel had been a good friend, a wise counsel. The least he could do was to offer the poor man a peaceful death.

Philippe reluctantly knelt down on one knee next to the bleeding Abbot. He disliked getting his clothes creased or dirty at the best of times but needs must, and the Devil had the whip which wasn't a bad connotation, considering…. "I will ask you one more time. How did Lady Amandine escape? Tell me the truth, and I will make this all stop. I will return you to your monks, and we can forget this ever happened. Just tell me, it is alright, I promise." He spoke these words for the audience, but he was confident that the Abbot would hold his tongue. But he foolishly hoped that the Abbot could come up with a plausible story that would be believed and then he wouldn't die on a pyre. Instead, the Abbot could die peacefully in a soft bed with the air smelling of incense and the prayers of his monks helping to ease his way.

The Abbot raised his head and looked at Philippe with frightened, pain-filled eyes. He looked every bit the sacrificial lamb.

"I did help her escape," the Abbot admitted, much to Philippe's shock and surprise.

The nobles gasped at such a confession, and even those who had had their doubts now stated that they had suspected all along that the Abbot was guilty.

"Devil worshiper," Lord Madec called out before spitting on the ground in disgust.

"I helped her. No one else. Just me." The Abbot said faintly. He closed his eyes and lowered his head as if his guilt was too heavy a burden to bear.

While the nobles digested this new piece of delicious intrigue, Philippe had continued to stare at the Abbot with disbelief. Abbot Daniel was beyond mercy now. His confession meant his death would be horrific. No monks. No bed. No gentle passing.

"Why?" Philippe whispered back, confident that his voice would not be heard over the noise of the nobles' gossip and condemnation.

"We are but sheep in the midst of wolves. I have given them what they want and besides, it is the truth, and well you know it." Abbot Daniel's voice was scarcely above a whisper. Philippe had to bend closer to hear him.

"Leave me now," Abbot Daniel ordered, his words were becoming harder to decipher as the blood continued to flow from his body. "Let the wolves come. Let them feast…"

Philippe breathed out unsteadily. He couldn't stand much more of this. He slowly rose to his feet as if he were an old man rather than a young one of two and twenty. The nobles' words and curses were lost to him as he looked down at the Abbot. His heart screamed no at what was to come next, but there was nothing he could do about it. Despite being the King of Brittany, he was powerless. He ruled in name only — that is what it felt like, anyway.

"I do not believe you acted alone. Who helped you? Was it Sister Mary Elizabeth?" Archbishop Verus asked with anger as he stormed across the Hall and pushed Philippe aside. He looked at the Abbot with contempt.

The Abbot scoffed softly, but he did not raise his head "Sister Mary Elizabeth never left Rome," he looked briefly at the Archbishop as he spoke.

"What did you say? I cannot hear you. Where is she? What have you done to her?"

Abbot Daniel breathed out shakily but did not answer. It was too taxing now for him to sit up, so he laid himself down on the floor of Benwick's Great Hall, surrounded by the smell of his own blood and the hum of his enemies.

"She possessed you, didn't she?" Archbishop Verus stated, taking a hasty step back in case evil was catching. "Lady Amandine poisoned you with her dark venom. Admit it. You killed Sister Mary Elizabeth so that Lady Amandine could escape. Search the grounds. Find Sister Mary Elizabeth," he ordered with a growing impatience.

The Breton soldiers looked to their King, Philippe tilted his head in consent, and the order was given.

"You serve the dark one now. You are one of the Serpent's demons," Archbishop Verus said on a snarl as he addressed the Abbot once more.

"Am I? What does that make you?" Abbot Daniel asked weakly. He closed his eyes again for it was harder to keep them open. He just wanted to sleep. Yes, sleep. There was peace in sleep. He began to shiver for he felt cold. Death was just a breath away.

The Archbishop scoffed and stormed back to his Bishop who was watching the events unfold with disinterest.

The Abbot raised his eyes to the King for the last time. Philippe stepped closer and bent his head so he could hear the Abbot's whispered words.

"The Dragon — you need to destroy it before it destroys you. The knights, you will need the knights… They are coming…"

"Shh," Philippe ordered softly. "Die quietly."

"Quietly, yes," the Abbot chuckled softly despite his pain. "I can do that…"

Philippe straightened and then with a tremendous amount of borrowed will, he turned his back on the Abbot. He wondered if it would be possible to draw out the judgement so that the Abbot could die on the Hall floor. The Abbot didn't have long, and it would be a better death than dying on a pyre. Philippe walked back towards his throne, grabbing a goblet of wine from a servant as he did so. He sat down heavily upon his throne, and his eyes rested on the Abbot.

"He must burn," Archbishop Verus made the words sound like a command. A few of the nobles agreed with him and then like sheep others followed until it seemed that everybody wanted to see the Abbot burn. They conveniently forgot all the good that the Abbot had done, and instead, they called for his blood. They called for his death. They had learned nothing in the years that had followed Jesus' death. How easy it was to cast that first stone and how hard it was to search your own soul for just a fragment of mercy.

"Are you sure you saw Sister Mary Elizabeth?" Philippe asked, turning his attention to the Archbishop, hoping to delay the inevitable. "None of us got a good look at her, did we? What if it wasn't her? What if she is still in Rome?"

"It was her. Of course it was her," the Archbishop replied. "I saw her with my own eyes."

You saw Amandine, Philippe bit his tongue to stop himself from uttering the words. The Archbishop only saw what he wanted to see. He wasn't the only one. Philippe was guilty of doing that once or twice as well. But now his eyes had been opened and he could see everything so much clearer.

"If not Sister Mary Elizabeth then who?" Mordred asked. "Who do you think it was, Sire?" His words were patronising, meant as an insult.

Philippe glared back at Mordred, how dare he take that tone with him, and in front of everybody as well. He was the king. He should be spoken to with respect not ridicule. "I have no idea. I am just speculating."

"It was an angel. An angel told me to save her," Abbot Daniel replied with a surprising passion and volume for one who was dying.

His answer silenced the Hall, for no one had expected that.

"An angel?" Archbishop Verus mocked, laughing albeit nervously. "If anyone were to see an angel it would be me, not some lowly godforsaken Abbot. Abbot Daniel is a liar, and he is now speaking in his native tongue. He does not hold to the truth, for he knows not what truth is. Burn him, and maybe then he will find salvation in Jesus Christ our Lord."

"But did not the angels present themselves to some shepherds on that holiest of holy nights?" Philippe queried, turning his attention to the Archbishop. He was determined to keep the Archbishop talking for just a bit longer. Abbot Daniel was very near to death. It was the least he could do.

The look on the Archbishop's face at been thus challenged should have made Philippe fearful, and yet he found it strangely amusing. How dare he, a simple king, challenge an Archbishop of Rome? But someone had to.

"I always found it curious how the angels bypassed the religious leaders and instead addressed the congregation. Now, why do you think they did that?" Philippe asked.

"I am not here to debate the scriptures with you. I am here to see a demonic woman burn."

"She is no longer here, so you cannot. Go back to Rome, Archbishop Verus, and take with you my sincere apologies. I can understand if the Pope no longer feels that my kingdom is deserving of a Papal Blessing, but I will not order the death of my Abbot because he listened to the command of an angel. His death would be a kind of sacrilege if I did. I would make him a martyr and that I will not do. Take him to the infirmary and let his monks, God willing, restore his health, and if they cannot then let him die in peace.

Despite his confession, Abbot Daniel has done a lot of good in his life. We must not forget that."

"No," Archbishop Verus stated. "There was no angel, unless it was an angel of darkness. He must die, right now, this instant. Or the nation of Brittany will be cursed. The seeds you plant will not germinate for the sky will turn orange and instead of water, blood will drip down from the heavens, tainting your rivers and killing your crops. Your animals will die, and famine will stalk this land. Your people will be struck by a sickness that knows no cure, and all the babies will be born dead. Your enemies will attack, but you will be like a blind man — you will be unable to lead your men to victory. You will be slaughtered, and your bones will be thrown out with the rubbish. I speak with God's authority, do not ignore my warnings."

"You hope there was no angel," Philippe contradicted. "But if there was and we execute him for doing what God asked, than you are right, my kingdom will be cursed. I would rather give him the benefit of the doubt, then risk angering God."

"Archbishop Verus knows more about God than you," Mordred stated.

"That is right," Archbishop Verus agreed, puffing up his chest with obvious pride.

"If he says that there was no angel, then there was no angel," Mordred continued. "Let us burn him and get it over with."

The nobles cheered and clapped at Mordred's words.

"Enough," Philippe held up his hand, and the Hall fell begrudgingly silent once more. He had no choice. He could not stand against Archbishop Verus or the will of his nobles. He could not go against Mordred. He could not stand against the Church. His gaze once more fell to the Abbot, and he felt sick. Everything inside of him rebelled at what he had to do. This was not justice. This was murder.

"Abbot Daniel, you have been found guilty of High Treason…" Philippe stated, each word pained him to speak. He felt as if his mouth was filled with stinging nettles and the more condemning words he spoke the more it stung.

The Abbot opened his eyes, but he did not try to raise his head to look at the King. Everything was blurry. It was as if he was looking through a great fog and the sound of Philippe's voice was just a murmur. He closed his eyes again and drifted into unconsciousness.

"I condemn you as a traitor to my throne, to my kingdom, to my people, and to God…" Philippe had a sudden fancy that he was Pilate and he was ordering Jesus' execution. He couldn't do this. He hesitated, not wanting to give the crowd their demanded sacrifice. Could they not see that this was wrong?

"You will be taken to the pyre where you will be burnt until you are nothing but dust. May God have mercy on your soul," Mordred stated, stepping in while Philippe wrestled with his own conscience.

"No. No mercy," Archbishop Verus disagreed. "Abbot Daniel, you were cursed when you came into the world and know that you are cursed when you leave it. Jesus does not wait for you. You are demon-possessed, and I spit at you," The Archbishop was good to his word. "You are nothing. I strip you of your position, of your power, and of your influence. Know that I will damn you. There will be no Mass said for your soul. You will be burnt and forgotten. You disgust me with your vile presence, and I no longer want to breathe the same air as you."

"If they persecute me, they will persecute you also," Abbot Daniel mumbled to himself as he came out of the darkness for the briefest of moments. *"Some trust in chariots and some in horses…* But I…" he chuckled softly as he thought of Sampson. *"It is finished."*

Mordred scoffed at the Abbot's words. The Archbishop raised his fist and shouted at the Abbot in anger. Philippe simply stared at him.

Abbot Daniel's chest rose one more time, and then he breathed out slowly. After that, his chest did not rise again. But no one apart from Philippe noticed the departure of the Abbot from this life. For the Abbot's words had, it seemed, enraged everyone, and they were too busy shouting curses at him to notice he was no longer with the living.

"Get him out of here," Archbishop Verus demanded, raising his voice in outrage. "I will not have him quote scriptures to me," he spat the words out. "You are not Jesus, nor are you David, how dare you speak their words. You defile them with your poisonous tongue."

"You are wasting your breath," Philippe said, his eyes had not once wavered from Abbot Daniel. "He is dead."

"Don't be ridiculous. He isn't dead," Archbishop Verus disagreed. "I know when a man is dead and when he isn't. He is pretending. He is pretending to be dead."

Mordred rose and walked over to the Abbot. Instead of checking for breath he simply stamped down on the Abbot's broken leg. "No. He really is dead," Mordred confirmed when the Abbot did not respond. "The Devil saved him from the pyre."

"He will burn anyway," Archbishop Verus stated with malice. "Get him out of here."

Bastian looked to the King, and Philippe reluctantly nodded his head. Bastian gave the order, but instead of Breton soldiers, Roman soldiers stepped forward, they grabbed hold of the Abbot by his dislocated arms and dragged him out of the Hall as if he were a piece of meat or an unworthy enemy.

"Burn the guards as well," Mordred demanded. "They were complacent. And pick out ten women from the crowd. We were meant to watch Lady Amandine burn today, that has been denied us, so ten others must take her place."

Again Roman soldiers were quick to follow his commands.

"No," Philippe disagreed, rising to his feet in anger. "I will not allow innocent women to burn. Lady Amandine's escape had absolutely nothing to do with the peasantry."

The nobles at last agreed with their King, although Lord Madec and Lord Prigent remained suspiciously quiet.

"And how would you know that?" Mordred asked as he stabbed his knife into another apple. "Is there something you want to confess too, Philippe?"

Philippe jutted out his jaw and glared at Mordred with contempt. Mordred stared back with an amused expression on his face and bit into the apple. Philippe hoped the apple would give Mordred the flux.

"Pick out ten women," Philippe stated with disgust. "I hope that appeases God," he did not take his eyes off Mordred as he spoke

"It appeases me," Mordred said with a grin. "For now…"

Chapter 4

It was said that the Church was built upon the foundation of the apostles and the prophets, but something had gone terribly wrong in the structure. The building was unsteady. It had somehow been corrupted along the way. Perhaps it was simply because they had forgotten to use Jesus as the cornerstone.

Brother Jagu lit the altar candles and knelt down. He held his shaking hands together and looked up at the wood carving of Jesus nailed to a cross. As he studied the tortured image of Jesus' final moments, a tear slid slowly down his cheek. He sniffed, trying to contain his tears, but little good that did.

He had seen Abbot Daniel as he made his way out of the Hall and that sight would haunt him for the rest of his life. He had not been allowed to speak to him, but Abbot Daniel had raised his head and smiled encouragingly, it was as if he was trying to say everything would be all right. But how could it? How could anything possibly be all right after this?

He felt a wave of nausea wash over him as he tried unsuccessfully to comprehend how anyone could do something so vile to someone who was so good. Abbot Daniel was the type of man who would go out of his way to help another, and that thought pulled him up short.

He was guilty. Abbot Daniel *was* guilty of the crime he had been accused of. He had helped Lady Amandine escape because he could not have lived with himself if he did not. He should have foreseen that Abbot Daniel would do something so foolish. He should have stopped him. He chuckled without humour, which quickly gave way to more tears. Abbot Daniel would not have listened even if he had tried to intervene. But did the Abbot's crime warrant the excessive abuse he had endured? Abbot Daniel was a man of God, for God's sake. Abbot Daniel was not a common criminal, and he should not have been treated as such.

Brother Jagu tried to comfort himself by recalling familiar prayers, but none came. He did not have the words. He was caught between anger and despair. Damn God and damn Abbot Daniel too. No. It wasn't God's fault. Abbot Daniel had often said that God could not be held responsible for the cruelty or the mistakes of man. *"How can you blame the father for the son's actions?"* But God should have stepped in. He should have stopped the Abbot. Unless, God had truly abandoned them, for why else would he allow such atrocities to occur to someone who was so devoted to him? And then he remembered Job.

Brother Jagu felt the pain of God's apparent abandonment deep in his soul, and for the first time in his entire life, he questioned whether there really was a God. He opened his eyes and stared once more at the image of Christ, hoping to find some answers in that intricately carved face, but the statue gave nothing away, for it had nothing to give. It was just a carving. It wasn't really Jesus.

He heard footsteps come up behind him but he did not turn his head, nor did he flinch when Brother Loïc rested his hand on his shoulder.

"Abbot Daniel is dead," Brother Loïc stated softly.

Those four words were the most painful Brother Jagu had ever heard. He felt a short, sharp pain in his heart and he placed his hand against his chest.

"They say he is a traitor and that he deserved a traitor's death. They have tied his body to the pyre that was meant for Lady Amandine, but that is not all. The soldiers who had guarded Lady Amandine's door have also been put to death, as have ten women who are condemned only because of their sex," Brother Loïc's voice broke as he relayed this news. "Not all the women are dead yet. Their suffering goes on…"

Brother Jagu groaned in agony. "No," he cried out in denial. "Dear God, no."

"Archbishop Verus told us all to come back here. He wants to give us religious counsel and guidance. He told me that he believes that we have been led astray by Abbot Daniel's teachings. He said that...that..." Brother Loïc began to sob quietly. "We have been told to wait for him in the Chapter House." Brother Loïc squeezed Brother Jagu's shoulder in a comforting manner, and then he too fell to his knees and began to cry in earnest.

"Though he slay me, yet I will hope in him..." Brother Jagu muttered the words with a shocking realisation. God always had a purpose, and although Brother Jagu did not understand it, he knew that God was wise and he had to trust in him. But how do you learn to trust again after such a gross betrayal?

Brother Loïc was beside himself with grief now, and yet Brother Jagu could not find the strength to comfort him. All he could think about was Job and the trials the poor man had to go through in order to prove his love to God. Was this a trial? Was this *his* trial? Was God watching him, judging him for his worth? Brother Jagu feared that he would fail where Job had succeeded.

"Get up."

Brother Jagu looked back up at the carving of Jesus and frowned. He could have sworn he had just heard someone speak. He looked at Brother Loïc, but the man was so lost in his grief that he could not have spoken the words. Brother Jagu looked back at Jesus with confusion.

"Get up, Jagu. Walk away. You need to leave."

Brother Jagu looked around, but there was no one in the Church except for himself and Brother Loïc. Where was the voice coming from?

"Now," the voice ordered.

Brother Jagu looked back at Jesus and slowly rose unsteadily to his feet. Was God speaking to him? Commanding him?

"Go," the voice ordered. *"Quickly."*

Brother Jagu did not think to question. Instead, he began to walk away from the altar. He did not think about where he was going. He just placed one foot in front of the other. It was as if he was in a dream. He had no control of his actions.

He opened the door and stepped into the Chapter House where his fellow monks had gathered. They spoke in agitated whispers about all they had seen and all they had heard, but when they saw him, they all fell silent. Compelled to keep walking, Brother Jagu did not even acknowledge his fellow monks. They may have spoken to him, said his name, but he did not hear them. He just felt this undeniable urge to get as far away as possible.

Keeping his head down, he left the Chapter House. His feet swiftly led him forward, through the cloisters and past the kitchens. Before he knew it he was standing in the empty dorter. All the beds were neatly made, and everything was in its proper place. He resisted the sudden urge to pull the covers off the beds and clear the desks of their contents. He wanted to reorganise the order and replace it with chaos. He balled his fingers into fists until the urge had passed.

He crossed to his bed and sat down heavily upon it. He stared unseeingly in front of him for a long time as he tried to make sense of all that had befallen the nation. When Philippe had taken the throne from Budic there had been a reason to hope. Budic had been a bad king. Budic had been concerned only with his own importance. Philippe, they had all thought, was different. How wrong they all had been.

Brother Jagu had no idea how long he sat there. He did not notice as the light began to fade, all he could think about was Abbot Daniel. He and the Abbot had been friends for a very long time. They had joined the monastery together, hoping for a better life than the impoverished one their once prominent families offered. They had learned their lessons together, but while Brother Jagu favoured the study of herbs and their healing qualities, Daniel had learned the art of illumination. Daniel had always had such an eye for detail. He could make even the mundane look beautiful. Many of Daniel's fellow illuminators would put down their brushes and watch as he carefully placed the expensive gold leaf onto the manuscripts. Brother Jagu decided there and then that *that* was how he would remember Abbot Daniel — bent over his work with a brush in his hand.

"All of them are to die, every last one. If they live, then they will make that bastard, Daniel, a martyr and that we can not allow."

Brother Jagu came back to the present with a jump. His mouth fell open in disbelief as he listened to Archbishop Verus speak.

"All of the monks?" Mordred Pendragon asked.

"All," Archbishop Verus confirmed.

Brother Jagu's mind yelled at him to stand up, to either challenge the Archbishop or make a break for it, warn his fellow monks, and then run far away from here and get help, but he felt as if a great weight was resting on his shoulders, preventing him from moving. He could not do anything but listen as the Archbishop ordered their deaths.

"Are you sure?" Mordred asked, his voice, for once, sounded uncertain. "The Pope—"

"The Pope will never know. I will tell him it was a tragic accident. He will not think to question my word. I have given him no cause to do so before. Mordred, once Daniel's monks are dead we can replace them with men of our choosing. They will preach our doctrine, and your name will be praised throughout the kingdom. We must do this. You cannot allow your enemies in the Church to turn the people against you. I believe it is our duty to cleanse the Church of all dissidents. This is God's will."

Brother Jagu listened, petrified, as he heard Mordred laugh.

"Just as it was God's will at Holywell. You should have seen those nuns run for their lives only to be cut down by Cerdic's men."

"The nuns at Holywell harboured an adulterous sinner. If they had not, then they would not have been put to the sword."

"I have waited years to kill her. He will be avenged," Mordred stated with passion. "I did not give that bitch a chance to talk. I cut her throat where she stood and moved on to the next. I am pleased to say that she had not aged well, I hardly recognised her."

"But you did…recognise her?" the Archbishop asked with a shadow of a doubt.

"Of course," Mordred spoke with confidence. "I would hardly forget my father's wife."

Brother Jagu stopped himself from gasping out loud as he listened to Mordred's confession. He had found her. Mordred had found Guinevere, and he had entered holy ground and killed her. So much for sanctuary. He guessed the rules of the Church did not apply to Mordred Pendragon or Archbishop Verus, for that matter.

"It is God's will that we separate the darnel from the rest of the wheat. When this monastery burns, the poisonous weeds will be destroyed once and for all. Come, let us hurry, time is of the essence. I told the monks to gather in the Chapter House, and I have kept them waiting long enough. It would do us no favours if they started to wander."

"How do you want them to die?" Mordred Pendragon asked in a

tone of voice that suddenly sounded very bored.

"I am sure you can think of something. But make sure it looks like an accident. I do not want the blame to come knocking on my door," Archbishop Verus stated.

A grey cat jumped on the bed beside Brother Jagu and began to meow.

"Shh," Brother Jagu pleaded as the cat put her two front paws on his lap.

"Did you hear that?" Mordred asked.

Brother Jagu heard a sword being drawn and to his horror the latch to the dorter's door lifted. Brother Jagu felt the strange weight lift from his shoulders. At last, he could move. He pushed the cat off his lap and as quickly and as quietly as he could, he lay down flat upon the floor and rolled under the bed, hoping the covering and the darkness would hide him from Mordred's all-seeing eyes. He held his breath as Mordred entered the room. Mordred steps were confident and sure as he made his way across the dorter. He paused every so often to rummage through the papers on the monks' desks and then he set to work. Brother Jagu trembled and bit his lip as he heard the clatter of books and parchment as they were thrown on to the floor.

"There is no one here," Archbishop Verus stated with impatience a few minutes later. "It was just their cat."

Mordred stopped what he was doing and glared at the cat with contempt.

The cat had curled herself up on Brother Jagu's bed and was watching Mordred with a detached disinterest. When Mordred approached her, she began to purr in contentment thinking that a petting was coming, for she had never felt a violent hand. Instead, Mordred picked her up by the scruff of her neck and shook her. The cat hissed and spat while trying desperately to wriggle free, but the more she wriggled, the tighter Mordred's hold became.

"I hate cats," Mordred stated, and without further ado, he broke the animal's neck with his bare hands. He threw the cat onto the floor by Brother Jagu's bed as if she were nothing but a dirty rag.

Brother Jagu had heard the crunch of bones, and he swallowed nervously. Sweat broke out upon his brow, and he began to shake. He closed his eyes and prayed fervently to God to spare him.

"What are you going to do about Philippe?" Archbishop Verus asked from the doorway.

"He has his uses," Mordred stated as he crossed towards the door.

"He is a blundering fool. He has a backbone the size of a sparrow. Crush him and be done with it."

"He amuses me. And besides, he is young and easily persuaded, and more importantly, he is terrified of me. He will do as he is told. I have backed him into a corner; there is no escape. I have nothing to fear when it comes to Philippe. I am content to rule through him, for the time being at least."

"Dogs are at their most dangerous when they are backed into a corner," the Archbishop warned. "Be careful he does not turn."

"Philippe is no dog. Do not worry about him. He is my concern, not yours. I think a fire will do," Mordred stated, changing the subject. "All those candles, it is an accident waiting to happen. I have always said that this church would one day go up in smoke. No one will suspect."

"A fire? Yes, that is the best way to destroy unwanted weeds. Let's get it over with then before someone sees. There must be no witnesses. Do you understand?"

"There will be no witnesses," Mordred stated. "When have I ever let you down before?"

"There is always a first," Archbishop Verus answered, but there was humour in his voice.

"Do not even jest of such a thing," Mordred replied, slamming the door of the dorter behind him.

***

Brother Jagu dared to breathe out slowly. It was only then that he realised he had been holding his breath. He needed to get up and warn his fellow monks. He could not lie here and let them die. But fear held him in her grasp, and he found he could not move. It was for the best if he stayed under the bed. What could he do anyway? He was but one man. He was not skilled in the art of warfare only in the art of healing. How could he even think to challenge the Archbishop and Mordred Pendragon?

He closed his eyes and felt the roughness of the wooden floorboards against his cheek. The air under the bed was stale and smelt of dust, mice and old straw. But all would be well, for soon the straw mattresses would be re-stuffed and the cats would chase the mice away. Everything would be as it should be. He must have fallen asleep. This was nothing but a bad dream. Abbot Daniel wasn't dead. The Archbishop didn't really want to kill the monks. How absurd. He chuckled, almost hysterically, for just a moment before he remembered that he was supposed to be quiet.

Tears began to slide out from behind his closed eyes even as he tried to convince himself that what had happened, and what was about to happen, was in his imagination. But the truth was that very soon everyone he ever loved, and everything he knew would go up in flames.

He had never given much thought to how much he valued his own life, until now. If he stayed here, then he would live — for a few more hours at least. But if he showed himself... If he tried to help his friends, then death would be imminent. Brother Jagu was not a brave man because he never needed to be. The Church was his salvation. It was his shelter. The monastery was a place of sanctuary, not a place of death.

"Fear and trembling have beset me; horror has overwhelmed me. Dear Lord, give me the courage to do what I have to do."

Brother Jagu took several deep, steadying breaths. How dare he hide while others died. And besides, he could not hide from the enemy forever. Better he faces him now and be done with it, then wait and face him later.

He forced his reluctant body to move, and with difficulty, he wriggled out from under his bed. Hesitantly he rose to his feet. His heart was pounding so fast in his chest that he felt momentarily light-headed. With a trembling hand, he reached for his desk, using it as a support while he battled to keep his balance.

He took a moment to look around the room. Mordred had not thought twice about reorganizing the order and replacing it with chaos. Holy books lay upon the floor, as did parchment and candles. It looked as if a thief had ransacked the room. But Mordred wasn't a thief. He was a man intent on murder.

The distance between his bed and the door was a mere six strides, but to Brother Jagu, the space was like a desolate desert, and he knew that when he opened the door, only death would greet him.

He tried to take courage from Abbot Daniel's example, but courage was not forthcoming. He stood there looking at the door as if it was something to be feared, for he fancied that it led to the shadowy world of Hades. He was frightened to move but also equally frightened not to.

"Do not be afraid; do not feel discouraged, for the Lord your God will be with you wherever you go..." Muttering those words under his breath, Brother Jagu bravely stepped forward. All his attention was centred on the door, but having only taken three steps he faltered and he turned to look back at his bed. He caught sight of the dead cat that lay next to it. The dorter was no haven. Death would find him here as surely as it would find him outside. But at least if he died outside then it would be because he had tried to stop a massacre.

With a deep and almost painful sigh, Brother Jagu made himself walk the small distance to the door. Once there, he reached out tentatively and touched it. The wood was surprisingly warm under his fingertips, and it gave him courage. He cautiously lent his ear against the smooth wood, but he could hear nothing. He opened the door, cringing as it creaked on its hinges. He then stepped out into the corridor and shut the door softly behind him.

Now what? He had no choice but to move forward. There was no going back. His path was set, and he would be true to it.

The monastery felt subdued. The peace and tranquillity had been replaced with a great sadness. It was as if the building already knew her fate and she grieved for all she would lose.

Keeping to the shadows, Brother Jagu made his way towards the Chapter House, and that is when he heard it. The gently crackling of a fire. Instead of hurrying forward he came to a jolting stop. And then the screaming started. The sound of his friends' screaming jarred him into action.

He crept as close to the Chapter House as he could, but the black smoke swirled around him as if it were a ghost that was sustained only if it sucked the life out of the air. Coughing violently, Brother Jagu valiantly continued, for he could hear the banging as the monks tried to open the locked and barricaded door that led from the Chapter House to the cloisters. But the closer he got, the thicker the smoke became. The heat coming from the building was blistering. *How did the fire take hold so quickly?* He asked himself over and over. This was no man-made fire. It was too intense. Too ferocious. Sweat poured down Brother Jagu's face as he desperately tried to drag away the many items that had been wedged against the door to stop it from opening. The screams for mercy intensified, as did the smoke.

The Angel of Death had paid the monastery a visit, and it would not be thwarted until it had claimed all the innocent souls as its own.

Brother Jagu's body was racked with desperate coughing, and he realised that there was nothing he could do. For too long he had lingered in the dorter, and this was the consequence of his cowardliness and his inaction. He hung his head in shame and slowly sank down to the floor. He willed the Angel to take him too for he did not want to live while his friends died, but a hand grabbed his arm and tugged him to his feet. He did not have the strength to argue for he could scarcely draw in a breath. He coughed so violently that he thought he would pass out but the stranger had a tight hold of his arm, and Brother Jagu knew that no matter what happened the stranger would not let go.

The smoke stung Brother Jagu's eyes so like a blind man he allowed the stranger to lead him through the cloisters and into the kitchens. The stranger let go of his arm and pushed him onto a stool. He then dipped a cloth in some water. Brother Jagu gratefully clutched the damp fabric to his eyes hoping to soothe the sting of the smoke.

"Drink this, but hurry, we don't have much time. We have to get you out of here," the voice was muffled as if hidden by a cloth.

Brother Jagu kept the damp cloth on his eyes while he blindly accepted the cup. He drank quickly, the weak ale eased his burning throat and helped to relieve his cough.

"Come on. We have to keep moving."

Brother Jagu once again felt a hand on his arm, but he put up no resistance as he was pulled back onto his feet. He dropped the damp cloth onto the floor and looked at his rescuer.

"You run with the hare and hunt with the hound," Brother Jagu stated in a very hoarse voice as he looked at his rescuer with surprise.

"Someone has to," Bastian stated as he ripped away the damp cloth that he had tied around his mouth and nose to protect against the smoke. Bastian swiftly took off his cloak and threw it over Brother Jagu's shoulders. He also thrust a bag of coins into the monk's hands.

"Head to Frank and then charter a boat to Cerniw. Tell Alden all of what has happened here. Tell him I was wrong. Tell him that I am sorry. Tell him that Brittany is lost. Tell him to raise an army and for the love of all that is holy, tell him to cross the water and liberate us.

Mordred will destroy Brittany if you do not."

Chapter 5

A heavy sea mist hung over the Kingdom of Brittany, but still, the monastery smouldered. Those who had so valiantly tried to tackle the flames had been forced back by the ferocity of the heat. There was nothing anyone could do but pray for rain. But rain was not forthcoming no matter how hard they prayed.

Archbishop Verus had stated that this fire was God's will and that they should leave such fire well alone for it would do them no good to meddle. Those were easy words for the Archbishop to say for he knew not the monks who were being burnt alive. The Archbishop was just a visitor and one, if the truth be told, whom they all would be glad to see the back of.

While the Archbishop spewed his hate, the servants and the soldiers had stood with tears in their eyes and watched as the flames quickly engulfed the entire building. Many years from now those who witnessed the fire would say that they did not know what was worse — hearing the monks' scream for help, or the silence that came after.

No one spoke. No one uttered a word. Instead, they stood or sat and kept their thoughts to themselves, although all of their thoughts ran along a very similar line. Abbot Daniel was dead and that in itself was a tragedy but to lose the rest of the monks as well... What was God thinking? Where did they turn to for religious counsel now? Where did they go when their children were sick? Where did they go when they were hungry? Where did they go when it was time to die? The monks were a huge part of the community, and under Abbot

Daniel's leadership, the monks had become a friend to the poor. They had become a necessity. They sustained life. But now they were dead. The Kingdom of Brittany should have burned along with them, then at least they would have all gone together.

Those who worked in the kitchens of the castle came out with a cauldron full of pottage and baskets of fresh bread. No one had told them to, and no doubt they would be reprimanded for daring to share a little of the King's wealth with these good people, but it was a risk they were willing to take. No one spoke as the food was handed out, but their faces showed their gratitude for the night had been very long, and they were all exhausted.

No one could say why they had felt compelled to stay and watch the building burn. The Archbishop had announced, when the night was at the darkest, that he was off to find his bed. He wasn't going to lose sleep over this. And that statement confirmed everything that the common man had feared. The Church of Rome would send men like the Archbishop to replace those who had perished. They wouldn't care about their parishioners like Abbot Daniel and his monks had.

Bastian instinctively accepted the bowl of pottage when it was handed to him, but he didn't raise the spoon to his mouth. Instead, he set the bowl down on the edge of the well and looked back at the charred remains of the monastery. The church roof had long since collapsed; the now black beams lay across the church floor like fallen Christian soldiers. When it was deemed safe, then Bastian would, with the help of a few chosen men, try to locate the burnt bodies of the monks. It shouldn't be too difficult to find the monks, after all, he knew where they were. He thought back to what he had seen when he had attempted to enter the Chapter House. The Archbishop was very quick to tell everyone that this was a tragic accident, but Bastian knew different. He had seen the barricade. This fire was premeditated. The monks had been murdered because of politics and religion, both of which had no place in a civilised world. Thank God he had managed to save Brother Jagu. Thank God there was someone who could stand up and testify to what really had happened this day. Brother Jagu had told him, between fits of coughing, what he had overheard. Bastian should have felt surprised by Brother Jagu's words, but he didn't. Abbot Daniel and his gentle ways were at odds with the Church's teachings. An Abbot was meant to control its congregation not sympathise with it. Abbot Daniel was a threat, and this threat had been well and truly dealt with. But regardless of what the Church thought, Bastian knew that the world was a darker place because Abbot Daniel and his monks no longer walked upon the earth.

"My Lord," one of the soldiers in charge of guarding the harbour called out to his general as he jumped off his horse. A few people looked his way at the interruption to the vigil, but no one said anything. They were beyond words now. Beyond hope.

The soldier was young, with a kind disposition. But his usual easy smile was missing from his face. Bastian watched as the soldier performed the sign of the cross as he looked upon the devastation.

The soldier had seen the fire from the harbour. Everyone had for it had lit up the night sky. But he had not expected this.

"Did anyone…"

Bastian shook his head. "We couldn't reach them. Everyone is dead."

The soldier closed his eyes, and when he opened them again, his eyes were filled with tears. *"Dead?"* he asked shaking his head in disbelief, and he took a moment to compose himself. "Are you sure?" he took a step towards the building.

"I am sure," Bastian reached out to stop him. "No one survived."

The soldier hung his head and began to cry. Bastian patted him awkwardly on the back and stepped away.

The soldier sniffed and rubbed at his tears with the back of his sleeve. "Abbot Daniel once told me that *outside is the sword; inside are plague and famine.* He told me to always be wary, for the enemy is not always the army outside of the walls. I never understood what he meant, until now. This was a little convenient, don't you think? This was no coincidence. Why would the Abbot and all of his monks die on the same day? And in such tragic circumstances. It doesn't make sense. I am sorry," the soldier stated quickly, his voice still heavy with tears. "I am speaking out of turn."

"If you had said that to anyone else then you would find yourself tied to the pyre. Keep your opinions to yourself. There have been enough deaths already."

"I am sorry. It won't happen again," the soldier promised. He coughed, clearing his throat. "May I ask, how much longer do we have to accommodate the soldiers from Rome? They are making us all uneasy."

"No, you may not ask," Bastian answered sharply and then he sighed deeply. "I don't know," he answered honestly. "I don't even know why they are here. Keep your head down boy, do as you are told, and maybe you will come out of this alive. Now, what did you want?"

"We found them."

"You found them? Found what?" Bastian queried with a frown creasing his brow.

"The oars," the soldier gave a hopeless shrug. "We found the oars."

"Have you retrieved them?" Bastian asked, his voice dropping an octave as he spoke, fearing they would be overheard.

"A few, not all."

"Keep it that way," Bastian ordered.

"My Lord?" the soldier asked, clearly not understanding why his general would want the oars to remain hidden. "But with the oars, we can man the boats…"

Bastian glared at the young soldier, and it curbed the soldier's tongue.

"What are your orders?" the soldier asked instead, standing up straighter and looking to the left of Bastian's shoulder — for he had forgotten that a simple soldier like himself had no right to look such a great man in the eye.

"I will give the order myself," Bastian replied.

"I'll get your horse," the soldier answered, and not waiting to be dismissed, he ran to the stables.

***

A little girl sat on the sand and looked with wide glassy eyes at the pyre. The fire had long gone out, but the memories would remain. Her long blond hair was matted and covered in ash. In her hands lay what looked like a pile of old rags but to the girl, she only saw her beautiful rag doll that her mother had given her. She held onto that doll so tightly that her fingers had gone white. An old woman walked up to the child, but when she touched the little girl on the shoulder, the child screamed. It was an abnormal ghostly scream that seemed to know no end. Philippe wanted to cover his ears and run far away, but he could not drag his eyes away from the child. She sat motionless even while she screamed. He had never seen anything like it. The old woman stepped back from the child, and the screaming stopped. The old woman shook her head and walked away.

He had done this to her. This was what his weakness had caused. The child had witnessed her mother and her older sister burn. She was the only surviving member of her family. There was no one else.

Philippe felt the old woman's judgemental eyes on him. He raised his head and looked at her. No one had ever looked at him with that much hatred — even Merton's glare had not been a match to this old woman's. He could not hold her gaze, so he turned his attention back to the child.

He knew he should be back at the castle, but he felt compelled to stay at this place of evil and watch over the young one, for a while longer at least. What would happen to her after he left was something he didn't dare think about.

Philippe had two guards with him, but he had wanted some time alone, so he had asked his guards to go back to the cliff face and wait. They had done so unwillingly, but damn it all he was the king. His men would do as they were told while he still possessed what little authority Mordred allowed.

He heard the sound of pounding horse hooves, but he did not turn to look. If he were in any danger, then his guards would let him know.

Sighing sadly, he turned away and looked at the pyre the children had made. They had not lit it, and the crude effigy of Lady Amandine remained untouched by flames. He rubbed his hand over tired eyes and looked back at the child. He had stolen not only her mother and her sister but also her childhood. What kind of monster would do that?

"Sire," Bastian said his name cautiously as he slowly dismounted.

"My general," Philippe turned and looked at Bastian with contempt. "Mordred's general," he added bitterly.

"Your general," Bastian stated, falling onto one knee in homage.

Philippe scoffed and turned away. He heard Bastian stand back up, but he did not turn to look at him.

"That little girl has been sat there all night. She has not moved. I find myself asking what kind of king would make a child suffer so?"

"You didn't have a choice," Bastian argued.

"Oh," Philippe chuckled, but without any humour. "We all have choices." He turned back around and looked at his general with accusing eyes. "Abbot Daniel escorted Lady Amandine from her room. That was *his* choice. When I saw her, with him, I did not say anything. I let her go. That was *my* choice. I am assuming, that when the two of them approached you at the portcullis, you opened the gate and let them walk out with their lives."

"I did," Bastian replied quietly.

"Then that was *your* choice. So do not talk to me of choices. We all made a choice, but it is this little innocent that has paid the ultimate price for those choices."

"The innocent always pay. That is the tragedy of life."

"No. It is not a tragedy. A tragedy would mean it was unintentional. We in power exploit their weakness. We think ourselves greater than them because we live in a fine castle. We have beautiful clothes and plenty of food. We do not think twice about our poorer neighbour. All we are concerned about is how much money the poor can make us. We tax them to such an extent that they cannot fill the bellies of their children. We ask them to fight and to die for us in wars not of their making, while we stand back and watch. And when they come to the end of their usefulness, they are nothing but a nuisance to us. When did we start treating our fellow man like animals? Those women had done nothing wrong. But we demanded their deaths, and so they died. Who are we to command such a sacrifice?"

"Have you stopped to ask yourself why Mordred wanted those ten innocent women to die?" Bastian asked cautiously.

"I know why they died. They died because Abbot Daniel died in my Hall and not on a pyre. I made another choice, don't you see? I did not want him to die by fire, so I tried to…" He didn't need to explain. He could see that Bastian knew what he had done. "But now it is I that will be condemned for this. It will be my name that is forever associated with butchery. My people will turn from me because of this. I will lose the kingdom because of this, and maybe I will lose my life as well, but quite frankly, right now, I don't care. I was just as responsible for Lady Amandine's escape. I should have died, not him, not them," he pointed to the pyre.

"We found the oars," Bastian said quietly.

"What use have I for oars?" Philippe replied with scorn. "All these people died because I wanted her to live. And yet, I cannot regret the small part I played in saving her life. I just regret what happened after…" Philippe's words faded away as his gaze once more rested on the child.

"We have yet to retrieve all of the oars. I knew you would not want to take up the chase. We will put them back where we found them because if Mordred gets wind of them, then he would lead the hunt and she will die."

Philippe did not speak, but he jutted out his chin and gave a quick nod of his head.

"Sire, do not let guilt destroy you. You need to be strong if we have any chance of defeating him. I am on your side."

Philippe frowned, for he very much doubted Bastian was on anyone's side apart from his own, but he kept such thoughts to himself.

Bastian bowed and gathered up the reins of his horse.

"Just out of interest, where are they?" Philippe asked, turning to look back at his general.

"That is the damnedest of things. They were under our feet all this time. The oars are under the jetty."

Philippe spluttered on a laugh and shook his head. "God, damn him," he muttered with realisation. "That bastard didn't die, did he? Only he would come up with something like that." He shook his head again as he thought about it. He looked into Bastian's face for just a moment, and he saw the truth for the first time. "You knew, didn't you? You knew he was alive."

"I knew there was a possibility," Bastian answered cautiously. "He was in a very bad way when… When I helped them escape."

"You and that monk?" Philippe asked, there was no anger in his face, just ironic amusement.

"Brother Sampson saved his life. The man we pulled from the dungeons and buried outside the castle walls was one of my men who had died—"

"Spare me the details. You say you are on my side but… You made a choice and now we are here," Philippe replied.

"I was Merton's sword master. He was like my own child."

"And then I asked you to kill him," Philippe replied, his voice etched with sadness as he recalled what he had done to Merton du Lac that day. "I should have known. Who was I to think I could kill

The Devil? He came for her?"

"He did," Bastian confirmed. "He came right up to the castle gates, and he looked me in the eyes. He did not even come with an army, just a small number of men and his usual arrogance and determination."

"He is with her?" Philippe asked.

"Yes," Bastian replied.

Philippe's gaze was drawn back to the little girl. "Then everything is as it should be." He walked towards the little girl, leaving his general behind. When he reached her, he knelt down on the sand, and he looked at the pyre. He heard her sharp intake of breath, and he could feel her confused eyes resting on his face. And Philippe realised that he would not have to wait to die, for his day of judgement had already arrived.

Chapter 6

When evil comes, it destroys and corrupts everything it touches. Even the gentle sound of the sea as it crept up the shore sounded offensive to Philippe's ears.

He knew not how long he had sat on the sand next to the little girl, and he knew not what the rest of the day was going to bring. Would he die too? Or would he find the courage to stand up to Mordred for once and for all? Would his army support him if he did? Or would they side with his enemy? Dear God, he had promised his kingdom salvation and instead he had delivered them into the hands of evil. Everyone had been better off under Budic du Lac's rule. Philippe had thought himself so clever. He had been so sure that he would make a better king than his cousin and yet, here in front of him was the indisputable proof that as a king he had failed.

He blinked back his tears. He felt like the little girl by his side — lost, alone, afraid. Did he turn towards a general he did not trust, or did he reach out to his kin and beg them for forgiveness? Perhaps he should run away and leave Brittany to her fate. He could change his name, start again, make a new life for himself somewhere far away from here. He could pretend the past had never happened. He could pretend it was nothing more than a bad dream.

He felt the little girl's gaze on his face, so he turned to look at her. A single big fat tear threatened to fall from her left eye. It was then that she did the unthinkable. She reached up with her tiny hand and touched Philippe on the cheek as if she could sense his grief and wanted to offer comfort. A great sense of shame washed over him. He hung his head and began to sob. The little girl's hand fell away, but she moved closer to him and then closer still until she had wriggled her way onto his lap. She put her little arms around his neck and hugged him tightly.

She did not know who he was, he realised, as he hugged her back. She didn't know.

***

Philippe made his way slowly back to the castle, the little girl still in his arms. He could not leave her on the beach to face her future alone. He had caused her great pain. It seemed only right that he would be the one to ease it and bring her comfort.

She had snuggled into his arms, and her thumb had found its way into her mouth, but she did not fall asleep, as he had expected — perhaps she feared sleep the same way he now did.

He stopped to look at the monastery. This fire had been no accident. Any fool could see that. Wisps of smoke still rose into the sky as if it was trying to find a way to Heaven. This sanctuary was desolate, no longer would the soothing smell of incense haunt this building. Likewise, the quiet footsteps and gentle chanting of the monks at prayer would no longer be heard. So *this* was how it would begin — with fire, brimstone, and a burning wind. He should not have felt surprised. Wasn't that how the Bible said it would occur?

"Philippe," Mordred's voice did not draw Philippe's gaze away from what was left of the monastery. "Philippe, we must prepare. Eric of Rennais has just arrived with his daughter. Today is your wedding day. There is much still to do. Archbishop Verus said he would preside over the wedding ceremony. We can hold it in the Great Hall. I was going to suggest holding the ceremony there, anyway. The church was always so draughty — more so now," Mordred laughed at his own joke. "Why are you holding a child? Put her down. You do not want to risk catching something from such a filthy little vermin. She is probably full of disease. Philippe, are you listening to me? I said put her down."

Philippe held the child a little tighter. He did not know if he did so because he was concerned for her welfare or because he was concerned for his own. He felt as if he had been thrown violently from a boat. The child was his flotsam, and she was all that was keeping his head above the water. He would never let her go no matter how much Mordred demanded it.

"There will be no wedding," he stated under his breath. He would be damned if he let himself be used any longer. He had no desire to marry the daughter of Eric of Rennais. He tore his gaze away from the monastery and began to make his way slowly towards the castle. He did not acknowledge Mordred. Instead, he walked straight past him as if he wasn't there. He felt as if a million eyes were watching him. He was used to the sensation for he was the King of Brittany, but this time he feared that everyone was waiting for him to make some grand speech — to either condemn or condone what they all knew had happened at the monastery. But he felt numb. It was almost as if the last day and night had been experienced by someone else. He climbed the castle steps, and he stopped. He was the king. He should turn around. Address his people. At least, thank them for their efforts at trying to put out the fire. But then he realised that they did not want his gratitude. They wanted him to lead them, but Mordred would never allow it. And so he continued into the castle and not once did he look back.

Archbishop Verus rushed up to him as soon as he entered the castle. The Archbishop was all smiles, and he put his hand on Philippe's shoulder as if to guide him towards the Hall, but Philippe shrugged him off, and he left the Archbishop standing there, frowning at him, as he made for the stairs.

Philippe took the steps two at a time. He then walked along the cold and unwelcoming corridor towards his chamber. He paused briefly outside the chamber Amandine had been held, and for a reason unexplainable to himself he pushed the door open with his foot and stepped inside.

The room had a mousy smell to it, which it had not had before. It also smelt of sickness and urine. It was a heady combination. Philippe repositioned the child on his hip as he walked further into the room. He stepped over the mess on the floor where Amandine had apparently missed the chamber pot while she purged her stomach. He could not imagine what her suffering must have been like. She must have been so very afraid. He noticed her dress, neatly folded and lying on a chair. He put the child down on the stripped bed and picked up the dress. He had given this to Amandine. She had looked so very beautiful when she wore it. It was at that moment, seeing her in *this* dress, that he had realised he had fallen in love with her. She had been so bravely defiant. So spirited. How could he not love her? He held the fabric to his face and inhaled deeply. Amandine's scent still clung to the fabric, and he closed his eyes to savour it. When he opened them again, he noticed that there were drops of blood on the wall, which seemed to culminate in the corner of the room. He put the dress back on the chair. Then, he cautiously knelt down. The mousy smell was stronger nearer the floor, and with it, he could also detect an earthy scent that was unmistakable — Hemlock? His heart recoiled at such a thought.

"Dear God," he whispered under his breath. Was that why Amandine had looked so ill when he had seen her with Abbot Daniel? He wondered who had given it to her, how much she had taken, and if she were still alive. If she died then all of this...

He pulled the sleeve of his tunic down as far as he could to cover his hand, for he did not want to get any Hemlock on his bare skin accidentally. He then carefully brushed the reeds out of the way.

Under the reeds, he discovered two names that had been crudely carved into the stonework of the wall. Amandine had been busy it seemed, for there as plain as day, was her name and that of her lover's, both of which were covered in blood. Her blood. He touched their names and then drew back his hand quickly because, as unlikely as it seemed, the blood was still wet. He looked at the blood on his finger with horror. Fire and blood. Death and destruction. He had caused this. Amandine's blood was on his hands, as was Abbot Daniel's, the monks, and those that had died on the pyre. And not forgetting Merton's blood — that was on his hands too. Shame was his burden to bear, but right now that burden seemed too heavy. It was very easy to say to himself that every man makes mistakes, but to do what he had done... Was there any way back from that? He quickly rose to his feet. It felt as if the walls were closing in on him and the smell of the Hemlock burnt his throat with each breath he took. The voices of those who had suffered because of him cried out, and images flashed in front of his eyes of Amandine, the Abbot... And Merton. Without pausing to think, he picked up the child and fled the room as if the Hounds of Hell were at his very heels. He slammed the door shut and leaned against it, trying desperately to catch his breath and calm the feeling of panic in his chest. The child moved in his arms and looked at him with terror, for his fear had set off her own.

"It is all right," he reassured. He closed his eyes and lent his head against hers. "It will be all right," he said again.

He could still hear the voices. They were calling his name, begging him for mercy. He shook his head as if that would help dislodge them and he backed away from the door. The voices became a whisper, and then there was silence. Like a wind, the voices had blown away. He would command that the door be nailed shut. He hoped that would be enough to contain the ghosts that lingered there.

Philippe hurried along the corridor, desperate to put space between him and Amandine's old chamber. He had never been more pleased to see the two guards who were stationed outside of his door. One of the guards opened the door, and Philippe ordered that the Royal Healer be brought to his chamber immediately. For he genuinely feared for the girl's health. The night air would have done her no good. It certainly had not done him any favours.

His chamber was warm, thanks to the fire and his nose began to run with the change in temperature. The child's nose ran as well, but she simply wiped her nose on his tunic. Yesterday, Philippe would have grimaced and thrust the child from him, but now he didn't care. He sniffed and made his way over to the hearth. In this room, this sanctuary, the flames chased away the cold, whereas out there, it embraced it. The child cried out in panic when her eyes fell upon the hearth.

"Shh," Philippe soothed, understanding her fear. "This is a good fire. It is nothing like the bad one who took your mother."

He pulled a chair up close to the hearth and sat down upon it. The child cried and tried to move away, but he would not let her. She needed the warmth if she were to survive.

"It is not going to hurt you," he promised. "I won't let it hurt you." But she didn't look convinced.

"Your dolly is cold," Philippe stated desperately. "I think she would like to warm her hands."

The little girl made a whimpering sound, shook her head and held her doll all the tighter.

"I am going to warm mine," Philippe said, but before he could move his hand, she had grasped hold of it in her own and again she shook her head. Tears began to fall from her eyes.

"What is your dolly called?" Philippe asked, desperate to distract her from the fire.

Her little lips were turned down and then she screwed up her face and began to sob in earnest.

"I will keep both you and your dolly safe," he heard himself make the promise, even though he had no right to. He could not keep Amandine safe, or Abbot Daniel, or the monks, or the people under his care. What right did he have to make a promise he could not hope to keep?

"Fire took away your family, but this fire will keep you and your dolly alive. I won't let it hurt you. I swear, with God as my witness, you are safe. We do not have to get any closer to the fire, but I am not getting up from this chair, for I am very tired and you are very heavy to carry about," he smiled, hoping to see an answering one in her face, but he did not.

Philippe did not have much experience with children so, in desperation, he began to hum a song from his childhood that he had all but forgotten. Thankfully, the song seemed to settle her, and it wasn't long before she lost her battle against sleep. Her eyelashes touched her cheeks, and with a great sigh, he felt her body relax.

Tears fell silently down his face as he rocked the child in his arms. He didn't know what to do. He felt like an animal caught in a trap. The only way to escape the pain was to die. But he didn't want to die. He had too much to atone for before he closed his eyes for the eternal sleep.

It wasn't long after, that there was a gentle knocking on the door and a young woman, of no more than twenty, entered his chamber. She had a basket hanging from the crease of her elbow, and her hands were carrying a tray of steaming broth and fresh bread.

She curtsied somewhat clumsily.

"Alwena?" Philippe sniffed back his tears when he saw his childhood friend. "What are you doing here? Where is Franseza?" Franseza was the Royal Healer and what she lacked in a bedside manner she more than made up for with her knowledge of healing.

Alwena did not answer immediately. Instead, she put the tray and her basket down on the table. She then crossed to where Philippe sat and knelt down next to his chair.

"Who is the child?" she asked gently, reaching out and touching the little girl's matted hair.

"I do not know her name. All I know is that her mother and sister died on the pyre. I don't even know how old she is."

"She cannot be much older than three. She is half-starved, bless her little soul. So maybe she is older. It is hard to tell sometimes. We should wake her and see if we can get her to eat something."

"Wait," Philippe reached out and caught Alwena's arm when she made to rise. "You didn't answer my question, what are you doing here?"

Chapter 7

The South Sea. One day later...

"*The sun rises and the sun sets, and hurries back to where it rises... All streams flow into the sea, yet the sea is never full. To the place the stream comes from, there they return again... What has been will be again, what has been done will be done again; there is nothing new under the sun.*" Brother Sampson sensed Merton's stare, so he turned his head to look at him. "*Is there anything of which one can say 'Look! This is something new?' It was here already, long ago. It was here before our time...*"

Merton frowned and turned his attention back to the woman who was asleep, her head resting on his chest. He fussed with the fur that was covering them, pulling it over the woman's shoulder.

The others in the boat had fallen oddly silent. The battle had been won. They had been victorious. They had got what they came for. After the exhilaration of outwitting the enemy and the feeling of relief that came with that, exhaustion had finally caught up with them all. The sound of the boat creaking and groaning as it skimmed the waves had an enthralling feel to it, anyway. Likewise, the gentle rocking of the vessel was a comfort, much like a mother singing sweetly to her child would be. No wonder so many of the warriors had fallen asleep. There was a rhythm to the boat as she rose and fell on the tide, a sense of quiet order. Sampson closed his eyes and took a moment to enjoy this feeling of peace. He valued it for what it was — a stolen moment. The calm before the storm.

If only they could stay in this moment forever. Sampson opened his eyes and looked back at Merton. If only he had the power to protect him, to take away his hurt, to ease his suffering, and make him whole again. He had saved Merton's life back in the dungeons of Benwick Castle, and now he felt obligated to look after him. No. That wasn't the right word. His feelings towards Merton were so much deeper than something as cold as an obligation.

Sampson had grown up in a monastery. He had been conditioned from an early age to love God. That had been no hardship. God was very easy to love. People, on the other hand, were confusing. They said one thing and then did another. They praised and cursed in the same breath. Sampson knew where he stood with God, but when it came to his fellow man, he was often unsure of their motives. If he did not have God to ground him, then he would truly be lost at sea. Forever adrift. He would have been the black sheep in a flock of white. Never quite fitting in. Perhaps that is why he and Merton were drawn to each other — Merton didn't fit in either.

The wind had been in their favour ever since they left Brittany. The Saxon mercenaries praised *Wade* for this act of mercy, but Sampson knew better. It was God that had given them the gentle wind. It was God that steered their vessel, although Sampson suspected Eadger would have something to say about that — it was, after all, his turn to be in charge of the steering oar.

Sampson smiled softly as he watched Merton kiss the top of Amandine's head. And to think he had harboured doubts about rescuing her. Abbot Daniel had been right all along. He had been blinded by a mortal man's fear of death. *"I am the resurrection and the life,"* Sampson whispered to himself. How God liked to test his faith, he swore silently that he would never doubt him again.

"Here," Alan handed him a stale biscuit and sat down beside him, the boat rocking gently underneath them as he did so. "Did you get any sleep?" Alan asked.

Alan was the Keeper of the Blade, the man whose duty it was to reunite Arthur's knights when the time came. That time had now come. Once he reunited them, then the prophecy would be fulfilled. But it was an impossible task, and Sampson feared that there was no way in Heaven or earth that Alan would be able to accomplish it. The knights were either dead or in hiding. Finding a needle in a haystack would be easier than finding Arthur's lost knights. Sampson did not envy Alan his task. But he kept his peace. Who was he to say it was impossible?

Sampson screwed up his nose and yawned. "A little," he answered. "She is still not out of the woods. I wanted to be awake in case either of them needed me."

He looked back at Merton and Amandine, and he felt compassion fill his heart. Merton could barely move without grimacing in pain and Amandine, the poor child, was hanging onto life. She had denied herself food in the hope that God would come for her before the executioner did. The road ahead of her would be a long one, but Sampson was confident she would recover, for she had a very good reason to live. Whereas Merton… How long did he have before he would be bedridden? His twisted back wasn't going to get any better. Sampson suspected it was going to get a lot worse. Everyone had thought that Merton would die in a battle in a far-flung place, but Sampson knew that Merton's enemy was no longer a warrior with a sword or an army intent on vengeance. *Time* was now Merton's greatest enemy. And everyone knew that time, like the tide, waited for no man.

"Did you?" Sampson asked, trying to free his mind of an uncertain future that no mere mortal could ever hope to foresee. "Sleep?"

"A couple of hours, maybe," Alan stated. "Land cannot come soon enough though. I am not by nature a sailor."

Sampson agreed wholeheartedly with Alan although he didn't say anything. Instead, he turned back to look at the sunrise.

"We did the right thing," Sampson spoke more to himself than he did to Alan. "But—"

"War is inevitable. It always was. Us rescuing Amandine just brought it forward a little, that is all. Mordred will not be content until he rules the whole of Briton. If he were to conquer, if he were to succeed, then everything and everyone we have ever loved will be destroyed. Mordred is…" Alan sighed deeply. "What he did to my father… What he did to the nuns at Holywell…"

"He will be punished," Sampson reassured. "God will punish him."

"I do not think we have the time to wait for God's judgement. And I do not think I have the patience."

"In the monastery, we are taught to forgive. We are told not to pay back a wrong with another wrong. We are told to turn the other cheek. Justice is for God to deliver, but I have seen enough to understand that there is a time for war, just as there is a time for peace," Sampson shook his head as he thought of the coming battle. He could almost taste the foul scent of death and destruction in his mouth. "But I wish that... I wish that we could find a way to live in harmony with each other. Why is it so hard to love our neighbour?"

"Because peace is a foreign word to men like Mordred. While men such as Mordred live, there will always be a reason to fight."

"I fear you are right, but then I look at him," Sampson looked once more at Merton. "And then I remember there is always a reason to hope."

***

Merton kissed the top of Amandine's head and then closed his eyes. But sleep did not come. It should have done. He was bone weary. He had not slept for days, but he didn't feel safe. Even on a boat full of friends.

He thought of Trace, whom they had left back in Brittany. Trace had been with him for almost five years. They had fought side by side in countless battles. So many memories. And now he was dead. Trace should have known better than to cross him. What had the fool been thinking? How dare he think to challenge him for the leadership of the men. He may be a cripple, but that did not make him incompetent, or somehow lacking in intelligence. He would not stand for disloyalty. Not even from a friend. Especially not from a friend. Trace was dead because he had killed him and thus eliminated the threat of revolt. But that didn't make his death any easier to live with.

Merton opened his eyes and stared across the deck at his dearest friend. Yrre was looking out to sea, lost in thought. It was a small comfort to know that if he had not killed Trace, Yrre would have. A long time ago Merton had thrown a fight to save Yrre's life, after that the two of them had been inseparable. Where there was one, the other was not far behind. They would always have each other's backs, and nothing would ever change that.

Yrre touched the woven leather band around his wrist, and with the sight one has when you have been in someone's company for a very long time, Merton knew precisely what Yrre was thinking of. Yrre was thinking about his wife and his children.

Merton used to envy Yrre his family. But now, at last, Merton had a family of his own. A proper family. That was if Amandine still wanted him after she learned the truth. Dear God, he hoped she did. He loved her so much.

Darker thoughts entered his mind. His brother, whom everyone thought was dead, had, after ten years, turned up alive. He thought back to his last conversation with Garren. They had parted on bad terms, and he hadn't wanted that. Garren had been lost to them for so long that it felt like a miracle to be in his presence again, but as with all miracles, it came with a price. He had to tell her. He had to tell Amandine that Garren still lived. And when he finally plucked up the courage to tell her the truth, there was a very great chance that he would lose her to him.

He would let her go, he told himself, if that was her desire. She was alive, and that was enough. If she were happy, then so would he be.

Who was he trying to jest? If she did not choose him, he would be devastated. Garren didn't love her. He never had. Merton felt a wave of possessiveness wash over him. She was his. *His.* Not Garren's. Not anymore.

Amandine fidgeted, trying to make herself comfortable and he moved to accommodate her. He still couldn't quite believe it. He had been told that she was dead. All those months of heartache, thinking he had failed her. Thinking she was dead. All that stolen time that they would never get back.

"Merton," she mumbled his name in a sleepy protest.

"Shh, go back to sleep."

She made a tiny kitten like sound, which filled his heart to overflowing with emotion. They were going to kill her. They wanted her to die on a pyre. *How could they?* He felt tears gather in his eyes as he thought of all the vile things they had done to her. The Church had shaved off her once glorious long dark hair. She had been beaten, ridiculed, damned. These thoughts made him hold her a little tighter. He wouldn't let anyone ever hurt her again.

A pain stabbed him in between his ribs, and he hissed in a breath. He needed more of his tonic, but he had taken the last of it last night. So in the meantime, he would have to grin and bear it. He just hoped Santo, his brother's Royal Healer, had a supply to hand when they anchored, for he doubted very much he would be able to walk without it. He feared it was a sign of things to come. Maybe he should let her go. What did he have to offer her? A body that was failing. A life on the run from his enemies. That was not what she needed. She needed stability. She needed a man who could protect her, not one who had to rely on others. He was selfish to even dream of keeping her with him. But by God, he loved her. He prayed that his love would be enough to sustain her, for it was all he had to give.

Merton opened his eyes and saw Sampson staring at him again. He wondered what was going on in that young monk's mind. Sampson gave him a reassuring smile, but he didn't return it. How could he? Until Amandine knew the truth about Garren, then nothing was settled.

"Thank the gods. Galahad. Look. Land," Yrre called out, with joy in his voice.

Those asleep roused themselves to see. Above them gulls flew, crying out to each other in sheer joy at being alive. As for Galahad, well that was the name Merton now went by. Merton du Lac had died that dreadful day when Philippe took the throne. It was better for everyone that he remained dead. The name Galahad had been Yrre's idea. At the time, Merton could not have cared less what he was called. All he could think about was how he had failed Amandine. The borrowed name was supposed to keep him safe, but Merton knew that one day his sins would catch up with him. It was just a question of when.

Amandine stirred in his arms again and opened her eyes. She tilted her head to look up at him, and Merton bent down and brushed his lips against hers.

"I feared you were a dream," she whispered, her voice filled with wonder as she raised her hand to touch the soft bristles and the raised scars on his face. "I was afraid to open my eyes. But you really are real," she laughed softly in disbelief. She touched a lock of his flaming red hair and pushed it back behind his ear. "Last night…" she studied his face intently for several seconds as if looking for something. "I am sorry if I hurt you. I didn't know who you were, and I didn't know where I was. I was scared."

"You certainly gave me a walloping," he grinned gently down at her, his grey eyes alight with humour. "I think you have the makings of a great mercenary. I might have to recruit you to my cause."

She smiled at his teasing, but then she began to trace the scars on his face with the tips of her fingers, and her smile disappeared. "Do they still hurt?"

"Yes," Merton replied. "But the pain I felt when I thought you were dead was a hundred times worse. Philippe had broken my body, but that was nothing compared to the pain in my heart. Without you, I was lost."

"That day… When they beat you. You were so brave," Amandine replied.

Her fingers felt like butterflies on his skin, so soft and gentle. He closed his eyes to savour the sensation.

"I never knew anyone could be that brave," Amandine continued. "You could have won your freedom and yet, you surrendered to their torture to save me. Why? I am but one person. Just one amongst so many."

"Why do you think?" Merton asked shakily, opening his eyes to look at her again, hoping she could see the depth of his love in his scarred and deformed face.

"I gave you these scars," Amandine stated with a painful realisation, her hand dropping away from his face. "You are like this because of me," her voice was thick with unshed tears.

"No, not because of you," Merton immediately contradicted. "My reputation, Philippe's greed, Mordred's hate, and Bastian's fear, gave me these scars—"

"I should not have gone back to your chamber. If they had not found me there, then they would never have known about us. If they had not known, then you would have had no cause to surrender. Bastian would not have taken your sword arm." Amandine touched what was left of his arm. "Philippe would not have lashed you." She touched his face again and shook her head. "I am to blame." She sat up and her eyes filled with tears, her hand fell away from his face. "I am to blame," she said again as a tear slipped down her cheek. "How can you stand to be near me?"

"I was marked to die that day," Merton answered. He reached up and cupped her face lovingly with his hand; his thumb gently stroked the contours of her cheek and brushed away the tear. "I was told to fight to the death, *my death*. Contrary to popular belief I am no devil, I could not defeat five thousand men, and Philippe knew that. Philippe gave me a choice, Amandine, and that choice was to fight or kneel. Either way, I would lose my life. There was no way I was ever going to kneel to him. I was under no illusion that I was going to come out of that fight alive. I just hoped that you and Alden would. Amandine, I once told you that loving me had consequences, but you did so anyway, and I did nothing to stop you because you gave me hope that I could leave all that I was behind me and maybe, become a better man. You had faith in me when I had lost all faith in myself. You loved me, even though I thought myself unlovable. I cannot even begin to describe what that felt like. I would have done anything to protect you, I still would. You are my world, Amandine. And I love you."

"You were so brave," Amandine said again as she took his hand in hers, entwining their fingers. "I tried to be brave," her voice quivered as she spoke. "I tried to be like you. You stood against five thousand as if it were an everyday occurrence."

"Believe me, that was not an everyday occurrence. I was terrified."

"I didn't want to dishonour your memory by begging for mercy," Amandine continued as if she had not heard him. "But they were relentless… I am so ashamed. I betrayed you. I condemned you. I would have said anything to make them leave me alone."

"Alan told me what they did to you," Merton answered, his voice filled with emotion. "You have nothing to be ashamed about. I am humbled that you tried to defend me against such overwhelming opposition. And I do not blame you for giving in to their demands."

"I pretended that you were by my side and for a time that gave me courage. But I was so scared. Sometimes I wished for death…" She touched the ragged scar on her neck. It was a reminder of her failed attempt at taking her own life, "…so that I could escape their torment. They didn't even tell me you were dead, I overheard. They wouldn't let me see your body. They wouldn't let me visit your grave. They wouldn't let me grieve."

"I am not dead. The body wasn't mine. It is over. You are safe now," he reached up and touched the scar on her neck. "And we are together. I will never leave your side again unless you ask me to. I swear it," he promised. "I love you." He cupped his hand around the back of her neck and kissed her softly. Their kiss tasted of tears and despair. When their lips parted, they stayed close. His forehead resting against hers, their eyes closed.

"I love you too," she said in a whisper, and he opened his eyes.

"I know you do," he replied with a tender smile. He shifted his position so she could lay her head upon his chest once more. He wrapped his arm around her and breathed out unsteadily.

Sampson cleared his throat loudly, and he drew Merton's gaze. Sampson's eyes were full of knowing. Was it too much to ask for a little time before reality intruded? This may well be the last chance of holding her close. If she chose Garren, then this was all he would ever have. Like a dying man, he wanted a little more time. Just a little more…

"Look," Merton moved slightly so Amandine could see over the saxboard. "Cerniw. Your new home." He smiled at the look of wonder on her face. Cerniw had a habit of doing that. The rugged beauty of the land could still take his breath away. Amandine looked back into his face for a moment and smiled, and then she went back to looking at the waves as they crashed against the rocks. If this were all he had with her, then he would make the most of it. He studied her face, committing every line to memory. But soon the thought of losing her became too much. He closed his eyes for a moment as his love for her almost undid him.

"It is so beautiful," Amandine whispered in awe.

Merton opened his eyes and smiled. He began to whisper the story about the exiles of Troy. He spoke of Corineus and how he had single-handily defeated the giant, Gogmagog, in an epic battle to the death. And in doing so, Corineus won himself a kingdom. The kingdom was Cerniw and the rest, as they say, was history.

"Thank you, for sharing that story with me," Amandine said when he had finished his tale. "Is there any truth in it?"

"I like to think so," Merton replied. "Corineus was the first King of Cerniw and thanks to his daughter, Gwendolen, it has been ruled by various members of my family ever since."

"That would explain a few things," Amandine answered thoughtfully.

"And what do you mean by that?" Merton quizzed when she began to giggle. It was the first time he had heard her laugh since they had rescued her. The sound gave his soul reason to hope.

"I was thinking of Hector, one of the princes of Troy," Amandine replied, still giggling.

"And what about him?" Merton asked, a smile pulling at the corner of his mouth.

"He was like you," she stopped giggling and smiled up at him.

"Brave. Kind. Loyal. He was a hero."

"Not to the Greeks he wasn't," Merton replied. "To them, he was a—"

"Devil?" Amandine asked. The word hung between them for a moment.

"They weren't Christians so that, I wouldn't know. Amandine, don't compare me to him. I am no Hector."

"But you are like him. You are honourable, and you would do anything for those you love," the smile fell from her face. "You stupid fool," she punched him softly on his chest. "Taking on the Breton army alone, what were you thinking?"

"I was thinking of you, mostly. I told you I would have to do something barbaric after you compared me to a sunrise."

Amandine giggled at the memory, and he bent down and kissed the tip of her nose. It was so good to hear her laugh. He felt his heart overflow with love. No more words were said as she settled her head back on his chest. Together they watched as the birds played on the currents in the air.

The feeling in the boat changed from exhaustion to one of eager anticipation. They were almost home. But instead of joy, Merton felt only trepidation. Sampson was right. He had to tell her. He was running out of excuses. He was running out of time. He held her a little tighter, and he tried to find the words, he really tried, but he could not voice them. Every part of him rebelled at the thought. He loved her, and she loved him. Why could Garren not have stayed away? Why did he have to come back?

Chapter 8

They followed the coast of Cerniw for some time. They could have docked at one of the many fishing or merchant harbours, but they chose to sail on to Dor. At Dor there was no harbour or jetty, for that had been destroyed many years ago, and no one had ever thought to rebuild it. Merton wished he felt a sense of belonging. Cerniw was where he lived, but it wasn't his home. He kissed Amandine on the forehead. His home was wherever she was. So if she chose his brother…

"We have been seen," Yrre stated, pointing to a lone rider who was urging his horse up a steep hill that was covered in coarse grass and copious amounts of sand. A small village was tucked behind the hill, out of sight, and behind the village was his brother's fort. Their long and arduous journey was about to come to an end, and all aboard were thankful. All, except for Merton.

This was it. He had delayed for long enough. He had to tell her.

"I'm scared," Amandine whispered unexpectedly, her blue eyes once again shimmering with tears.

"There is nothing to be scared of. No one will hurt you here. This land belongs to Alden. This is du Lac land. This is where you belong."

"Brittany was du Lac land," Amandine stated quietly. "But everyone there hates me and hate is always catching, have you ever noticed that?"

"Yes," Merton replied, his heart breaking anew at everything she had been through. "But hate will not follow you here."

"The things they said. The things they accused me of. They wanted me to die. They called me a whore. They said I worshiped the Devil, and that I had been possessed by a demon. My death was to be a celebration... I do not understand how my love for you made them hate me so much that their only answer was to burn me."

"They didn't hate you. They hated me," Merton answered softly, but inside he raged. They would pay dearly for what they had done to his beloved. He would make sure of it. "Their hate should have died when I did, but the problem with hate is that it is irrational and very difficult to let go of. I was dead, and you loved me, so it was very easy for them to transfer that hate onto you. You did nothing to deserve their hate. It is a reflection of them, not of you. You are no more possessed by a demon than I am. Hate has a lot to answer for."

"The things they said about you. They made me pray for your damnation," she shook her head as the tears came yet again. "I didn't want to... But they beat me. Starved me. Ridiculed me. I didn't mean what I said..."

"Shh, I know," Merton soothed. If he ever saw Philippe again, he would not kill him for the things he had done to him, but for the things he had done to her.

"Forgive me?" she begged.

"There is nothing to forgive. I am not going to hold you accountable for the things they made you say. They were in the wrong, not you."

"But still I said them," Amandine stated. "I should have refused. I should have suffered the consequences. I betrayed you more thoroughly than anyone else ever has," she shook her head in horror as she looked at him. "I love you. I should have defended you. I should have defended you to the death, but I didn't."

Merton had never seen such grief before in another, and the fact that she grieved because she feared she had wronged him was unexpected. They said that love was stronger than hate, but Merton knew, at that moment, that love could be just as condemning. He could see that condemnation, that guilt, in Amandine's eyes.

"You didn't betray me," he spoke past the lump in his throat.

"They said I had betrayed Garren... They said so many things. They said I was an evil person. A sinner. They made me question myself, and I began to believe that maybe I was the evil person they portrayed me to be."

"They knew what would hurt you and they used that to their advantage," Merton replied. "They exploited your caring heart and turned it against you. You are not evil, far from it…"

"I was told so many times that I was in the wrong. Philippe would say the same thing over and over again about how wicked you were. He would talk about the things you had done. That barn… All those people."

Merton sucked in a breath at the reminder. There was no room for that barn and all the ghosts that accompanied it, on this boat.

"Even Brother, I mean Abbot Daniel said you were a monster, and by the end, I began to wonder if maybe they were right."

"Do you still think that?" Merton asked, holding his breath as he waited for her answer.

"Philippe made me like him, you see. He was my only friend when Alan left," she said, not answering his question.

"He wasn't your friend, he was using you," Merton replied. He could do nothing to hide the pain in his voice. How could she even think Philippe a friend after everything he had done? "He was just using you."

"That is what I thought too, but there were times when he seemed so honest and sincere."

"He ordered your execution," Merton reminded her, a little more harshly than he had intended. He had expected a battle when it came to Philippe. Alan had told him how the new King of Brittany had manipulated her. But to hear her call Philippe a friend and himself a monster cut to the quick.

"He saved my life," Amandine stated. "He saw me with Abbot Daniel. He knew what we were doing. There were soldiers everywhere, but he did not alert them to my presence—"

"He saw you? Are you sure?" Merton could not believe what he was hearing. Why would Philippe let his prized prisoner escape?

"Philippe spoke to me. He said he would try to delay the execution for as long as possible so that I could escape. If he was simply using me then why would he do that?"

A million reasons raced through Merton's mind as he looked at her. Had she been sent to spy? He immediately dismissed such a thought. Amandine was a du Lac. She was the love of his life. She must have imagined Philippe's generosity. It was the only explanation. "Amandine, when Alan carried you onto the boat you were unconscious. Perhaps you dreamt—"

"It wasn't a dream," she said again as if trying to convince herself as well as him. "I know it wasn't. He gave me a silk purse." She sat up and searched for the said item, but she could not find it. She must have dropped it.

"I think you dreamt it," Merton stated as he stilled her searching hands and tucked her back in, for she was wearing only an old and mouldy tunic, which would do nothing to keep the fresh sea air from her skin.

"It wasn't a dream. I know what he did. Here, look at this ribbon," Amandine pulled up her sleeve and showed him a ribbon the colour of the summer sky. "He gave that to me the night he told me I was to die. I think I must have known, deep down, that he wouldn't do it. I knew he wouldn't go through with it. He spared me, Merton."

Merton looked at the ribbon and it felt as if a bit of him died in that moment. "Take it off," he demanded softly. "Please, I can not bear to see it."

Amandine looked down at the ribbon and then back into Merton's face.

"It was a gift," Amandine replied.

"It is a lie," Merton countered. "Everything he said, everything he did was a lie. I heard he was to receive a Papal Blessing with your death. That is no small thing to be thrown away without regard."

"I know it doesn't make sense. But he didn't want me to die. I know he didn't."

"And why would he not want you to die?" Merton asked with a growing suspicion. "What are you not telling me? Why did he give you this ribbon? Why did he give you a silk purse?"

"I don't know," Amandine said a little too quickly. "Hold me. I am cold."

He wrapped his arm around her and pulled her closer towards him. But by doing so, he could feel the quickness of her panicked breath. She was keeping something from him, and he wouldn't allow that.

"I don't want there to be any secrets between us," he breathed the words into her hair. "Why do you think Philippe spared you?"

"You wouldn't understand," she said with a small sigh.

"Try me," Merton encouraged. He tried to ignore the pit of dread that made his stomach feel heavy.

She gave a brief nod and breathed in deeply. On a long sigh, she released her breath and wet her dry lips with her tongue. "Philippe told me that if he were not the King of Brittany and I had not been your whore, he would have married me."

Never had words wounded so profoundly. Merton felt as if someone had grabbed him by the throat and was strangling the life out of him. This could not be happening. Why would Philippe have said something like that? Unless...

"Are you trying to tell me that he loves you?" his voice broke on the words. "He beat you. He hit you. I saw it with my own eyes. How can you..." A sudden dark thought entered his mind, and although his heart rebelled at voicing such a question, he had to ask. He had to know. "Tell me you did not share yourself with him? Please God, tell me you didn't." Merton almost gagged on the words, and the thought of Philippe's hands on her made him want to turn the boat around and wring that bastard of a King's neck.

"No. Of course not. It wasn't like that. He kissed the back of my hand several times, but nothing—"

"He kissed you? And you let him?" Merton asked. He felt like he had been kicked in the stomach and he felt as if his heart was being unmercifully torn into two. "He tortured me, Amandine. Look what he did to me."

"I know what he did, but there were reasons—"

"Reasons? Amandine, for God's sake. He beat you. He gave you to the men. Everything that has happened to you has done so because he either ordered it or turned a blind eye."

"You know nothing." Amandine glared up at him as she spoke. "You were not there. You do not know him as I do."

"Tell me you didn't fall for him and his lies. Tell me it is not him you wish were holding you now."

"No," Amandine replied shakily. "No. Of course not. How can you even think that?"

"What am I supposed to think? You are defending the man who took everything from me. He almost took my bloody life. Perhaps you wish he had."

"Of course I do not wish you dead," she reached up to his face with her hand but he raised his head higher to avoid her touch, and her hand fell away. "I knew you wouldn't understand."

"What is there to understand...?" Merton could not hold her gaze. He shook his head in disbelief and looked away. "He was going to kill you and yet you wear his token."

"The Church was going to kill me. Philippe didn't have a choice. Merton, don't," she grabbed hold of his tunic, preventing him from getting up. "I don't love him. I have never loved him. I love you. You said no secrets. I just wanted to be honest with you. But you have to understand, Philippe isn't all bad. He has been mistreated too. Mordred is—"

"*He* has been mistreated? Am I supposed to feel sorry for him?" Merton interrupted. He was hanging onto his temper by a thread. "Look what he did to me."

"He made a mistake."

"*He made a mistake?* Well, that is all right then. We all make mistakes. By God, can you hear yourself speak? You are praising the man who tortured me and who abused you."

"He didn't abuse me. He took care of me. It was the Church..."

Merton had had enough. He pushed her gently from him with the intention of getting to his feet, but his body had other ideas. When he tried to move, pain shot across his back and down his legs. Without Santo's tonic, he was going nowhere.

"Merton..." Amandine grabbed hold of his tunic again and refused to let go.

"He has got his claws in you, hasn't he?" Merton's voice trembled as he spoke. This was not how he imagined their reunion to be. "Alan said he had, but I didn't want to believe it. I thought you were stronger than that. I thought you were wiser. He lied to you. Everything he said to you was a lie."

"Including the part where he told me he envied you because even in death I was faithful to you...?" She raised her eyebrows briefly and then glowered at him. But then her expression softened. "Merton, I was always faithful to you, despite the things they made me say. I would never go to his bed willingly and nor would I have ever been his queen." She let go of him, and quickly undid the knot that held the ribbon on her wrist. "Philippe gave me this, when I first refused the silk purse and the necklace that was in it. I know you don't want to hear it, but Philippe became my friend. I can't pretend that he wasn't. Don't ask me to. But if you rather I throw the ribbon away, then I will..."

"It is your ribbon to do with what you will. Throw it away or keep it, it is all the same to me."

"Please don't be like this. Merton, I can't explain how it feels to be able to see you. To be able to touch you." She raised her hand to his face, this time he did not try to move away. He allowed her touch. Encouraged, she leant forward and kissed him.

He did not draw away, and yet he did not kiss her back either. He did not know how to respond to her. So much had happened to them both. She was foolish if she thought a simple kiss would erase all the damage that her words had just done. He was foolish to think they could go back to how it was.

"So this is how it is going to be," Amandine said as she looked into his eyes. She looked out to sea for a moment and then she tossed the ribbon overboard.

"Don't you dare hate me too," Amandine begged when she turned back to look at him. "I am just being honest. These many months have been nothing more than a living death," she began to cry, and she had trouble getting her words out. "I was on my own, Merton. You left me on my own. You left me behind."

"Amandine, we didn't know you were alive. Alden was told you were dead."

"Perhaps he should have checked..." Amandine answered, almost hysterical now. "And then maybe we wouldn't be having this conversation."

"Amandine—"

"I cannot change what happened, Merton. When Alan left, I only had Philippe to talk to. Can you imagine what that was like? Can you even begin to imagine how awful I felt every time he made me laugh? Knowing, that he had killed you. Knowing that my life was in his hands. I had to trust him, but now...I don't know who to trust. I don't know what is right. HE WAS MY FRIEND. He said he was my friend. I don't understand. I don't..."

"Merton," Alan warned cautiously. "That's enough. She is not strong enough—"

"Do not get involved," Merton snapped back, not bothering to look Alan's way, although he knew Alan was right and that he had to put an end to this, now. For her sake and for his.

"Who can I trust?" Amandine asked again. "Tell me that. Who

can I trust?"

"You can trust, me..." Merton stated, reaching for her. She came willingly, in a flurry of tears. "I'm sorry. Alan is right, you are not strong enough for a stupid interrogation. You have been through so much. I had no right... I'm sorry. I'm so sorry. Don't cry. I am sorry."

"Please don't hate me," Amandine begged. "I could live with everyone else's hate, but not yours. Please..."

"I don't hate you," Merton reassured, his voice, like hers, was thick with tears. "It is hard for me to hear you praise him, that is all. He ruined my life, Amandine. He took my sword arm. He took my strength. He took you. I should have been there. I should have protected you like I had promised to do. You should hate me because I hate myself."

"I do not hold you responsible—"

"I should have seen you safe before I tried to free Alden. I should have... When we anchor you should... You should run from me and never look back. I failed you."

"But when you found out I was alive, you came for me. I would be dead if it were not for you."

"I thought it was—" Merton bit off his reply. It was obvious now that she was confused. One moment she was praising Philippe for her escape from death and now...

"You would never have found yourself in such a situation if it wasn't for me," he said instead. He breathed out unsteadily. He had to tell her about Garren. He was afraid though. Not for himself so much now. But for her. He had no idea how she would take the news. "Amandine, I have to tell you something."

"There is another woman?" Amandine guessed. Her eyes beseeching him to say it wasn't so. "I understand. You thought I was dead."

"No, you don't understand. As if I could look at another woman after you. You mean everything to me. Dead or alive that would never change. No other woman would ever take your place in my heart. I don't want another woman. I want you. But, I cannot pretend that there is not a rival for your heart. And I will not lie to you."

"I do not love Philippe."

"I wasn't talking of Philippe," Merton replied, dropping his voice to almost a whisper.

"Well, then who?" Amandine asked.

Merton could see the confusion on her face. But again, he found he could not say his brother's name.

"The only man I ever loved, apart from you, was Garren."

"I know," Merton's words were stilted.

"Garren is dead," Amandine stated. "He has been dead for a long time. You have nothing to fear from his memory."

"What if, like me, he isn't dead?" Merton asked. "What if you had to choose between us? Who would you choose? Him? Or me?"

Chapter 9

The Kingdom of Cerniw.

How many times had he watched a boat carry Merton away? How many times had he looked to the horizon and prayed for Merton's safe return? Alden du Lac, King of Cerniw, had spent many long years living in fear that one day his brother's boat would return without him in it. It had always been a possibility. Merton was reckless with his life at the best of times. Even as a child he seemingly had no fear of death or injury. He had always been one for taking unnecessary risks. With age, Merton had become a formidable warrior; some whispered on par with Alexander the Great — although Alexander's greatness was always a matter of opinion. Merton had no interest in forging an empire for himself or for conquering the world as Alexander had. He was instead, in it for the money, and some said the glory. But both men had been referred to as demons. Both had been, rightly or wrongly, accused of many wicked things. Alexander had made it to two and thirty — his friends had cried poison. Merton had almost lost his life at three and twenty — but there had been no poison. Just a mallet and a whip.

In that stinking dungeon in the bowels of Benwick Castle, Merton had died. Even thinking about it brought tears to Alden's eyes. But God, in his great wisdom, had shown clemency and restored Merton to them. Brother Sampson had said it was a miracle, but as the months passed by, Alden wasn't so sure. The man God returned wasn't the same as the one he had taken. Merton had changed. He had become a shadow of himself. Merton was alive, but he was also dead. He was living between two worlds, but he participated in neither. He was nothing better than a ghost. It had been a terrible thing to witness.

"Please God, let her be with him," Alden spoke this simple prayer under his breath. He wished with all his heart that things had turned out differently to the reality they were all having to face. Why had he taken the word of a traitor as truth? With Merton injured, it had been his responsibility to ensure Amandine's safety. He had failed her. Just like he had failed Merton.

"ALDEN. NO." His brother's voiced came from the past and echoed through his head. He felt the unwelcomed heat of the fire and the sickening smell of blood and death. He could feel the sting of a whip as it tore at his flesh. And he could hear the mocking laughter of his torturer. The sensations and images disappeared as quickly as they came, and Alden came back to the present with a frightened gasp. His heart was pounding in his chest, and he felt sweat upon his brow, despite the coldness of the day. How many more years did he have to suffer this torment? Wasn't it bad enough that Wessex had taken him from the battlefield all those years ago? Why did he have to keep reliving it? Unfortunately, these images had been coming more frequently of late. He fisted his hands to stop them from shaking, and he took a deep calming breath of the cold sea air. He closed his eyes, determined to let the terrifying images go. He would not be held to ransom by his memories. He would not let the past command his future.

He cursed his own arrogance and stupidity, just as he had cursed it when Wessex had taken him prisoner. He should have known Bastian had lied to him about Amandine. For the love of God, that man made Judas look like an angel. Unlike Judas, however, Bastian had never really been loyal. And as for Josephine... Alden still had not decided what he was going to do with her. He wanted to send her back to her husband. But Annis had asked him to wait until Josephine had birthed her child. They could decide what to do with her after that.

Alden stepped into the surf, not caring if he got his shoes and trousers wet. The tide tugged at his legs, and he gritted his teeth against the cold of the water, but he was not tempted to step back out of the sea. He watched as the men battled with the current as they rowed closer to the shore. Alden narrowed his eyes against the glare of the sun and stepped further into the sea until it was up to his thighs. He involuntarily began to shiver, for the water had a freezing bite to it. But he was committed now. He would not leave the water until he knew the truth. Alden was so desperate to see if Amandine were with them that he contemplated swimming out to the boat. But better sense prevailed. He would know the truth soon enough, no point catching a cold.

"Sire," James, the general of his army, called his name to get his attention.

Alden frowned, but he did not turn to see what his general wanted. The only thing he was interested in was the boat and the people in it.

As the vessel neared, Alden ignored common sense and waded out further. He heard the splash of horses as they too were urged into the sea, but again he did not turn to watch. He battled on through the current until it was up to his waist. He then reached out and touched the smooth damp wood of the boat just above the waterline, and he closed his eyes very briefly and thanked God for small mercies. The boat had made it home, and that was always a reason to celebrate.

"Need a hand?" Yrre asked with a grin as he leant over the boat and extended his hand for Alden to take. "Or are you just looking at the workmanship? I know a very good boat builder if you have it in mind to build a fleet. Although, I hear he is expensive, and he's an Ascomanni," Yrre said the name as if it were a curse.

Alden looked up with questions in his eyes and a frown on his face. "What the hell is an Ascomanni?"

Yrre chuckled. "It translates as *ashmen*. It is just what we call the men from the north. We call them a few other things as well, but that is not fit for the ears of a king. Are you coming on-board or not? I think your brother would like a word."

"Lady Amandine?" Alden asked, holding his breath as he did so. For some strange reason, it felt as if the fate of a nation was resting on Yrre's answer. If not the nation, then Merton's fate was certainly resting on it.

"We got there just in time," Yrre stated. A hard look came into his eyes. "They were going to burn her." The hardness in his eyes lifted and was replaced with amusement. "But Galahad came up with this fabulous idea of dressing the Monk up as a woman."

The relief Alden felt at hearing Amandine was alive was swift but quickly replaced with outrage. *They were going to burn her?* Execution by fire had been outlawed in Brittany during his father's reign. What the hell was Philippe doing bringing it back? While his mind was still in turmoil, he forced a smile. "What is it with my brother and his obsession with dressing everyone up in women's clothes?"

"I don't know. You will have to ask him," Yrre answered with a grin. "Come on. Let me help you up."

Alden grabbed Yrre's offered hand, and with Yrre's help he pulled himself up and onto the boat. His eyes immediately sought out Merton's. His brother was sitting near the stern of the boat, and there, cuddled into him, was a woman wrapped in furs. Bile rose up in Alden's mouth as he looked at them, but he swallowed it down. He was a king, not a coward. It was time to take responsibility and own up to his mistakes. If he had to get down on his knees and beg for her forgiveness, then so be it.

Alden quickly glanced around at the boat's tired crew, making sure that everyone had returned. It was one thing for the boat to make it home, but it meant nothing without those who had originally made up the war party.

"Where's Trace?" Alden asked, looking to Yrre for an explanation.

"He became acquainted with Galahad's axe," Yrre explained with a careless shrug. "It is a long story but needless to say; he got what he deserved. I would have killed him if Galahad had not beaten me to it. Traitorous bastard." Yrre then turned his attention away from his King. He threw a rope at a waiting horseman and then he jumped overboard into the surf. The other warriors followed in his wake, for all hands were needed to pull the boat up onto the beach and with these waves, a horse could only do so much. A dog started barking from the shore in sheer joy, and before anyone could catch her, the dog ran headlong into the surf. With her tail wagging, she jumped over the waves, barking the entire time, for she had spotted her master. Vernon, the youngest of Merton's warriors, gave a shrill whistle, and the dog swam out to where he stood dripping wet.

"There you are. Did you miss me?" Vernon asked his pet, picking the sopping wet animal up out of the sea and hugging her tight. In return, the dog licked his face, his ear, and then his face again.

Trace was dead? Alden frowned at the thought. Yrre must have been jesting when he said Trace died by Merton's hand. Merton could not even pick up a sword, let alone an axe.

"Sire," Brother Sampson bowed his head with respect. He then handed Alden a fur, which Alden gratefully accepted, for that water had been cold, and he was shivering. Sampson looked back at Merton and Amandine. "They are both going to need looking after," Sampson lowered his voice for Alden's ears only. "Lady Amandine especially. That first night, I feared for her life. But she has a strong heart. I think it will see her through."

"Yrre said Philippe was going to burn her? Is that true?" Alden queried, with a frown. Although he did not know why he felt the need to ask for Sampson's confirmation — Yrre had never lied to him before. Well, there was that little white lie about Clovis that Yrre told, but the least said of that, the better.

"She had been condemned by the Church. They said she was a demon worshiper. They lied," Sampson spoke with an angry passion. "I cannot be a part of a Church that justifies the wicked and condemns the righteous."

"What will you do?" Alden asked, looking at the young monk with concern. "I can not imagine you without the robes of God—"

"God has spoken to me, and I will take heed of his word. He will lead and I will follow. It has always been our way. Do not concern yourself with me."

"You are a true disciple of the Lord," Alden stated.

"I try my best," Sampson said with a grin. "You should go and speak to your brother. I need to go and find Santo, Merton ran out of his tonic last night."

"Thank you," Alden said, touching Sampson's arm, preventing him from leaving. "Thank you for helping my brother. Yrre said that he made you dress up—"

"We don't need to speak of that," Sampson interrupted, a look of irritation passed across his face.

"No. Of course not," Alden replied, trying to stop the smile that was threatening to form. Only his brother could convince a God fearing monk, such as Sampson, to wear the clothes of a woman. He wished he had been a fly on the wall for that conversation.

"It is good to be home, Sire." Sampson patted Alden on the back, and then he made his way over to the side of the boat. Sampson gingerly perched on the saxboard, which made the boat rock terribly and if it were not for the warriors holding onto the other side, the boat would have capsized. Sampson was about to throw his legs over the side when Yrre's arm wrapped around his middle and pulled him overboard. Sampson fell into the surf with a tremendous splash. He came up spluttering amidst the laughter.

"I baptise you, Monk," Yrre said with a mocking bow.

"Baptise me?" Sampson spat out water as he yelled. "How dare you—"

Yrre pushed the monk back under the water. This time when Sampson surfaced, Yrre helped the monk to his feet.

"Sorry. I couldn't resist," Yrre replied, still laughing.

Sampson growled and muttered something that Yrre could not comprehend. He then pushed past Yrre and made his way towards the beach.

"Oh, you have upset him now," Eadger jested.

"I have only just started," Yrre replied with a grin.

"Leave the boy alone," Rand stated, he had been the only warrior who had not laughed, and the look on his face was one of extreme disapproval. "I like that monk."

"So do I," Yrre said, still smiling. "So do I…"

***

Alden carefully made his way across the rolling deck to where his brother sat. His shoes were full of water, and each step was accompanied by an undignified squelching sound, but Alden didn't care if the leather shrank, he had other shoes.

When Alden reached the couple, he got down on his knees. His damp trousers chaffed his thighs, but he ignored the discomfort. Amandine had turned and was looking at him with wide, frightened eyes. She had never looked at him that way before. In fact, no woman had ever looked upon him as if he were something to fear. Her bottom lip was trembling, and he felt tears gather in his own eyes. He had done this to her. Trusting fool that he was. She broke eye contact and bowed her head in respect.

"No. Do not bow to me," Alden stated, his voice was hoarse with emotion, so he cleared his throat. "I am unworthy of your respect."

She raised her head, and Alden looked into her gaunt face and her haunted eyes. He wondered what she had experienced and what she had witnessed. He reached out and touched the short strands of her hair with a trembling hand. She flinched as if he were about to hit her.

"What has he done to you?" Alden asked, his hand dropping away from her hair to clasp her hand, he was pleased when she did not snatch her hand away. "What has he done…?"

She looked down for a moment as if ashamed, and then she raised her eyes back to his. She was like a hunted doe who was too exhausted to run and had now turned to look at her attacker. He wondered if her life was flashing before her eyes as she looked at him.

"I am so very sorry. I was told you were dead. I would never have left Brittany without you if I had known. You have to believe that." He raised her cold hand to his lips and kissed the back of it. "Amandine, I am sorry."

"Sire…" she began to speak, but her words faded away.

"Come here." He thought for a moment that she was going to refuse his request. But on a sob, Amandine went willingly into his arms. Alden sighed with a mixture of equal parts guilt and joy. He closed his eyes, and held her tighter, although he was mindful of his wet clothes. He did not want her to catch a chill because of him.

She was so thin — it was like holding a sparrow in his hands. She felt delicate, breakable. How had she survived this long in the face of such apparent hardship? How dare that bastard starve her. Philippe would pay for all the damage he had done. He would pay… "We are going to have to fatten you up. Don't worry. I'll make sure Annis does not cook for you." he stated, trying to make her smile. "If she did, you would stay this thin forever."

"Her cooking has not improved with time. If anything, it has got worse." Merton added, winking at Alden as he did so.

His jesting had the desired effect, and Amandine hiccupped on a laugh.

"He speaks the truth," Alden agreed. "Even our children know better than to come to dinner when their mother has cooked."

"We should use Annis as our new secret weapon," Merton stated. "If she cooked for the enemy, then they would all be dead within a month. It will save us a job. I don't know why I had not thought of that before."

Alden scoffed at Merton's words, but what he said was true, although he would never consent to his wife going behind enemy lines.

"I can't…I can't believe I am here," Amandine pulled back so she could look into Alden's face. "It is like a dream. I never thought I would see any of you again." She turned towards his brother and held out her hand. Merton leant forward and clasped her hand in his. "All these months… I thought he was dead. I thought…"

"Many have tried to kill him, but he is still with us," Alden smiled at her. "He is like a limpet. No matter how rough the sea is, he will not be defeated. He will hold fast to that rock."

"Thank you for such a vivid analogy," Merton stated, with a rather bemused expression on his face. "I was once compared to the Devil, and now you are comparing me to a limpet. How times change."

Amandine giggled again, but her laughter soon gave way to tears.

"It's all right. It is over now. You are safe." Alden stated with a small smile, and he took her back into his arms. "We need to get you inside and get you to a bed. It is too cold out here," he took her tear-stained face between his hands and raised her head, so she had no choice but to look at him. "I promise, you will never want for anything ever again. You will be under my protection until he decides to make an honest woman of you," Alden smiled down at her as he spoke. But then a sudden coldness travelled up his spine. It was as if death had brushed past him. He dropped his hands from her face and sat back on his heels and looked at her. Was this a bad omen? He had never believed in such things before. It was probably nothing more than his wet clothes, he quickly rationalised. There was nothing to fear. Not in this moment. Nothing at all.

"She knows she just has to say where and when and I will be there," Merton replied, but there was a catch in his voice, and Alden raised his eyes to look into his brother's face. He was surprised by the quiet anger that greeted him.

"I need to see Garren, first," Amandine stated.

Alden breathed out unsteadily, well that explained Merton's anger. So he had told her. This was a conversation that Alden had hoped to save until later.

"We should get the pair of you off this boat," Alden said, quickly changing the subject.

"Alden, I need to see him," Amandine said, catching hold of his tunic with her hand.

He looked down at where she held him and shook his head. "He is gone. He left the same night Merton did," he raised his eyes briefly to Merton's as he spoke. "We had a disagreement. He…" Alden thought back on their quarrel. He wished he knew where it was all going to end. What hope did they have in defeating Mordred and his supporters when they were so busy fighting amongst themselves? "I don't know where he is," Alden admitted. He did not need to look into his brother's face to see the anger that statement had met with. "And before you start," Alden said, looking back at his brother, "I asked Casworon to follow him. If he so much as spits in the wrong direction I will know of it."

"Merton told me Garren challenged you for the throne," Amandine spoke with caution.

"It was a long boat trip, we had a lot to talk about," Merton said in his defence.

"I don't understand him," Alden admitted. "He's different. Garren is not the man we knew. You need to forget about him, Amandine. You have cried too many tears for him already."

"He was my husband," Amandine said quietly.

"Yes, he was. But he isn't anymore. Come on, let us get you back to the fort. Give yourself time to settle in and then we will talk of Garren some more."

Amandine reluctantly nodded her head.

"Can you walk?" Alden asked, with a concerned frown.

"No, she cannot," Merton spoke for her.

"I can," Amandine argued, while a blush brought some much-needed colour into her face.

"No. You really cannot," there was a finality in Merton's words as if he was daring for her to argue with him.

Alden had to bite back a grin when he saw a spark of determination in her eyes. He was glad to see that Amandine was still more than a match for his brother.

"I think I should know if I am capable of walking or not," Amandine huffed. "They are my legs after all."

"Amandine, I don't want to argue with you, but—"

"Then don't," Amandine interrupted, glaring at Merton as she did so.

Alden needed to step in before things got out of hand. Without asking for permission, Alden swept Amandine into his arms and stood up.

"You are as bad as he is," Amandine complained, while she frantically tried to pull the fur that was wrapped around her, over her exposed legs.

"Stop squirming and be quiet. For the love of God, I am going to drop you if you don't stay still," Alden jested. "And besides, I am the king, and if I want to carry you, I will. I need not ask for permission."

Amandine placed her thin arms around his neck and glared up at him. He smiled at her expression. "It is bloody good to see you, Amandine. Welcome home."

The glower slid from her face, and she smiled. "Thank you."

Alden smiled back at her and then he turned his attention to his brother. "Can you walk? I am not sure I could carry you both, but I could give it a go," Alden spoke with good humour. "I just need to fling this piece of sackcloth over my shoulder."

"Don't you dare," Amandine warned, gripping onto his neck all the tighter.

Merton did not answer as he braced himself for the pain that movement brought. Alden watched, feeling helpless, while his brother tried to rise. He knew better than to offer help. Merton hissed through his teeth as he slowly rose to his feet. Alden pretended not to notice how long it took his brother to do something that was so ridiculously simple.

"Can you walk?" Alden asked, when Merton had, with a grunt of pain, picked up the stick he used to help him walk.

"Hell, no," Merton replied with a frustrated growl, and this time there was no humour in his words and his face portrayed his pain.

Chapter 10

Was this now his home? Was it possible for the Keeper of the Blade to have a home? Alan kept his distance from the rest of the party as they made their way towards the fort. He felt like an intruder. He didn't belong here.

Alan had been born in Londinium, but he had spent the better part of his thirty years of life in Brittany. Cerniw was a foreign country to him. He knew nothing of their language or their customs. Reason said that Cerniw could not be that different to Brittany — they had belonged to the same Royal House after all. But Cerniw felt different. And Alan could not fathom why.

He caught the eye of James, the general of Alden's army. James bowed his head, ever so slightly, as a sign of respect. Alan returned the sentiment. But he did not feel encouraged to step forward and speak to the old knight. Instead, Alan retraced his steps and climbed up the sandy embankment. Once at the top, he stopped and looked at the sea. It was cold up there, the wind having picked up speed. And as the waves crashed to the shore, the sky darkened with the threat of rain. Alan felt a wave of hopelessness wash over him. Rescuing Amandine had been the easy part, now his fate awaited him. He could not ignore it any longer. Mordred was gathering an army. It was time he did likewise. But where to start?

His father had said that Percival resided in Northumbria. As for the rest of Arthur's knights, they could be anywhere. They could be dead. Alan sat down on the damp sand. He rested his arms upon his knees, and he stared moodily out to sea. The cold whipped around his body, and because he was still somewhat damp from helping to pull the boat ashore, he could not help but shiver.

Northumbria was a big country, and it wasn't exactly the most stable of kingdoms. Northumbria's neighbour, Bernicia, was yet another kingdom to fall under Mordred's influence — not that such a thing had been acknowledged, but the signs were there. Mordred's influence was vast indeed, as were his coffers. And money could pay for all kinds of evil. The King of Bernicia, Æthelfrith, had made his intentions with regard to Northumbria very clear. And because Æthelfrith had the superior forces, it was only a matter of time before the House of Deiran fell. Alan did not want to be there when that happened. But what choice did he have? He had to find Percival.

Alan groaned aloud as the first drops of rain began to fall from the sky. Everything was against him — even the weather. He allowed his mind to drift, which was never a good thing. He thought of his father, lying in that bed, the smell of sickness in the air. His father had appeared so weak, so defenceless, and yet with a few simple words, he had brought Alan to his knees. His father had chosen to share the most intimate family secret on his deathbed. Alan wished that he had not. Some secrets should remain secrets. That is why they were secret in the first place. But the damage had been done. He now knew a terrible truth. And now the secret was his to share or bury.

The secret was one of lineage and Alan had been left speechless when his father had finished speaking. From the age of twelve, Alan had been a loyal soldier to the House of du Lac. Arthur Pendragon and his knights had been the enemy. They were the monsters that Breton mothers used to threaten their children with if they misbehaved. *Off to bed or Arthur will gobble you up.* The name, Pendragon, was little better than a curse word. And for a good reason. Arthur had brought his army over to Brittany, and Lancelot had to fight to keep his throne. The du Lacs had won that battle —

although Lancelot had once said that no one had won that day. How could there be a victor when the very ground they stood on was saturated with the blood of men who were once friends? Bastian had said that Lancelot was never the same after that battle. And because of that, Alan had hated Arthur, even though he had never met him. Lancelot had inspired that kind of loyalty. He had been the kind of king any soldier would willingly lay down his life for. Alan had never met anyone like Lancelot before. He had been an inspiration and Alan had wanted to emulate him. Everyone in the Breton army had. Lancelot had been the perfect soldier and the perfect king.

That was why it was so hard for Alan to hear that Arthur was his uncle. Which in turn meant that Alan was a Pendragon and the rightful heir to Wessex. Alan would have rather his father had told him he was a bastard son. Better that, than a noble prince of a House he hated. He didn't understand why his father had told him in the first place. What difference did it make? He was a prince without a kingdom. There was no Camelot, not anymore. A Saxon sat on the throne that was rightfully his. But it did mean that Mordred was kin. That knowledge hurt more than a sharp blade to the heart ever could.

It began to rain harder, and Alan watched as the sky darkened so much that the sun disappeared. Was this a sign of things to come? He hoped not.

Alan rose to his feet, brushing the wet sand from his damp clothes as best he could. He took one long last look at the sea, and with reluctance, he turned away. He had wasted too much time already. He needed to organise his supplies, borrow a horse and set off on the long trek north. Even without the threat of war, Northumbria was a vast kingdom to navigate. Percival could be anywhere. Alan had absolutely no idea where he was going to find him. It would be like going into battle blind. No one wanted that sort of disadvantage. It did not inspire confidence.

Alan followed the path from the beach to the village. When he had first caught sight of the Kingdom of Cerniw, he had felt momentarily overcome by its beauty. He had thought Brittany wondrous to behold, but Cerniw was something else altogether. There was a wildness about the place, and it was easy to believe the stories this kingdom inspired. No wonder Alden had fought so hard to win her back from Wessex all those years ago.

A few of the villagers stopped what they were doing and watched as Alan navigated his way around the roundhouses and the animal pens. He wished he could communicate with them, greet them with a good morning, but he knew only a handful of words and no doubt he would pronounce them wrong, so he chose silence over ridicule. The truth was, he had never been one for picking up a foreign tongue, and he wasn't good at conversation. Put a sword in his hand, and that was a different matter, but it wasn't his sword that he needed, not if he wanted to reunite Arthur's knights and lead them under a common cause. But even if he did manage the impossible, would the knights follow him when they found out his intentions? Many had stood with Arthur and fought against Lancelot and his kin. Now Alan was going to ask them to do the complete opposite. He just hoped their collective hatred for Mordred would be enough to sway them to pledge their swords to the du Lacs.

On a hot summer's day, the shadow of Castle Dor's high walls would fall upon the village. But today, everything was shrouded in a depressing dullness. Alan looked up at the battlements. Soldiers with arrows nocked looked back down at him.

Two very fierce and rapidly flowing rivers surrounded Castle Dor. They were more of a deterrent than any man-made moat. But Alden had not been content with that. He had also ordered dry ditches to be dug out as well, and if an encroaching army had somehow managed to navigate the ditches and survive the rivers, then a regiment of wooden pikes awaited them. After that, it was just a case of scaling the battlements while arrows and burning sand rained down from above. Castle Dor seemed impregnable, but then so had Benwick. And yet, Benwick had fallen.

Alan crossed the wooden drawbridge, the soldiers on duty recognised him and allowed him to pass into the fortress without question. It had been a different story only days earlier when Alden had taken him prisoner. Alan, thankfully, had truth on his side and Alden had always been one to listen to reason. Thank God.

For a moment, Alan was unsure where to go. The Great Hall was where everyone would gather, he knew that, but he didn't want to be a part of Alden's court. So instead he headed towards a cluster of roundhouses on the far side of the fort's extensive grounds. He passed the Church. It was nothing like the one in the grounds of Benwick Castle. It was smaller to start with, not so ostentatious, and it did not support an order of monks. Although it was, for the time being, playing host to some displaced nuns.

He headed towards the roundhouse where the nuns were taking shelter. He felt responsible for them. The nuns had looked to him for guidance when the Saxons had come to Holywell. But he had been just one knight, and against such a force, they had no choice but to run for their lives. Mordred had led these Saxon barbarians — he had wanted to silence the Prioress. For she knew things about Mordred that he did not want to be repeated. But Mordred had been unsuccessful in his endeavours. And in his rage, he had allowed his men to rape and murder the nuns they had taken prisoner. There had been no mercy and no compassion. If that was not bad enough, Alan had watched as his frail father was dragged from the Church and handed to Mordred. Mordred had not hesitated; he had taken his knife and slit Alan's father's throat. Alan's footsteps faltered as he thought of that terrible day. He had to find those knights and put an end to this madness. It was then that he noticed Sister Bernice. Sister Bernice carried a bucket in one hand and was leading a goat in the other. She smiled when she saw him, and she immediately tied up the goat. He watched as she stepped into the roundhouse. Moments later she came out again, this time without the bucket, and began to walk towards him.

Alan felt his heart speed up at the sight of her, and he hoped the coldness of the morning air would keep the blush from his cheeks at bay. He had never been romantically involved with a woman before.

At thirty years-old Alan was still innocent in the ways of women. He wasn't naive; he knew the basic facts about lovemaking, but he had never put this knowledge into practice. He was a warrior, first and foremost. Up until now, he had been content with that. He had never felt like he was missing out on anything. That was until he had met her. *She's a nun.* He silently berated himself. And she wouldn't be interested in him even if she were not a nun. No woman was. He was too shy. And he never knew what to say. Women liked men who could turn a phrase, who could shower them with compliments. He was not that kind of man. And besides, what did he have to offer her, or any woman for that matter? He had no home. No money, not since he deserted from the Breton army. He knew not how to be a husband. Soldiering was all he knew. And not forgetting, he was also the Keeper of the Blade. He was responsible for the safety of the kingdom. He had no time for love and all that comes with it. Men like him did not marry. They did not settle down and live the rest of their lives in marital bliss, especially not with a nun. The idea was so ludicrous that he almost laughed. Sister Bernice was devoted to God, who was he to think he could compete with a deity?

Then Sister Bernice smiled at him, and it was as if the sun had suddenly come out. He felt warm inside, despite the dampness of the day. *He must not fall in love with her,* he reminded himself. If he did, if he allowed himself to love, then he would never leave. And he had to.

"You are back, thank the good Lord," Sister Bernice said, and she touched his arm very briefly with her hand. "I was so scared that something had happened to you."

He could not find his tongue, and like a mute, all he could do was stare back. Sister Bernice was so very lovely, and her sparkling green eyes portrayed her kindness and her generous heart. It was sinful therefore to dream about taking her into his arms and tasting her lips.

"How is Guinevere... I mean the Prioress?" Alan stammered over the words, and he coughed in embarrassment.

The smile slipped from Sister Bernice's face. "She is unresponsive.

She does not speak. We have to force her to eat. She just sits there staring at nothing. Brother Sampson is with her now. I hope that he can bring her back to us. If he cannot, then…" she gave a hopeless little shrug.

"She is a strong woman," Alan said, trying to reassure. But he had seen such things before, especially amongst young soldiers after their first battle. Some called it cowardliness. Alan knew different. They had all seen and heard things they had wished they had not that day at Holywell, and no one had come away from that place, and that moment, without scars. But Guinevere had suffered more than most, for she had been responsible for the nuns, and they had died because of her and the secrets she kept. If Guinevere remained lost to them, then Mordred would have got what he wanted all along. The irony was not lost on Alan. "What happened at Holywell will not best her." He said the words with more force than he intended, and he felt the heat rise in his face.

"I think it already has," Sister Bernice disagreed sadly. "Will you walk with me a while?"

The request was unexpected, but not unwelcomed. Alan's blush deepened. "Of course."

Sister Bernice smiled and began to lead the way towards the battlements and Alan, like an obedient puppy, followed in her wake. He tried his best not to notice the softly rounded curves of her hips, or how the rain dampened her long blonde hair and made it curl. She was a nun, for the love of… It was sinful to think of her this way. He tried to concentrate on something else — the rain as it fell from the sky, the soldiers as they patrolled the battlements — and yet it did no good. All he could think about was her.

They climbed the stone steps of the battlements, and together, they strolled along the walkway until they came to a pretty view of the moor, and here they stopped. It was still raining, but softly, almost as if God were weeping.

"Brother Sampson said you had saved the woman…"

"Lady Amandine, yes," Alan confirmed.

"I envy her," Sister Bernice stated quietly, so quietly that Alan thought he must have misheard her.

"Envy?" Alan asked, not understanding.

"If something like that happened to me, there would be no one who would charge to my rescue. Forgive me," she laughed nervously. "A silly girl's daydream of a life denied."

"Do not envy her. She has suffered greatly."

"I meant no disrespect," Sister Bernice quickly stated.

"Are you unhappy?" Alan asked as he tried to decipher the meaning of her words. "I am sorry, that was an insensitive question, after everything that has happened. Of course, you are unhappy." *Why did he not keep his mouth shut? He was making himself look like a fool.*

"The Queen has been very good to us. I must say she has taken us all by surprise. We did not expect such generosity from a Saxon."

Sister Bernice spoke too fast, and she never spoke fast. What wasn't she telling him?

"Do you not want to be a nun anymore?" Alan asked, trying his best to second-guess. She would not look at him as he spoke, and he wondered if he had guessed right.

"You can change your mind," Alan continued with caution, but inside his heart came alive with hope. Perhaps she did have feelings for him. The day suddenly felt a lot warmer than it was. "God will not think less of you if you do. You do not need to spend the rest of your life behind the high walls of a convent."

"I cannot leave my fellow sisters," Sister Bernice said with too much passion. "They are my family. I have known no other. I am an orphan. I was left on the doorstep of the Priory. I was not even wrapped in a blanket. I guess my birth mother did not think me worthy of such consideration. I mean, why should she? She didn't want me."

"Maybe she didn't have a choice," Alan stated softly. "I cannot imagine anyone ever willingly walking away from you." He longed to reach out and brush a stray strand of hair from her face, but he refrained from doing so, for he had no right, and he feared his attention would be unwanted.

"As a child, I did pretend," Sister Bernice admitted as she tucked her wayward hair back behind her ear. "I pretended that I was a daughter of a noblewoman and that she had no choice but to leave me behind," she laughed softly at her foolishness, but Alan could hear a lifetime of heartbreak behind that laugh. "I would wait for her," she continued. "I convinced myself that one day she would return to claim me but… No. No one came. It is hard not knowing who your parents are. Not knowing where you come from."

"It is not always easy when you find out," Alan stated, thinking of his father and what he had told him.

"And besides," Sister Bernice continued. "I did not need a mother. The nuns gave me everything I needed. My childhood was a happy one."

"Just because the nuns raised you, it does not mean you have to become a nun as well," Alan replied. "Do you really want to spend the rest of your life living as a nun?"

Sister Bernice laughed and looked at him with amusement in her eyes. "You make it sound like a disease."

"I am sorry," Alan felt the heat rise in his face yet again, and he turned his attention away from her and tried to concentrate on the view.

"Until the day I met you, I would have said yes," Sister Bernice admitted. "I would have been content to live my life as a nun. I had no desire to leave Holywell. It had been my home for so long. It was the only life I knew."

"Holywell is no more," Alan replied softly.

"As is the life I knew. Sister Helena quotes from John over and over again. She says, *In this world we will face many troubles. But take heart! I have overcome the world.*' These words comfort Sister Helena, and yet, they do not comfort me… Where was God when we needed him?"

Alan had no answer for her, so he did not insult her intelligence by saying it was part of God's great plan or some other such nonsense.

"When all this is over… Will you take a wife? I mean… I know you have to find the knights and unite them. And I know that war is… I was just… Before the Saxons came to Holywell, I was resigned to my life, and now I am not. I think that is because of you…" she laughed nervously and dared a glance at him.

Alan could not believe what he was hearing, and he lost the power of speech, all he could do was stare at her in astonishment.

"Do not get me wrong," she continued. "I am very grateful for everything the nuns have done for me, but I am no longer—"

"Content," Alan finished her sentence for her, and then he swallowed nervously. Cautiously he touched her hand with his, when she did not draw her hand away, he felt encouraged. The touch was innocent enough, but it seemed to fascinate them both. Alan longed to pull her into his arms, but he was all too aware of the soldiers who patrolled the battlements and besides she wore the clothes of Christ. He dared not touch her like that. It would be a sacrilege.

"You have to leave," Sister Bernice stated as she looked down at their joined hands. "You have to find the knights so that the prophecy can be fulfilled. If you want, I will wait for you."

A frown marred his brow as he listened to her words. It was so much more than he expected. Far more than he deserved. He didn't know what to say, and even if he did, he wouldn't know how to say it. She squeezed his fingers and let go of his hand. He wanted to snatch her hand back, but he knew that would be unwise.

"God go with you, Alan," she whispered and raised her eyes to his. "Come back to me."

All he could do was nod. No more words were spoken between them, and she left him standing on the battlements.

***

Smoke from the fire pits stung Alan's eyes as he entered the King of Cerniw's Great Hall. Alan had expected the Hall to be busy, but instead, he found it suspiciously empty, and he wondered where everyone was. However, he was not so curious as to go and look for company. He was in no doubt that at some point during the day Alden's court would gather here. All he had to do was wait. Alan sat himself down next to one of the fire pits, and he allowed the heat to warm him. He watched the flames, and he welcomed this fragile gift of solitude. It gave him time to gather his thoughts and plan his long journey north. Never mind finding Percival, the journey north was going to be a challenge in itself, for there were many kingdoms between here and his final destination, and some of those were Saxon. He breathed out unsteadily. Why was he even thinking of going? No one believed in the prophecy, anyway. Arthur's knights would never ride again. It was nothing but a dream. And yet…

A door opened at the back of the Hall, and Alan looked up. Alden, his Queen and her ladies-in-waiting entered the room. Alan stood and bowed at the royal couple. When he raised his head, he saw Alden kiss his Queen on the cheek. With a smile in his direction, the Queen and her ladies left the Hall.

"Please, sit down," Alden invited as he picked up a pitcher of ale and two clay cups.

Alan sat back down and accepted the cup the King gave him. Alden poured the ale and sat down opposite him.

"Thank you," Alan said.

"It should be me that is thanking you," Alden replied. "Because of you, Lady Amandine is safe."

"All I did was tell you she was alive. Her rescue was all down to Mert…Galahad," Alan quickly corrected himself. "I have never, in my life, met anyone like your brother," Alan admitted. "How he thinks… He sees everything, doesn't he?"

"Sometimes he sees too much," Alden stated, taking a sip of his ale.

Alan did not know what Alden meant by that, but Alden's expression did not encourage questions.

A grey dog wandered into the Hall. He sniffed the air and then made his way over to where they sat, his tail wagging absentmindedly.

The dog sat down next to the King and yawned.

"I am glad I had a chance to speak to you alone," Alden said as he placed his cup of ale down on the bench beside him. He began to play with the dog's soft ears. The dog tilted his head, obviously enjoying the petting. "With everything that has happened, I was wondering, what your intentions are. I don't need to tell you that you will no longer be welcomed in Brittany. If you went back, you would be accused of High Treason, and you would hang, or burn."

"I will not be going back to Brittany anytime soon. I have to find the knights."

"Do you really think it is a wise thing to chase ghosts?" Alden asked. "I mean, you don't really believe in all of that nonsense. Do you?"

Alan unstrapped his blade and handed it to Alden. He watched as Alden traced the engraving on the golden sheath — a knight on top of a horse. The blade was a promise. Alden pulled the blade free of its sheath, and the silver blade reflected the firelight.

"Draíocht," Alan stated. "One of the sixth ancient weapons of Briton. When the Blade, Sword, Shield, Spear, Cauldron, and Stone are reunited, then Arthur's knights will ride again."

"That is just a story," Alden said as he studied the blade.

"It is a prophecy, not a story, and the people of Briton believe in it. And they will rise up and fight the aggressor. They will fight Mordred. It is the only way we can defeat him."

"Do you really think we can defeat Mordred with a group of old men and a handful of relics? Mordred would laugh us off the battlefield, and then he would slaughter us all."

"That may happen anyway," Alan stated with all seriousness. "But the knights will give our army confidence. Tell me you would not feel more assured going into battle if you had your father by your side."

"My father is dead. Mordred killed him." The amusement had gone from Alden's voice, and he handed the blade back. "Alan, it could take you years to track down the knights. Mordred could have burnt Briton to the ground by then. I think your time would be better spent here, commanding a regiment of my men."

Alan had not expected such a proposition. "Sire?" he shook his head in wonder and for the second time that day he found himself lost for words. "I am honoured that you would—"

"You have proven your worth," Alden stated. "And I reward loyalty."

Alan was sorely tempted. He could stay here, marry Sister Bernice and live a good life. Of course, none of them would live for long if Mordred invaded. Alan looked down at the weapon in his hands. The blade felt warm to his touch as it always did. He could hear the blade's silent call to arms. To deny the blade's call would bring nothing but disaster. "I am honoured," Alan said again, dragging his gaze away from the blade to look at the King. "But I am the Keeper of the Blade. I cannot turn my back on my destiny or my promise to my father. He wanted me to find the knights and bring them together. It was his dying wish. I am sorry, but I must decline your generous offer."

Alden did not reply straight away, and Alan had the distinct impression that the King was taking his measure.

"I can see that there is nothing I can say that would change your mind," Alden finally said. "Where are these knights of yours?"

Alan could not hold the King's knowing gaze, so he looked back into the flames.

"Do you even know?" Alden asked.

"Percival is in Northumbria."

"Percival is dead," Alden contradicted. "He died a long time ago. Leodegrance murdered him in cold blood."

"And you know this for sure?" Alan asked. He could not hide the panic in his voice, for Percival was the only name his father had given him. "Leodegrance has been dead for a long time. My father would have known of Percival's death if that was the case."

"My father was not in the habit of lying," Alden stated. "Was yours?"

Alan closed his eyes at Alden's words. Alan's father had lied to him about who he really was for the entirety of his life. Surely that should have been a warning in itself? But Guinevere had not contradicted Kay when he spoke of Percival, and she would have known if he was dead, surely?

"As I said, you are going to be chasing ghosts." There was concern in Alden's voice as he spoke. "You need to forget about your promise to your father. It is going to bring you nothing but heartache and disappointment."

"I cannot," Alan said, opening his eyes and looking at the King. "Percival is dead? If that is so then, I have to find his grave. For he has the Shield."

"If it is a grave you seek, then I suggest you start in Wessex," Alden stated as he rose to his feet. "But please reconsider. If Cerdic catches you in his kingdom, you *will* wish for death."

Chapter 11

Amandine's father had once said that life was full of tragedy. Amandine knew that he had been thinking of her mother when he spoke those words. She could not recall her mother's face, for her mother had taken her place beside the angels a long time ago. But she could remember her mother's smile and how it felt to hold her hand as they strolled barefooted along the beach. She could recall waking from a nightmare, and her mother rushing into the room to comfort her. She had sobbed into her mother's shoulder, and her mother had soothed her with tender words and a warm embrace. What she would give for her mother's comfort right now.

"You are safe."

Amandine had lost count how many times those words had been said to her since she had arrived in Cerniw. She wondered who they were trying to convince — themselves or her? She wasn't safe. No one was. Not while Mordred lived. He would not let such an insult go unpunished. Someone would have to take the blame for her escape. She just hoped it wasn't Abbot Daniel or… Philippe.

Please God, not Philippe.

Amandine had never felt so conflicted. She knew what Philippe had done. She had felt the sting of the back of his hand and Merton was a living witness to the monster that hid in him, but Philippe was a contradiction. There was good in him. At least she thought there was. Not that anyone here wanted to hear that.

Alden had given up his chamber for her, or maybe it had been Merton he had given it up for. Alden had said so much to her, in such a short space of time, that she couldn't remember. She had tried to feel grateful, but there were too many opposing emotions going around in her head. One moment she felt relief that she had escaped death and on the other... Amandine had prepared herself for death, she should be feeling joy and celebrating, but she felt numb and confused. *Where did she go from here?*

The King had carried her into this room and placed her down on the bed, and that was where she had remained. She had felt no inclination to look at all the fine swords that adorned the walls. Nor had she wanted to warm herself by the fire pit. The flickering beeswax candles, which gave the room a warm and homely feel, were of no interest to her. She had not felt compelled to sneak a peek at the important documents that were stacked, one on top the other, on a beautiful oak table. Even the round wooden bath, which the servants had dragged into the room, and then filled with steaming water, did not rouse her curiosity. A bath was an extravagance that she could live without. The warmth of the fire should have been a comfort, but instead, it reminded her that the Church had wanted to burn her alive. Beeswax candles were not necessary. A cheap tallow candle did not burn less brightly. And as for the swords and the documents, they were none of her concern. She was a guest in this foreign land. Just a guest.

"You are safe."

Amandine had been surprised by Castle Dor. She had an idea in her head of what Alden's castle looked like. Amandine had imagined a small comfortable fort, nothing on par with Benwick Castle. She could not have been more wrong. Dor was only a fraction smaller than Benwick. Alden was no provincial king. Cerniw was not a second-rate kingdom. How foolish she had been to think it was. How foolish and naive.

The presence of armed soldiers had not gone unnoticed. They were everywhere. Just like they had been everywhere in Benwick. The soldiers had looked at her with undisguised interest as their King had carried her through the fort to this room. Amandine did not want to be looked upon. She did not want to be seen. She wanted solitude, to live somewhere quiet and out of the way. She wanted to hide away from people, away from everything. Amandine wanted no reminders of a life at court.

When Alden's Queen came running into the room, it took every ounce of what little strength Amandine had left to stay seated and not flee from the Queen, and everyone else for that matter. She did not want to see their happy faces or hear their words spoken ten to the dozen.

"You are safe."

The Queen had embraced her, and Amandine had tried her best not to cringe or flinch. It had just been a friendly hug, meant to reassure. But it did the complete opposite. It had been hard to pretend to be brave when faced with her enemies, but it was so much more difficult to be brave when faced with people who were once her friends and who were still offering friendship.

Annis must have sensed her hesitation, although she did not say anything and none of her actions betrayed her knowledge. However, Annis had not tried to embrace her again and for that, Amandine was thankful.

Annis had spoken of many things, but mostly she spoke of how relieved they all were that she was alive. The King had agreed with his wife, and he had kept winking at Amandine as if to say that sometime soon this would all be normal and that she was safe here. Amandine had wished he would stop. She didn't need his reassurance. She just wanted them to leave her alone.

Annis had brought Amandine some clothes that she no longer wore, with the promise that new gowns would be made for her. What did she want with new gowns? Amandine didn't understand the Queen's generosity. She wasn't worthy of such gifts. Why did no one here understand that? What was the matter with them all? She was the daughter of Satan... Or so she had been told over and over again. Amandine briefly closed her eyes. She wasn't the daughter of Satan. She wasn't. It was just a poisonous lie the late Abbot had made up to make her feel inferior and unworthy.

The Queen's welcome could not have been more gracious. Amandine was lucky to have ended up here and yet... She did not feel lucky. She felt as trapped in this room as she had done in her chamber in Benwick Castle. But at Benwick her room had been hers, and hers alone. No one else apart from Alan, Bastian, Abbot Daniel, and the King had ever entered that chamber, whereas here, it was like being stuck in the middle of a busy crossroads. There seemed to be so many people coming in and out of the room that they had all blurred into one. They had worn the same smiling faces. They had said the same reassuring words.

"You are safe."

The chamber began to feel too small, too crowded. There were too many conversations, too many smiles. Even the water being poured into the bath sounded offensive to her ears.

A beautiful grey *Cú Faoil* wandered into the room. His tail was wagging as he looked for a petting. But the sound of his claws as they pitter-pattered on the wooden floor sent shivers down her spine. Amandine couldn't stand it. This welcome, as lovely as it was, overwhelmed her. Over the past year, Amandine had become used to her own company, and she now longed for that solitude with all her heart. She just wanted everyone to leave her alone. It was peace that she needed, not reassurance.

"You are safe."

"*She is a common criminal. A witch. A demon worshipper. A follower of Satan...*"

"You are safe."

"*An adulterous. A whore...*"

"You are safe."

The words of Archbishop Verus came back to haunt her. Amandine wanted to curl up in on herself, cover her ears and scream, but she couldn't, not here. So instead, she wrapped her arms around herself and began to rock. Back and forth. Back and forth.

"You are safe."

Back and forth. Back and forth. She couldn't stop. If she didn't rock, she would surely die.

"Go. Leave us," Amandine heard Merton's voice from a distance, but she did not raise her eyes to look at him. She couldn't. She had to rock. Yes, rock. The motion was soothing. She wished her mother were here to rock her.

"I will come back with a tonic to settle her nerves," Amandine heard the healer say. "It is to be expected. She has suffered a great trauma. What she needs is time and patience. I will help her to recover her wits. You have my word."

"Amandine," Annis touched her gently on the arm and this time Amandine did flinch. "I am not going to hurt you. You are safe here."

No, she wasn't. Why didn't the Queen understand? She wasn't safe because her haters were still in her head.

"Let me settle her," Merton stated. "You can come back later, Annis."

The bed shifted as Annis stood. Amandine could feel the Queen's concerned gaze on her, but she didn't care. She focused on a corner of the room and continued to rock, for that was all she could do.

***

It was only when the key turned in the lock that Amandine felt like she could breathe again. She was safe in a locked room. She wasn't safe anywhere else.

Merton sat down next to her, and although she longed for him to touch her, he did not, so she continued to rock.

He got up abruptly, and she wanted to protest, fearing he would leave her alone in this perpetually fearful state. But he came back a moment later and with difficulty, he knelt down in front of her.

"Give me your hand," he stated quietly.

She wanted to comply but she couldn't, and he must have known because he gently prised her fingers lose of their determined hold on her own body. He took her hand in his, kissed the back of it. And then, to her surprise, he began to wash her hand with a warm damp cloth.

Amandine looked down at her hand as he ran the cloth between her fingers, and over her knuckle. Such a normal everyday task. So simple. God, she loved him. Only he would know how to break through her fear. She concentrated on the feeling of the damp fabric and the gentle touch of Merton's hand. He was alive. She was alive. They were together. Slowly the panic began to subside, and she ceased to rock.

Merton took hold of her other hand and began to clean that too. He didn't say anything. He didn't need to for his actions spoke far louder than any words ever could. He would take care of her, no matter what. Could she say the same for Garren?

There was a discreet knock on the door. Merton stood and went to answer it. Without his touch, the darkness returned, and she began to rock again.

"This will help calm her down. Be sure she drinks it all," she heard the healer say.

"What is in it?"

"Chamomile. Just Chamomile. It should take the edge off her fear. If it doesn't, then for the love of God, let me know and I will give her something stronger."

Amandine heard the door close again, but she did not watch as Merton made his way towards her. She had to rock. If she rocked, then everything would be all right. Merton once again knelt down next to her and placed the cup on the floor.

"Stop rocking," Merton said with a concerned voice as he held her hand again. "I am here. I am not going to let anything happen to you. You need to stop this, Amandine. You need to listen to me and do as you are told. Stop it. There is no need for this. Stop it."

She willed her body to cease its motion, but it was like swimming against a tide. The odds were against her. It was only a matter of time before she drowned.

"Sip this," Merton encouraged, picking up the cup and placing it against her lips.

The taste was fresh and earthy with a subtle hint of apple. It was refreshingly good. She licked her lips and sipped again.

"Good girl," Merton praised. "That's right. Drink it all. It will help."

By the time she had finished she no longer felt this all-consuming desire to rock. She felt tired though, but at least she could think clearly.

"There you are," Merton said with a grin as she raised her head and looked into his eyes.

He placed the cup back on the floor and reached for the damp cloth. He began to wash her face with the same care as he had washed her hands.

"The King..." Amandine stammered, looking into Merton's face with a dawning horror. What must Alden think of her? What must everyone think? She began to tremble. Would they condemn her because she had been unable to control herself? Would she be banished? Ridiculed? Burnt?

"Alden understands. Don't worry about it," Merton reassured. "Everything is new for you here. Cerniw is vastly different to Brittany—"

"I can't stay here," Amandine interrupted with a voice that

conveyed her desperation.

"I know how you feel," Merton replied. "I know what it feels like to think you are alone amongst friends. Let me reassure you. *You* are not alone. Amandine, you are safe here. And you know I do not say such words lightly."

"No place is safe. I can't stay here." *Please understand* she wanted to beg, but she held her tongue.

"Then we will leave." Merton leaned towards her and kissed her softly on the forehead. "But not today," he tilted her chin up with his finger and kissed her lips. "I am not well enough to travel, and neither are you. Let us take advantage of my brother's hospitality for a couple of days and then I will take you somewhere a little quieter. I promise."

"There are too many people here—"

"I know," Merton reassured. "And Alden and Annis know that too. Do not think they judge you, for they do not. We know what it is like to—"

"You must think me a madwoman."

"I always thought that," Merton stated. Laughing softly, he took the cloth away from her face and dropped it next to the discarded cup. "But you are *my* madwoman, and I love you." He held her hand again. "How do you feel? Has the tonic helped at all?"

"I don't know," she stated honestly.

"Perhaps it needs more time. Santo knows his herbs. He is a good man and very knowledgeable. He has earned his place as Royal Healer. You are in safe hands."

"Do not say safe… I can't abide that word, for it is a trickster, and it delights in its mischief. So many people have told me I was safe. The Church. Philippe. You." she shook her head. "But you all lied. What you meant was I was safe for the time being. I went to sleep in your arms thinking I was safe. I awoke to a pounding on the door, and then it crashed open. Soldiers poured into the room. One of the soldiers grabbed my hair and pulled me from the bed. I was dragged into the Great Hall, and there I saw Wann, hanging from the rafters. And I knew… I knew you had failed to rescue Alden. I knew that both our lives would be forfeited. I expected them to get a rope and hang me, but they didn't. They…" she bit her lip and closed her eyes against the memories. "You told me I was safe. But I wasn't."

"Amandine, I," Merton shook his head and looked away from her for a moment. When he turned back, she could see that tears had gathered in his eyes. "I am sorry. Philippe took me by surprise. I didn't think anyone would break into my chamber. If I had known that was going to happen, then I would never have left you there."

"But you left me there because you thought I was safe. I don't blame you. I thought I was safe too. But surely you can understand why I think the word *safe* is an imposter? I don't want you to tell me that I am safe because I won't believe you."

Merton briefly nodded. "You are right. I won't belittle your intelligence by saying you are safe. But believe me when I say you *are* out of harm's way."

"Isn't that the same thing?" Amandine asked.

"No. It is completely different. The words are pronounced differently, spelt differently—"

"You are so stupid," Amandine replied, smiling despite herself.

"But I made you smile, and that is the main thing. And besides, you wouldn't have me any other way."

"You are right. I wouldn't."

Merton smiled and placed another kiss on her forehead. "Come on, that bath is not getting any warmer."

Merton stood with difficulty, and he took a moment to find his balance before holding out his hand for her to take. She grasped his offered hand, and she felt a sense of rightness and relief as his fingers closed around hers. This is where she belonged. Not in the fort of a great king. She belonged with him. Amandine rose unsteadily to her feet. The difficult journey and her recent emotional response had taken a toll on a body she had abused. But Merton had a firm hold of her, and he helped her to cross the room.

The scent of lavender rose with the steam. Amandine reached out with her hand and touched the water, causing tiny ripples. The warm water was certainly tempting. She tried to raise the tunic that she wore, but she felt so weak, like an old lady beset with illness.

"Let me help," Merton stated, and like a toddler she let him undress her. She felt no embarrassment. No shame at being stood naked in front of him. She listened, fascinated, as he cursed and then touched the scars on her back that had been left by the lash.

"I have scars too," she said with a simple shrug, as if the scars were of no consequence, although she would remember the humiliation and the pain of that torturous day for the rest of her life.

"You do. It is a good job the bastard who gave them to you is dead."

"Mordred buried him alive," Amandine stated with a shiver as she remembered.

"Mordred was far more generous than I would have been," Merton stated with a cold and barely suppressed rage.

Amandine dared not think what Merton would have done. She knew of Merton's past. He would not have been merciful.

With Merton's help, she climbed into the bath. The warm water was a comfort against her cold legs, and with a sigh of pure pleasure, she lowered herself into the bath. But the pleasure quickly turned to a disappointed groan of agony, for although the water was warm and soothing, she was too thin to enjoy it for long because the wood was too hard against her starved, pathetic body. Merton must have seen her discomfort for he immediately reached for the soap. And like he had done once before, he washed her with a care and diligence that told her that she was loved.

Once she was clean, he helped her from the bath and dried her with the same care she had seen in him all along. He helped her into one of the nightgowns Annis had given her, and he pulled back the covers of the bed. Amandine was so tired that she had trouble keeping her eyes open. Perhaps the tonic was beginning to take effect.

"Stay with me," she begged, as she lay upon the bed. He made much of tucking the covers in around her.

"I am not going anywhere," Merton promised. "You are well out of harm's way. I'll be here when you wake up."

With such reassurance, Amandine allowed sleep to claim her.

Chapter 12

A waning candle always burns brightly until that very last moment. And then… Darkness. Amandine opened her eyes and stared up at the unfamiliar rafters. Her body ached from where she had stayed in the same position for so long, but she did not have the energy to move. The candles were burning low, and some had already burnt out. Music and muffled voices interrupted the sacred quiet of the room. It must be the evening meal, she concluded. For that was when a king's Great Hall was always at its busiest. Someone laughed with raucous, and a dog began to bark with excitement.

"Merton?" she called his name, feeling a moment of blinding panic when he didn't respond. She forced her aching body into a sitting position and looked around the room. Merton was sprawled in a chair by the fire pit. His eyes were closed, and the glow of the fire made shadows fall on his already scarred face.

Amandine stopped herself from calling his name again. He needed his sleep as much as she did. With a grimace of pain, she rolled her shoulders, waking up aching muscles. She needed to relieve herself, so she quickly pulled back the furs and got up. She felt momentarily dizzy and more than a little nauseous. Her stomach ached with hunger. She needed to find something to eat. But first, she needed to take care of her personal needs.

When she had finished, she walked towards where Merton slept. Amandine looked down at him for a long while, rejoicing in the fact that she could. Despite the circumstances, this was a dream come true for her. Never had she loved a man as she loved him. Her tender gaze fell upon Merton's face, the curve of his lips, the scars that hid perfection. His eyes were closed, his breathing was even, and yet, his slumber did not look like a peaceful one. Every so often he would grimace as if he were in pain although he did not wake. Perhaps he had taught himself how to sleep through it — if such a thing were possible.

Amandine allowed herself to remember him as he was. Strong, brave, heroic. His eyes alight with laughter. A ready smile. A comforting embrace. An endearing arrogance that for some reason she had found so appealing. Merton had always been so sure of himself, and his confidence had inspired her own. But now there was something different about him that went much further than his scarred body. Wisdom, perhaps? How can you go to Hell, come out the other side and not be wiser for the experience? Amandine fancied that they had been in Hell at the same time. Hell, however, was so vast that they had not seen each other as they both battled with their own personal demons. Amandine would go there again, despite what she knew of Hell, if it meant Merton rested in Heaven. For if anyone deserved peace, then it was him. When she looked into his face again, she did not see the scars that the world saw. How could she? Love does not recognise such trifle imperfections.

An unexpected smile pulled at the corner of his mouth, and she wondered what he dreamt of. Perhaps he dreamt of her, the way she used to dream of him. How she had longed for the night to come when she had been a prisoner. For in dreams she had lived. Her dreams had taken her outside of her chamber and reunited her with people that she loved. But Merton had come for her. He had rescued her. He still loved her. Amandine had no need for dreams anymore.

Merton opened his eyes and looked at her with confusion for a moment. Then his eyes filled with love, and he smiled.

"Amandine," he said with a yawn. "Sorry, I must have fallen asleep."

Amandine did not speak straight away but instead stared at him in awe. Those grey eyes of his had always been her undoing. Amandine had thought never to look upon them again, and now that she could, she found she could not look away. He did not withdraw his gaze from her. And the two of them looked upon each other as if fearful someone would come and snatch the other away at any moment.

"Amandine."

Her name sounded like an intimate caress when it came from his lips. She had never heard anyone say her name the way he did. The way he was looking at her made her feel warm inside and something more. Desire. Want. Need. Feelings she had thought never to feel again.

A log crackled on the fire, and Amandine realised that she had been staring at him as if she had fallen into a trance. "How… How long have we slept?" she asked, feeling the heat of embarrassment rise in her face.

"A couple of hours," Merton answered with another yawn. "How are you feeling?" He asked as he fidgeted in his seat, trying to make himself comfortable.

Amandine shrugged. "I don't know," she answered as honestly as she could. "Happy. Sad. Scared. Confused. Afraid. In love…" she smiled then.

"You are in love, are you?" Merton asked as he reached out and entwined their fingers. "And who is the lucky man?" he asked as he pulled her towards him.

"You," Amandine replied. She squealed in surprise as he pulled her down to sit on his lap.

"Me?" Merton asked as she made herself comfortable. "Well, I can't say I blame you. I would love me too, if I were a woman."

"You don't change, do you?" Amandine asked as she lay her head on his shoulder. She closed her eyes and breathed in deeply. She could very quickly become intoxicated with the way he smelt — all leather, and horses, and wood smoke. Amandine savoured the sensation of his hand as it absentmindedly traced patterns on her back. Was there anything quite as good as being held by Merton du Lac? Amandine very much doubted it.

"You cannot change perfection," Merton replied with an easy smile, but that smile fell from his face as quickly as it came and his whole body stiffened.

"What?" Amandine asked, raising her head and looking into his face with concern.

"It's nothing… Just… *Sard*…" he cursed under his breath. "As much as I want to hold you, you are going to have to get up."

"I'm sorry," Amandine stated, quickly rising to her feet. "What is it? What is hurting?"

"It's just my back. Don't worry…" Merton said as he made to rise also, but on a gasp of pain he sat back down. "I shouldn't have slept in the chair…" he breathed out unsteadily as he looked at her. "It's my own fault… Damn it," he groaned as he tried to make himself comfortable. "It's like being stabbed," he gritted his teeth and gave a short, sharp laugh. "It is frustrating, to say the least."

Amandine couldn't bear to see the pain in his eyes. "What can I do?" she asked desperately. "What do you need? Should I get the healer? Where would I find him?" Her fear of the unknown and the many people in Alden's court vanished in the face of Merton's need.

"I don't need Santo. It will pass. It is just unpleasant while it is here. Take a seat. It is all right. It is easing now."

Amandine was not convinced, but she pulled up a chair and sat next to him. She cautiously reached out to touch him. She hoped her touch would not cause him more pain. He caught her hand in his and brought it to his mouth where he lovingly left his kiss.

"Does it hurt often?" Amandine asked with grave concern.

"No. Just all the time," he closed his eyes and sighed deeply. "But it is true what they say…" he opened his eyes and looked at her. She felt a small sense of relief when she saw humour lurked underneath the pain in his eyes. "It is amazing what you can get used to."

"I do not like to think of you in pain," Amandine replied desperately. "There must be—"

"Then do not think of it," Merton interrupted. "It is just how it is for me. Although," he moved in his seat again, grimacing as he did so. "I don't think all that time sat in a boat did me much good."

"I am sorry," Amandine replied, feeling the weight of guilt settle upon her. He was hurting because of her.

"So you should be," Merton replied with a chuckle, kissing the back of her hand again. "The things I have to do for you."

"I am sorry that you have to do them," Amandine replied. "What happened earlier… I am not making life easy for you, am I?" Heat rose in her face again as she recalled her actions. She had humiliated herself. How could she look the King and the Queen in the eyes ever again?

"You have wounds that do not mar the skin, but that does not make your pain any less real than mine. Amandine, despite all the odds, you survived. Most women, and men for that matter, would not have been able to endure what you did. I am not going to tell you to forget all the horrendous things they said to you or did to you because you can't. But know this, I understand what you are feeling and what you are going through. You are not alone. Not anymore."

Amandine bit her lip as his words brought tears to her eyes. "I love you," she whispered through her tears.

"I know," he smiled at her. "I didn't say those words to make you cry. Come here," he leant across the chair and gathered her into his embrace. She closed her eyes and sobbed into his neck.

"It's all right," he whispered into her ear. "I've got you."

She raised her tear soaked face to look at him. "I do want to marry you."

"As I said back on the boat…" Merton smiled and then ran sweet kisses from her mouth to her ear. "You just have to say the words, and I'll be there."

"I will say them."

"Once you have seen Garren. I know." Merton whispered in her ear.

"I have to see him," Amandine replied, pulling back so she could look into Merton's face.

Merton sighed heavily and sat back in his chair. "I understand. I do."

She stared at him for a moment longer and then she looked away, unable to maintain eye contact. She felt guilty that her hesitation in marrying him was hurting him. But in this, she didn't have a choice.

"It is you I want to marry," Amandine said, watching a candle on the other side of the room. The candle flared incredibly brightly just for a moment, and then it went out, leaving only a thin trail of smoke to mark its passing. "You said Garren had been taken prisoner and sold into slavery."

Merton sighed again. Amandine knew he did not want to talk about Garren, but there were things she needed to know.

"That is what he said," Merton replied. But there was an edge to his words that she did not fully understand. "He ended up in the Holy Land."

"The Holy Land…? He walked where Jesus once walked? Breathed the same air? My goodness. Imagine that," her tone was one of wonder.

"He wasn't visiting," Merton stated.

"No. He wasn't. It must have felt like a blessing as well as a curse. To be in the presence of all that history, but to do so in bondage... It does not bear thinking about. How he must have suffered..."

"He was strong, Amandine. He got through it. And he won his freedom. I do not know all the details. What I do know is that he came back to claim his birthright. He wants *this* throne. He wants to be crowned King of Cerniw. He pretended that he didn't. He pretended that he was just thankful for being here. But, we saw through his apparent sincerity. I saw the ambition in his eyes. We are brothers. We are meant to stand together. But Garren and Budic... They march to a different drummer than Alden and I. They always have."

"They may follow a different beat, but they are still your brothers," Amandine answered wisely.

"My brothers are Alden and Yrre. Eadgar and Vernon. Rand. My brothers are the men who stand by my side, no matter what. It is a common misconception, but blood does not make one a brother. Budic and Garren are not my brothers. I denounce them as such. They are just people I once knew. But they are strangers now."

"They are your kin," Amandine replied.

"And what does that mean? What is kin? Are we meant to stay loyal to people we dislike because we happen to have the same blood? I am sorry, but that is nonsense," Merton stated. "Why should I be loyal to them? Budic is responsible for what happened in Brittany, but will he take responsibility? No. *You* paid the price. *I* paid the price. But Budic... He escaped Brittany with nothing but an injured pride and a small cut on his arm. That was nothing in comparison to you and I. And yet, Budic is the one who has been so grievously wronged. And now he looks at Cerniw and has decided that by right, the kingdom is his. He thinks Alden should step down and hand it over. And Garren, he thinks the same way. Garren regards Alden as a custodian of Cerniw. Not a king. Budic, in his twisted mind, sees Alden as a usurper. But they are both wrong. Alden is the king. And as long as there is breath in my body, the king he will remain."

"Do you think Garren will side with Budic?" Amandine asked.

"I doubt it," Merton replied with an unamused grunt. "Garren despises Budic and for a good reason. But, I do not know what Garren intends. I do not know where he has gone. I was never privy to Garren's counsel."

"Do you fear Budic?" Amandine asked.

"Budic?" Merton laughed. "No," he shook his head.

"What about Garren? Are you afraid of him?" Amandine asked with a small frown as she digested all of what Merton had told her.

The laughter died on Merton's lips. "Yes," Merton admitted on a breath of honesty. "Of course I fear him. He was your first love. I fear that when you see him, you will choose him over me. It doesn't matter how many times I tell you that he is not worthy of your love, it is ultimately up to you to decide. I do not want to throw you into his arms, but I have to tell you that I think he would renew your marriage vows if you asked him to. I am not going to tell you that he would make you happy because I don't think he will. He would be a devoted husband for a while, no doubt, but he has eyes that wander. He is always looking for his next conquest — the next woman who would share his bed. In that, he has not changed. His current mistress is Josephine, and before you it was Anna. Goodness knows how many women he has had since then. I very much doubt him being in bondage dampened his appetite. And he always had a way with women."

"I find it hard to believe that Garren slept with the Queen. Anna never said anything."

"Why would she?" Merton asked. "You loved him. You were in mourning. We all saw how you grieved for him. She spared you the pain of knowledge. Sometimes it is better not knowing…"

"I would rather know the truth, no matter how painful," Amandine stated. "This last year I have been fed nothing but distorted truths and outright lies. That is no way to live. From now on I demand honesty."

"Then I will be honest with you," Merton stated. "While you were sleeping, I was watching you and thinking that maybe I am wrong in wanting to keep you with me. I thought that maybe I should let you go. And that maybe you would be better off married, not to Garren, but to someone else. Alden has a Hall full of noble knights. I thought that with time, you might choose a husband from their number."

"What are you talking about?" Amandine asked on a cry of despair. A sudden sense of disbelief washed over her and made her heart ache. Amandine had not been sure of Alden or the welcome she had received, but she had been sure of Merton. It felt like he had suddenly pulled the rug from under her feet. The pain of desertion was like nothing she had ever experienced before. The thought of losing him again was beyond comprehension. "Why… Why would you even think that? I thought you loved me—"

"I do, love you," Merton stated, his eyes alight with pain and sincerity. "I love you more than life, and you know that. You asked for honesty. I am being honest—"

"You are being cruel," Amandine contradicted. "I do not want to choose a husband from Alden's knights. I want you. Just you. Please, don't leave me. Please… I can't…" she began to cry. Why was he doing this? She didn't understand.

"Shh," Merton soothed. "I am not saying these things to hurt you. I don't want to leave you. I don't want you to marry someone else. It would destroy me. But, I am not going to allow you to agree to marry me with your eyes closed. I am not the same man I was. I am not the man you fell in love with. You need to know the truth about me."

"I know everything I need to know," Amandine stated, as the tears slipped heedlessly down her cheeks.

"No. You don't." Merton rose to his feet with difficulty, but he seemed determined and would not be thwarted in his effort to stand. "You need to see what Philippe did to me," his voice shook as he spoke. "And you need to see my back." He undid his belt, and he tossed it aside.

"Merton…" Amandine shook her head and rose unsteadily to her feet as well. She reached out to touch him, but he stepped back. "You don't have to do this," she stated in a voice that trembled as he began to pull up his tunic. He ignored her and continued to disrobe. She averted her eyes, looked the other way. Better that, than see the condemning truth of Philippe's cruelty. Or the shame in Merton's eyes.

"Look at me," his voice was heavy, full of emotion.

"No," she shook her head and closed her eyes tight shut.

"Look. At. Me," Merton said again. "Please…"

It was the *please* that undid her. She took a deep breath and raised her eyes to his.

"I told you to look at me," Merton stated.

"I am," Amandine answered, her eyes not leaving his. She raised her chin defiantly.

"No, you are not. You are looking into my eyes. That is not what I want you to look at. Look at me."

"I don't want to," Amandine replied, as her tears continued to fall.

"If you do not look, then I am going to walk away from you. Is that what you want?"

"That is not fair, Merton. Don't make me do this," she begged. "Please don't."

"It has to be done," Merton replied. "Better now, than—"

"I hate you," Amandine threw the words at him. "I hate what you are doing. Stop it."

"Look at me," he whispered.

Amandine closed her eyes briefly. *Why was he doing this?* She didn't understand what he was trying to prove. Did he really think she would turn away from him because of a couple of scars? She opened her eyes and looked in to his. Gone was the ever-confident Merton du Lac. And in his place, stood a man who was unsure. A man who was waiting for condemnation from the woman he loved. Well, she would see about that. Her eyes dropped to his chest, and before she could stop herself, a small gasp escaped from her mouth. His chest was a mass of raised red scars. The path the whip had taken was forever etched into his skin. There were so many scars, more than could be counted. How could any man heal from such a trauma? Amandine looked up into his eyes with horror and then she looked back down at his chest. She heard and saw him take an unsteady breath, but she could not take her eyes away from the terrible scarring. Her gaze travelled to what was left of his arm. He had endured so much. So very much. His right arm was nothing but a stump of angry scars caused by a burning blade that had sealed the wound shut. This is what Philippe had done. This was the damage he had caused. Merton had been held down, unable to defend himself. The only choice he had was to endure. No wonder, Merton had been so upset when she had tried to defend Philippe. What a naive fool she had been. She had been defending the Devil to God. She had not understood properly, until now. Philippe had been using her. Lying to her. Toying with her like a cat does a mouse. Philippe had not been her friend. It had all just been a game to him.

"Pretty, isn't it?" Merton choked out the words with self-mockery and scorn. "But this is nothing compared to my back." Merton turned around slowly and revealed the terrible truth.

Amandine had once heard the late Abbot preach about deformity.

He had said that it was a divine punishment. A physical payment for sins committed. He had said that all such men should be shunned. He was wrong. The late Abbot had been wrong about many things.

The distance between her and Merton was no more than an arm's length, but something had changed between them. That distance now felt as wide and as treacherous as a gorge. She raised her hand to touch him. But her hesitant hand could do no more than hover over his spine. To touch him, would be to break him. She did not know how she knew that, but she knew. Her hand fell away.

"It curves at the bottom as well," Merton whispered. "So now you know," Merton spoke with self-mockery as he turned back around to look at her. "I can see the disgust in your eyes. I can see—"

Amandine slapped him hard across the face. So hard, in fact, that his face turned with the blow. She had not even realised she was going to strike him. It had been instinctive, something beyond her control. But with his words, came an anger the likes of which she had never felt before.

"You bastard," so great was her rage that the words came out like a poisonous hiss. "You think me…" She shook her head in disgust. "You think me so shallow that I would let something like a scarred chest and a damaged back make me love you less? I am not in love with your body, you fool. I am in love with your soul."

Merton looked at her in astonishment, but she was far from finished.

"I am in love with the way your eyes light up when you look at me. I am in love with the way you touch me as if I am something precious. I am in love with you because you fought for me, you were willing to die for me. You came for me, and you saved my life. You make me laugh when I want to cry. You defend me when I need defending. You do not judge me, even though others have and still are. Earlier today when I wasn't myself, you didn't run from me, you stayed and helped me. Merton—"

"Galahad," he interrupted tenderly, his eyes were soft with a timeless love as he looked at her.

"I am in love with you because you are you. I don't care about the way your back looks. I care only about the pain it causes you. I do not look at your chest and arm with disgust. I look at it with pride because those scars tell me that you are strong and loyal to the love we have for each other. They are a part of you, Merton. And therefore they are a part of me too."

"My name is Galahad," he said again, although this time he reached for her. He pulled her closer to him and bent his head to kiss her, but she raised her fingers to his lips to stop him, for she had more to say.

"You say that Garren would renew our vows if I asked him to, but he didn't sail over the sea to rescue me."

"I told him not to," Merton replied somewhat sheepishly. "I am sorry. I know I had no right to say that to him but—"

"And did no one tell you not to?" Amandine interrupted. "Did no one say that your injuries would prevent you from rescuing me?"

"Yes," Merton replied, frowning slightly. "Yes, they did."

"But still you came. Despite what others said."

"I came because I love you," Merton stated.

"If Garren loved me, then there would have been nothing you could have said that would have stopped him. He would have come anyway. I just want to see him. I have no intention of marrying him. I don't want one of Alden's able knights. Don't you understand? I could never love another man the way I love you."

"My actions may have proved my love, but Amandine, we have to be realistic. My back isn't going to get better. Santo reassures that I am not going to get any worse, but look how bad my back has become within a year. What is it going to be like this time next year? I have gone from being the most feared warrior of our time to a man who has to take vile concoctions of God knows what so that I can walk a few steps with a bloody stick. Love they say is all well and good, but will you love me when I am bedridden? Will you love me, when the money runs out, and we have to rely on my brother's generosity to keep a roof over our heads? Will you love me when we have nothing?"

"Do not talk to me of nothing. I spent two weeks locked in a cell. I had no fire, no blankets, no food, no freedom. My days were nothing but a torment, and my nights were filled with torture. I was only allowed out when the Abbot wanted me to pray for your damnation. I had nothing, Merton. Nothing. And yet I still loved you."

Merton reached up and touched her cheek with the back of his hand.

"It's always been you," Amandine admitted, as much to herself as to him. He bent down and kissed her. She immediately wrapped her arms around his neck and kissed him back. But there was more she needed to say, so she broke the kiss. "Even when I was with Garren, deep down I knew that it was you I wanted. Garren was kind and considerate, and he brought me many gifts. How could I not love him? But... You were so wild. So full of life. You were everything I could never be. If you had been my husband, you wouldn't have showered me with gifts. You would have taught me how to ride bareback through the waves. You would have taught me how to climb a tree and steal into the kitchen to pilfer one of Cook's fabulous pastries."

"I would have been a terrible influence," Merton agreed as he stole another kiss.

"Despite what you think of Garren he did make me feel cherished. But you.... Your very presence in my life makes me feel alive. I cannot describe what I feel when you hold me close. When you kiss my lips. I don't ever want to lose this feeling."

For as long as she lived she would never forget the look in his eyes when she spoke those words. He looked humbled, but in true Merton style, he quickly recovered.

"I fell in love with you when you taught me to dance," Merton stated, his eyes once again sparkling with amusement. His hand curved around her neck and he drew her closer still.

"You were with Josephine then," Amandine reminded him.

"That came later, and I was drunk. It was you I wanted. I thought myself unworthy of a woman like you. When you offered to teach me to dance, I felt like I had conquered the world. I acted the fool. I pretended I was truly hopeless, so that those lessons would not end."

"Are you trying to tell me that all these years you pretended you couldn't dance?"

"Not initially, I was pretty hopeless."

"Merton, the more I taught you, the worse you became," Amandine reminded him.

"It was the only way I could legitimately spend time with you," Merton replied with a narrowing of his eyes. "I don't think you understand, those sacred hours I was with you were some of the best times in my life. I didn't want our dance lessons to end because that would mean you would have no reason to spend time alone with me."

"Why didn't you say something?" Amandine asked.

"I was younger than you. I still am younger than you. I was fourteen, Amandine. And you were my brother's widow. I had never been in love before. I had never kissed a woman. That brief kiss we shared was my first. I know it was clumsy, but inside I was shaking. I was so scared you wouldn't feel the same. I was afraid I was going to make a complete fool of myself."

"That never deterred you before," Amandine replied with a smile. "And besides, I wasn't that much older."

Merton chuckled. "I loved dancing with you."

"I loved dancing with you too," Amandine admitted. "Although I have to admit, I wasn't so keen when you stood on my toes."

"I had to make my incompetence look believable," Merton said in his defence. "I am sorry that I will never be able to show you how accomplished I really am." He winked at her with amusement. "My dancing days are over."

Amandine burst out laughing, and she hit him playfully on the top of his arm. "That is convenient for you. Oh, you had me there for a moment. You are such a liar. No one can pretend to be that bad at dancing."

"We will never know now, will we," Merton replied with a grin.

Amandine continued to giggle.

"I love hearing you laugh," Merton stated as he looked deep into her eyes.

"No one could, or has ever, made me laugh as you do. I needed you back then. I need you now. My need for you is never going to change. Even if you do end up as a grumpy old man tied to our bed," Amandine stated with all seriousness. "I will still want you. I will still love you."

"I said nothing about tying me down," Merton said, with a disapproving scowl, which made Amandine giggle again. "Although now you come to mention it, I am intrigued as to what you are planning to do once you have tied me to our bed."

Amandine blushed at his words. "That is not what I meant, and well you know it."

There was a sudden loud knock that made Amandine jump. And they both looked at the door.

"Let's ignore it," Merton stated as he began to kiss the side of her neck. "I am sure Alden has some rope about this room somewhere so we can practise."

She turned to look back into his eyes, but before she could say anything to the contrary, he covered her lips with his. His kiss was desperate, and she returned that desperation. Amandine put everything she had into that kiss and then more still. And at that moment nothing else mattered. There was no past. No future. Just them.

The key turned in the lock, and the door opened, but they were so lost in their kiss that both were blind to it. Amandine's hands were in Merton's hair now, and she stood up on her tiptoes in a bid to get closer to him.

A man cleared his throat. Merton broke the kiss and looked at her. Both of them were breathing heavily as if they had run a great race.

"I should not have taken the key from the lock," Merton said quietly, glancing at the table where he had left it. "I didn't realise there was another key. I'm sorry," he whispered.

"I have summoned the war council," Alden stated, getting straight to the point. "I am sorry to drag you away, but I need you."

"I will stay with you, Amandine," Annis said. There was amusement in her voice. "I brought some sewing. I thought you would be in need of something to occupy your hands. But I can see that you already have your hands quite full," the Queen continued. And the King snorted with a laugh.

Merton scoffed at the Queen's jest, whereas Amandine turned an alarming shade of red. Amandine made a conscious effort to untangle her fingers from Merton's hair.

"Stay with Annis. I won't be long," Merton promised as he kissed her softly on the side of her mouth. Her lips tingled at the touch.

Amandine shook her head. Panic replaced embarrassment. Amandine grabbed hold of his arm, determined not to let go. She didn't want to be away from him. Ever.

"I am going to be in the next room," he reassured. "I am not going to be far."

"No," Amandine whispered desperately. The feeling she had experienced earlier today reared its ugly head again. It felt as if a thick mist of fear was swallowing her up. "Don't leave me alone."

"Annis will be with you."

"Merton… Please, don't. Don't leave me."

"I need him, Amandine," Alden spoke gently and with

compassion. "When I have finished with him, I will bring him back. I swear."

"No. No…"

"Then come with me," Merton stated.

"Galahad, that is not wise," Alden's voice held a warning to it.

"I have some tunics of Galahad's that need taking in. As his future wife, I thought you would like the honour of sewing his clothes," Annis said with an encouraging smile.

Amandine looked at the Queen and the pile of clothes that she held in her arms, but it did nothing to quell her panic.

"Galahad we need to go," Alden stated. "And please, put some clothes on."

"Stay with Annis," Merton urged. "For the love of God, do not let her anywhere near my clothes. Her sewing is only marginally better than her cooking."

"I heard that," Annis said with mock abhorrence.

"You were meant to," Merton stated with a grin as he looked down at Amandine.

"You won't be long?" Amandine begged. The fear of abandonment was there for all to see in her eyes. But she knew, deep down, that she was fighting a losing battle. Merton had to obey his King's orders.

"I will try not to be, but Alden does like the sound of his own voice. When I come back, I promise to teach you how to pilfer pastries from the kitchen. *That* is a lesson that is long overdue."

"I will hold you to it," Amandine stated nervously.

"I won't be long," Merton promised as he bent to kiss her. The kiss was brief and over far too soon. When he pulled back, it felt as if part of her soul had been ripped from her. She watched as he struggled back into his tunic. She couldn't do this. She couldn't…

"I will have him back before you know it," the King promised.

Merton caught her gaze and winked. She had to bite her lip to stop herself from crying out. She watched as he and Alden left the room and when the door shut, she wanted to scream.

The room fell silent, apart from the sound of the fire popping as Annis tossed another log onto it.

"Come and sit down," Annis encouraged. "Have you eaten recently?"

Amandine made herself look at the Queen even though she

wanted to watch the door. "No," she managed to mumble.

"I will tell the servants to bring us both a little pottage. How does that sound?"

"Whatever you desire, your Majesty," Amandine stated, watching that closed door with longing.

"Amandine, Alden will bring him back to you. Please sit down."

But Amandine could not. She had to watch the door. Her life depended upon it.

"Did I ever tell you about the time when Merton got stuck down a well?" Annis said in a conversational way as she threaded a needle.

"What?" Amandine asked, looking back at the Queen with confusion. "He got what?"

"Stuck down a well," Annis stated with a smile. "Why don't you come and sit down and I will tell you the story while we sew…"

Chapter 13

Merton had once heard someone say that war was experienced on the battlefield, but it was felt at the hearth. Never had truer words been spoken. Nightmares plagued him. The ghosts of those he had killed had been constant companions for more years than he cared to count. But he had kept that tortured side of him hidden, for he had a reputation to uphold. He had to remain strong. Fearless. Confident. He had to pretend.

Benches and chairs had been pulled up around the fire pit, and here everyone had assembled. They spoke in whispered conversations as if they feared someone would sneak in and listen as they speculated about the coming war. A few of them shared nervous jokes, while others drank deeply from their cups.

Brother Sampson took a seat next to the Bishop of Cerniw. Sampson did not speak. Instead, he bowed his head, clasped his hands together, and began to pray. Merton wondered if Sampson prayed for peace or victory. Perhaps he prayed for wisdom. *Let it be wisdom.* Merton glanced up at the rafters of the Hall, seeking the Heaven that Sampson so liked to speak of. But all he saw was seasoned oak and a few cobwebs.

Merton leant heavily on his stick. He felt terrible. His whole body ached — each muscle complaining about being used. He also needed much more than a few hours sleep in a chair, to drive off exhaustion. To make matters worse, Santo's tonic had not worked as well as it usually did, but he didn't want to admit to that. How could he in a

Hall full of able bodies? How could he admit that his body was well and truly broken? For it was a known fact that a broken body meant a fractured mind. No one wanted to listen to the opinions of a cripple. And because of this Merton did not feel inclined to sit down with the other men. He stayed back, hiding in the shadows, for that was where a man such as he belonged.

Merton did not want to be here. He wanted to be back in Alden's chamber with Amandine. He hated leaving her alone. She needed him.

Amandine had frightened him this morning. Seeing her like that — rocking back and forth — felt like a punishment. To see the person he loved most in the world suffering, had broken his heart. They couldn't stay here. He knew that. Amandine needed somewhere quiet to recover, they both did. And he had promised…

Merton felt a sense of guilt about what he had just put her through. His own fear had festered inside of him until he had to give it a voice. It had been difficult for him to understand just why she loved him when he had been whole. He had been the Devil. He didn't deserve her love. But now… How could she possibly love a man like him? But she did. She had proved him wrong with an almighty wallop. He smiled to himself at the thought. It was more than he deserved. He should not have doubted her.

By God, he did not want to talk of Mordred, kingdoms, and war. He wanted to talk about love, and happiness, and peace — words that had been foreign to him for so long. But that was not to be. Merton sighed, thoroughly fed up.

The Bishop started the proceedings with a prayer. Everyone bowed their heads and said *"Amen,"* and *"Thanks be to God,"* at the appropriate time. Everyone that is, apart from Yrre — who looked upon Christianity with a kind of contemptuous amusement.

Alden thanked the Bishop for his words, and then he decided to tell those gathered everything that they already knew. Mordred was their enemy, as was Philippe, as was Wessex. They had to be defeated. They had to win the war for the sake of Briton and so on and so forth. But Merton did not see any of the other Kings of Briton sat around the fire pit. No one had answered Alden's call to arms. The other Kings were either too afraid or had allowed their coffers to be filled with Mordred's gold. Where was Constantine? Where was Aergol, Serwyl, and Commius? They should all be here, but they were not. Their absence was telling.

"Let me tell you a story," Alden stated as he poured himself some mead. Alden sat back in his chair and looked at his men with a confidence that Merton knew Alden wasn't feeling. Alden knew how to play a part too — *'it was the curse of the Du Lacs,'* their father had one said. To always pretend that everything was fine when it was clearly not. Some men might call such a pretence, arrogance, but they didn't understand. It wasn't about arrogance or self-importance. It was about survival. The Du Lacs had always been very good at that.

"Some of you are old enough to remember when Arthur brought his army to Brittany," Alden continued. "They outnumbered my father's army ten to one. But my father, he did not think to surrender. He fought. He defended what was his. The battle was terrible with a great loss of life on both sides. But, despite the odds, my father was victorious. He had something worth defending, you see. Something worth dying for. I feel the same way about Cerniw as he did about Brittany. I would rather die fighting than surrender to Mordred Pendragon as so many of the other kingdoms have done. My father sent Arthur running home with his tail between his legs. I will do the same to Arthur's son."

There was a murmur of agreement to Alden's words.

"It was not so long ago that Cerniw fell to Wessex," Alden reminded his knights, even though they needed no reminder. "I think we can all remember what living under his yolk was like. Living under Mordred's rule would be a hundred times worse. He wants to wipe out the Du Lac name. He would put my entire family to the sword. I will not give him that satisfaction. He will not take this kingdom. But... I need your help. I cannot do this alone."

"You have it, Sire," Sir Austol said. Others began to pledge their allegiance to Alden and Cerniw once more. Alden's knights were loyal. If he went down fighting, then so would they.

Merton was the only man among them that remained silent. He felt Alden's gaze fall upon him, but he did not return it. All that Alden said was true, but Cerniw was alone. No one came to their aid when Wessex attacked. Why should *this* be any different?

Mordred was a shrewd strategist. If all the other kingdoms were in Mordred's keeping, then they would face a war on all fronts. Cerniw did not have the men to defeat such odds. It truly was a desperate situation, and yet, Merton knew it wasn't hopeless. For he had faced such odds while fighting in Burgundar. But, to claim the victory, the Cerniw army would have to be introduced to a different type of warfare. Merton wasn't convinced that Alden's army was ready for such a radical change.

"We should take this war to Philippe. I say we sail to Brittany and hit him with everything we have got. He will not expect such a bold move from us," James stated with the wisdom of old age.

There was cheering and a general agreement at James' words, but Merton did not cheer, and neither did Yrre. Yrre glanced Merton's way and shook his head at the stupidity of man. But Merton knew better than to interrupt or disagree. He was always of a mind to let the old men speak their words first, for they deserved such respect. They had seen much, or so they liked to remind everybody. They knew many things. However, in this instance, James had completely missed the point. It wasn't Philippe they needed to defeat. It was Mordred. And although Merton was not against taking this war to Mordred, he did not agree with James' suggestion.

"Alan, I am glad to see you here," Alden said with something very close to sounding like relief, as Alan entered the Hall. Alden spoke in the tongue of the Britons, as Alan had not learnt the Cerniw tongue. "James has just suggested that we should take this war to Philippe. He believes that Philippe would not expect such a bold move from us. I would be interested in your thoughts on such an idea?"

Alan frowned as he took his seat. His hair was damp from the rain that continued to pour down from the heavens. Before answering the King, he reached for the mead and filled up a goblet. His actions were slow and seemingly deliberate. But no one could drag their gaze away from him, for Alan had been part of the Breton army since the age of twelve. He knew things that they did not. All eyes watched Alan as he took a sip of his mead. Alan sighed in appreciation of the mead, and then he looked at James. "If it were Philippe, you were really talking about, then I would agree. He is a weak king and an appalling ruler. You may well be victorious before the sun set. But Philippe isn't whom you are talking about. Philippe is not your concern. He is nothing. A puppet king at best. However, *Mordred* is no easy foe. And he has eyes everywhere. He sees all. He will see you coming."

"He didn't see *you* coming when you rescued Lady Amandine," James replied, and a few of the knights murmured their agreement with their general.

"Maybe he did," Alan allowed with a shrug.

Merton, who had been absentmindedly studying the reeds that were scattered on the floor, looked up sharply at that statement for he had not been expecting it.

"Maybe it was all part of his plan," Alan continued. "Maybe we are playing right into his hands. Maybe we will all die." Alan raised the goblet to his mouth again.

Merton frowned, and he saw that Yrre's expression reflected his own. Mordred's influence was significant, but surely not so significant as to be able to influence his enemies' decisions? Was Mordred so astute at King's Table that he could predict his opponents move before they had even thought of it?

Alan's statement was met with a wall of silence, and all contemplated what he had said. A few nervous glances toward their King showed that Alan had touched a nerve in many of them. *Let them know fear here, in the safety of the Hall,* Merton silently thought *because only then can they understand the value of courage on a battlefield.*

"Mordred will be expecting us to come to him. So we must stay here. We must do the unexpected," Alan finally said. "We must do nothing. At least until I have reunited the knights—"

"No," James interrupted, stopping Alan before he could say any more. "We should do as I suggest. Attack Brittany now while they are still reeling from their defeat. We do not have the time to wait for you to do the impossible. The knights of Arthur are dead. And dead men are of little use in battle."

"What defeat are you referring to?" Alan asked with a puzzled expression on his face. "We rescued one woman, we did not defeat an army. We have annoyed Mordred, not vanquished him. Do not make our achievement appear more than what it was. We did not go there to fight but to rescue. We were but a few men, not an army. We slipped into the crowd. We did not stand apart. What you are talking about doing is something completely different. Sire," Alan turned his attention to the King. "You know as well as I that Mordred would see our boats long before we thought to heave to. Archers will be waiting along the cliff tops to give us an undoubtedly frosty and painful welcome. And if... *If,* by chance, we so happened to make it to the castle itself, what then? Do you propose we lay siege? And if so, for how long? Must I remind you that the last time Benwick came under siege, she held out for an entire year. So I ask you this, what happens to your kingdom, Sire, while you are pretending to be Joshua? I can tell you this for certain, Benwick is no Jericho. Her walls will not crumble — no matter how many soldiers we take with us. But Dor's walls will fall. And you will be too far away to prevent it. It is madness to go to Brittany. Only a fool would suggest such a thing."

James rose to his feet at such an insult. "Say that to my face."

"I am," Alan stated, standing as well. "What you are suggesting will get us all killed."

"How dare you come into this kingdom and tell us what to do. You are a deserter. There is no honour in you. Or maybe you are a spy, sent amongst us to cast doubt and cause disagreements. Why should we listen to anything you have to say? Get out. You are not welcome here."

"I was summoned to this council by the King," Alan stated, glancing at Alden as he spoke. "I thought it unwise to ignore the summons. You would be choosing suicide—"

"You have said your piece. Now go," James snapped, his eyes flashing with rage.

"I will go when Alden tells me to."

"Then I suggest, your Majesty," James stated, turning to his King. "That you send this man on his foolish quest to chase phantoms." He turned back to glare at Alan. "Be gone with you, *Keeper of the Blade,*" he said the title with mockery. "We do not ask for your opinions, and we certainly do not want your help."

"But I will give you my opinion and my help, for it is mine to give," Alan stated. "I have an invested interest in seeing Mordred fall. I will not let incompetence stop me from seeing justice done."

"You have some gall," James snarled. "To come here and speak like this to me," he reached for his sword. "Who the hell do you think you are?"

"Enough," Alden stated, glaring at them both. "Sit down. You are supposed to be giving me wise counsel, and yet all I see are two grown men squabbling like children over a broken toy."

Both men reluctantly sat down, but James continued to glare at Alan with malice.

"Alan is right. I think that it would be very unwise to send our army across the sea to Brittany," Yrre dared to voice an opinion.

"Why would it be unwise?" James snarled like a dog defending his corner from an aggressor. "Now is the time. We have shown Mordred and Philippe that Benwick Castle can be breached."

"We have shown Mordred and Philippe nothing of the sort. All we have shown them is that they have traitors in the nest. You forget James, none of us apart from the Monk," Yrre nodded his head in Sampson's direction, "stepped one foot inside Benwick Castle."

"I say we should sneak inside the stronghold of Benwick Castle and kill both those bastards while they sleep," Sir Cadar suggested. His words were met with strong agreement.

Yrre scoffed and shook his head. "You are dreaming of an easy victory against a formidable opponent. What you speak of is impossible. They would be well guarded. We would die long before we reached their chambers."

"We should bring this war to Mordred," James said again, speaking over Yrre as he did so. "Before he brings it to us. Do you want to see a war on the beach? Because if we do nothing, then that is what will happen."

"Of course I do not want to see that," Yrre replied. "I do not want to see the blood of my people spilt upon the sand—"

"Your people?" James ridiculed. "You are Saxon. You are not of Cerniw."

Merton frowned at James' words, for Yrre had bled for Cerniw. He had earned the right to call Cerniw his home.

"My wife and my children are of this kingdom," Yrre stated rising to his feet.

"And yet, you are still a Saxon," James said, rising to his feet again.

"Is that right?" Yrre asked. "I will tell you this for nothing—"

"My wife," Alden stated with a touch of anger, "is also a Saxon. Is she not of this kingdom? Is she not your Queen?"

Merton silently thanked his brother for his quick intervention, for the knights of Cerniw were not yet ready to hear the truth about Yrre's lineage. Merton caught Yrre's gaze and mouthed the word *No*. Yrre glowered back, but Merton trusted him enough to know that he would say no more. God knows what the knights would do if they knew that the half-brother of the King of the Franks sat amongst them. Yrre was no Saxon, even if he did act like one.

"Yrre is one of my most loyal subjects," Alden continued.

"He is loyal to Galahad," James contradicted. "He is not loyal to you. He will fight only if Galahad tells him to. You cannot rely on Galahad's band of Saxon butchers, and you should not take heed of anything they have to say. And you should especially not listen to him," he jabbed a finger in Yrre's direction.

"What gives you the right to say that?" Yrre growled.

"I can say what I want about a slave," James replied with contempt.

"I am not a slave," Yrre stated with a growing anger. "I won my freedom."

"Only because Merton let you win."

"That is enough," Alden shouted as he pushed his chair back and stood up. "What is the matter with you, James? Where is this anger coming from?"

"I am trying to protect you and Cerniw. These men give you unwise counsel. You must ignore them and do as I say. Or we will lose everything."

Merton had heard enough. This meeting was dividing them not uniting them, and therefore it served no purpose. Alden should dismiss the council and allow heated tempers to cool, before trying again tomorrow.

"Galahad, you have been unusually quiet. What do you think we should do?" Alden asked.

"What does he know?" James asked dismissively. "I don't even know what he is doing here. You are no longer a warrior, Galahad. Go back to your woman and let war be planned by able men."

Merton snorted with a laugh at James' words. *That took less time than he thought.* He had not even opened his mouth and yet his words were not welcomed because he was a cripple. Well, good luck to them. If they were not open-minded enough to listen to wise counsel, then they deserved to lose this war.

"Galahad," Alden demanded an answer.

"You do not need me here," Merton stated. "You have counsel enough. What could I add to the conversation other than telling you to listen to Yrre, for he is an experienced warrior, and he knows what he is talking about. And you should listen to Alan, for he was the second in command of the Breton army. If you will not listen to them, then why would you listen to me?"

"I was fighting long before any of you were born," James shouted his frustration. "I know how to plan a war."

"That is true," Merton agreed. "I would never dispute your prowess in battle, for I have fought by your side. I have bled by your side. But you have fought only the Irish and the Saxons. Mordred is neither. He is of Rome and what experience do you have fighting them?"

"What are you talking about? We are not going to war with Rome. Rome is all but dead. Rome no longer possesses the men to make war with anyone. And besides, she is not interested in Cerniw. She never was," James stated. "That was the reason the Empire never sent her troops into our kingdom. That, and the fact that those brave invaders feared our army."

"Rome is far from dead. She still holds her Eastern Empire."

"Eastern Empire be damned—" James argued, but Merton interrupted him.

"They never feared our army," Merton stated coldly. "They wanted to trade. And we were willing. That is the only reason she left Cerniw alone. But Cerniw still has tin and silver running through her veins. She is still a worthy prize. Especially for a crumbling Empire, whose dazzling sun is about to set. Can you imagine the reception Mordred would receive if he rode into Rome, or perhaps Constantinople, and told all his fellow countrymen that he had not only secured Briton, but a thousand years worth of tin? They would celebrate his success. His name would be written down for posterity. Whereas us — the defeated — would be forgotten. Make no mistake. If we go to war with Mordred, then we go to war with Rome."

"Just what I would expect from the mouth of a cowardly cripple," James sneered.

"My general you may be, but speak to him like that again—"

"I can speak to him any way I want," James interrupted Alden's reprimand. "You need me, Sire. You cannot win this war without me. It seems that I am the only man here who is not afraid of Mordred Pendragon."

"Then you will die a noble fool on Mordred's blade," Merton yelled. His words echoed in the silence that followed. "We cannot allow our army to face his. If we do, our losses will be absolute."

"Then what do you suggest we do? Give up?" James shouted back. "Would you have Alden suing for peace? Would you humiliate your brother and demand he kneels to the man who murdered your father?"

"I said nothing about surrender," Merton replied. He took several deep breaths to regain control of his temper. But it was difficult when arguing with someone so set in his ways and so stubborn in his beliefs.

"Then what do you suggest?" Alden asked.

Merton glanced at Yrre. Yrre grinned in encouragement, for he knew as well as Merton did what kind of war was needed to secure the victory. With another deep breath, Merton looked back at his brother. "Isn't it obvious, Sire? We fight the way our forefathers fought."

"We hit, run, hide," Yrre stated, picking up his goblet. "I'll drink to that." And he did.

"You are asking us to break every rule of war?" James asked in angry amazement. "You would have us break every rule of the Knights' Code? Only a savage barbarian would suggest such a thing. We are knights. We meet on a battlefield, and may the best side win. We fight fairly. We fight like—"

"What? Roman soldiers?" Merton asked. "Is that what you are suggesting? Shall we line our army up into three columns? Shall we hide behind a *testudo* while arrows fly around us? Shall we die on our feet because you are incapable of reason?"

"The Knights' Code is sacred," James stated. "If we do not follow it, then we will go to our graves without our honour. *You* would turn us all into nothing better than mercenaries. *You* would lead us straight to Hell."

"So you would rather play into Mordred's hands and lose the kingdom? I think you value your place in Heaven too much to be any good to the people of Cerniw." Merton turned his attention to the Bishop of Cerniw. "Bishop, tell me, did God write the Knights' Code?"

"Well…" the Bishop looked uncomfortable at being thus addressed. "No. But—"

"No?" Merton's gaze flickered back to James. "Think on this, my Lord. The Knights' Code did not do much for Natanleod and his army of five thousand, did it?" Merton scoffed and took a step closer to the throne. "I witnessed that battle. I saw Natanleod die. I saw no honour. His army was slaughtered because they chose to follow the Knights' Code. Let us not make the same mistake as Natanleod did. Hit, run, hide — that might just snatch us victory."

"You suggest we become demons?" Alden asked quietly.

"If that is what it takes to win," Merton replied. "We should harry our enemies. We should give them no peace. Our attacks should be unpredictable and unprecedented to anything that has come before. We have to make them fear us so much that the soldiers will start to desert. It is the only way to win against such odds."

"This is nonsense, Sire. Surely you are not taking such a suggestion seriously?" James shook his head in disbelief. "I have heard the rumours of your kind of war," James said, turning to address Merton once again. "You were unmerciful. How many people have you murdered? How many children? How many innocents must die to curb your appetite?" he turned back to look at his King. "This is not warfare Galahad is suggesting. It is savagery."

"It is survival," Alden contradicted. "And I will sign a pact with the Devil himself if it means Cerniw and her people are spared the torment of calling Mordred, master."

"Then you and I, we have nothing more to say to each other," James stated. "My debt to your father has been paid—"

"What debt?" Alden asked, sitting forward in his chair.

"I will not be a part of this," James carried on speaking as if Alden had not asked a question. He unsheathed his sword and threw it at Alden's feet. "Find yourself a new general, for I am done." And with a contemptuous stare at Merton, James stormed from the Hall, slamming the door behind him.

The silence that followed James' departure was the same kind that filled a room when someone died a sudden and unexpected death. There was an air of disbelief. A sense of foreboding. They were a ship without a steering oar. A horse without a bridle.

"That went well," Yrre said, breaking the silence in a way that only he could.

Merton found himself stifling a laugh.

"Sire, I must intervene," the Bishop stated in all seriousness. "James is your general. You need him. Go after him. Pacify him. We cannot win this war without his expertise."

"Of course we can win it," Merton stated, stepping forward and sitting down in the seat James had so recently vacated.

"You would resurrect the Devil?" the Bishop asked, looking at Merton with horror. "You will bring such disaster on Cerniw that the ears of everyone who hears of it will tingle."

"I think you are getting Cerniw mixed up with Jerusalem and Judah," Merton replied with a frown. "But if you want to battle in scriptures, then I will say this… *Praise be to the LORD my Rock, who trains my hands for war and my fingers for battle…*"

Chapter 14

Disappointment ripped at Sampson's very heart as he heard Merton's words. He had thought to save Merton's soul, but how could he when Merton was so intent on following where the wicked one led?

Sampson had naively believed that the Devil, that evil part of Merton, had died. He should have known better. He felt tears gather in his eyes and he looked down at his shaking hands as Merton and the Bishop continued to argue. This was not how it was meant to be.

The Bishop's words were becoming more passionate. Sampson could feel the heat of the Bishop's anger as clearly as he could feel the heat of the sun on his face on a warm summers day. There was anger in the very air itself that Sampson breathed. Such a feeling was suffocating in its intensity. Sampson knew he should intervene. Calm the situation. But he could not find the strength of will to do so. And besides, he didn't know what to say to these great men who were gathered around this fine fire pit. He was no warrior. He knew nothing of war. He knew nothing of warfare. What help could he be? He wished Jesus were here, for he would know what to do.

Sampson raised his head and looked back at Merton. There was a fire in Merton's eyes that had not been there for a long time. Sampson had thought the fire had been extinguished, but it had not. It had been smouldering, waiting for a breath of wind to rekindle it.

Merton would never inherit the earth, and such a realisation felt like a physical blow to the young monk. Merton would not receive mercy because he was not ignorant of his actions. Merton knew what he was doing. And he knew what he was asking. And he knew where it would lead.

When Sampson had taken his seat earlier, he had closed his eyes and prayed. He had prayed so hard that this very thing would not come to pass. He had prayed for the Lord to keep Merton out of the war. But war was like a religion to Merton. And he was faithful to his cause. In front of armed men, was where Merton preached his sermon. Merton would lead his congregation towards certain death, and his loyal subjects would follow without question. Merton could take them to Hell, and still they would place their feet where he did. Merton was the kind of man who lost sheep flocked to.

Sampson wondered if this feeling, this despair inside of him, was the feeling God had when he threw that ancient serpent and his dark angels out of Heaven. Sampson loved Merton, but right now he despised him. For Merton was taking everyone down a path that Sampson could not follow. Such knowledge hurt unbearably.

The Bishop stood up abruptly. He pointed his finger at Merton while shouting at the top of his voice. He was so angry that his words became somewhat incomprehensible. Merton remained seated, and apparently undisturbed, while the Bishop raged down at him.

"He is evil," the Bishop yelled, jabbing his finger in Merton's direction again. "Sire, you must not listen to him. He is the serpent, brought here to lead you astray. He will corrupt you and anyone else he touches. He is mad, insane. He is possessed by demons. You are taking advice from the Devil himself. You must cast him out."

I know you can stop this, Sampson continued to pray desperately. *Please… Do not let Merton be drawn back to the evil one. Save him from himself, I beg you.*

"I will cast you out before I cast him out," Alden threatened as he too rose to his feet. "I mean to win this war, by whatever means necessary. Galahad, Yrre, and Alan are right. To set sail to Brittany with my army would be nothing short of suicide. I cannot, I will not, choose that for my men. I do not have the right."

"Then do not set sail to Brittany, wait for Mordred and his army to come here. Defeat them on the beaches, if that is what needs be, but do not listen to him."

The knights rejected the Bishop's idea rather vocally. For no one wanted to see a war at home.

"You will bring ruin to Cerniw and shame to your throne if you act on his advice," the Bishop continued, unperturbed, as he shouted his opinion over those of Alden's knights. "Is that what you want?"

"I only care for victory," Alden answered coldly. "I care not how it is achieved."

"Then you are damned," the Bishop stated with an air of doom. "You are all damned. There will be no coming back from this, for any of you."

"What does it mean to be damned?" Yrre asked. "Does that mean they will not enter the great Kingdom of Heaven? It seems to me all the best people are in Hell, anyway. Why would anyone want to go to this Heaven of yours? There are no warriors in Heaven. Only weak men live there. There are only men who wear robes such as yours."

"I would not expect a savage to understand the Kingdom of God," the Bishop spat in outrage. He looked at Yrre as if he were something vile. Like dog faeces on the bottom of a shoe.

"Then perhaps you should explain it a little clearer. That is what you are here for, isn't it? You are here to give religious counsel. From what I have seen, you have given no such counsel. You shout at Galahad, and you yell at the King, but you do not make any suggestions as to what they could do that would win this war and secure the kingdom. We do not want to fight Mordred's army on the beaches. We do not want him in our kingdom at all. And that is why Galahad's plan is so perfect. I know what a few well-trained men can do. It was my privilege to fight amongst such men. If we approach this war as Galahad suggested that we do, then we can fight Mordred anywhere at any time. We will have the advantage."

"I can foresee only failure at such an approach," the Bishop answered with apparent wisdom. "Your men will be scattered. There will be no way to communicate with each other—"

"You foresee nothing," Yrre interrupted. "I have met plenty of seers in my time. You, my holy friend, are not one. I think you are a very arrogant man who has started to believe in his own self-importance."

"How dare you speak to me in such a way." The Bishop was clearly astounded by Yrre's words. For never had he been spoken to in such a tone. But Sampson was not so surprised, for Yrre was an outspoken man at the best of times. Sampson still felt a quiet rage towards the Saxon after what he had been subjected to earlier at the beach.

"I can speak to you any way I choose. You are a man, a mere mortal. That gold cross that hangs around your neck does not make you a God. I have watched you, and I see how the peasants and the nobility alike bow to your apparent wisdom because you can read your God's written words in a book. You act as if you are the King of Cerniw."

"That is a preposterous lie," the Bishop yelled in his defence. Sampson could understand his rage. To be accused of acting like a king was considered an act of treason. The penalty of which was death. Yrre had no right to imply such a thing.

"I think it is a strange thing for a God to write down his rules in a book," Yrre continued. "I do not understand why he needed to write it down for you to comprehend his meaning. My Gods have voices. They can speak. They can guide us. They show us things. Is your God a mute? Or, perhaps he does not like his creation. Is that why he leaves you all alone with only a book to guide you? I wonder, have you ever considered that maybe your God did not write your book at all?"

"Just what I would expect from someone who does not understand the one true God," the Bishop replied with a scowl. "You worship false gods, and you deserve to be—"

"I deserve to be what? Stoned? Will you spill my blood while praising your one true God? And then, when you gather your followers, will you tell them not to kill for it is a sin? Sin is a very strange word that you Christians like to throw around whenever the mood takes you. As is the religion that you all follow. I do not think Christianity will last for long. Someday, someone will burn all your books, and you will not remember your God and his 10 rules—"

"There are 613 commandments in the Bible, not 10," Merton interrupted, with an edge of humour in his voice that Sampson found disturbing. Back on the boat, Merton had asked Sampson to teach him how to pray. And yet now, Merton was mocking the very religion that could save his soul.

"*613?* You surely jest?" Yrre's face showed his surprise.

Merton shook his head. "613 and counting..."

"Then forgive me for my mistake. You will not remember your God and his *613 commandments,*" Yrre corrected himself while raising his eyebrows at such a number. "You will not remember your precious Jesus Christ who apparently died on a golden cross so that you can keep on with your precious sinning."

"Jesus shed his blood on that cross for us. He took our punishment unto himself. And in return he offered us his righteousness," the Bishop corrected with much passion.

"I do not understand what you say," Yrre stated with a frown. "Why would your God bleed for you? I think you must have misread that passage in your Holy Book. That makes absolutely no sense."

"NO! I have not misread the scriptures," the Bishop went so red in the face that Sampson feared his heart would give out, but still, Samson remained seated. He did not intervene. He did not help the Bishop defend their religion or their God because he knew that Yrre was beyond salvation. Yrre would never accept the true God. What was the point in wasting your breath for a lost cause? And besides, they were not here to speak of religion, but war.

While the Bishop continued to rage at Yrre, Sampson looked at the King. Alden had already decided. There was no conflict in Alden's face. Instead, he looked like a man who was sure of his path. Alden would make Merton his general, and they would fight the war Merton's way. Therefore, they were, as the Bishop so rightly said, damned. And there was nothing Sampson could do about it.

Sampson turned his attention back to Merton. He wished he could see the man he had come to know. But all he could see was the man Merton had been. The Devil was back from the dead although Sampson now doubted whether he really died in the first place. Merton must have sensed his gaze for he looked into his face, and into his eyes. And much to Sampson's surprise, he saw a silent plea for understanding. *This wasn't what Merton wanted.* This new knowledge made Sampson gasp out loud. Merton was battling the Devil inside of him at this very moment for dominance. Merton didn't want this. He didn't want such responsibility. He didn't want to be here.

"*Help him,*" Sampson begged under his breath with desperation. *"Help him, please. I will do anything. Anything... Please do not let the Devil consume him again."*

But it was too late. Alden had stood, and he agreed with his brother. He announced that Galahad would replace James as the general of his army. They were to fight this war Galahad's way. Something shifted in Merton's eyes. Sampson wondered if it was disappointment. Regret. Why had no one else come up with a better idea? Surely someone else could lead the army? Galahad was a cripple after all. He was not well enough to lead men. What was Alden thinking?

"If you listen to him, you will be fighting fire with fire," the Bishop barked.

"What other way is there to put out such a fire?" Alden asked.

The Bishop's mouth dropped open in shock at the King's words. Even Sampson was surprised by them. Did Alden not know that to fight fire with fire meant that both sides would be extinguished? All that would remain would be a burnt kingdom and a pile of ash.

"All who draw the sword will die by the sword..." Sampson mumbled under his breath. When he looked back into Merton's face, he saw a terrible truth. Merton knew. He knew that such a war would end with no victor. But still they would fight. Still, they would die.

"Then there is nothing more I can say," the Bishop said, admitting defeat. "But be careful Sire, for the Devil promises much but, unlike God, he never delivers."

"I have heard your words," Alden replied briskly. "And I thank you for your wise counsel. Now leave us."

The Bishop went to protest but then thought better of it. He huffed with indignation as he left the Hall. When he shut the door to the Hall, he made sure the wind took it. The sound of the door slamming reverberated around the room.

"Nation will rise against nation, and kingdom against kingdom," Sampson stated in the silence that followed the slamming of the door. Yrre had been right in what he said, but for the wrong reasons. The Bishop was no seer because he did not need to be. For everything that has been, and everything that is, and everything that is to be, is written in the Holy Book. Time had run out for everyone. Revelations was upon them.

As these great men began to debate the best way to win this war, Sampson continued to stare at Merton and Merton... He stared back. Sampson discreetly shook his head as he continued to stare. He saw something shift in Merton's eyes, the fire of war suddenly burnt less brightly, but it had been such a brief change, and for such a scant moment of time, Sampson thought he must have imagined it.

"We need to bring down the Breton army from the inside and thus eliminate the threat they pose to us. I for one, do not want to go up against their cavalry, especially if we have to fight a Roman Legionary as well," Alden stated. "Alan, how would you describe the mood in the Breton army?"

"They are on the brink of mutiny. Philippe promised much and has delivered much, but discontent continues. Bastian is losing control of the men. It would not take much to kindle a rebellion, although such a rebellion may not work in your favour. Galahad," Alan turned his attention to Merton, "when you were forced to fight, you killed several men and injured many more, and then you, Sire," he looked back at Alden, "had the audacity to escape. They have not forgotten that. Nor will they forgive it. Soldiers have long memories even if their commanders do not. I do not think they would desert the Breton army for the Cerniw one."

"You did," Cadar replied as he refilled his goblet.

"I am the Keeper of the Blade. I do not fight for Alden. I fight beside him. I have not joined your army."

"It makes no difference if they desert to Cerniw or not. I just want the Breton army to be in such a state of disorder that they cannot make war. Is there anyone you would trust to lead such a rebellion?" Alden asked.

"I can think of a few... Menguy, possibly Ronec."

"I know Ronec," Alden replied. "Could we get a message to him?"

"No, we should not involve Ronic," Merton stated.

"Then who?" Alden asked.

"Bastian," Merton broke eye contact with Sampson and looked back at his brother.

Sampson, so confused by the conflicting messages he saw in Merton's eyes, once more looked down at his hands.

"Bastian?" Alden scoffed. "You are suggesting we should do what? Make a deal with the bastard who took your arm? Are you asking me to trust him after everything he did? I don't think so. He is Mordred's cousin."

Alan fidgeted in his seat, and he drew Sampson's gaze. Alan suddenly looked very uncomfortable. He looked like a man who wished the ground would swallow him up. Sampson wondered what Alden had said that had provoked such a reaction from Alan. But he did not have the time to dwell on it, for Merton was speaking again.

"He helped Amandine escape. And he helped you, and I, escape," Merton continued to address his brother.

"Only because he felt guilty."

"Then we play on his guilt."

"No," Alden stated in no uncertain terms. "No. I cannot bring myself to ask for his help. I will always be wondering if he will betray us—"

"I am sorry to interrupt. Galahad," Annis' gentle voice rose above the debate.

The talking stopped abruptly, and Galahad turned in his seat to look at the Queen.

"She needs you," Annis stated simply with a small shrug of despair.

Merton looked back at the King, seeking permission to leave. Alden narrowed his eyes at the silent request. Sampson could see that the last thing Alden wanted was to grant such a request, but what choice did he have? The King sighed heavily, making his feelings known, before reluctantly nodding his consent.

For someone who was in a great deal of pain, Merton rose to his feet very quickly. Sampson caught Merton's eyes only briefly with his own, but what he saw gave him hope. The fire was gone from Merton's eyes and in its place was concern. Love. Perhaps this was the way to save Merton from himself. Perhaps Amandine had her part to play in Merton's salvation. Abbot Daniel had been right; God had wanted Amandine to be saved from the pyre, but not for her sake. God had wanted her spared for Merton's. Sampson picked up his cup and took a sip of the weak ale, and as he did so, he came to a sudden decision. He rose abruptly from his chair, knocking it over in his haste, and yet he did not react to the noise or the curious stares from those gathered.

"I must go, Sire," Sampson muttered. Alden raised his hand up as if in apparent disbelief as his war council deserted him. But Sampson saw none of this, for he was already following in Merton's footsteps.

Sampson followed Merton and the Queen towards Alden's private chamber. What he had seen in Merton's eyes had given him hope. And he would rejoice in that hope and be consistent in his prayers. He had vowed to save Merton du Lac's soul. And nothing. Not even a war. Not even a king was going to get in his way and stop him from doing God's work.

"I tried to distract her with stories of your wayward life, and for a time it worked. But then we heard shouting coming from the Hall…"

Annis was talking rapidly when Sampson caught up with the pair.

Merton did not wait to hear more. He quickened his pace, but even so, his steps were awkward, and Sampson feared he would fall.

Merton yanked the door to Alden's chamber open, and he crossed the room to where Amandine sat, rocking. Merton approached her, and with gentle words, he encouraged her back to her feet. Sampson watched with sympathy as Merton guided Amandine to the bed. Merton's every word, every action, was that of a compassionate man. He was a complete contrast to the man who he had been just moments before. Sampson touched the Queen's arm gently. The Queen looked up at him with questions in her eyes.

"I think it is for the best that we let Galahad take care of her," Sampson stated quietly. "Let us leave them to it."

"Yes. You are probably right," Annis followed him out of the chamber, and she shut the door behind her. It was dark in this corner of the Hall, and only the flickering lights of several candles illuminated their faces.

"Amandine was fine one moment," Annis stated, her voice trembling with emotion. She hastily wiped a tear away from her cheek. "And now… This. Tell me the truth, Brother Sampson. Do you think she has lost her wits? Is she beyond help?"

"No. No, to both questions," Sampson was quick to reassure. "Lady Amandine is simply afraid. She was to be burnt on a pyre. We must not forget that."

"Do not think me unsympathetic. My heart aches when I think of the ordeal she has had to endure. I know what it feels like to be afraid. When I helped Alden escape from my father's dungeon, all those years ago, I learnt what it felt like to be a hare running from the hounds. My father's men hunted us unmercifully. They would have killed us if they had caught us, I am sure of it."

"I have heard your story," Sampson replied with sympathy in his eyes. "You were very brave. Your story is an inspiration. And it proves that good always conquers evil."

"And then when Alden sought sanctuary in Kent, we were betrayed by King Oeric. If it were not for Merton's quick thinking we would have died," Annis continued, lost in her memories.

"You have been through so much," Sampson commiserated. "And yet you have come out the other side so much stronger."

"Not to mention all that trouble with Budic in Brittany and the rebellion here. I almost lost my life, and that of my unborn child's that terrible day when the peasants revolted. I look at Jowen every day and thank God that he survived. He was such a strong baby. He will make a strong king. One day... Although may that be a long, long time in the future."

"I am sure Jowen will make a fine king. Your Majesty, I do not mean to speak out of turn, but are you comparing the situation you found yourself in, to the one Lady Amandine found herself in?" Sampson asked with a small frown.

"Perhaps," Annis admitted.

"Then, I suggest you stop," Sampson advised wisely. "You have suffered greatly. There is no disputing that. But throughout your many trials, Alden never left your side."

"Apart from when Budic took him prisoner," Annis contradicted.

"But then you had Merton," Sampson replied. "Or so I have heard."

"Yes, you are right. I did. Amandine was also a great comfort to me. As was Josephine."

"You were surrounded by friends. Lady Amandine had no one. She had no friends. In Brittany, they were calling for her blood as if she were nothing but a sacrificial lamb from days of old."

"She is frightened," Annis replied with a small shake of her head. "I understand that. I just do not understand the rocking and the staring at nothing. I have never seen anything like it. What is wrong with her? It is as if she is possessed or something? Do you think that maybe a demon—"

"No your Majesty, I do not," Sampson was quick to interrupt. "I have seen demons. Amandine is not displaying any signs that a darker force, other than fear, possesses her. I think she is confused and very scared," Sampson spoke slowly and with caution. "She thought," he lowered his voice, "Merton was dead. There is no demon, Annis. Be careful not to start a wild rumour. Or you may find that one day soon the people of Cerniw will also be calling for her blood as well."

"I would never say such things to anyone but you," Annis assured. "If you do not think she is possessed, then I am reassured. But why does she rock?"

"She has been under siege this past year, and by the sounds of it, she has remained strong. Now there is no need for her to be strong. She is safe. But such a change in circumstance can take some getting used to. I believe that she rocks because she does not know what else to do."

"Yes. Yes, no doubt you are right. But you must tell me, what can we do to make her feel more secure? How do we convince her that she is safe here? I cannot stop the servants from talking. If they see her behaving in such a way, it will be all over the castle by the end of the day. And then her reputation will be…"

"We must trust in God. He is our refuge after all," Sampson said with a smile.

"I do trust in our dear Lord, and I believe in the power of prayer, but I still fear for her. I have this terrible feeling. A feeling that I do not truly understand."

"Then please, tell me of this feeling, and I can help you interpret it and if not, then at least I can share the burden of your concern."

"I fear that Castle Dor is not where Amandine should be. Her being here is making me feel very uneasy."

"In what way?" Sampson asked, not really understanding what the Queen was trying to tell him.

Annis shook her head ever so slightly as her husband approached her. Whatever it was, it was obvious Annis did not want her husband to know.

"Is everything alright?" Alden asked with concern.

"We were talking about Lady Amandine," Sampson stated. "The Queen is very concerned for her health."

"We are all concerned," Alden replied, looking at his wife as he spoke. "What happened?"

"The same as this morning," Annis sighed sadly. "She began to rock…"

"I used to walk," Alden stated, giving his wife a hard look that Sampson could not interpret. "Can't you remember how I was?" He dropped his voice as he looked into Annis eyes and Sampson wondered what they were speaking of.

"You did not rock," Annis stated in an equally quiet voice.

"She is frightened," Alden said simply as he reached up and touched his wife's face with the back of his fingers. There was an intimacy to the touch that made Sampson feel a little uncomfortable. The two had eyes only for each other. "As was I. When I looked into her face this morning, it was like looking into my own. I know what she is going through. When I get my hands on that bastard, I am going to gut him alive for what he did to her." Alden's hand fell away from his wife's face.

Samson saw Annis' face pale at her husband's words although Alden did not seem to notice. It was as if the King was looking inward. His eyes had glazed over as if he was seeing something that no one else saw.

"I think Sire, that we need to talk about the possibility of sending Lady Amandine and Galahad away from court for a time," Sampson dared to speak. He watched as Alden's eyes came back into focus.

"And why would we need to do that?" Alden asked. "Santo is the best healer in the kingdom. Amandine needs to be here with the people that love her."

"The walls are too thin. It was the raised voices that upset her," Annis stated. "Brother Sampson is right. We must send her away."

"With Galahad," Sampson was quick to add.

"When she has recovered her wits, she can come back."

Alden sighed deeply. "I cannot lose Galahad. He is my general now. I need him here. I cannot allow them to leave."

"I am not suggesting that Galahad should leave and never come back. But surely you can spare Galahad for a little while at least?" Annis asked. "We can not send Amandine away without Galahad accompanying her. I am sure that once he has settled her into her new home, then he will come straight back to you. Please, Alden, I cannot bear to see her like this. For her own sake, we must send her away."

Alden scoffed softly under his breath as he listened to his wife's words. "I need Galahad by my side if I am to ensure victory."

"I am sorry Sire, but Galahad is not God. Only God can ensure victory," Sampson reminded the King.

"I wish that were true," Alden replied.

"Alden please," Annis persisted as she grabbed hold of her husband's tunic. "Galahad will be away for a few days at most. Just enough to get Amandine settled. And in the meantime, Yrre can advise you. He knows as much about warfare as Galahad does."

Alden sighed again. "And I suppose you have somewhere in mind for the two of them to go."

Sampson smiled his relief. He had not thought the King would be so easily persuaded. Thank God for the Queen.

"To Galahad's Druid. She will take them in, I am sure of it,"

Annis stated with a smile.

"I would have to protest at that," Sampson stammered, this was not what he had hoped for at all. It was the complete opposite in fact. Galahad's soul was in a very vulnerable state. If he stayed with the Druid and she practised her magic on him, she could drive him even further away from God. Surely that was not what God had in mind? No. Merton must not be in the company of that woman again. It was bad enough the last time.

"Amandine is hardly going to feel comfortable in a convent, is she?" Annis argued back.

"And Galahad would not be that far away," Alden mused as he thought upon the plan.

"Tegan's it is then," Annis stated. "I will make arrangements for them to leave as soon as Amandine is able."

"Your Majesties, please," Sampson continued to protest, but his words were met with only deaf ears.

Chapter 15

Benwick Castle, The Kingdom of Brittany.

Philippe fell to his knees before the fire, closed his eyes and began to pray. Praying was all he had been doing. He had been praying for days. *Why did God not speak to him? Why did he remain silent?* Philippe had prayed desperately for forgiveness. Tears had fallen unheeded down his face, but God had uttered not a word. God had not offered his forgiveness or his guidance. He offered nothing.

He was a fool. He was a fool to keep praying to a God who had turned his back on him. Philippe felt a sudden and uncontrollable anger towards God — an anger that was as destructive as his guilt and just as pointless. He knew, deep down, that it wasn't God's fault that he found himself in the situation he was in. After all, God had nothing to do with it.

Philippe opened his eyes and wearily looked at the fire. However, Philippe did not see the comforting flames of a fire in a hearth. All he saw was a pyre. He could still hear the screams of the dying and the smell of roasting flesh. Bile rose up into his mouth unexpectedly. The taste was bitter, burning, like the flames before him. He swallowed it back down, and then wished he had not, for it continued to burn in his stomach. It was an unquenchable fire that was burning him from the inside out. The taste of sickness lingered in his mouth, but he did not rush to pour himself a drink because he knew that there wasn't enough water in this entire world to quench the burning pain inside of him. He absentmindedly rubbed at the pain in his chest as he rose unsteadily to his feet. He had spent enough time on his knees these past few days. If God had abandoned him, then so be it. It wasn't as if this was the first time he had been left to fend for himself. He had always somehow managed to muddle through. Why should this be any different?

The child and Alwena were asleep in his bed. The only light in the chamber came from the fire. The darkness was fitting, for it matched his black soul.

Philippe's mother had told him on her deathbed, many years ago, that it was always darkest before the day dawned. She had died that night. She had never seen the dawn. Philippe had thought that his life could not possibly get any darker than it did the days that followed his mother's death. How wrong he had been. *This* was his darkest hour. Or maybe *this* was his final hour. What was it all for, anyway? Everyone died eventually. It was just a question of when.

Alwena muttered in her sleep, but Philippe did not strain to listen. In truth, he did not know why she was still here. Alwena had said she was here for him and the child. There was more to it, he was sure. But every time he brought the subject up Alwena evaded his questions. She would change the subject and Philippe did not have the strength to demand an answer.

The child had kept her silence too. It was a terrible thing to look into her young face. Her eyes were dry, but her terror was real. Her grief was eternal, and yet not once did she cry. She did not call out for her mother or her sister, not even in dreams. In fact, she did not speak at all. Not one word had made it past her lips. Philippe wondered if she ever would recover her voice. And if she did, what would she say? Would she blame him for her mother's and her sister's deaths? Would she condemn him with a few choice words? How he wished she would, for he deserved such condemnation.

Alwena had managed to get the little girl to eat some pottage, so that was something. But the child showed no pleasure in eating. She showed no pleasure in anything. She just held tight to her flea-infested doll and looked at him as if she carried all the tragedy of the world on her shoulders. Philippe knew not her name, nor if she had any living relatives. Philippe knew nothing about her, other than the fact that her life had been utterly destroyed by him.

As for Mordred, he had kept his distance. Philippe had expected him to demand an audience, but he had stayed away. Everyone had stayed away, and as a king, Philippe knew that did not bode well. While he had been hiding in this chamber, had Mordred claimed the throne in his absence? Was his court laughing at him at this very moment? Were they raising a goblet to his imminent demise?

Philippe tossed another log onto the fire, and he realised he didn't care. If Mordred was so desperate to have the throne, then it was his. Philippe had had enough of being a king. He had had enough of everything. If his court were laughing at him then what concern was it of his? Why should he care? He would be like God and act indifferent.

With a shaken faith, Philippe rose to his feet. At least he had tried to communicate with God, but God was either not listening or did not care.

Philippe breathed out unsteadily. Life was unbearable. The guilt was killing him. He dared not sleep, for every time he closed his eyes the ghosts would come calling. He could not eat, for every time he ate he felt sick. He didn't want to speak to anyone. He just wanted to hide away and pretend that all of this had happened to someone else. But that was not an option. There was only one way this agony could end…

With clarity, Philippe knew what he had to do. He knew how to stop this endless cycle of torment. Alwena and the child did not stir as Philippe made his way towards the door, for his footsteps were light, even if his heart was heavy with grief and guilt.

The soldiers who were on guard outside of his door looked at him with surprise as he stepped out into the cold dark corridor. He must have looked a sight. He had not changed his clothes since the executions, and a comb had gone nowhere near his hair. But for once, such concerns were of no interest to him.

"No one goes in," Philippe whispered his last order under his breath, although he did not look at the two men as he spoke. He had already convinced himself that Alwena would see the child to safety. She would look after the little girl. She may even become the child's mother, in time. What did either of them need him for?

"Sire," both soldiers acknowledged their King at the same time, but Philippe was already walking down the corridor by then.

Philippe paused outside of Mordred's chamber. Mordred had a

fondness for the servants. The moans that were coming from his chamber suggested that this particular servant was not unaffected by Mordred's charms. Her screams rose higher as she reached her pleasure and Mordred's moan of contentment soon followed. How any woman could lay with that monster was beyond Philippe. But then he guessed some women liked the idea of all that power, and some were attracted to evil. An image of Josephine came to mind. Josephine and Mordred would have made a good pair. They were suited to each other. Perhaps he should have arranged an introduction.

With trembling fingers, Philippe touched the door. He wished he had the courage to push the door open, unsheathe his knife and slit that bastard's throat. But he was all out of courage. His hand fell away from the door, and he took a step back. *Merton would have done it* — the voice in his head mocked him. Merton would have pushed that door open without a second thought. But Merton wasn't here. Although one day he would be, Philippe was sure of that if nothing else. Merton would hold him to that flame, and he would not be merciful. Just like *he* had not been merciful to Merton. Knowing Merton was alive was like living with a tumour. Merton would kill him. *If,* his guilt did not do so first.

A woman giggled from inside the chamber, and Philippe heard the slap of skin against skin. The moaning started up all over again. It made him feel sicker than what he already felt. With a shake of his head, Philippe continued on his way. Down the stairs, he went, although when he reached the bottom of the staircase, Philippe could not recall how he had gotten there. The Great Hall door was wide open. The stench of sweating bodies coming from the room was so intense that his eyes watered. He had been absent for three days, and the castle had descended into chaos. Thankfully, the Great Hall was not Philippe's chosen direction. However, the idea of his so-called loyal court awakening to see their King hanging from the rafters appealed to his melancholy mood. But he resisted such a temptation, for there were better ways to die. He made his way outside where the damp night air greeted him like an old friend.

Night cloaked the earth with her dark essence. The weather was overcast. There were no stars in the sky. There was no moon. It was the perfect setting for the vilest of crimes.

Philippe went where his feet led, and they led him to the ruins of the monastery. The air here still smelt of ash and something else. Something more sinister. There was an evil here. Philippe could feel it. The hairs on the back of his neck stood up in warning, and he unconsciously shivered.

"The dragon will breathe his fire on the Kingdom of Brittany, and all that is good will be destroyed," Bastian prophesied in the darkness.

Philippe did not respond to Bastian's words, but he heard them. He understood them. The fire at the monastery had not been an accident. Darkness may shroud Philippe's soul, but he wasn't blind to the truth. Mordred did this. *"Remove the opposition,"* Mordred had once said to him. Mordred heeded his own advice very well.

Philippe turned away from the ruins, and with a new determination, he made his way to the stables. Thankfully, Bastian had not lingered. Philippe was walking in the shadow of death, and that was a path he had to walk alone.

The door to the stables was shut for the night. The grooms were asleep. There would be no one to wait on him, which suited Philippe just fine. Philippe pushed the door open. The smell of horses, leather, and hay was a welcomed distraction to the smell of an ash-filled night.

Philippe did not bother with a torch. He made his way to his horse's stable by touch and memory alone. Philippe knew in which stall his horse stood and he did not need a saddle or a bridle. He could ride just as well with a headcollar and a rope. For once, he was grateful for his ancestry. The du Lacs' had always been excellent horseman. Philippe was no exception.

Philippe rode out of the castle grounds at a gallop. He met with no resistance. No questions as to what he was doing, or where he was going at this ungodly hour. No one suggested an escort for their King. Even the soldiers who guarded the portcullis did not think to stop him. The Devil was at work this night, and he would have both blood and death.

The wind whipped into Philippe's face and dragged at his clothes. Usually, Philippe felt a sense of exhilaration when he rode into the wind. But tonight he felt nothing. Only despair. The air was cold on his exposed skin. It was cold but welcoming. Philippe kicked his horse on harder. The animal, despite the dark, was surefooted and more importantly fast. Philippe steered off the road and began to gallop towards the edge of the cliff. If anyone had happened by, they would have witnessed the final moments of a king.

The air was colder here and tasted of salt, but that did not deter Philippe. He kicked his horse on again, asking for more, demanding more. The horse was blowing hard, but he did as he was asked. He kept on running. Philippe yanked the horse towards the very edge of the cliff. He yelled at the animal to get on. Death was tempting. And at that moment Philippe thought that it was the only escape from this terrible reality.

But then God parted the clouds, and a moon, bright and full, shone down upon the King of Brittany and the horse as they raced headlong towards disaster. The horse, now seeing the direction he was asked to run, began to falter. Philippe, however, would not let the horse check his speed. And the horse had no choice but to obey his master.

The horse's long strides ate up the ground. Relief was Philippe's for the taking. Five strides. Four strides. Three strides. Philippe pulled back on the makeshift reins with such force that the horse screamed as it came to a skidding halt at the very edge of the cliff. The sea pounded the rocks below them. Above them the clouds regrouped and hid the moon. God had won this battle. There would be no death this night. The Devil would have to wait to take his prize.

Philippe's breathing matched that of his horse. Exhausted and shaking, he lent forward and laid his head upon his horse's sweat-soaked mane. He apologised to the animal, and slowly slid off the horse's back. His legs immediately gave way, and he fell upon the damp ground.

Huge sobs racked Philippe's body. "God, please. Please forgive me. Please."

***

The sky was the colour of summer lavender as Philippe led his horse back towards the stables. Philippe felt numb. Like the kind of numbness that warriors feel after a terrible battle. Philippe had fought his own demons this night and, like with any battle, it had left its scars.

A groom came running towards him with a relieved look on his face. "We were just about to send a search party, Sire. We feared someone had broken in and stolen him."

The groom looked at his King with questions in his eyes, but Philippe did not have the energy to do anything other than hand the lead rope to the groom. But the horse seemed reluctant to go with the groom. He planted his hooves firmly on the ground and refused to move. Perhaps the horse could sense Philippe's need for non-judgemental company.

"Bring him out, keep him walking," the head groom, an old man whose name Philippe could never recall, ordered as he threw open the stable doors.

A horse was brought out of the stables. The animal was reluctant to walk but instead desperately pawed at the ground. He was in a state of obvious distress. His breathing was rapid, and every so often he would pause and look back at his flank. He began to kick at his stomach with his hind hoof as if there was a foreign body inside of him that needed telling off.

"I will give him a good rubdown, Sire," the groom stated, bowing respectfully. "Will you need him again today?"

"What horse is that?" Philippe asked instead. His attention entirely focused on the horse that was ill.

"That is Logodenn," the groom replied with a heavy sigh. "He was one of a pair that Lord Pendragon..." the groom sighed again, for it was not his place to criticise his so-called betters.

"Mordred destroys everything he touches," Philippe said as he watched the grooms desperately try to keep Logodenn on his feet.

"Yes," the groom agreed under his breath, feeling confident to do so now. "We have noticed that. You could not ask for a better horse than Logodenn. He is so easy to take care of and has such a pleasant attitude to his work. One of a kind, you might say."

"Get me a blanket, quickly," the head groom yelled. A blanket was quickly thrown over the bay horse that had survived Mordred's sickening abuse in the chariot. The blanket covered up the healing wounds, but it did little to warm the animal. The horse was sweating profusely, and steam was rising from his body to mingle with the morning sea mist. Very soon the blanket was soaked through with the horse's sweat.

The horse began to yawn excessively as if he were fatigued, but Philippe knew better as did everyone else who was watching.

"Has the healer been called for?" Philippe asked, for horses were an expensive investment, and one that deserved looking after.

"Franseza is still ill, and no one can find Alwena. We are reluctant to summon Tanguy, for he has a heavy hand and is drunk more times than not. We managed to get some bitter apple down him, but it hasn't done anything."

Philippe would not allow Alwena to leave the child alone, even for a horse as deserving as this one. He kept his silence about Alwena's whereabouts.

"Let him stretch," the head groom yelled as he took control of the lead rope. The horse stretched as if he was about to urinate, but no urine came.

"We need to keep him moving, lads. Let's see if we can walk it out of him. But one thing is for certain — if he goes down again, I don't think he will get back up."

"Colic," Philippe said in recognition, for he had seen it many times before. Sometimes horses survived. Most times they didn't.

"Colic," the groom agreed. "We hoped it wouldn't happen," the groom said tight-lipped as he watched his fellow grooms battle to keep the horse on his feet.

Philippe's horse chose that moment to whinny loudly, and Philippe wondered if his horse was trying to encourage his ill stablemate not to give up. Many would mock him for such a thought. Animals didn't have feelings. They were dumb beasts, incapable of forming attachments. The arrogance of man knew no limits.

"When a horse suffers a trauma of any kind, it always goes to his stomach," the groom continued as he patted Philippe's horse. "Gaël has said that many times."

Gaël, of course, that was the head grooms name, Philippe silently thought. *Why did he keep forgetting?*

"We thought we had made it past the time of vulnerability," the groom continued. "But he picked at his food yesterday, he passed very little, and his stomach was very quiet. Young Neven slept in his stall, to be on the safe side. The boy woke us just before dawn. He told us that the horse was down and would not get back up."

"Get me a whip. We must keep him on his feet," the head groom bellowed, but no one ran to do his bidding, for they could see what Gaël did not want to see. "Come on you bastard, keep moving. Keep moving. You can do it. I am not going to lose you too."

Unfortunately, the horse could not keep moving for the pain was too great. With great violence the animal threw himself on the floor, yanking the lead rope from Gaël's hands.

"NO," Gaël yelled, picking up the lead rope and trying desperately to get the animal back on his feet. The horse complied, for it was in his nature to be obedient, but as soon as he was back on his shaking legs, he threw himself to the ground again.

"No," with tears in his eyes Gaël tried again to make Logodenn rise. But the horse was beyond that now. His gut had twisted. It was just a matter of time. The horse rolled, thrashing with his legs in a demented like manner, but there was no escape from the pain, and somewhere in the horse's wise mind, he knew that.

How long Logodenn thrashed and rolled for, no one knew, for no one was keeping time. But eventually, Logodenn came to rest on his side. His breathing was erratic, the whites of his eyes were showing, and a continuous groan of pain came from somewhere deep inside of him. *There was nothing worse than the sound of a horse crying out in pain,* Philippe fleetingly thought as he watched. But then he remembered the pyre, and Abbot Daniel dying in his Hall.

"Get me another blanket," Gaël demanded in a very gruff voice. "And Neven, go and wake Erwan. He will put an end to Logodenn's suffering. I'll not have the poor beast suffering any more than he already has. It could take hours for him to die, and I'll not have that."

Philippe turned away from the upsetting scene. He felt a fire in his heart that didn't burn. He was angry, but this time he would direct that anger on the man who deserved it.

Chapter 16

Philippe had not gone back to the castle, instead he found himself stood at the foot of his uncle's grave. He had never visited the cemetery before. The thought of being surrounded by his ancestors' bones had always made him strangely nervous. It wasn't because he feared for his mortality. He did not fear death. But he did fear what came after. Would all these people lying in the dirt one day stand before him with accusing eyes? Would they judge him, condemn him, before he had a chance to defend himself? Of course, they would.

He touched the top of Lancelot's tombstone. The stone was surprisingly warm, and he hadn't expected that. Philippe withdrew his hand quickly as a strange sensation travelled up his arm. A sensation he did not understand. All he knew was that the old ones said that Lancelot had been one of those people who had always shone brightly. Lancelot had been too alive to die. Much like Merton had been. Only Merton wasn't dead. *Dear God, why didn't he die?*

Philippe had never been close to Lancelot. He couldn't even remember what he looked like. But Philippe needed answers, and as God was stubbornly quiet, Lancelot was the next best thing. Philippe knelt down on the dew-damp grass and looked at Lancelot's name. He gingerly reached out again, and this time he traced the inscription with his fingers. *Lancelot du Lac, King of Brittany.* Underneath that, almost hidden by the grass, was a very small script. Philippe flattened the grass down with his palm and lent in closer.

Be loyal. Be brave.

Philippe read the words several times before sitting back and staring at the tombstone with bewilderment. Philippe did not understand why the motto of King Arthur's knights was inscribed at the bottom of Lancelot du Lac's tombstone. Lancelot had broken faith with the knights and Arthur. And yet, even in death, Lancelot proclaimed his loyalty. Mordred had preached that Lancelot had been dishonest. He had been a knight with no knightly qualities. Mordred had once said that it was no surprise that Merton had turned out the way he had. He was merely following in his father's footsteps. But the inscription... It didn't make any sense.

"Uncle," Philippe said the words out loud and then felt foolish for doing so. What possessed him to think that Lancelot would want to listen to anything he had to say? Philippe had stolen the crown from one of Lancelot's sons and tortured another. He was wasting his time, and yet he did not feel compelled to move. It felt good being here. It felt right.

Philippe sat where he was, mindless of the dampness of the grass, for a long time. He heard not the birds as they welcomed the dawn. Nor did he hear the sound of the soldiers and the servants as they too awoke and began their day of work. Philippe looked for answers to his many questions in the blades of grass the covered the grave. He sought the truth in the inscription of Lancelot's name. But there were no answers, and there was no truth. Instead, there were more questions. So many questions.

Philippe had just wanted what was best for Brittany. Budic was not a great king. Everybody had said so. Even Alden. Budic was selfish. He was arrogant. Philippe had brought about change. He had made life better for his people. Philippe had thought he was doing the right thing. But now he knew he had been ridiculously naive and far too hopeful in a golden future that had never been promised.

When Lord Jenison had introduced Philippe to Mordred Pendragon, Philippe had initially harboured doubts. He, like everyone else, had thought Mordred was dead. The two of them had written to each other long before they had actually met. Philippe had been impressed with Mordred's honeyed words. Looking back, he now understood. Mordred had flattered him. Agreed with him. And that had made Philippe feel important and confident. Mordred made him believe that the bastard son of a disgraced brother could rise above his station and lead a nation to greatness. But when he met Mordred in secret just days before he usurped Budic, Philippe knew he had made a terrible mistake. He did not admit it to himself, not even then. But now, he did. Mordred had fed him one lie after another. Mordred wasn't his friend. He had never been his friend. He was just using him.

"How did you defeat him?" Philippe asked the silent grave. "How did you defeat Arthur? I need to know because I made the same mistake you did. I trusted a Pendragon. I know I have no right to ask you. But you are my last hope."

Like God, Lancelot said nothing. The dead took their secrets to their grave. Everyone knew that. Philippe was wasting his breath.

With a deep sigh of frustration, Philippe was about to stand up when a bird, a magpie, landed on top of Lancelot's grave. The bird tilted his head to one side and regarded Philippe with curious eyes. Philippe watched as the bird flapped his wings and flew to another tombstone.

Philippe rose slowly to his feet. "I am sorry to have intruded on your rest, great King," he stated, looking down once more at Lancelot's grave. "Sleep easy, uncle. I will see you soon. And then I will explain all, I promise." He touched the tombstone briefly with his fingers as if to seal the promise he made.

There was nothing left for Philippe to do but to head back inside and confront his court. He just hoped that his fate would not be the same as the Abbot's, and the monks', and the horses'.

The magpie was still sat on the tombstone, and out of curiosity, Philippe crossed to where the magpie was perched, to his surprise the bird did not protest. This memorial was smaller. It looked like a rock sticking out of the grass. Philippe knelt down and looked at the engraving. *Tristan du Lac,* this one read. Tristan had not only been Lancelot's cousin, but he had been his best friend, or so they said. How Philippe wished he had a best friend. What must it be like to have someone who is always on your side, no matter what?

"What are you trying to tell me?" Philippe asked, looking at the magpie. The bird had not moved. But it did look at him with eyes that seemed to mock him. Then without warning, the magpie flapped his wings and flew away.

"They won't help you," Bastian stated and Philippe turned to look at him. "The dead. They won't help you."

"I thought I was alone," Philippe said as he looked back at Tristan's tombstone.

"In Benwick Castle?" Bastian scoffed. "There is always someone watching. You know that as well as I do. Why are you here?"

"I came looking for answers."

"Did you find any?" Bastian asked with cynicism.

"No."

"I didn't think so."

"Lancelot was a brave man, wasn't he?" Philippe mumbled the question more to himself than anything else.

"As was Tristan," Bastian agreed.

"Did you know him? Tristan, I mean."

"A little. He kept himself to himself for the most part. He was wounded you see, during the battle of Benwick. He lost the use of his legs. He couldn't walk. But he…" Bastian smiled as he remembered. "He was very wise. And he was happy to share that wisdom. I liked him. Although not everyone did. After Tristan died, there was talk. Some said he was a liar."

"What did Lancelot say?" Philippe asked.

"I cannot imagine Lancelot being friends with someone who lied to him. But he neither condemned nor defended Tristan. He kept his own counsel. What are you going to do, Philippe?"

Philippe looked up at the sky. The lavender hue had changed to a blue one. He never appreciated how beautiful the sky was, until now. The day promised to be a warm one, but Philippe felt chilled.

"What would you do?" Philippe asked, as he rose to his feet and looked at his general.

"You have two choices. You can abdicate. Hand him the throne. Or…"

"Or…" Philippe encouraged.

"You could kill him," Bastian said with a shrug.

"So could you," Philippe stated. "Which then begs the question, why haven't you?"

"Why haven't you?" Bastian asked, turning the question back on Philippe.

"He owns me, Bastian. I am bought and paid for," Philippe said, admitting the terrible truth that he had been too frightened to admit before. "I am the so-called King of Brittany. I am responsible for my people. You saw what Mordred did to Abbot Daniel. You saw what he did to the monks and to those women. If I challenged him and lost, can you imagine what he would do to Brittany? So the only path I can take is to abdicate and hope and pray that he is merciful to the people he will rule."

"No, you must not. It is prophesied that he will burn Brittany anyway," Bastian replied. "Do not shame your ancestors by giving that bastard an easy time. You must try to hold onto your throne, at all costs. You owe it to your people to at least try."

"You are right, of course. I will try. I will do everything in my power to prevent the prophecy from coming true," Philippe made this promise here with the dead as his witnesses. Bastian was right. There was no way he could hand his throne over. Not now. He would not give anyone cause to call him a coward. He had to fight. He had to defend his kingdom. "I must protect my people from the dragon."

"And I will help you," Bastian promised.

"I will hold you to that."

Philippe left Bastian staring at the tombstones. He felt a new purpose inside of him. But as he came in sight of the castle entrance, he felt his courage waver. Who was he to stand up against such a dragon? He was a pathetic excuse for a man. Who was he trying to convince? Philippe sighed and looked down at his feet.

Tufts of grass were fighting their way up through the pitched paving. Nature always won. No matter what man did to try to contain it. Nature found a way in through the cracks and the crevices. Perhaps that was how he could defeat Mordred — with little acts of defiance. Philippe pondered on this as he reluctantly climbed the steps and entered the castle.

It was cold inside of Benwick. Colder than a tomb. The Great Hall was coming back to life with laughter and a few groans of protest as nobles awoke. The servants were up and about. They carried large buckets of steaming water for the nobles to wash the sleep from their eyes. Later they would return with food and the day would begin properly.

"Philippe?"

Philippe looked up as Mordred made his way down the stairs. He felt hatred in his heart as he looked upon Arthur's only son. How dare Mordred look refreshed after all the crimes he had committed. How did that bastard sleep easy at night?

"You look awful," Mordred stated, as he looked Philippe up and down with an assessing gaze.

Mordred made Philippe feel like a naughty child who had been caught playing in the mud in his best clothes. But Philippe could not allow himself to feel like that. He had to remain strong. No more thoughts of suicide. No more thoughts of running away. He had created this mess. It was up to him to clear it up.

"There was a horse that took ill in the night," Philippe stumbled over the words. Where was that conviction when he needed it? Was he so afraid of Mordred Pendragon that fear froze his emotions? "He was a prized member of my stables," Philippe heard himself ramble on. "We lost him."

"You are rich enough, you can buy yourself another," Mordred stated without compassion. "I suggest you go and get changed. You do not want the nobles to see you like this."

Mordred turned away from Philippe as the servant girl, who he had obviously spent the night with, came down the corridor. She carried a bucket of water, just like the other servants did. Mordred closed the distance between him and the girl. He took the bucket from her and placed it on the floor. She smiled up at Mordred; obviously pleased he was still taking an interest in her, for it was common knowledge that Mordred liked variety. He never slept with the same woman, or man for that matter, twice. Mordred took her hand and led her to where Philippe stood, watching.

"What you need is a woman," Mordred stated with arrogant confidence. He moved so he could stand behind the girl. "She is pretty, isn't she?" Mordred ran his hand suggestively over her body. When he cupped one of her breasts in his hand, she gasped with pleasure, and her head fell back onto his shoulder. "She is very good. I have broken her in. Why not have a taste, Sire? She will satisfy you, I am sure. She will make you forget about your dead horse."

"I do not bed prostitutes," Philippe stated coldly. Inside he was shaking, but he had had enough of Mordred's whores, and the wine, and the promises. And perhaps this small act of defiance would show Mordred that he wasn't going to lie down and be ridden over. Not anymore. "Get out of my castle, you are not paid to sleep with my guests," Philippe glared at the girl as he spoke. He directed his hatred of Mordred towards the girl. He knew it wasn't fair. But then life never was.

"No," the girl began to protest, but Mordred pushed her away from him with a force so great that she stumbled into the wall.

"You heard him," Mordred stated, his voice as cold as Philippe's. "Get out of the castle and do not come back, you filthy bitch."

"I need the money," the girl cried. "Please Sire, I am sorry. It won't happen again. Please. My family depend on this money." The girl began to sob as she begged to keep her position.

"Oh, for God's sake," Philippe mumbled under his breath. He meant to insult Mordred with such a declaration, but the man was beyond reproach. He pushed past Mordred and the girl and made his way into the Great Hall.

As he entered, the Hall fell silent. The Hall stank, and he was about to order the Hall to be cleared so the servants could clean it when he noticed an effigy of himself hanging from the rafters. He looked up at it in a stunned silence. His fleeting thought about hanging himself from the rafters suddenly took on a new meaning.

"What is the meaning of this?" Mordred's voice bellowed behind him.

No one answered as they stared at their King.

"Who did this?" Mordred demanded, his voice ringing with what sounded like genuine anger. "I shall beat every single one of you until I get an answer."

Philippe stumbled as he made his way towards the effigy. A hand reached out and stopped him from falling, but he did not pause to thank whoever it was who had helped him. The crude effigy was calling him forward. It was mocking him, with its sackcloth face and its mass of straw hair. Someone had stolen one of his tunics and dressed this grotesque representation. On its head, was a crown made of thorns. Philippe knew what it meant. It was not an attack on Jesus, but an attack on his own authority.

"I mean it," Mordred continued to yell. "I shall start with you," Mordred pointed to an aged man who had only just woken up and had absolutely no idea what was going on.

Philippe reached up and touched the effigy of himself. It was one thing longing for your own death. It was another altogether when others longed for it too.

"This is the Devil's work," the Archbishop stated with too much force. He had just come into the Hall and had made his way towards Mordred.

Did the pair of them really think he was that stupid? They could both pretend outrage and demand answers, but Philippe knew where the blame really lay.

"Someone cut that abomination down, now," the Archbishop ordered.

But nobody moved.

Philippe pushed the effigy out of the way and with the grace of a drunk, he crossed the Hall to where his throne was. Although stunned, he did not feel intimidated. Anger, yes he felt that. But it had also given him that final push to do what he should have done all along. He would rule from now on the way he wanted to rule. Things were about to change, one way or the other. The Kingdom of Brittany's fate would be decided within the next few moments.

"To wish for the death of your sovereign King is—"

"Treason," Mordred finished the Archbishop's sentence for him.

An orange cat had made himself at home on Philippe's throne. Philippe felt more disturbed by seeing that cat than by the hanging effigy. Elouan, *was that the cat's name?* The animal had once belonged to Lady Amandine. Dear God, he missed her. And he feared for her.

Elouan looked up at him and began to meow. Philippe, whose hatred of cats was well known, did something so out of character that those who watched would later talk about it amongst themselves. Philippe reached down and picked up the cat. He held it close to his chest as he sat himself down on the throne that Lancelot had once sat on. Elouan curled up on his lap, and as Philippe began to pet him, the cat began to purr.

"This is treason," Mordred said again. "The penalty of which is death."

"It is always death, isn't it?" Philippe stated. There was no anger in his voice, but a strained and tired patience. He did not look at Mordred as he spoke but continued to stroke the cat. "If you steal some bread because your children are hungry then you are sentenced to death. If you poach some wood from the forest because your family needs a fire to warm themselves and to cook their food, the sentence is death. If you are a woman and you kiss a man who is not your husband, it is death. If you disagree with the king, it is death. If you make an effigy… Once again the sentence is death. Why not chop off everybody's heads and be done with it? Or perhaps you could set fire to the Hall. We could barricade the doors, like my cousin, Merton du Lac did when he murdered that entire village in Frank." *Like you did to the monks,* Philippe wanted to add but thought better of it.

"We are not barbarians," Archbishop Verus stated with an angry passion.

"Are we not? So what was that the other day? Why did we burn those innocent women?"

"They were not innocent. They were witches," the Archbishop replied.

"Witches? Really? How strange. I thought they died because Lady Amandine escaped justice. I thought they died because Abbot Daniel died in my Hall."

"They were witches—"

"Why do you hesitate, Lord Pendragon?" Philippe asked, turning his attention back to Mordred. The Archbishop's disgust at being interrupted was clear for all to see, but Philippe did not care. "Why not kill them all? You can start with Lord Madec."

"My Lord," Lord Madec immediately began to protest with alarm, but he did not look at Philippe as he spoke. He looked at Mordred. "I did not make the effigy. I have done nothing wrong. You know this."

"Why do you look to Lord Pendragon for mercy, Lord Madec? Why do you direct your plea to him?" Philippe asked. "Only I can grant pardons. I am your king. Mordred is not your king. Do not look to him for help. You should be looking to me."

"Mordred, please," Lord Madec continued. "I am your most humble servant. We were only doing what you told us to."

Many gasped at Lord Madec's confession.

"Mordred?" Philippe narrowed his eyes as he looked at Arthur's son, but he did not feel surprised. Of course, Mordred had ordered the effigy to be made and hung. Time was running out, Philippe knew that. Death was approaching. But if he were to die, he would not die quietly. "I cannot believe you would do such a thing."

"How dare you implement me in your disgusting crimes. I will take your tongue as well as your life," Mordred threatened as he pulled out a vicious-looking knife.

"Sire," Lord Madec turned his terrified face towards Philippe. "Mordred wants your throne. He wants—"

Mordred threw his knife. The blade hit Lord Madec to the left of his stomach with a sickening thud. Lord Madec instantly fell to his knees, but Mordred was not finished with him yet. For he had vowed to take his tongue and take it he did. Lord Madec screamed as Mordred pulled the knife from his body and forced his mouth open.

Philippe looked down at the cat as Mordred butchered one of his own. Lord Madec's scream was bloodcurdling, and the iron scent of blood did nothing to improve the smell of the Hall.

"The tongue of a traitor," Mordred yelled triumphantly, as he held Lord Madec's tongue in the air. No one cheered. A few of those in court instead, purged their stomachs.

Bloody and dying, Lord Madec fell forward. The Hall was filled with the sound of Lord Madec choking on his own blood, and as he did so, no one dared to speak. For all feared that maybe they would be the next victim. It was better to hold your tongue than lose it.

"Get rid of this vermin," the Archbishop ordered as he stood over the dying man. "He deserves no Christian burial. Throw him away with the rubbish."

"Cut off his head and stick a spike into it. So all can see what happens to traitors," Mordred stated. He threw Lord Madec's tongue to the dogs, who fell upon it snapping and biting.

"Lord Prigent," Mordred said the man's name with malice and intent.

Lord Prigent looked like he was about to pass out and he stared at Mordred with wide, frightened eyes.

"You were very close to Lord Madec, was this your doing too?" Mordred pointed at the effigy with the tip of his bloody knife.

"No," Lord Prigent was very quick to deny. "I would never do such a thing, your Majesty," Lord Prigent, would not make the same mistake as Lord Madec. He directed his words at Philippe, as he fell to his knees. The rest of the court followed his lead, and soon everyone was kneeling. Even the servants.

"Have I not been a generous king?" Philippe asked, as the cat jumped off his lap. "I have granted you all favours. I have given you land. Titles. Gifts. And now you want to hang me? That seems a little ungrateful," Philippe sat back on his throne and regarded all the bowed heads. He then looked back at Mordred and the Archbishop. They were the only two men who had chosen to remain standing.

God, if you can hear me, give me courage, Philippe silently pleaded. This was it. This would be the defining moment of his reign. All he had to do was stand up to Mordred. He could do this. He could. He counted to five in his head and put his trust in God. "But remember, I am the King of Brittany, and I will have total obedience. Mordred, your men, I want them gone from my kingdom by the end of the day."

"What men?" Mordred asked with a hint of contempt that he didn't bother to conceal. It was obvious by the look on his face that he did not like being addressed so. Philippe had not thought he would. He was playing with fire. Provoking the dragon. Such things never ended well and Philippe knew that. If he came out of this unscathed, it would be a miracle.

"The one behind you for a start," Philippe stated.

Both Mordred and the Archbishop looked behind them at the soldier dressed in the colours of Rome.

"Those are my personal guards," the Archbishop stated, as if he was talking to a simpleton. "I never travel anywhere without them."

"Then I suggest you leave with them," Philippe said with a touch of annoyance "There is no longer a need for you to be here. Lady Amandine has escaped. And I no longer have any plans to marry. There is nothing here for you to oversee. Please send my compliments to the Pope."

"I must stay until a new monastery is established. I can not possibly leave you without religious counsel."

"I am sure we can manage," Philippe stated coldly. "I have dismissed you, my Lord. That usually means you must leave my presence, pack your bags and get out of my kingdom."

"How dare you speak to me—"

"How dare you speak to me," Philippe spoke over the Archbishop, with a growing anger. "Leave on your own accord, right now, with your dignity intact. Or I will have my men throw you out."

"Touch me, and you will feel the wrath of Rome."

"Ignore me, and you will meet God sooner rather than later."

"You forget who I am—"

"Mordred, if you would, silence the Archbishop the way you silenced Lord Madec."

"You will regret this," Archbishop Verus stated as he picked up his skirts. "You will regret it," he said again as he stormed from the Hall.

The air in the Hall seemed charged as the sky does before a great storm. War was coming… If it were not already here.

"Everyone, please," Philippe said, raising his hands in the air for his court to rise. As he did so, he looked into Mordred's eyes. Mordred stared back, but Philippe could not decipher his expression.

"A good king admits when he makes a mistake. A bad king does not. I was wrong to listen to the advice of Lord Pendragon and Archbishop Verus. Those women should not have died. That was a mistake and one I will not make again," Philippe continued to look at Mordred as he spoke. "I no longer want to listen to my chief advisor, for he does what he wants. Mordred, I never permitted you to kill Lord Madac, and in my Hall of all places. How dare you. You think you are greater than I am? You think to rule Brittany?"

Mordred smiled menacingly back and Philippe felt his heart miss a beat. This was it. The dragon was awake, now it was a matter of waiting to see what he would do.

"Philippe, you fool," Mordred laughed. "I do rule Brittany. And your short reign is about to come to a rather abrupt end."

Chapter 17

The Kingdom of Cerniw.

"Whoa," Alan whispered under his breath. "Steady." His horse, a dapple grey gelding that Alden had kindly given to him, flicked his ears forwards and backwards as he listened to Alan's command. The horse snorted softly, and he tried to pull the reins from Alan's hands, for there was some very tempting looking grass growing by his hooves that he longed to taste.

Alan cautiously dismounted and led his horse further into the thicket. Someone was following him, and they had been for a couple of days. But as of yet, they had not shown themselves or declared their intent. Alan thought, at first, to outride them, for he had no desire for a confrontation, nor did he have the time. However, he had not managed to shake off his pursuer. Whoever it was, knew how to track.

Alan let the horse have the reins, and the animal immediately stretched out his long neck and began to graze. What to do? That was the question. Should he ride on? Or should he wait? He decided to wait. It was always better to know your enemies.

Alan quietly placed the reins over a timeworn briar. Keeping to the shadows of the mighty birch trees, he crept closer to the abandoned road, unsheathed his knife, and waited. He had had enough of playing the part of the prey. It was time for the hunter to become the hunted.

Time marched on, and the sun rose higher in the sky. The road was blessedly empty. There was no sign of the stranger. But he was out there. Alan knew that he was. Some roe deer crossed his path, grazing on the tender new blades of grass. They seemed unaware that Alan was there. Or maybe they did not see him as a threat. Alan watched the deer for a moment, and then closed his eyes and listened. Around him, birds sang. A doe barked at her fawn to keep up, but apart from that, there was nothing out of the ordinary. No blackbird issued a warning. For now, there was nothing to fear.

Sighing softly, Alan opened his eyes. He flicked away a fly as it buzzed annoyingly around him. "Come on," he whispered to himself. "Show yourself."

A twig snapped behind him, and he turned quickly in the direction of the sound, but he could not see anything, and the birds did not seem concerned. It was probably a deer or perhaps a boar. Alan hoped it wasn't the latter, for boars were dangerous animals to cross. He frowned as he looked about him, but there was nothing there. He turned back around just in time to see the deer gallop back to the woods. Something had startled them. A moment later Alan heard what the deer had. The two-beat gait of a horse in trot.

It wasn't long before the horse, and his rider came into view. The man had his head hidden by a hood, but the horse seemed familiar. Alan could have sworn he had seen that horse in Alden's stables. Was this a messenger from the King?

The man pulled his horse up short and quickly dismounted. As the stranger bent to trace the tracks of Alan's horse, his hood fell away from his head, revealing a mass of long blonde hair.

"What the hell?" Alan mumbled under his breath, hardly believing what his eyes showed him. "Sister Bernice, what the hell do you think you are doing?" he asked as he rose to his feet and began to walk towards her.

"Alan," Sister Bernice straightened, and a smile lit up her whole face when she saw him. "You have given me a merry chase. Please don't be angry. I can explain."

"Has something happened? The Prioress—"

"No, Guinevere is fine. Well, as fine as she can be."

"Alden?"

"He is fine too. At least I think he is."

"Then I don't understand," Alan's eyes searched hers. "What are you doing here? Why have you been following me? What on earth are you wearing? Why are you dressed in a man's clothes?" Alan had never seen anything so shocking. The trousers hugged her legs and made him imagine things he had no right in imagining.

"I..." A blush kissed her cheek, and she stumbled over her words, although she did not look away from him. "I am no longer a nun. You were right. I wanted to tell you that. I wanted... I wanted to be where you were," Bernice finally admitted. "I wanted to be with you. I knew you would never allow me to accompany you. I know the quest you are on is fraught with danger. But..."

Alan reached up and touched the softness of her cheek. She inhaled sharply at his touch, and her blush deepened to that of a wild rose.

"Please don't be angry," Bernice pleaded softly as she reached up and touched his hand. "I just wanted to be near you."

"I am not angry. I am way beyond that," Alan stated, stepping a little closer. He looked down at her lips, and he almost gave into his desire to kiss her, but he did not want their first kiss to be instigated by rage. "What were you thinking? Do you know how dangerous the roads are for an unarmed woman? Even dressed as you are, you would not fool anyone into thinking you are a man." He dropped his hand away and began to march back the way he came with the intent of retrieving his horse. "I am going to have to take you back. I don't have the bloody time for this."

"I am not going back," Bernice stated defiantly as she and her horse followed in his wake. "I am going with you."

"Over my dead body," Alan stated over his shoulder. "And who the hell taught you to track?"

"Please stop swearing," Bernice reprimanded. "There is no need for such foul language. And if you must know, Sister Agatha taught me to recognise the footsteps of all the animals in the local wood. I whiled away many a long afternoon, playing in the woods and tracking the animals. Tracking a horse is nothing compared to tracking a wood mouse."

"*A wood mouse?* Bloody hell. You shouldn't have come," Alan stated as he picked up the reins of his horse and threw them over the animal's head. "I can't even begin... You saw what happened at the Priory. Not all men in Cerniw are good. You could have been attacked. You could have been raped."

"But I wasn't," Bernice reassured. "And now I am with you. So there is nothing for me to fear."

"I am taking you straight back to Dor."

"You will not," Bernice stated, planting a hand firmly on her hips as she glared up at him. And once again Alan saw his avenging angel as she had been on the beach when they had landed in Cerniw and had, to their dismay, received an icy welcome. Bernice had argued with Alden until she got what she wanted. Alan would be damned if he would give into her so easily.

"I can help you. I… I don't want to be apart from you. When you left, I felt an ache, here," she placed her hand upon her chest where her heart lay. "I cannot go months, years, without knowing how you fare. I have just found you. I never thought I would find a man who I could love. I am not going to let you walk away from me."

Alan was not expecting a declaration of love, but now that she had said such a sacred word, he felt his anger evaporate. "Bernice, I have absolutely no idea what I am walking in to. I am going to Wessex."

"Oh," Bernice's face lost the red hue of embarrassment and anger. "I didn't know," she took a step back and would have tripped over a tangled bramble bush if Alan had not reached for her. "Why are you going to Wessex?" she asked with a genuine fear in her eyes. "It was Cerdic's men who attacked the Priory. You'll be killed if they discover you. Please… I am sure your father never meant for you to risk your life."

"I do not know what my father meant, but I have reason to suspect that Percival is not in Northumbria but instead, lies in a grave in the very heart of Wessex. I need to find that grave. I need to find the Shield."

"No, you don't," Bernice pleaded. She grabbed hold of him firmly by his tunic. "You don't have to do this at all. It was your father's responsibility to unite the knights, not yours. I cannot bear the thought of you alone in that kingdom, surrounded by your enemies."

"My father is dead."

"And so are the knights," Bernice interrupted. "Everyone says so."

"No, they are not. Bernice, if we want to win this coming war against Mordred, then I do not have a choice, I must find them," he stepped back, hoping to put some space between them, but his angel held on tight to his tunic. "Get back on your horse. I am taking you home."

"If you are going to Wessex, then so am I," Bernice stated with conviction.

"No," Alan replied, shaking his head. "You are not going to Wessex, and that is final."

***

The Kingdom of Dumnonia. Four days later…

Alan poked at the fire with a stick and leant back on his elbows. Overhead an owl hooted and the first of the season's crickets sang to the moon as she settled in the shape of a crescent in the sky above them. Somewhere hidden in the woods beyond, a vixen screamed, the sound all too reminiscent of the cries from the nuns in the Priory as Mordred and his men butchered them. Alan pulled the fur a little tighter around his shoulders and willed his mind to think of other things.

His gaze settled on Bernice. She was curled up on her side, a hand resting on her cheek as she slept. Alan got up and silently placed his fur over her sleeping form. The night was warm enough, but he did not want her catching a chill.

He sat back down and sighed into the darkness. So much for taking her back to Dor. Bernice was annoyingly persistent, and he was too weak to deny her anything. It was a mistake taking her with him. He knew that. But then maybe this whole quest was a mistake. Tomorrow they would reach Wessex, and they would be in the very heart of Saxon territory. It wasn't something Alan was particularly looking forward to. Cerdic of Wessex was not known for his hospitality. Ideally, Alan would slip into the castle grounds, locate the graveyard, and slip out again with Cerdic being none the wiser. But Alan suspected it would be more complicated than that. He had been to Wessex only the once, and that was when he was a child. He knew not the topography of the castle for he had never visited it. And apart from a few greetings that Yrre had kindly taught him, he could not communicate in Saxon. Which might prove to be a problem if they were stopped and questioned.

The vixen cried out again as she desperately sought out a mate. He silently wished her luck as he laid his head upon the hard unyielding earth and closed his eyes. He needed to sleep so that he could face tomorrow fresh and alert, but there were so many things that could go wrong that he did not find rest easily.

He was still awake when the sun stained the sky a blood red. He lay on his back and watched the dawn through the green canopy of the trees. There was a moment of silence, as if the earth was inhaling, and then the birds began to sing as they praised a God that only they knew.

Bernice stirred under the furs and Alan watched her with something close to fascination as she sleepily opened her eyes. She smiled when she saw him.

"Good morning," she yawned as she stretched and sat up. "Do you hear the birds?" she asked, her voice ringing with joyful delight.

"I would have to be deaf not to," Alan said as he too sat up. He rolled his shoulders, willing away the ache.

"I just need to…" Bernice stated as she stood and scanned the shrubbery for somewhere that would grant her some privacy.

"Don't go far," Alan instructed.

While she was gone, Alan checked on the horses. They looked well rested and content. He took them down to a small stream so they could quench their thirst and graze on the soft shoots that grew there. By the time he got back to the camp, Bernice had a small fire going and was busy warming up some water. They had stopped in a village when they had first crossed the river Tamar into Dumnonia. The villagers had been more than welcoming, and they had purchased some hard cheese and fresh eggs. Bernice had carefully wrapped the eggs and placed them in her saddlebag. Alan had not thought the eggs would survive the hardship of the journey, but miraculously they had.

"Did you sleep?" Bernice asked, as she carefully unwrapped the eggs and placed them into the water.

"Not really," Alan replied as he tethered the horses.

Bernice sat back and looked up at him. She had to squint for the sun was in her eyes. "It will be all right. God will look after us." She grinned as he handed her a wine skin that he had just filled with water from the stream. "This is a strange land, isn't it? All moors and forests. So different to where I grew up." Her smile fell from her lips as she remembered, but she bravely forged on. "This Island of ours is full of surprises. It is very beautiful, though, don't you think."

"There is a reason why it is so sought after," Alan stated. "And so fought over."

"God's Eden, perhaps?" Bernice offered. "A worthy prize indeed."

"Perhaps."

"Why don't we just stay here, Alan? Build a house. Grow old together."

"That sounds very tempting," Alan said as he sat down beside her. "But I am—"

"I know," Bernice laid her hand on his arm. "It is not easy being in love with the Keeper of the Blade."

"It is not easy being the Keeper of the Blade. Bernice… What if they don't want to be found? What if I can't find them?" Of all the things this was what Alan feared the most. Failure was a very real possibility.

"If anyone can find them it is you," Bernice reassured. "I have faith in you. Have faith in yourself."

Chapter 18

The Kingdom of Wessex.

"What is this place?" Bernice asked as she looked at the horizon with trepidation. From where they were sat on the horses, the ground dropped away and before them, floating in the mist, was an island. And on that island was a stone circle, which no one needed to tell them, was as old as time itself.

Alan had no answer, for like Bernice, he had never seen anything like it. Wessex was a big kingdom, and they had been crossing her vast moors and rolling hills for almost four days. Alan had known it would take time, for the journey through Wessex wasn't something to be rushed. They kept off the roads as much as they could for they did not want to risk meeting fellow travellers and having to converse in a language they did not understand. Last night the rain had forced them to take shelter in one of the many caves they had come across during their journey. Bernice had not slept easy, fearing what lurked deeper in this mysterious cavern. Alan had passed the night in restless sleep as well, but not because he feared the unknown. The people of Briton, whether they knew it or not, depended upon him for their freedom. If he failed, the consequences did not bear thinking about.

"Let's keep moving," Alan said as he nudged his horse on with his heels. "We will follow the tracks of the goats."

"And walk into the mist?" Bernice asked with panic in her voice.

"What if it swallows us up?"

"We will be careful," Alan replied, for what else could he say? They had to move forward. Going back was not an option. Not for him, anyway. "Stay close."

The ride downhill was steep and fraught with danger, one misplaced hoof, and that would be that. Alan had contemplated dismounting and leading the horses down the hill, but then he had thought better of it and trusted in the horses' surefootedness.

Neither of them spoke as they rode, for the ride took all of their concentration. The lower down the hill they rode, the thicker the mist became. It was like trying to navigate through a forest, blind. The damp mist swirled all around them, and all Alan could see was the top of his horse's ears. The occasional bleat of a goat was the only sound apart from that of the horses breathing. Bernice's horse slipped on the soft mud, but thankfully the horse found his footing straightaway and none were the worst for the mishap.

"Tighten your reins," Alan stated, daring to glance back at Bernice, although he could not see her clearly, for the mist hid everything it touched. "It may stop him from falling again."

"They are as tight as they can be," Bernice replied. "I know how to ride a horse," she added under her breath. "Sister Agatha taught me."

It seemed Sister Agatha had taught Bernice a great deal. Alan smiled to himself despite the danger they were in.

"Alan, I think we should go back."

The fear in Bernice's voice tempered his smile. He did not like the idea of her being scared.

"We have travelled too far to head back," and unfortunately that was the truth. Alan knew that this wasn't what she wanted to hear, but they were committed to their path now. The time for turning around and heading back to Dor was long gone.

"You are a mist that appears for a little while and vanishes..." Bernice quoted from the Book of James, nervously. "Why will it not vanish?"

"I do not know. But I am not planning on dying today. Are you?" Alan asked, halting his horse and waiting for Bernice to catch up. He didn't have to wait very long. The mist lifted for just a moment, and he saw how pale she was, how frightened. "I knew I should have taken you back to Dor. I am sorry. The nuns are probably worried sick. If they knew you were here—"

"It was my choice to come," Bernice stated bravely. Alan heard the conviction in her voice, but he wasn't fooled. She was terrified, and the truth was, so was he. There was something unworldly about this place. He feared that God had abandoned it.

"Let's push on," Alan replied, for what else could they do?

Neither spoke after that, for the path thinned to a single track that was littered with rocks and the burrows of rats.

As the hill levelled out, Alan breathed out deeply, and he heard Bernice give a similar sigh of relief. He dared to look back up the way they had come, but he could see nothing but blinding whiteness.

"Are you all right?" he asked Bernice. Bernice's face was still as white as the mist. She managed a quick reassuring nod. "Wait here," Alan ordered. "I am going to ride a little ahead and see what the terrain is like."

"Alan, no," Bernice cried out in panic. "You will never find me again. The mist is too thick."

Alan frowned for she had a point. "Yes, I fear you are right. You must keep up, and watch where your horse is putting his feet."

"Believe me, that is all I have been doing."

They continued to follow the path of the goats until it ended in a land that was lush with grass but boggy underfoot. Alan dismounted swiftly and immediately pulled up a tuft of grass. "Peat," Alan stated, throwing the grass away from him in disgust and with it came a terrible realisation. "Damn it. Damn it. Damn it. DAMN IT." How the hell had they ended up here?

"We are lost?" Bernice's voice trembled as she spoke.

"No, we are not bloody lost," Alan growled with annoyance. "We are in bloody Avalon. DAMN IT. I didn't want to come this way."

"Avalon?" The fear lifted from Bernice's voice and was replaced with wonder. "We are in Avalon?"

With a deep sigh of frustration, Alan looked back at the woman who had stolen his heart. He saw her smile, and her eyes now looked about with barely concealed excitement.

"I have heard of Avalon," her face practically beamed as she tried to see through the mist. "The Summer Lands — that is what the Prioress calls it. The island floating in the mist is no island, is it? It is the Tor," she smiled. "Guinevere once described to me the temple that was built on the Tor in the times of old. I never thought I would ever see it. We really are in Avalon, aren't we? We are in the place where the apples grow…"

"And where the natives die," Alan replied bitterly, and he turned away from her. "This is a dangerous place, Bernice. We need to find the road. I suggest you get down."

"But I thought we were avoiding the roads?" He could sense Bernice's frown without having to see it.

"We were, but now we are in Avalon, and that changes everything. The land is treacherous. The ground is soft. We have to use the road. I suggest you pray to God that a Saxon patrol does not see us. Now, get down from your horse, I am not going to tell you again." He bit back another curse. He had no right to talk to her like that, no right at all. But she had to understand the danger this place represented to them.

Alan did not wait for Bernice to do as she was told, but instead, he led his horse along the bottom of the hill they had just descended. The mud stuck to his boots and made a squelching sound with each step he took. He heard, rather than saw Bernice dismount but he did not turn around to see.

It was cold in the mist and damp. Alan looked at his feet, being ever careful where he placed them, and he strained to hear past the goats bleating. He prayed that he and Bernice were the only two people foolish enough to try to navigate Avalon when the mist was upon her.

"Have you been to Avalon before?" Bernice asked as she struggled to keep up.

"Once," Alan replied. "With my father." He did not elaborate, and Bernice had the good sense not to ask further questions. Mordred Pendragon had soiled his father's memory. Alan could not think of his father anymore without reliving those desperate last moments.

∗∗∗

It felt like they had been walking for hours, but time had no meaning here. Finally, the mist began to rise, and as it did so, it revealed a world that one only ever heard of in stories. The land was vast and flat, although in the distance the rising hills looked like cliffs. It was said that the sea had once claimed this land for her own, but for reasons untold she had relinquished her claim. But the sea was known for her fickleness, one day she would claim it again. Alan hoped it would not be this day.

The dawn chorus was like nothing either of them had ever heard. The noise was deafening, as each species of bird tried to compete with the other. It wasn't so much about welcoming the dawn here, but more about who could sing the loudest.

"There is no road," Bernice stated, her voice sounded strained. Gone was the joy of discovering she was in a magical land.

"Not the kind of road we are used to. This is Avalon. Nothing is simple in Avalon. Look," Alan pointed to something up ahead. "Can you see that wooden track?"

"I can see nothing but grass, and brambles, and trees," Bernice stated.

"There. Look where I am pointing," Alan tried to hide his frustration.

"That wooden thing?"

"Yes," Alan stated with an irritated sigh. "*That* wooden thing. That *is* the road."

"That is not a road," Bernice stated with a look of horror. "That is just some planks of wood, held up by stakes."

"Not only is it a road. It is the *only* road," Alan replied.

"Don't be ridiculous, that is as far from a road as you can possibly get."

"Bernice, please… Just… Just believe what I am telling you."

"But it is so narrow. It's…"

With another sigh born from frustration, Alan turned to look at her. "You followed me. You told me that you knew that the journey with me would be hard. So do not moan when the journey becomes not to your liking. I did tell you to go back to Dor. You should have heeded my words."

"And I am beginning to regret not heeding them," she stated under her breath as she led her horse forward. "Of all the men in the world, why did I have to fall in love with you?"

Alan's frustration and upset were vanquished by her words. "And of all the women in the world, why did I have to fall in love with a stubborn, opinionated nun?"

He heard her laugh and for a moment he forgot about the danger they were in. He glanced back her way and smiled at her. Her answering smile warmed his heart.

The horses were reluctant to walk upon the wooden track for

never had they been asked to do such a thing before. But once Alan had managed to coax his beast to cooperate, Bernice's horse was happy to follow. The wood creaked and seemed to sink under the horses' weight. But it was far easier to walk upon the wooden track than on the wetland.

"Are you sure this is safe?" Bernice asked for the hundredth time.

Alan did not bother to reply, for his answer would be the same as it had been for the other nine-and-ninety times.

With the sun now shining overhead and the mist a distant memory, the moor became a breeding ground for flies. The air was alive with the sound of their little wings. So much for the mist obscuring the view, now it was these little demons that filled the air and plagued both horse and man alike. The flies swarmed around the horses' eyes and bit their sweaty rumps. The swish of the horses' tails did little to discourage the bloodsucking devils.

"I am being bitten alive," Bernice complained. Her temper was becoming more frayed by the minute.

"There is a bee on the floor, be careful," Alan warned, as he narrowly missed stepping on the little creature. "We don't want it to sting the horses."

"I have never seen so many insects in my life. No wonder there are so many birds. Alan," Bernice shrieked his name and came to a sudden halt.

"What?" he turned to look at her in panic, fearing she had turned an ankle.

"I saw a snake."

Alan looked to where she pointed and saw the retreating dark green tail of the snake in question. "It won't hurt you, that is a grass snake. It is probably more scared of you than you of it."

"I know what it is. Sister—"

"Agatha," Alan said with a grin. "If you know what it is, then you also know there is no reason to fear it. It is non-venomous."

"But it's a snake," Bernice stated as if that explained her fear. She did not look at all convinced by Alan's reassurance, and neither did her horse. Her horse kept a wary eye on the snake and shied dramatically around it as Bernice tried to lead him forward.

"Better a snake than a Saxon army," Alan whispered under his breath. "We are too exposed here. We have to keep moving, come on."

***

The sun rose higher in the sky, beating down upon them with an intensity that neither of them had expected. They had filled up their wineskins and watered the horses at a secluded little river that they only found by following the distant call of a kingfisher. Here, up-winged flies gathered in great numbers, as well as brightly coloured dragonflies. The bees swarmed together on the muddy ground, moving almost as one mass as they quenched their thirst at the water's edge. This river was a haven for many a creature. If memory served Alan correctly, then this was the River Brue. But where was the small, yet bustling market village that he and his father had once stayed the night in? Alan concluded that either he had lost his sense of direction or the village was no more. Alan feared it was the latter.

"How much further?" Bernice asked with impatience.

"You sound like you are five years old," Alan teased, but he too wanted an answer to that same question. They were following a road that seemingly had no end. However, they had no choice but to push on. Thankfully, they seemed to be the only people using the road this day.

As the last ray of sunlight lit up the sky, they finally found themselves in the shadow of the ancient Tor. But neither had the energy to congratulate themselves on the day's achievements. There was a small stream that surrounded the Tor *"A natural moat,"* Alan had jested. But it was the smell that they had not expected. The air was sickly sweet with the scent of many wildflowers. It was a truly magical place.

"It isn't one hill, is it?" Bernice said, as she looked up at the Tor. "It is like lots of hills one on top the other. Look at the ridges, have you ever seen anything like it?"

"In dreams, maybe," Alan replied. "We have come all this way, do you want to climb to the top? We can watch the sunset."

"You may have to pull me up," Bernice stated with a laugh. "But yes, I would like to tell our children what it is like on the top of the Tor."

"Children?" Alan asked with a small frown. "When did we discuss children?"

Bernice's answering smile made his heart yearn for such a thing.

What would their children be like? What would he teach them? He caught her hand with his, and together they attempted the steep climb.

They stopped many times to rest as they climbed, but burning muscles and tired legs would not thwart them. As they reached the summit, the wind unexpectedly picked up, and when they were finally stood next to the ancient stones, the wind was so strong that it stole their breath and refused to give it back.

"A temple, just like Guinevere said," Bernice stated as she touched the ancient stones. "Look at the roof. I wasn't expecting it to have a roof. And look at the ground." Bernice knelt down so she could study the mosaic that seemed so out of place but at the same time so fitting. She tried to make out the images. Some of the tiles were cracked and, in other places, they were missing. Bernice traced the drawing of what looked like two fish, and she tilted her head as she tried to interpret what looked a little like a ram. "Alan, come look at this."

When he didn't respond, she looked up. Alan was standing next to a standard, whose wooden staff had been stabbed into the earth. Bernice stood and brushed off her clothes.

"Roman?" she asked, as she reached out and touched the golden carving of what she assumed was a depiction of an animal.

Alan shook his head. "Saxon."

Bernice's hand dropped away from the carving, for she did not want to touch anything made by the hands of such an evil race.

"That is where we are heading," Alan raised his voice to be heard above the wind, which had picked up again and blew at their clothes and their hair. "Can you see the castle?" he pointed.

Bernice gave a brief nod while hugging her arms to herself. "I do not understand why the Saxon King who has so much, would want more." She sat down on the tall grass and continued to look at the view.

Alan sat down next to her and put his arm around her shoulders. "It is said that those who love money, never have enough. The same can be said for land. Greed is a powerful master and a difficult one to disobey."

"Do you think Mordred paid Cerdic to kill us…?" her voice broke when she spoke and Alan gently tugged her into his embrace.

"I wish I knew," he stated. He stared at the distant castle, and he felt a deep hatred in his heart. He wished he had come here with an avenging army. He wished he could pay back the favour Cerdic had given the nuns at Holywell. One day, perhaps.

"Shall we head back down?" Alan asked as the wind picked up speed again. Neither of them wanted to watch the sunset now.

Bernice raised her head from his chest and nodded her head, for the magic of this place was gone. Without another word, Alan stood and helped Bernice to her feet. They silently walked back the way they had come.

The way down was just as hard on their legs as the way up had been. But the excitement of reaching the summit was not with them. Gone was the exhilaration of discovery and in its place was the dark despair of grief.

"We will stay here the night," Alan stated as they finally made it to where they had left their horses. "Although I do not think we should light a fire. I don't want to draw unnecessary attention to ourselves. Sit yourself down," Alan encouraged. Bernice did not need to be told twice. She sank down onto the soft grass with a small disgruntled sigh.

"We have some of that cheese left," Alan said as he rummaged through Bernice's saddle bag. "Are you hungry?" He turned to look at Bernice, but she was already asleep. He knelt down next to her and tucked a wayward strand of hair back behind her ear. A lone tear clung to her eyelashes. And in that moment he couldn't help himself. Daringly he bent and kissed her cheek, surprised by the softness. "Sleep tight, my love," he whispered. "I love you."

Chapter 19

The Kingdom of Cerniw.

Josephine du Lac watched from a distance as Merton mounted his horse. She observed with a quiet rage as the Queen hugged Amandine as if she were a sister. It had been a long time since Annis had embraced *her* like that.

Alden helped Amandine to mount and then he handed her Merton's child. Josephine hated that child. She had never hated anything more than that little boy. Why had Brianna died while Tanick thrived? It wasn't fair. But such wrongs were easily remedied. Brianna was dead. There was nothing Josephine could do about that, but she could do something about Tanick. And she would… When the time was right. Merton would know what it felt like to lose a child that he loved. By God, he would know, and maybe then he would understand.

Alden laughed at something Merton said and, like a she-wolf, Josephine bristled. Let them laugh, for the time was coming when they would have nothing at all to laugh about. They thought her harmless. Little did they know. It wasn't Mordred that Alden and his army should fear. It was her.

Annis began to cry as Merton turned his horse and rode towards the portcullis. How pathetic. What did Annis have to weep about? It wasn't as if she were in love with Merton. Or maybe she was. Perhaps it was Merton's child that Annis carried — it wouldn't surprise Josephine one bit if that were true. That thought almost made Josephine smile. Oh, Merton would know what suffering really was. For she would kill every man, woman, and child, who had ever dared to love him. Merton would have no choice but to fall on to his knees in front of her and beg her forgiveness and cry for her mercy. And when he did that, she would spit in his face. Although she suspected she would also take him to bed and then they could begin again. They could have another child. One just like Brianna.

Annis' sobs grated on Josephine's nerves. Annis did not deserve to be a Queen. There was nothing regal about her. Crying was a private affair, not a spectacle for the world to witness. Josephine was pleased to see that the tears did nothing at all for Annis' complexion. She was all red and blotchy. Even without the tears, Annis was fat and ugly. Annis had the most awful unruly curly hair that looked like she had been dragged through a hedge. Josephine had the strongest urge to grab a knife and cut the offending hair off Annis' head. All Annis was good for was producing children, and even they were disagreeable to look at. What Alden saw in her was anyone's guess. Perhaps Annis was an easy ride. Passive. Josephine had heard that some men like that.

Josephine dared to take a step forward. She deliberately put herself firmly in Merton's horse's path. He would not ride away from her, not with that harlot and his bastard child. Merton was hers. HE WAS HERS. But, Merton didn't even look at her. He urged his horse into a trot and rode around her as if she wasn't even there. Inside she fumed at such an insult. Merton would live to regret his decision this day, she would make sure of it.

Amandine looked at her, though, and she halted her horse just in front of Josephine.

"What do you want?" Josephine's voice was heavy with loathing.

"All I ever offered you was friendship," Amandine stated softly.

"If you expect me to speak to you, you have another think coming," Josephine snarled back. "Philippe should have killed you."

"He almost did. What did I do to wrong you so?"

"What do you think?" Josephine growled as she glared up at Amandine and the child. The child stared back down at her with his father's eyes. With Brianna's eyes. It was almost too much to bear. She had to fist her hands to stop herself from grabbing the child and wringing his neck. She had never wanted anyone to die as much as she wanted that child to.

"I didn't ask him to fall in love with me," Amandine said quietly.

"He isn't in love with you," Josephine turned her attention away from the child and back to Amandine. "How could he love someone like you? It is *me* he loves. Merton is *mine*, not yours. One day soon he will come to realise that."

"Merton was never yours," Amandine whispered. "He never went to your bed willingly. You had to get him drunk."

Josephine felt a boiling rage at Amandine's words. How dare Merton disclose such information. That was private. But she would not let Amandine see how much her words had affected her. "Is that what he told you?" Josephine began to laugh, as if she had found something funny in Amandine's words.

"No, you told me."

"He was more than a willing participant," Josephine continued, choosing to ignore what Amandine had just said. "You should have heard him moan my name. But then perhaps you will — that's if he can stomach making love to you. He will be imagining it is me when he sards you, I can promise you that. Oh dear, have I said something to make you cry?"

"Amandine," Merton rode towards her. "Do not speak to this creature, for she is not worthy of your attention."

"Do you know how ironic that sounds coming from you?" Josephine snapped back.

"Stay away from my wife," Merton stated, glaring at Josephine as he spoke.

"She isn't your wife, she is your whore. And besides, *she* came to me, not the other way around. I have nothing to say to her."

"Make sure it remains that way. Come on," he urged.

Amandine nodded her head and nudged her horse on with her heels.

"Stay away from us," Merton warned as he turned his horse and followed his betrothed.

Josephine put her hands on her hips and glowered at the retreating couple. "I promise I will succeed where Philippe failed," Josephine said under her breath. "And then, Merton, you will be mine."

Josephine did not understand what Philippe had been thinking? Keeping that bitch alive showed how weak a man Philippe really was.

He should have slit her throat or at least cut off her nose and her ears so the world could see that Amandine was the adulterous whore that everyone knew her to be. Josephine had even offered to do it for him, but Philippe had declined. Amandine should have been disfigured — Merton would not have wanted her then. But, no. Amandine is a delicate flower that must be protected. She can do no wrong. Sweet Amandine. Lovely Amandine. Kind Amandine. It was always about Amandine. Well, damn Amandine to Hell. Josephine spat on the ground in front of her with disgust. Even thinking about how Merton had ridden to Amandine's defence just now made her skin crawl. How could he love a woman who could not stand up for herself?

For the life of her, Josephine could not understand what Merton saw in Amandine. She was nothing to look at. She was timid and shy. Amandine couldn't make Merton laugh the way *she* once could. And just by looking at her it was easy to tell what Amandine would be like in bed. It would be like making love to a corpse. Merton would soon realise his mistake. He would set Amandine aside and come running back to her. It was only a matter of time. But Josephine was not known for her patience.

"Josephine," Alden said her name in that contemptuous way he always said it.

Josephine was tempted to ignore him. How dare he speak to her. He had no right. She was the rightful Queen of Cerniw, not that fat cow Alden had married. Annis' father wasn't even from this country. He was a Saxon. Annis being crowned Queen was a joke. A bad one.

Josephine turned reluctantly around and glared at the King.

"Yes?" she barked, not bothering to hide the disdain in her face.

"Now he is gone, you are free to dine in the Great Hall again."

"Am I?" Josephine snorted the words. "Tell me, Alden, why would I want to do that? Why would I want to break bread with you?"

"It is an invitation. You do, of course, have the right to decline."

"Then I must decline. You are a pretender, Alden. This throne is not yours. You must stand aside immediately—"

"And just who should I stand aside for? Your husband? Or perhaps your lover? Josephine, neither Budic nor Garren will ever be the King of Cerniw, so get any fancy ideas about you becoming the next Queen out of your head. It is not going to happen. Now get out of my sight. I am sick of you already."

"I have been sick of the sight of you for a good deal longer. How could you let Merton go off with a bitch like Amandine? She is a spy, sent by Philippe. She will kill him. She will kill you all."

"I feel really sorry for you, Josephine. I do. You used to be such a sweet girl. But now your heart is black with jealousy and bitterness. Amandine has done you no wrong, and yet you have wronged her grievously. How could you lie to him like that? How could you look into his eyes and tell him she was dead when you knew she wasn't?"

Josephine snorted again and looked away. She didn't have to explain herself to anyone.

"The only reason you hate Amandine is because Galahad loves her. He loves her, Josephine, and you can't stand that."

"Merton does not love her. Amandine is a witch. She has cast her spell on him. He is enchanted."

"You say Merton's name again, and I will cut out your tongue," Alden warned.

"Josephine, please," Annis spoke softly. "Amandine is no witch."

"Of course she is," Josephine continued, ignoring Alden's warning. "Did you not see the way she looked at your husband? But at least you can be assured that while you are round with his child, Alden will not need to look far for a lover."

"Your heart is evil," Annis stated, although she looked panicked by Josephine's words.

"It is more than evil," Alden took his wife's hand in his and turned away. "Annis come on. Let us leave Josephine to wallow in her own bitterness."

"That is right, run away because you can not abide the truth. Your loving husband will betray you, Annis. Amandine is a witch, I tell you. A WITCH."

Josephine was pleased to see she had attracted quite an audience with her outburst. She glared at all who glared at her. This sorry looking lot did not intimidate her. "Lady Amandine is a spy," she announced again.

"That is enough," Alden stated, dropping his wife's hand and marching back to where Josephine stood. "Speak one more word, and I will send you back to your husband today."

"And kill a baby? You know as well as I that my time is close and such a journey could kill us both. Oh, come, Alden, you are too weak to send me back to Dyfed in this condition. Your conscience won't let you."

"Do not try me. Get out of my sight. NOW," Alden commanded.

Josephine raised her chin. She was not at all cowed by the rage she saw in the King's eyes. "You should ask your wife whose child she carries. I would wager it isn't yours. Perhaps it is your precious Galahad's. He said he would steal her away and have his way with her, can you remember? I can. I think he already has. She is his whore more than she is your wife."

Annis gasped in outrage, and Alden took a menacing step towards Josephine. Josephine looked at him with contempt and held her ground. "What's the matter, Alden? Are you not man enough to hear the truth? Your wife is a Saxon whore. She always has been, and she always will be. Get off me," Josephine glared in outrage at the knight who had caught hold of her arm. "Unhand me this instant, you disgustingly vile man. I am a royal princess. I will have your head for this, Enyon." She tried to shrug herself free from Enyon's grasp but to no avail.

"Take Josephine back to her chamber," Alden ordered. "And see she doesn't leave it."

"Back to being a prisoner, how surprising. Your wife is a whore, Alden, and you are not a king. You should have abdicated when Budic told you to. You will rue the day you went against him."

"Hold your tongue and keep walking," Enyon hissed in her ear as he marched her towards her prison.

"Lady Amandine is a spy, I tell you. She is a spy," Josephine yelled for all to hear.

***

Enyon manhandled her all the way to the house where she had been kept a prisoner. As she approached the roundhouse, Josephine's temper burned even brighter, and rage blinded her. The baby chose that moment to kick inside of her. How dare it… How dare it move? She had not given it permission to.

Enyon pushed the curtain aside and pulled her into the roundhouse. He let her go and went over to the fire pit that burnt in the middle of the room. He breathed out unsteadily as if he was trying to control his anger. Josephine almost smiled — she liked it when a man lost his temper.

The smoke from the fire swirled upwards and escaped through the roof, which was the only good thing about the house. The house, if you could call it that, was depressingly dark, not at all suitable for a princess. Alden had some gall keeping her prisoner in such inadequate accommodation.

"What the hell do you think you are doing?" Enyon demanded to know. He turned swiftly back around, grabbed her by the shoulders and shook her so hard that she bit her tongue. But the blood tasted good, and besides, she did not mind a little rough handling now and then.

"Oh, Enyon," Josephine grinned. A small trickle of blood seeped out between her lips. Enyon appeared shocked by the sight of her blood and Josephine watched as he took a hasty step away from her. Josephine wiped her mouth with the back of her hand and crept closer to him. With confidence, she reached up and curled her hand around his neck, bringing his head down to her raised one.

Enyon pushed her roughly away from him, as if he did not want her touch, but she knew better.

"That was a reckless thing for you to do," he rebuked. "You should not have given Alden any cause to doubt you. You were told to behave humbly. Gratefully. The lie will only work if you do as you are told. Your husband will be displeased."

"What care I for Budic?" Josephine asked as she continued to stalk her prey. "He wanted me to run away with Garren." She reached out with her hand and placed it firmly on Enyon's groin. Enyon hissed in a breath, but he did not turn away. "Budic told me to seduce Garren," she said as she began to fondle him through his clothes. "And then he told Garren that he would kill our baby if it were not born with red hair and Garren, the fool, believed him. On my husband's order I have shared my body. It is *I* who had to endure Garren panting all over me, although I have to say, he was rather good. No, Enyon, you are mistaken in your allegiance. Budic will not reward you as I would. Hear my words, Budic will never sit on this throne. This throne is mine. I have earned it. Now enough talk. I need you to sard this baby out of me, for I am fed up of carrying Budic's seed."

***

"I need to go," Enyon stated as he rose from the bed mere moments later.

Josephine huffed and glared at him but said nothing. Enyon was a disappointing lover. She had expected better. He had not waited for her to find her pleasure and he had done absolutely nothing to bring it about. But still, he had his uses, and he was under her control, for now. *Forever.* Men, on the most part, were so easy to manipulate. You just had to spread your legs and promise them your undying love.

"I need you to do me a favour," Josephine said as she sat up. The fur fell about her waist exposing her ample bosom to Enyon's appreciative gaze.

"What do you want?" he asked as he dropped the clothes he had just picked up.

Josephine threw the furs off her body altogether and looked at him through her eyelashes.

"A little poison," Josephine smiled sweetly as Enyon climbed on top of her again. He rolled them both over, so she was sat upon the part that ached.

"And what do you need a little poison for?" Enyon asked as he positioned himself beneath her.

"That is for me to know," Josephine stated with a coy smile. "And for you to find out."

Chapter 20

That woman. Alden had never met a woman more disagreeable than Josephine. Garren had no right bringing her here. No right at all. He wished he could send her back to her husband. She and Budic were made for each other. But Josephine was right. He would not risk an innocent child's life. But as soon as she had birthed that baby, then she was leaving. That day could not come quickly enough for him.

Annis had been quiet as she walked by his side. Alden hoped that Annis had not taken anything that bitch had said to heart. He risked a glance at her and saw that she had. It didn't matter how many times he had proclaimed his love. There was still this little part of Annis that doubted his words. Alden blamed her father for that. Cerdic had never wanted a daughter — he had made that perfectly clear to Annis while she was growing up. It had left her with a feeling of unworthiness. But if she could only see what *he* saw when he looked at her, she would know her worth, and she would never doubt him again.

They stopped when they reached the Queen's Hall, and Annis slipped her hand from his. The Queen's Hall was significantly smaller than the Great Hall. It was more intimate, a place of retreat. Home. Alden far preferred the comfort of the Queen's Hall to his own.

"Will I see you later?" Annis asked, but she seemed to find something rather fascinating with the pitched paving as she spoke.

Alden felt a weight sit heavy on his shoulders when he looked at her. He loved Annis. He loved her to distraction. But he wished that he didn't always have to be the strong one in the relationship. Why did she still doubt him, even after all these years? What would it take for her to believe that no matter what happened, he would never willingly leave her?

"I think we need to talk," Alden stated quietly.

"About what?" Annis asked, although she still would not look at him.

"You know what." Alden laced his fingers with hers again and walked into the Hall. He gave her no choice but to follow. Annis' ladies-in-waiting turned from their looms and curtsied respectfully, but Alden did not pay them any attention. He crossed the Hall and entered the Queen's private chambers.

Annis once again slipped her hand from his and walked over to their bed. She made much of straightening out the furs on the bed, even though she had already done so this morning.

"I would never have an affair with anyone, let alone my brother's future wife," Alden stated, feeling it best to say it quickly and get it over with.

"But Josephine was right…" Annis replied quietly, turning her back on him.

"Right about what?"

"You know what," Annis stated.

"No, I really don't. What I do know is that I have never met anyone as poisonous as that woman. Josephine would say anything to get a reaction. You know not to take heed of anything she says."

"But in this Josephine is right. I have eyes. I have seen the way you look at Amandine," Annis stated, daring a glance at him. "Everyone has seen it. It is the talk of the fort."

"I care for Amandine. I am responsible for what happened to her. I thought she was dead. I should have made sure that the information I was given was correct. She has suffered because of me."

"You love her," Annis accused.

"As a sister, yes—"

"You were going to ask her to marry you at one point," Annis turned to look at him. Her eyes, that were usually so loving, now looked at him with accusations.

Alden groaned in frustration and sat down heavily in a chair that had been pulled up to the fire pit. "Annis, you are my wife. I married you despite everyone, apart from Merton, telling me not to. I would have given Cerniw up for you — I almost did. I married you because I love you. You are the mother of my children. You are my Queen. I have never even looked at another woman—"

"Until Amandine—"

"NO," Alden rose to his feet. He tried desperately to keep his anger under control, but sometimes his wife was so infuriating. "Not even then. I feel sorry for her. I can sympathise with what she has gone through. I understand how she feels. Annis, she was tortured, just like I was. They were going to kill her, just like your father was going to kill me. What kind of man would I be if I did not feel moved by her plight?"

"You two have a lot in common," Annis agreed. "You always have."

"Stop it, Annis. Please. This is ridiculous. Do you see me accusing you of having an affair with Galahad?"

"I am not having an affair with Galahad," tears gathered in Annis' eyes as she spoke.

"But you love him," Alden contradicted. He wanted to go to her. He wanted to wipe her tears away but at the same time, he was incredibly annoyed with her. How dare she accuse him of having feelings that he did not.

"Not like that," Annis argued.

"I do not love Amandine *like that*. I wanted to marry her, yes. And you know the reason why I wanted to marry her. But that was before you."

"You wanted to protect her from Budic," Annis shrugged. "But we both know there was more to it than that—"

"Don't," Alden shook his head as he spoke. "Don't you dare twist my words and find lies instead of truths. I have done nothing wrong. I have not betrayed you. I will *never* betray you. I did not look at Amandine as a man looks at a woman he wants. Josephine is—"

"Fine," Annis snapped, turning her back on him again. "It is just me being ridiculous. Ignore me, that is what you usually do."

"For the love of God," Alden sighed in frustration. "Is this how it is going to be throughout this pregnancy?" It was the wrong thing to say — Alden knew that as soon as the words had come out of his mouth. Her whole posture stiffened. He waited with baited breath for her response.

"My pregnancy has nothing to do with it," Annis shouted as she turned swiftly back around to face him. "It is to do with you and the way you looked at her. Why are you here anyway? Don't you have a war to plan? Get out. I have nothing more to say to you."

"I am not leaving you until we have sorted this out."

"There is nothing to sort out. I am not blind. You want her, don't you? Just admit it."

"I am not going to admit to something that isn't true. Tell me this isn't the reason why you were so keen for Galahad to take Amandine somewhere far from here?" Alden asked with a dawning realisation. "Oh my God, that is it, isn't it? Did you think that if she were out of sight, I would not be tempted to what? Betray you? Betray *us*? For the love of God, Annis. Do you have any idea how hard today was for me watching him leave? Galahad isn't coming back. You do know that, don't you? I am never going to see my brother again."

"What are you talking about? Of course, he is coming back. It has all been arranged. Galahad will settle Amandine in her new home and come straight back to you. He would not leave you to face Mordred alone."

"And yet, that is exactly what he has done. We are not going to see him again, Annis. Galahad is lost to us. He is never coming back."

"You are lying," Annis stated angrily.

"Am I? Why do you think Galahad told me to offer the position of General of my army to Yrre?"

"I didn't know that he did," Annis stated in a quiet shock. "Alden—" she reached out with her hand, but he ignored her peace offering.

"Annis, believe what you want — you always do. And as you said, I have a war to plan. When you start believing in me, let me know." The sound of her sobs accompanied him from the room.

***

Alden stormed out of the fort. He needed to get away from everyone for a while. He needed a little peace and a little time to gather his thoughts.

Yrre called out to him, but he ignored him and continued walking. How could she accuse him of having feelings for another woman?

Did she not know him at all?

She is pregnant, he argued with himself. *She is emotional.* But damn it all, her accusations cut deep. Very deep.

He slowed his pace as he walked through the village that stood in the shadows of Dor. The village, as always, was busy, but he looked down at his feet as he walked and hoped that no one would stop him to air a grievance or pass the time of day. He wanted to be alone. He did not hanker for conversation or company.

Thankfully, no one bothered him, and as he climbed the dunes, he felt his anger lessen. The sea always calmed him. He stared out at the infinite blueness and marvelled at the oceans timelessness and beauty. Alden closed his eyes and listened as the waves crept up the shore. Here he found his peace. This was his place of calm. Here he could breathe. Here he could think.

***

"I was looking for you."

Alden opened his eyes and was surprised to see the sun now sat high in the sky. He had lost track of time. There was so much to do, so much to prepare. He did not have the time for such self-indulgence. However, he did not feel compelled to come away from the dunes and the sea beyond.

Alden turned and watched as Brother Sampson climbed the dune. The climb was steep, and Sampson took a moment to catch his breath when he reached the summit.

"I thought I would find you here."

"Did you say goodbye to Galahad?" Alden asked as he looked back out at the sea. A cormorant flew overhead, his large black wings casting a shadow on the ground below him. Alden watched the bird and silently wished he too could fly. How great it must be to be able to fly away from your troubles.

"No," Sampson shook his head. "I have no intention of ever saying goodbye to *him*. I cannot…"

"You love him," Alden stated as he continued to watch the bird as it flew out to sea.

"Don't we all?" Sampson replied with a simple shrug. "However, I fear Tegan will corrupt his soul with her false teachings."

"I don't think my brother is the kind of person who can be

corrupted."

Sampson laughed softly. "No. Probably not. Can I ask you something?"

"Of course."

"When I am troubled, I kneel and take my concerns to God. When you are troubled, you come here. Why?"

"The ocean gives me peace," Alden stated honestly.

Sampson began to laugh.

Alden felt slightly affronted by such a reaction — it was not what he had expected. "Does that amuse you?" Alden asked, not bothering to keep the irritation from his voice.

"No. No, of course not. It's just... God made Heaven and the earth..." Sampson turned to look at Alden with humour in his eyes. "And the oceans. He made everything. This is his creation. The peace you speak of comes not from the sea. It is a gift from God."

Alden breathed in the sea air slowly. He did not respond to Sampson's words in any other way. God was everywhere — Alden knew that. But sometimes, God seemed so very distant.

"Alden, a message came from Caldey," Sampson's face lost all signs of humour and his eyes shone with an unwanted duty.

"The Abbot wants you back," Alden guessed. Sampson had been gone for a long time. It was no wonder that the Abbot wanted him to return.

"Abbot Pyr is dead," Sampson said the words with an angry sigh.

"I am sorry for your loss," Alden said the only thing he could say at such unwelcomed news. "I did not know he was ill."

"Abbot Pyr lived a life of debauchery, lust, and drunkenness. He was drunk when he died. He wasn't ill. He fell down the well and broke his neck. It was a wasted life. A pointless death. I sometimes wondered if his love for wine was greater than his love for God. His death, I believe, shows where his true allegiance lay."

"No man is perfect," Alden said for want of something to say. "And there are many reasons why a man turns to drink."

"You are right. No man is perfect. But God is, and Abbot Pyr knew that. He chose drink over God. I can not understand why he would do that."

"He must have had his reasons," Alden stated. There were many times where he had used alcohol to numb the pain of the past.

"He was an Abbot," Sampson contradicted. "He knew better. He had no excuses. I do not understand why he chose not to follow Jesus' example. Why is it so hard for some people to live a good life?"

Alden hoped Sampson wasn't expecting an answer, for he did not have one. God had, in his wisdom, given each man free will. But sometimes too much freedom was as destructive as too little. You just had to see the state of affairs to see that *that* was true.

"I have to go back," Sampson stated with an edge of bitterness.

Alden closed his eyes briefly. First James, then Merton, now Sampson. When he needed them the most, those closest abandoned him.

"Do you have any idea who will replace Abbot Pyr as Abbot?" Alden asked, instead of voicing his despair. Sampson had his duty, as Alden had his. Alden could not ask him to stay. Just like he could not ask Merton to stay.

"Some fool who has no idea what he is taking on. I would not want to be the Abbot of Caldey," Sampson stated in no uncertain terms.

An uncomfortable silence followed Sampson's words. And both men thought about their lives, and how other people dictated how they had to live them. Alden did not want to fight, but Mordred had given him no other choice. And Sampson did not want to go back to Caldey, but he felt it his duty to return.

"How is Guinevere?" Alden asked, feeling the need to break the silence that followed.

"Now that Sister Bernice has decided to run away, presumably with Alan, the only person who can wipe Guinevere's tears away is Jesus. She clings to her faith, for that is all she has to cling to. What Mordred did at Holywell… I do not think she will ever get over it. She blames herself, of course."

"Isn't it strange how the victim always does?" Alden replied as he looked out to sea. "Why was the Saviour so easy to kill and yet Satan continues to elude us?"

"Jesus sacrificed himself. He died for us so that we would be forgiven. Satan wants to see us fail and fall. He has no love for us —"

"Unlike Galahad," Alden interrupted with a frown as his thoughts lingered on his brother. "I miss him already."

"Although I do not like where he has gone," Sampson spoke with caution. "You were right to let Galahad go. He doesn't belong here,

Alden. You know it. I know it. That particular Devil is dead. And long may he remain so."

"I thank you for your words. But I fear I have made a terrible mistake in letting him go."

"Galahad cannot win this war for you. Only God can do that."

"I am not so assured of God as you are. My faith is weak."

"Faith does not have to be strong for miracles to occur. Can you remember what the Lord said to the disciples about a mustard seed and a mountain?" Sampson smiled as he spoke. And as Alden looked into his eyes, he could see an ancient wisdom that was older than time itself.

"*...if you have faith as small as a mustard seed, you can say to this mountain, 'Move from here to there,' and it will move. Nothing will be impossible for you,*" Alden recited. "Then I pray that my faith will be enough and that God will allow me to do the impossible. If we do not win this war…"

"That isn't going to happen. You have God on your side. You must believe that."

"But Mordred has Satan."

"Do not fear Satan, Alden. God is by far the stronger of the two."

Alden nodded his head, and he felt a lightness in his heart at Sampson's words. But then he remembered that Sampson was leaving. "You will come back, won't you?"

"God wants me to bring his words and his wisdom to as many people as I can. He has also asked me to do something else. Something special. You will think I have lost my mind, but, God has asked me to form a new Church," Sampson's eyes lit up as he spoke.

"A new Church?" Alden queried. Such a thing was impossible.

"One that does not fall under the influence of Rome. The Roman Church has forgotten her true purpose. God has told me to start afresh and do things a little differently. Jesus did not have to demand or threaten his congregation into obedience. And I think that says it all. Talk of being thrown into the pits of Hell if you do something wrong, does not, in my opinion, make believers. It conjures only fear. God does not want his children to fear him. That is the last thing he wants. He offers us only love. My Church is going to be built on the foundation of his love."

A shaft of light fell from the sky as Sampson spoke, and Alden watched, in amazement as the light fell upon the young monk, illuminating him like one of the drawings in the manuscripts the monks painted. A warm gentle wind swept over them both. God was here. There could be no doubt. God had given the monk his blessing. The light faded and disappeared. Alden would wonder later if he had imagined it.

"I wish you well with your new Church."

"Thank you," Sampson replied with a smile.

"Then I guess this is goodbye to you too."

"No. Not goodbye. Do the swallows not have their nests? Do the foxes not have their dens?"

"What does that mean?" Alden asked with a frown. He hated it when Sampson started talking in parables. He could never keep up.

Sampson turned to look at him. "It means what it means. This isn't goodbye, Alden. Our paths will cross again. One day…"

Chapter 21

The Kingdom of Wessex.

"We will leave the horses," Alan stated, slapping at another fly that had landed on his arm as he did so. Was there no end to these pests in this kingdom? Never had he seen so many flies. He had a nasty bite on his left arm that had swelled considerably during the night. It itched like the Devil, but it was the least of his concerns.

Alan dismounted swiftly and with an edge of purpose. They were almost in the heart of Cerdic of Wessex's realm. Today they would find the Shield, *if,* all went well...

The night had been cold and eventful. As the evening wore on the insects had become more vocal. And they had feasted, not only on the horses that stood with their heads close together but also on Alan and Bernice. As the moon rose in the night sky, the sound of the insects had been replaced with something far more sinister. It had been hard to tell how far away the wolves were. Sometimes they sounded as if they were many *mille passus'* away, and at other times they seemed uncomfortably close. Bernice had awoken with a gasp at the first spine-tingling howl, and Alan had fleetingly wondered if he should light a fire. But he had instantly dismissed the idea. He knew that they would have a better chance of surviving an attack from a pack of wolves than if they found themselves surrounded by Saxon warriors. When the wolves had finally stopped howling Alan and

Bernice had fallen into an uneasy sleep. A high pitch growl and the sound of scampering amongst the grass had awoken them both. Alan had cautiously sat up, reached for his knife, and looked about him. The moon had hidden behind a cloud, and everything was so black, so devoid of light, that it made seeing almost impossible. But then a flash of white ploughed ungracefully through the grass and the sound of animals chattering had made Alan smile.

"Look," he had whispered to Bernice, "badgers."

They had crept closer to look at these nocturnal creatures, and for a time, weariness was forgotten as they watched the badgers forage for food. When the badgers had moved on, Alan and Bernice had once again tried to settle down to sleep. But without the warmth and the protection of a fire, all either of them did was, at best, doze.

When dawn was just about to break on the horizon, they both decided to give up on sleep. Alan had suggested that they climb the Tor and watch the sunrise, which they did. As the sun rose over Cerdic's kingdom, they ate the last of the cheese. It was a peaceful start. Now it was just a case of seeing what the day would bring.

Bernice had given the horses a quick brush over when they had returned to camp and, while she did that, Alan had counted his coins with a growing concern. There was one golden Roman coin in his purse — where that came from he didn't know — there were also a few Breton coins and a handful of Cerniw silver. Alan realised that if Cerdic's men caught them, they only needed to look in his purse to find out where they came from. He couldn't use such coinage here. Damn it. He should have brought something to trade. They were low on supplies. They needed to buy food, but that was not going to be possible, not in Wessex anyway. Alan had pulled the ties of his purse together and sighed heavily at his lack of foresight. Bernice had asked him if there was something wrong, but he had forced a smile and shook his head. He would figure it out, no need for Bernice to worry about it, she was concerned enough about the quest ahead as it was.

From the top of the Tor, Cerdic's stronghold had not looked that far away, but the distance was deceiving. It was close to midday when they finally saw the wood smoke from the village of Hordon rise up to the heavens. The smell of pottage drifted in the air, and this made both their stomachs grumble. The cheese had not chased off their hunger for very long.

"I think it will be safer to go on foot from here," Alan did not relish the idea, but it was for the best.

"What if someone steals the horses away?" Bernice asked, as she too dismounted. Her hair was a tangle about her face, and there were black rings under her eyes. Alan cursed himself again at giving into her demands. He should have taken her back to Dor. He should have been stronger. He should have listened to his intuition. But she was here now. There was nothing he could do about that.

Alan had thought long and hard about what to do with the horses. They needed the horses — there were no two ways about it. They were not going to get very far without them, and Alan did not have the coins to replace them. "I think that is a risk we are going to have to take. These horses are well bred. They will only draw attention to us. We will hide them…" He looked around at the shrubbery and the long sweet grass. "Over there." Alan pointed to a small wooded area that was far enough away from the road that he doubted many travellers ever ventured near it. He did not wait for Bernice to agree. He merely clicked his tongue and led his horse forward off the road.

They were on the edge of Avalon now, and the peat had given way to red clay. Some said the soil had been stained red by the blood of those who had fallen to the Saxons sword. You wouldn't know, to look at it, that this place of beauty had once been a battleground. Under the grass, the bones of those who had been slaughtered lay. The soil was, however, firmer underfoot than it had been in Avalon. The grass was long, and in places, it came up to the middle of Alan's thighs. The horse, forever an opportunist, immediately began to snatch at the grass with a seemingly insatiable hunger. Grasshoppers chirped a warning as Alan, and his horse, made a path through the long foliage. Gnats swarmed just above the grass line and several bumblebees flew from one flower to the next, collecting nectar to take back to their nest. There was also a rich variety of butterflies. So much life now lived where so many had died.

"If it was obscurity we were after, then perhaps we should have set out on donkeys," Bernice stated in all seriousness.

Alan turned as he walked and smiled at her. "Donkeys?"

"A fitting breed for the Keeper of the Blade, don't you think?" Bernice replied. The concern on her face was replaced with mirth. But the smile that hovered on her lips turned to one of worry. "Alan, we are leaving a trail."

Alan scowled, for it was true. They were. There was no point hiding the horses if they were going to be so obvious about it. "We will come back the way we came and brush the grass forward—"

"Because if we are seen doing that, we won't look at all suspicious," Bernice stated with a roll of her eyes as she looked back at him

"Do you have any better ideas?"

"Sister Agatha always said—"

"Sister Agatha? Really? Again?" Alan asked with a hint of cynicism. "Is there anything that woman didn't know?"

"No. I don't think so," Bernice said with a reluctant smile. "She was very wise."

"So tell me, what would Sister Agatha advise if she were here?"

"She would say the best hiding places are usually the least obvious ones."

"Why do you think I want to hide them in the woods?" Alan asked, trying to keep the humour from his voice.

"No. You don't understand. She would suggest taking the horses with us—"

"Bernice, that is madness—"

"I should imagine that the graveyard of Arthur's knights is going to be in the castle grounds. The only way you are going to access those grounds is if you pretend you are a man of importance. Or, if you pretend that you have found these horses and are seeking their owners."

"I am sorry to say that for once, Sister Agatha's advice would lead us to nothing but trouble," Alan stated as he mulled her words over. "Firstly, I have no intention of announcing I am in Wessex. And secondly, if I say I have found these horses then questions will be asked, and the horses will be taken from us. Either way, we lose the horses. I would prefer to hide them. Let us stick with my plan."

"Here was I thinking you didn't have a plan," Bernice replied with a touch of amusement.

***

They tethered their horses beside a fast flowing brook. The animals immediately stretched out their long necks and began to graze. They swished their tails and occasionally shook their heads to dislodge the flies that found their sweat soaked skin so appealing.

"We will hide the tack and our supplies as best we can," Alan announced as he unbuckled the girth and gently dragged the saddle from his horse's back. Bernice followed Alan's lead without saying a word.

They hid the horses' tack and supplies under a bed of ferns, and they prayed that no one would notice. With one last look at the horses, they headed back to the road, brushing back the grass, with two long sticks, as they did so.

"Are you ready?" Alan asked when they were back on the road. He adjusted his cloak, making sure his weapons were hidden from prying eyes. "You could stay with the horses if you want," he looked down at her trouser-clad legs with a glower of disapproval. He did not like the idea of taking her into the lion's den with him. If this all went wrong, which was a very real possibility, he did not want Bernice to be hurt.

Seeing where he looked, Bernice defiantly pulled the hood of her cloak over her head. "I have no intention of staying with the horses. We are in this together, Alan. I will not leave your side."

"If we are caught—"

"Then we are caught."

"You saw what they did to your fellow nuns at Holywell. The Saxons are barbarians."

"I am not afraid," Bernice stated firmly. "God is with me."

"Like he was at Holywell?"

She gasped at his words, and when he looked into her eyes, he saw a terrible hurt.

"I am sorry, I shouldn't have said that," Alan reached for her hand in a fumbled attempt at an apology. Her hand was so small, so delicate compared to his, although it was no soft hand his love had. The skin of her palm was calloused, from all the gardening she had done when she lived at Holywell. Bernice was no weakling, despite appearances. She was a strong woman. A brave one. "I love you," he said simply, looking at their joined hands. "I don't want anything to happen to you."

Tears sprang to her eyes at his words, and she reached up and touched his face. Alan breathed out unsteadily and looked into her eyes.

"I couldn't live with myself if you were hurt. Stay with the horses. Please. I beg you."

Bernice shook her head ever so slightly, and then she stood up on her tiptoes and kissed him.

His eyes closed and his lips parted when her lips touched his. He didn't know what to do, but he soon realised a kiss was a little like sword practice. She lunged. He parried. Their lips caressed. He advanced. She did not retreat. They surrendered to each other. He had been wrong — kissing was different to swordplay. It was intoxicating. He was aware of everything about her. Her hands. Her body. Her lips. When her lips moved, his followed. His hands reached up to her face and caressed her cheeks. He could taste her breath on his lips — never had he tasted anything so sweet. It was like the finest of nectars. And Alan, unlike when he was in a fight, lost all sense of where he was and what he was meant to be doing. He kissed her again, taking the lead this time. The taste of her. The feel of her in his arms… Why had he waited so long to experience such sensations? His hands were in her hair now. Her hair wasn't rough like a horse's mane. It was soft, so very soft, like the finest of silks. Everything about her was soft, gentle. She moaned, and he pressed his lips a little harder to hers. She pulled back in surprise, and he feared he might have frightened her with his eagerness, but then she was kissing him and, *Oh, sweet Jesus,* her tongue had found its way into his mouth.

"Alan," she breathed his name, and she clung to him as if her legs could no longer support her.

"Where the hell did you learn to kiss like that?" Alan asked breathlessly. He felt like he had been running, but they had not moved even a footstep.

"Sister Agatha," Bernice said, giggling softly.

"What?" Alan asked in breathless surprise. Surely she was jesting?

"I am sorry, I couldn't help it," Bernice said with another giggle. "Sister Agatha would not have approved of what we just did. No one taught me how to kiss. Just now, with you… That was my first kiss," the humour left her eyes and in its place vulnerability lurked. "Was I any good? I mean…"

"I have never kissed anyone before, so I have nothing to compare it to," Alan spoke with honesty as his cheeks heated with colour. "But I liked it. Very much. Did you?"

"Yes. Oh, yes," Bernice replied eagerly. "And I am now looking forward to my second kiss."

"So am I," Alan said as he lowered his lips to hers again. He kept the kiss gentle and light, but it was nevertheless as intoxicating as the first kiss had been.

"You are going to marry me, aren't you?" he asked, a little unsure as he pulled back to look at her.

Bernice laughed at his question and nodded her head. "Yes."

"Good," Alan said with a relieved sigh. "I was just checking. You can never be too careful with nuns."

She hit him good-naturedly in the chest, and he laughed at her expression of mock outrage. "Come on," he took a step back from her. "Before someone sees us and stones me for being indecent with a boy." He looked down at her trousers again. "This isn't going to work. Why didn't you pack a dress?"

"I can not fight in a dress," Bernice stated.

"You cannot fight at all," Alan replied.

"And I can not track, or hunt, or...."

"*Sister Agatha?*" Alan asked with a groan and a raised eyebrow.

"She knew her way around a sword," Bernice confirmed, trying hard not to smile. She held out her hand as if expecting Alan to present her with something.

"Are you sure Sister Agatha was a nun?" Alan asked. He looked down at her outstretched hand and back to her face.

"That is what she said," Bernice said with a grin. "Although I often wondered. Come on, I need a weapon of some sort."

***

The village of Hordon was nothing like Alan had imagined it to be. It was large, almost a town in size. But there was no structure. No uniformed pattern in the buildings as one often saw in towns such as Aquae Sulis and what was left of Londinium. There was a mixture of old native roundhouses and new Saxon settlements here. However, they did not seem to sit comfortably with each other. And why would they? The Saxons and the natives of Briton being forced to live side by side — in what world would that ever work? The land had been divided into small enclosures, and here sheep and goats grazed. Silver-grey chickens scratched at the earth, as they looked for insects that were invisible to the eyes of men.

The village seemed deserted. The only sign of life was the smoke and the smell of cooking. *Where was everyone?* A child came out of a dilapidated roundhouse and began to throw grain and scraps at the birds. They cooed and clucked as they ran towards her.

Alan pointed discreetly at the girl and began to walk towards her. She was singing softly to herself in a language he did not understand.

"Pardon me. Do you speak Briton?" Alan asked, approaching the girl. His only experience with children was with the young lads that he had taught to fight when he had been in the Breton army. He smiled at her with what he hoped looked like reassurance.

The girl jumped at the sound of his voice and dropped the food she was carrying. The chickens did not care; they surged around her feet like the sea does when it encounters a rock on the beach.

The child looked like she was no more than ten summers at a guess, but Alan couldn't be sure. She was dressed in threadbare clothes that didn't fit. She had nothing at all on her feet, and her stick-thin arms were covered in bruises. Her tears had left tracks down her dirty face. Alan felt a growing anger as he waited for her to speak. Only a coward abused a child. In Alan's opinion, it was one of the vilest of crimes; it stood alongside rape and torture.

"Do you speak Briton?" he asked again, trying not to portray his anger at her treatment in his voice.

The child took a step back, almost tripping over a chicken as she did so. The chicken squawked, flapped her wings and then carried on pecking at the grain.

"Don't be afraid," Alan held out his hand towards her, and then thought better of it as the girl continued to slowly back away from him.

"We have travelled far," Bernice stated, coming to Alan's rescue. "What beautiful chickens you have. They are a credit to you," Bernice smiled, and she bent to pick one of the birds up. "Does she have a name?"

The child shook her head.

"You do not name your chickens? At the priory, we had several chickens, and they all had names."

"What do you want?" the girl asked shakily in Briton.

Bernice put the chicken back down. "We are looking for something."

The child looked at Bernice with wide eyes. "Why are you dressed as a boy?" The child asked as she took a cautious step towards

Bernice.

"Can you keep a secret?"

"I keep many secrets," the child replied. "If I did not, then I would lose my tongue."

"I am in disguise. Shh!" Bernice put her finger to her lip.

"Why?"

"Because..." Bernice paused. "I am on a secret quest—"

"Then my prayers have been answered. There really is a God. You have come to liberate us." The hope in the child's eyes was painful to witness.

"I am sorry, no. We just came to find a... To find a grave. We are looking for the graveyard where Arthur's knights are buried," Alan explained. He felt regret when he saw the disappointment in the child's eyes.

"I understand," the child bowed her head. "We are the forgotten ones. Our King abandoned us, and so has our God. You are Christians," the child stared at them both with an air of hopelessness. "You mustn't be here. It isn't safe. We have to worship the Saxon Gods. No other type of worship is allowed. The King hates Christians. My parents were Christians. I do not know where they are now. I pray that they are dead."

"Why would you pray for such a thing?" Bernice asked, horrified. Did the child not know that wishing her parents dead was a sin?

"What else do slaves pray for when freedom is nothing but a dream that won't come true? We were taken from our kingdom and sold in a market along with the cattle and the sheep. I once foolishly prayed to God for wisdom, and now I am wise. I know how the animals feel. I know their fear. Their pain. For there is nothing different between us. I am like them, and they are like me."

"How old are you?" Bernice asked.

"I think I was eight when they came. My sister was seven, and my brother was five. They killed him. Stamped on his head with their boots. And as for my sister... They attacked her. Forced themselves upon her. They did the same to me, but I was stronger than she was. And then they burnt everything."

"Where are you from?" Alan asked, almost choking on the lump in his throat that had been brought on by her words and the way she had said them so matter-of-factly, so devoid of emotion.

"The land of tin. I miss the sea and the sound of the sea birds. I miss speaking in my own tongue, not that I can remember it very well. It has been so long…"

"Cerniw," Alan stated quietly. "You were taken prisoner when Wessex invaded Cerniw."

"What is your name?" Bernice asked.

"They call me Aisly, but that is not the name my parents gave me."

"What did your parents call you?"

"Does it matter?" the girl asked. "I am Saxon now."

"Alden returned to his kingdom and liberated his people," Alan spoke the words softly.

The girl turned to look at him. "He didn't liberate me. Or my parents. Or any of the others that were taken. He left us here to rot. When he escaped, we were punished. The King was so angry," her eyes took on a faraway look and she turned to walk away. "I suggest you leave before you can't. There is nothing for you here."

"I need to find the graveyard first," Alan stated, daring to touch her. She did not flinch under his touch. She showed no signs that his touch was unwelcome and that disturbed Alan more than anything else. He quickly withdrew his hand.

"The graveyard is in the castle grounds," the child pointed towards the towering walls of the castle that once went by the name of Camelot. "But it is a forbidden place. A Christian place. No one is allowed to visit the graves. The penalty for all who do is death."

Death. Of course, the penalty would be death. That was the Saxons answer to everything. Alan glanced at Bernice.

"You must not go there. You must leave before you are seen," the child looked nervously about her as she spoke. "I am being watched. I am always being watched. I really have to go."

"Wait. Do you know any way of getting into the castle without the guards seeing?"

The child's eyes darted to a building that had long since been rendered to ash. All that remained was the scarred black stones of what was once a forge.

"There is no way to get inside the castle without being seen — not anymore," the girl said, drawing Alan's attention back to her. "There were tunnels, but they have been filled in. I know because I helped to fill them. The only way in is through the portcullis. I am sorry, I really must go." The child turned on her heels and ran back to the house she had come from.

"She is five and ten," Bernice stated with a catch in her voice. "She has been starved and beaten. Alan, we have to help her."

"I have to find the knights," Alan whispered. "I'm sorry. If I could help her, I would, but I can't. Come," Alan took her arm in a gentle grip. "We cannot stay here. We are beginning to attract attention."

Several villagers had come out of their houses and were looking at them with undisguised interest.

"Alan," Bernice spoke with urgency. He looked up and saw a man approaching them. The skin on this man's face looked as if someone had stretched it over his cheekbones. And his eyes looked large and out of place.

"Who are you? And what do you want?" The man asked in Briton with a rasping voice. He did nothing to mask his distrust and suspicion. The smell of mead coming off the man was overwhelming as was the smell of a body decaying.

"I am looking for someone," Alan replied with caution, blinking back the water that had formed in his eyes because of the stench of the man before him. There was a river nearby — did these people never wash?

"Who?" the man asked.

"Someone long gone," Alan replied.

"If he is long gone then why are you looking for him?"

"I am looking for his grave."

The man snorted at Alan's answer. "If you have come here looking for a grave, then a grave you will find. But it will be your own," the man began to cough. "Strangers are not welcomed here. Take my advice," he wheezed, "turn around and go home."

"That I cannot do. I heard a story once of how a great King escaped Cerdic's dungeon. It seems to me that nothing is impossible in Wessex. If that King could get out, then I can get in. I have come to find a grave. I cannot leave until I have seen it."

"Whose grave is so important that you would risk your life in seeing it? You are a foreigner," the man stepped closer still. "And my King does not like foreigners."

"I am looking for the grave of one of Arthur's knights," Alan said, taking a step back to keep a distance of space between them. If the man got any closer, Alan feared he would empty his stomach. Even his dying father had not smelt as bad as the man stood before him now.

"Arthur had many knights, which one, in particular, are you looking for?"

"Does it matter?" Alan asked as he reached for his purse.

"You think to bribe me?" the man asked, although he rubbed his hands together, and he did not look away from the purse Alan had in his hands.

"How much?" Alan asked as he tipped a few coins into his hand. "Take me to the graveyard, and I will pay you generously."

The man snatched at the money, but Alan closed his fingers over the coins and took another step back. The man licked his thin cracked lips and held out his hand. The man's hand was black with years of ingrained dirt.

"One, for now, the rest when you take me to the graveyard," Alan said as he placed a single silver coin onto the man's palm.

"These are not Saxon coins," the man stated in annoyance. He raised the coin to his eyes so he could see it better. "This is du Lac money." He did not say the du Lac name with disgust, only intrigue.

"It is." Alan heard Bernice catch her breath at his confession. It was a risk admitting such a thing. However, Alan did not know what else he could do. He had to find that grave, no matter what. He had to find the Shield.

"I cannot buy anything with this except, perhaps, an early death," the man gave the coin back, but something shifted in his eyes. "Come on," the man tilted his head towards the direction of the castle. "If it is a grave you seek, I shall show you where to find it."

Chapter 22

Alan couldn't shake off the feeling that this stranger was leading them towards the gallows. He could almost feel the tightness of the rope around his neck, and the wobbly wooden box underneath his feet. The village, so quiet before, suddenly came to life. Those who had sought shelter in their homes now stood on their thresholds and watched with suspicious eyes as the trio walked past them. Alan wondered if the villagers would cheer when the box was kicked from under him, and he found himself dangling on the end of a rope.

Bernice had the good sense to keep her head down, but Alan met the villagers' gazes. If they were being led to their death, Alan would be damned if he did so with a bowed head. He would look his accusers in the eye so that after he was gone, they would not forget his face.

The stranger bent down, plucked a long blade of grass from the earth and put it between his teeth. He looked like a horse that had bitten off more than he could chew. He disgusted Alan with his foul smell and strange ways. The stranger stopped walking when they drew near a small enclosure where a couple of sheep contentedly grazed, while their lambs danced and pranced around them. He leant against the fence and moved his lips up and down, the blade of grass moved as well. Alan fought back the urge to snatch the offending blade of grass from the man's lips.

"Why do you risk your life to find a grave?" the stranger asked, not bothering to remove the grass from his mouth as he spoke.

"That is my concern, not yours," Alan replied tight-lipped, as he placed a hand on the rough wooden fence and looked at the sheep. He did not trust this stranger. He did not like this stranger. But, he had to find the Shield... Somehow.

"When were you last in Cerniw?" the man asked with a curiosity that made Alan immediately suspicious. "How is Alden? Well, I hope? How is his wife? Dead, I hope?"

Alan refused to comment. He would not be drawn into a conversation with such a creature.

"Not very talkative, are you?"

"I am not here to talk," Alan replied guardedly.

"No, you are here to find a grave," the man snorted in amusement. "Do you like one-sided conversations? Is that why you seek an audience with the dead? Or perhaps you do not come here to talk but to steal. You will be disappointed if that is your reasoning for risking your life. There is nothing left to steal. Wyrtgeorn plundered the graves after his victory over Arthur. Anything of value he took and squandered. There is nothing in the graveyard but ghosts."

Alan breathed out unsteadily, this was not what he had wanted to hear, but it was something he had secretly feared. But the Shield... It had to be here. It had to be.

"There is still time," the man said. He took the blade of grass from his mouth and dropped it carelessly on the ground. "You can turn around, go home. No one will be any the wiser that you dared step a foot in this cursed kingdom. If you are from Cerniw, then I would advise you to rethink this madness and leave the dead well alone."

"I am not from Cerniw," Alan stated, turning to look at this sorry excuse of a man. "Are you going to show me where the graveyard is or not? If not, then leave us be, and we will find someone else to show us the way."

"Check your purse before you please yourself," the stranger replied. "If you had dared place that coin in anyone else's hands then you would have found yourself being marched to the dungeons. And believe me, you don't want to see the inside of Cerdic's dungeons. Those who do, rarely live to tell the tale."

"I am not asking for your advice—"

"It was not advice I offered, I was stating a fact. Turn around and go back to Cerniw or wherever you came from. There is nothing here for you except for death. Even if I could get you into the castle grounds, which is unlikely, I will not be able to get you out again."

"It is a risk I have to take."

"And you are willing to risk your companion's life as well?" the man asked with a raised eyebrow. "Or is she as suicidal as you are?" the stranger scoffed and raised his wineskin to his mouth.

Alan was concerned that this man had seen through Bernice's disguise so easily. He also felt revulsion as the man drunk seemingly insatiably in front of him. Red liquid oozed from the corner of his lips and dribbled down his chin.

"You judge me," the man stated as he lowered the wineskin and wiped his mouth with the back of his dirty sleeve. "You see, a slave. A drunk. A villain. A dirty old man. A man not to be trusted. And yet you gave me a silver Cerniw coin. Why? Did you think I," he pointed to his head, "am simple? Insane? Did you think in my inebriated state that I would not notice? You wouldn't be the first to think that. I can play the drunkard. I can play the fool. I have been doing it successfully all of my life. Why do you think I have lived so long?" He raised the wineskin to his mouth again and took a large draught. "When Cerdic came back the conquering hero, and with Alden in chains, I thought that was the end. I stole several small barrels of Cerdic's wine and I feasted. I remember hearing the bell tolling and angry shouts that the prisoner had escaped, but I was so drunk that I didn't care. I was more concerned about the barrel of wine I had not drunk. I decided to hide it in the abandoned tunnel that was under the stables. And then, there they were. Alden and that Saxon whore, in my hiding place, asking for help."

"You helped Alden escape?" Alan asked, and he felt a reluctant respect for the man before him.

"I got him, and his whore, to Bors. Bors did the rest. But... So many people died because Alden escaped. Cerdic took it out upon the Cerniw prisoners. He took it out upon the villagers. He took it out on everyone. And it left me wondering if one man's life was worth the sacrifice of so many others. If I had not helped Alden, then..." the man sighed with apparent defeat. "And now you are here, with your Cerniw coin and your request to see a graveyard that no one dares go near anymore, and I wonder if I should help you, or if I should hand you over to Cynric. Who are you? And what is so important in that graveyard that you would risk everybody's life to see it?"

"My name is Alan, and I am the Keeper of the Blade—"

"*Keeper of the Blade?* There is no Keeper of the Blade — there never was. It is just a story we Britons tell ourselves in a bid to holdback despair. It is utter nonsense. Next, you will be telling me that you intend to awaken Arthur and his knights from their slumber. Is that why you are here? To chant some words over a graveyard? Go away," the man turned away from Alan, his voice heavy with defeat. "Go back to where you came from, you will get us all killed."

"I am not here to raise the dead," Alan stated. He glanced at Bernice, and he realised he sought her permission to tell this man, this stranger, the truth. But before he could speak, the man began walking towards the castle again.

"Come on," the man spoke over his shoulder. "I am dying anyway. I want to see you raise the dead. I want to see the knights reunited. I want to see the look on Cerdic's and Cynric's faces when they realise they have to battle ghosts. Maybe your actions will even provoke a revolt, and we will be able to win our kingdom back."

Alan and Bernice shared a concerned glance at each other. They were not here to raise ghosts, or start a rebellion.

"Well, come on. What are you waiting for?" the man called. "It is actually your lucky day. Cerdic rode off with Alden's kin. And he did not say where he was going. So, if you are caught, it is only Cynric you have to worry about. You could probably buy his silence with your purse of silver. You wouldn't be the first."

"Cerdic has ridden away with Alden's kin?" Alan asked, hoping he had misheard him.

"Yes. The dead one. Garren du Lac. He was here. I saw him. He and the King have gone on a journey, but no one knows where. Even Cynric does not know where. I wonder if Alden du Lac knows where they have gone?"

"So do I," Alan said under his breath as dread settled in his stomach. What game was Garren du Lac playing? "So do I."

***

Alan heard Bernice suck in a breath as her eyes fell upon what was once Arthur's great fortress. From a distance, the castle had looked foreboding, but up close it was something else entirely. Never had Alan seen a castle of such size and grandeur, it was beyond anything he had ever imagined. The high walls made of Sarsen stone looked like they could stand an attack against anything. It had not one, but two dry moats. And here, hares nested. It seemed a precarious place to give birth, but the hares had been nesting in this land for centuries. Why should they move on when it was man who had invaded their territory? Alan could see the tips of the black ears of the leverets. These young hares trusted in the grass to hide them from all predators. Alan watched with unease as a cat stalked ever closer. As he watched, he felt as if a shadow crossed his path and that he too was waiting for death to catch him unawares.

Alan looked up at the battlements, but he quickly looked down again for he realised archers were watching them. These archers had their arrows nocked, and that never boded well.

As far as Alan could see, there was only one way into the castle grounds, and that was through the portcullis. How had such a castle fallen to a band of opportunist Saxon warriors? It didn't make any sense. What had gone so drastically wrong in Arthur's court that this Saxon takeover was the consequence?

"Alan," Bernice whispered his name.

"Keep your head down. Keep it covered," Alan advised under his breath. If they realised Bernice was a woman…

There was a wooden bridge over the dry moats. It seemed sturdy and in good repair. Nevertheless, Alan took a deep breath before he stepped upon it and he heard Bernice do the same. This was ridiculous, what were they doing? Alan knew he had to go forward, but everything in him urged him to turn around and run away, which was unusual for him because he wasn't a coward.

"David," one of the Saxon warriors approached them as they made their way towards the portcullis. This warrior was a formidable-looking man with long blonde hair and arms as thick as tree trunks. His nose had been broken, not once but seemingly twice. And he had a scar across his chin. His eyes were a startling blue, and they saw everything. "Nodin is looking for you," the warrior stopped speaking and began to gag. "By the gods' man, you stink. Have you been rolling in hogs *scitte* again?"

"Aye, 'twas a good day for it," David replied in a voice that was suddenly heavily accented and it also made him sound somewhat dim-witted. David bowed awkwardly which made him stagger and almost fall over.

"You drunken bastard," the warrior said in disgust. "Who are these people that you bring to our great King's castle?" The warrior looked at both Alan and Bernice. "Market day is on *Tiwes daeg*. You are two days late. Come back next week."

"I do not think they are here for the market," David said, reaching for his wineskin.

"Then why are you here?" the warrior asked.

"They are from our King's nephew's, cousin's, brother's, army," David said proudly in one long breath. He raised the wineskin to his mouth again, but the warrior grabbed the skin and tore it from his lips.

"Hey, that is mine," David protested, staggering forward and reaching for his wineskin.

"Nothing is yours. You are a slave. Exactly whose army do you belong to?" The warrior asked Alan and Bernice, but he became distracted when he sniffed the contents of the wineskin. He turned back to David with a look of outrage on his face. "This smells like our King's mead. Did you steal this?"

"Why would I steal from the King?" David asked, his attention fully focused on the wineskin. "I have served him loyally from the beginning. I am a 'onest slave. I have stolen nothing."

"Then where did you get it from, and who are these people?"

David's face portrayed his puzzlement at such a question. "I cannot recall. How strange... Let me think. I was with the 'orses, and I were... What were I doing? Oh aye, I were mucking them out, that was what I were doing. I took me one-wheeled cart to the dung heap. I love that one-wheeled cart I do. Couldn't ask for a better one. Here, I wrote a song about it. You wanna hear?" David did not wait for the warrior's consent; instead, he began to sing with a deep, but off-key, voice. *"I had a cart. I had a cart, with a wheel. I had a cart, with a wheel that went round and round and round."* He inhaled sharply and off he went again. *"I had a cart. I had a cart with a wheel—"*

"ENOUGH! That is quite possibly the worst song I have ever heard."

"Here, hang on, there's another verse... *I had a torch. I had a torch, and it were bright. It were so bright. It lit up the sky. It lit up the sky. My torch. I had a—"*

"SHUT UP! By the gods, man. I asked you where you got the mead."

"I fell over, didn't I? I banged me head. See," David pulled up his greasy hair from his forehead to show a round and protruding lump. "I got up, felt a bit dizzy... Then what did I do? Oh, I know. I were sick. And then I ran into these two. Well, I didn't run. Stumbled would be a better word. Fell upon them actually. It were them that gave me the wineskin. I think that is what happened, anyway. But... I could be wrong. *I had a cart. I had a cart with a wheel...*"

"By the gods," the warrior shook his head in disgust. "Perhaps I will get more sense out of them?" he turned to look at Alan and Bernice again. "Who are you? What do you want here?"

Alan had never wished for anything more than being able to speak and understand Saxon. He had no choice but to look to David to translate.

David turned and glared at Alan and Bernice as well.

"I told you. They are our King's brother's, cousin's, sister's, father's, nephew—" David began only to be interrupted.

"Enough from you. Does he not have a tongue?" the warrior bellowed. "Can he not speak for himself?"

"We were sent here with a message for the King. But we were set upon by masked men. They stole everything, our horses, and our supplies. We have been walking for many days to get here."

Alan looked back at Bernice in surprise. Her head was still lowered, and her hood was still up. She had tried, rather unsuccessfully in Alan's opinion, to sound like a man. But it seemed the warrior was fooled.

"What is the message?"

"The message is for the King's ears and his ears alone. Are you the King?" Bernice asked, her voice heavy with sarcasm.

"The King isn't here," the warrior replied.

"We have orders to deliver my King's message to King Cerdic and to him alone. So, we will wait for his return."

"If that is your pleasing. Where were you set upon? What did these masked men look like?"

"They had masks on," Bernice's voice became even more sarcastic. "As for where we were set upon, do we look like travelling bards? Are we supposed to know our way around this backward kingdom? We took the Londinium road to get here. We stopped at a crossroads, and it was there that we were set upon."

"There are many crossroads on the Londinium road. You will have to be more specific."

"What is this? An interrogation?" Bernice snapped in apparent outrage. "But if you must know there was a gibbet where several bodies were hanging. Does that bring anything to mind? I thought Cerdic commanded the entire southeast of Briton. We were assured we would not meet with any trouble. My King will be most displeased when he hears how we were not only set upon but how we had to endure such questioning when we finally reached our destination. Tell me, is this how you treat all your honoured guests?"

"I do not know your names, so I do not know if you are honourable or not. Who is your king?"

"King Elesa von Sachsen," Bernice stated.

The warrior took a step back at the mention of King Elesa's name.

"Please forgive me," the warrior pleaded, and he lowered his eyes, like a submissive puppy. "David will show you the way, and I will inform Cynric of your arrival." The warrior took to his heels and almost tripped over himself in his haste to get as far away as he possibly could.

"King Elesa von Sachsen?" David asked with a hint of humour.

"It was the only name I could think of," Bernice replied. "I did not expect such a reaction."

David chuckled, although his mirth quickly turned into a hacking cough. "Elesa is a temperamental bastard, or so I have heard. But then, all of Cerdic's relatives are."

"What just happened?" Alan asked.

"Your friend has just put the fear of God into… I have never seen him run so fast," he started laughing again. "That was the best thing that has happened to me in a long time. I am glad I lived to see this day. *You,* I like very much. *Him,*" he pointed to Alan, "not so much."

Alan frowned at Bernice. She just shrugged, but as she looked up at him from under her hood, he could see that she looked very pleased with herself.

"Where did you learn Saxon? And why didn't you tell me?"

Bernice gave another little shrug.

"Sister Agatha?" Alan guessed.

"You have bought yourself some time," David said through his mirth. "Everyone, even Cynric, will avoid you for as long as they can. But still, it is best not to linger. If you want to see the graveyard, then we must hurry."

As they entered the portcullis, Alan dared to look up at the murder-holes that were directly above him. It reminded him of Benwick Castle, but it was on a much grander scale. They entered a large courtyard. A dog barked at them and rushed forward with teeth snapping, only to be jerked back when he came to the end of his rope. The dog fell to the ground and immediately jumped back up. He began to growl and snap at them again.

"Don't mind him. He hasn't killed anyone in months. This way," David stated with an urgency that had not been in his voice before.

"Alan," Bernice's voice shook as she spoke. Gone was her boldness. She was frightened and by God, so was he.

"Just keep walking. Don't make eye contact with anyone."

There were warriors everywhere, and they were all looking at them. It seemed that news travelled fast. When Alan dared to make eye contact with a few of them, they all lowered their gaze in respect. Alan wondered who this King Elesa von Sachsen was. And he wondered why Cerdic's men would fear him. But even though that for now, they would be left in peace came the terrifying knowledge that they were in the very heart of enemy territory. And that Cerdic's army would rip them to shreds if they discovered their real intent. He prayed that the Saxon warriors, who had attacked the monastery, would not remember his face.

"DAVID!" an old and weather-worn man came running from the stables, his face contorted with anger. He had apparently not heard who these special guests were.

"I think we will go this way instead," David quickly did an about turn and walked incredibly fast in the other direction for one so apparently sick and pretending drunkenness.

"DAVID!" the man yelled again, but he did not take up the chase.

"Where are we going?" Alan demanded to know under his breath. "Why the sudden change in direction?"

"That is Nodin. He is as much a slave as I am, but he has been given responsibilities and so he thinks he is in charge of me. He and I…" David laughed softly. "We do not see eye to eye. He thinks me lazy. I would have to agree with him. But why break your back to gild another man's pocket? Come… the graveyard is quite a walk."

David led them around the perimeter of the castle and Alan, if he had not been so terrified, would have been in awe of what he saw. Never had he seen a castle of such magnitude before. Alan guessed it had not lost any of its beauty through the long years of Saxon possession. Cerdic had looked after it.

"Over there," David pointed to a piece, of what looked like, scrubland. It was covered in a thick layer of brambles and weeds. Unlike the castle, the graveyard had been neglected for a very long time. Alan felt his heart sink when he looked upon it. This wasn't what he had expected. This wasn't what he had expected at all.

"That is your graveyard," David replied with a small shake of his head. "I hope you find who you seek."

"No," Alan shook his head as he spoke. He took a step forward, but brambles blocked his way. It would take weeks to clear this graveyard, for it was no small site. Weeks and weeks and weeks of backbreaking work.

"What did you expect?" David asked with a hint of ridicule. "Cerdic has dedicated his life to hunting and destroying what was left of Arthur's knights. Do you think such a man would respect the resting place of Arthur's dead?" David chuckled to himself. "Were you expecting grass cut with a scythe? Tombstones on all the graves? You fool. Whoever it is you are looking for, has long since been lost. You will never find him. Never."

"Alan, I think we should go," Bernice tugged on his arm, but Alan ignored her.

"You should listen to your friend. The longer you are here, the more likely you are to run into trouble. But just out of interest, who are you looking for?"

"The Keeper of the Shield," Alan stated with a defeated sigh. It was no point pretending anymore. His quest had been doomed from the start. He should never have left Cerniw.

"You will have to be a little more specific. Does this Keeper of the Shield have a name?"

"Percival," Alan stated quietly.

David started to laugh. "How innocent you are. This is a Pendragon graveyard. Only the knights who were loyal to Arthur are buried here. Percival's sword master was Tristan, and Tristan was a du Lac. It is the du Lac graveyard you want, not the Pendragon one."

Alan turned to look at this slave of Cerdic's with a growing anger.

"The two great Houses were never really united," David explained when he saw Alan's face. "They would never share the same burial plot."

"Then where is the du Lac graveyard? Take us there immediately."

"I cannot take you there, Cerdic extended the barracks a couple of years ago, he built over it. But that is by the by, Percival was not buried there either."

"But you said…" Alan breathed in deeply in a desperate bid to control his temper. "Then where is he?"

"Somewhere else," David replied unhelpfully.

"Northumbria?" Alan asked, recalling his father's words. He should have listened to him and not to Alden.

"Northumbria?" David began to laugh again. "Why would he be in Northumbria? Who have you been listening to? I am sorry to say, but you have been fed a dish of lies."

Alan feared that David was right, but he would never admit to that. "Where is Percival's resting place?" He hissed the question angrily between his teeth.

"Why does it matter? Percival was never a Keeper of anything. Someone is making a fool out of you."

"I was told he had the Shield. I was told he had *Ochain*."

"Percival was ten and four when he died. Do you not know your history? You are no Keeper of the Blade. You are no Keeper of anything."

Alan hesitated for a moment, and then he slowly withdrew Draíocht. The blade caught the sunlight, and for a moment it glistened like a jewel. "Then what is this?" Alan asked, holding the knife out for David to see.

David's mirth faded to nothing. "I am so sorry," he said, and he appeared sincere. "You intentions are no doubt noble. But—"

"Do you know where Percival is buried?"

"No," David replied. "But I know where the Shield is. At least, I know someone who might know, because I heard something once, from my cousin's, sister's, brother's, cousin."

"Take us to him," Bernice commanded.

"It is not that simple."

"Why not?" Alan demanded to know.

"Because I'm not talking to my cousin's, sister's, brother's, cousin." David stated. "He said I stole his mead. Bloody liar. I never stole anything, and my cousin isn't really my cousin, and as for his sister…"

"You see this knife?" Alan held up the blade again.

"Mighty fine knife it is," David stated.

"How would you like to see it embedded in your stomach?" Alan threatened.

"Alright, alright, I'll take you to him. No need to get all violent. Christ! Threatened with a knife? I have never heard the likes."

"Can I kill him?" Alan whispered under his breath to Bernice. "Please, let me kill him."

"I had a cart. I had a cart, with a wheel... This way, follow me… *I had a torch. I had a torch, and it were bright…"*

Chapter 23

Goon Brenn. The Kingdom of Cerniw

The moor had swallowed all sounds except that of the wind and the call of a skylark as she flapped and flitted across the vast expanse of sky. At first, Amandine was staggered by the moor's splendour. She had never even imagined such a place, but the novelty soon wore off. The moor was vast, and there was no horizon. It was endless.

They had stopped to rest at a place where an ancient monument stood, tall and proud, over the surrounding area. Merton told her that the locals called this place *The Giant's House*. He had then woven her another elaborate story about his ancestors and how they had battled the giants for dominance. When looking at such a monument, it was very easy to believe in the tale. Perhaps there really had been a race of giants. Perhaps the stories that parents told to their children were not really stories at all.

Amandine yawned with fatigue. How she longed to be in a bed, with the furs wrapped tightly around her. However, she kept such thoughts to herself. Amandine had assured Merton that she could make this journey, but she would have said just about anything to leave Dor. She had felt trapped there. It had been as if she were suffocating slowly and silently. Each passing moment had felt like a piece of her was dying. Amandine wished she had felt differently. She wished she did not have this burden of fear. Alden had been so kind to her. He had welcomed her into his home, given up his bed and in return, she had stolen his brother away. Alden had told her that he understood and that made it all the more difficult. Such thoughts brought tears to her eyes, but she quickly brushed them away, for she did not want Merton seeing.

Her thoughts turned to Josephine. Amandine did not know what possessed her to try to talk to the woman — a desperate desire to understand, perhaps? All Amandine knew for sure was that she would never have done to Josephine what Josephine had done to her. She would never subject anyone to the pain and the humiliation she had been forced to endure at Benwick.

"I am the daughter of Satan," the wind of the moor tore the words from her mouth and took them far away to a place where they could not be uttered anymore. But even so, Amandine wondered if she would ever be free of the late Abbot.

She reached down and stroked her horse's neck. The animal's soft breathing soothed her, and she willed the memories of the Abbot away.

Vernon had long since tied a lead rope to her horse's bit ring, and he had taken the wriggling Tanick from her arms. She had felt gratitude, for although she surprised herself with how much she loved Merton's child, she was not strong enough to amuse an infant for the long hours that was needed in the saddle to get to their destination. Vernon was talking to Tanick now in that strange Saxon tongue that Amandine wished she could understand. Vernon pointed at the skylark above them, and Tanick squinted up at the sky and pointed as well.

"How much further?" Amandine had been desperate to ask that question, but she had resisted, fearing she would expose her lie — *she was not strong enough for this journey*. It was taking everything she had to stay on top of the horse.

Merton turned in his saddle so he could look at her. She saw the concern on his face that he did nothing to mask. "Not long," he reassured, "a couple of hours."

Amandine sighed with tiredness. She repeated in her head what Merton had just said. *It was just a couple of hours*. This time tomorrow this journey would be in the past and forgotten. She could do this. She could pretend that she was fine, and that she was coping.

"Do you want to stop again for another rest?" Merton asked with a concerned watchfulness. She had not fooled him with her pretence of wellness. She should have known better than to try to hide the truth from Merton du Lac. He saw everything.

"I want to get there," Amandine replied, which wasn't exactly true. She was terrified of meeting this Tegan. Merton had told her so many things about the old druid that Amandine could not help but feel apprehensive. She had never met a druid before, and she wasn't too sure how to make friends with one. She wasn't sure how to make friends with anyone anymore if the truth were to be told.

Merton turned his attention to Vernon and talked rapidly in Saxon. Vernon looked back at her, and she knew they were talking about her. Amandine wanted to protest, to chastise Merton for speaking in a language she could not follow, but she simply did not have the energy.

Merton halted his horse and, with a stiffness of joints, he dismounted.

"I don't need to rest. I am fine," Amandine protested as Merton limped towards her.

"Maybe you do not, but the horses are tired, especially yours. Poor thing, what torture it must be to carry your weight upon his back."

"Really?" Amandine asked with concern. She had not thought herself heavy, but then she did not know a great deal about horses and what they could and couldn't carry.

"No," Merton replied with an easy grin. "You are so light your horse probably does not even realise you are on his back."

"Then why did you say… You are not funny," Amandine reprimanded.

"Tanick thinks I am," Merton replied as he held out his hand to help her down.

"Give it a few years and he will change his mind," Amandine warned. "I do not need to rest, I can carry on," she persisted.

"You may, but I can't," Merton admitted quietly.

Amandine only now noticed the fresh lines of pain around Merton's eyes that had certainly not been there this morning. And with that realisation came the guilt. She had been so desperate to leave Dor that she had not thought to consider if Merton was well enough to travel. How much more selfish could she get? With a sense of shame, Amandine closed her eyes and dismounted. When she hit the ground, she forgot to bend her knees and jarred them most painfully.

"Are you all right?" Merton asked with concern when a small gasp of pain escaped her.

"It is just a long way down," Amandine attempted to smile.

Merton pulled her into his gentle embrace. She closed her eyes and savoured the sensation of being held by the man she loved.

"We are almost there," he reassured as he pulled back a little. "And I know Tegan will fuss over us all," he smiled as he looked down at her. "She is going to love you. Just like I love you."

"I do not know about that," Amandine stated nervously. "What if she doesn't?"

"She will," Merton smiled at her. He leant forward and left a kiss on her forehead. "I need to help Vernon with Tanick."

Amandine nodded and let him go. There was nothing for her to do, the men seemed more than capable of taking care of everything, so she walked to where a rock, covered in moss, jutted out of the ground as if it was a spear that had been thrust into the body of an animal and left there to fester. And here she sat. The rock was no more comfortable than the saddle was, but she did not have the strength to walk about and loosen weary muscles.

Amandine closed her eyes and welcomed the gentle breeze upon her face. She had missed this. She had missed the smell of the air and the sound of the birds. How cruel Philippe had been to lock her in a chamber and deny her all of this. She willed the tears away, although she felt them slip from underneath her eyelids. She just wanted to be free of him. Free of the past.

She felt Merton sit down beside her and she leant into him.

"Shh," he whispered into her hair as he put his arm around her.

"I am sorry." Amandine opened her eyes and sniffed in a bid to stop the tears. With frustration, she wiped the tears from her face with the back of her hand. "I was just thinking—"

"Alden should pass a law and stop you from doing that," Merton jested gently.

"I wish he would," Amandine agreed as more tears threatened to spill. "I'm—"

"You don't have to tell me. I know."

The skylark flew above them, calling to her mate, or maybe she was praising God in the only way she knew how. To Amandine's ears, the bird's song sounded strangely melancholy. Almost like the tolling of a bell at a funeral.

"Look," there was humour in Merton's voice as he pointed to Tanick. Vernon had given the child a piece of bread that he had dipped in honey. Vernon's dog was sat next to Tanick with her head to one side waiting patiently for the child to share. Tanick took a piece of the chewed up bread from his mouth and gave it to the dog. The dog licked the food from his fingers as if it were the finest of delicacies. Tanick giggled, the sound travelling on the wind.

"That is disgusting," Amandine could not help but smile.

"The dog doesn't seem to mind, and there are worse things than sharing your meal with a creature such as her. I am a little concerned I must confess, I have no idea what Lowen is going to make of that dog."

"Who is Lowen?" Amandine asked. She thought that Tegan lived alone. It was hard enough to find the courage to meet Tegan, let alone someone else.

"It is Tegan's cat. Oddest damn cat I have ever seen. Tegan dotes on him as she will on you."

Amandine felt relief at his words, but also concern. "I do not want to be a burden to her," Amandine replied quietly. When Merton had agreed to take her away from Dor, she had initially thought that they would go somewhere alone, just the two of them. But now she realised that was never his intention. Amandine did not know what hold Tegan had on him, but it was strong. And it was a hold that Amandine had no argument against.

"I thought the same," Merton stated. "But, Tegan, she is different from other people. Not once did she make me feel like a burden. She did not look at my deformities and judge me because of them. She saw through them. She saw me. The real me, the one that you know, not the devil everyone else remembers. Tegan is probably the most extraordinary person I have ever met. She saved my life."

"Then I love her already," Amandine stated, wishing that what she said were true. Was she grateful to Tegan for what she did for Merton? Yes. But at the same time, there was this foreign feeling of jealousy. Tegan and Merton shared something that she could not. Both had been warriors. Amandine was as far from being a warrior as you could get. When Merton spoke of Tegan, he spoke of her bravery and courage. Tegan would not have allowed herself to be intimidated by an Abbot. She would not have allowed herself to be broken. Merton had never said such things, but Amandine did not need him to say it. Compared to Tegan, she was nothing. Self-doubt plagued her soul and with it came the ghosts.

She breathed in the fresh air deeply and gathered up her courage to ask Merton something she needed an answer to. "Merton?"

"Hmm?" he asked, there was a smile in his voice as he watched his son.

"What do you do when the ghosts continue to torment?"

Merton breathed out unsteadily as the question hung between them. Amandine immediately wished she could take the question back, but it was too late for that. She turned to look at him. He was frowning as he looked at Tanick.

"Merton?"

"Fight them," he replied simply, turning to look at her. There was a determination in his eyes, as well as a flame of anger.

"That is easier said than done," Amandine replied shakily.

"What other choice is there? You cannot let them win. Every day I battle my ghosts and every day I win. If you stop fighting that is when they will take all hope and twist it and distort it and make you wish for death. You must never stop fighting, Amandine. Never."

There was nothing more to say after that. Merton got up and limped to where his son and the dog sat. Amandine pulled her knees up to her chest and wrapped her arms around her legs for she suddenly felt very cold. She watched as Merton sat down next to his child. The child climbed onto his father's lap and like before with the dog, Tanick took some chewed up bread from his mouth and offered it to his father.

"I don't think so," she heard Merton say on the breeze, but the boy was persistent, and in the end, like the dog, Merton accepted the humble gift. Amandine giggled softly to herself.

Merton must have heard her because he turned to look at her.

"Your turn next," he winked. "Why don't you give some of your bread to your mother?" Merton asked the child. "It is her favourite. Shall we find her a piece that has not been in your mouth? No. You eat that. I don't want it. No. Tanick. Really?"

Amandine laughed as Tanick forced another piece of half chewed bread into his father's mouth. She loved that Merton already regarded her as Tanick's mother; it was something she had not expected. Not until they were married at least. Amandine rose from the rock and crossed to where the two people she loved most in the world, sat.

***

The Standing Stones rose eerily up from the earth. How long they had been there, nobody knew. And as for their purpose, that too remained a mystery — to some, anyway. Brittany had her fair share of standing stones; such things were not new to Amandine. But there was something about this place, something familiar. It was almost like the Stones were welcoming her home.

"This is where we must wait," Merton announced as he halted his horse. Tanick had started to cry for the journey had been tiring for one so young, and there were only so many birds and animals he could look at.

"How long must we wait?" Amandine asked above the noise. She hoped it wasn't too long, for her thighs felt bruised and battered and a great fatigue threatened to overcome her. She was also concerned for the child — like any mother would be.

Merton frowned as he looked at her and she could almost see the thoughts going around his head.

"It is not far. Just…" he shrugged. "She said to wait."

"How will she know we are here?"

"She has her ways. Her gods talk to her all the time. They tell her things. I know… It sounds strange, but… I have witnessed it. When you meet her, you will understand. There is nothing to fear. Please do not think there is. She is no witch — I would not take you to someone who is dangerous. Tegan is different, that is all. And her gods are different to our God."

Amandine felt unnerved by Merton's words. He said she had nothing to fear, but what if he was wrong? What kind of woman was he leading them towards?

"Is this where she wants us to wait?" Vernon asked with impatience, for he did not speak Breton and therefore he could not follow their conversation. "You know where she lives, don't you? What is stopping us from going there? I say we carry on."

"She said to wait." Merton replied in Saxon.

"Is the great Merton du Lac taking orders from a woman, now?" Vernon asked with a teasing grin.

"And what is that suppose to mean?" Merton asked.

Amandine could detect a hint of annoyance in Merton's words, although she could not understand their meaning. Vernon must have heard it too, for apart from an annoyed sigh, Vernon chose not to answer.

As they spoke the sky began to darken, and the first drops of rain began to fall. There was no shelter here, apart from one old oak tree.

"If we all die of cold, then it will be your fault," Vernon stated as he pulled his hood up and adjusted the child, so Tanick was sheltered from the storm.

"So be it," Merton stated under his breath. "We will ride to where she lives. I just hope we do not live to regret it." He then repeated his words for Amandine to understand, but he left out the whole *regret* part.

"But I thought you said—"

"It will be fine," Merton was quick to reassure Amandine. He smiled at her with what Amandine assumed was encouragement, but she was too tired and too anxious to acknowledge that encouragement.

Amandine held onto the pommel of the saddle as her horse followed Vernon's. Amandine concentrated on the speck of white in her horse's brown coat to distract herself from the aches of her body. She doubted very much she would be able to stand at the end of this journey.

The rain continued to fall. However, it was not like the rain of winter. It was not cold and damning.

Tanick's cry became even more distressed. Amandine wished she had the strength to comfort him. She hated this fatigue and the feeling of hopelessness that accompanied it.

"He will be asleep soon," Merton reassured, glancing with concern at his son. The journey had been very hard on the child. Tanick was also, no doubt, missing Emma — the woman who had fed him and taken care of him when his own mother had abandoned him and then later tried to kill him. How anyone could kill an infant was beyond Amandine's comprehension. What was wrong with the world? What was wrong with the people in it?

As Merton had predicted, eventually the child fell into an uneasy sleep. His dear little face was red from all the crying. Amandine had already silently vowed to herself that she would do everything in her power to be a good mother to the child. She would love him with all her heart. She would be the one he would run to if he scraped his knee. She would be the one to comfort him if he awoke from a bad dream. She would be his mother in every sense of the word. Amandine lost herself to daydreams of a future that she had once lost hope in ever seeing.

***

Merton spoke quickly in Saxon to Vernon as they approached the edge of the wood. Vernon attached the lead rope to his saddle, knotted his reins, readjusted the child and reached for his shield. Amandine's tiredness was forgotten as she picked up on the agitation of the men. Something wasn't right. A warrior only knotted his reins for one reason and one reason only. Danger.

"What is it?"

Her question met only silence.

"Merton, answer me," she demanded with a growing fear.

"This isn't right... Something is wrong," Merton stated as he narrowed his eyes and scanned the wood.

"How do you know?" she whispered back. Merton did not answer. Instead, he nudged his horse on, but the horse had barely taken two steps when Merton halted him again.

Amandine looked about her, but whatever it was that Merton saw was lost on her. She could see no movement in the woods. She could see no apparent threat.

The dog began to growl. Amandine turned to look at her. All the hair along the dog's spine was raised. She obviously sensed what Merton and Vernon did.

"Look to the sky," Merton yelled suddenly as an arrow flew through the air and embedded in the ground by the front hooves of his horse. Merton's horse cried out in terror and reared. Amandine's horse, decidedly unnerved, shied, and if it were not for the lead rope, Amandine suspected her horse would have bolted. As it was, Amandine found herself clutching to the neck of the animal.

"Stay down," Merton ordered. "We need to get out of here."

Another arrow flew through the sky, this one found a home in the earth, behind them. In quick succession more arrows followed. Effectively stopping their retreat. They were trapped. There was no going forward. There was no going back.

"This isn't good," Vernon stated as he raised his shield to protect the now screaming child in his arms.

"Stay down," Merton yelled the words again.

Amandine could not have sat up if her life depended upon it. She clutched to her horse's neck, too terrified to move.

"Merton," Amandine squeaked his name, but he did not even look at her. Another shower of arrows flew over their heads. It was like a condemnation from Heaven. One of the arrows found its mark in the hindquarters of her horse. The animal bucked, unseating Amandine, who was thrown heavily onto the ground. She narrowly missed hitting her head on a small, seemingly unobtrusive rock. With the wind knocked out of her she watched with a helpless sense of doom as her horse reared. Vernon was quick to untie the lead rope, freeing the injured horse from his own, but Amandine saw none of this. She just saw thrashing hooves, and all she heard was the sound of her crying son, and the aggressive bark of the dog.

"Amandine, get out of the way. You are going to be trampled," Merton yelled. But she couldn't. She couldn't move. Fear had paralysed her. Merton dismounted from his horse with a swiftness that she had not seen since they had been reunited. He grabbed her horse's reins, as another arrow embedded into the animal's sleek neck. The horse screamed and pulled the reins from Merton's grasp. And with the arrows still embedded deep into his body, the horse, with much bucking, galloped back the way they had come. It wasn't just man that, when injured in battle, longed to die at home. Horses did too.

"Get them out of here," Merton commanded in Saxon as he pulled Amandine to her feet. With difficulty, Vernon held out his hand, and with Merton's help, Amandine found herself sat behind Vernon on his horse.

"I am not leaving you," Amandine stated desperately.

"You will do as you are told," Merton replied before turning his attention to Vernon. "Vernon, go. I will meet you at the Stones." He smacked the rump of Vernon's horse as soon as he had finished speaking.

"Merton," Amandine cried as Vernon kicked his horse into a gallop. The dog followed on behind. Arrows rained down around them, but Amandine could not think about that because this time it wasn't her that was left behind. It was Merton.

Chapter 24

Life was given by God. Death by the serpent. With no shield and no means to defend himself, Merton knew that this was where his story ended. He had survived Philippe's torture, but he wasn't going to survive this. The arrows kept on coming.

He had not stopped to think about dismounting when Amandine was thrown from her horse. As always, his only concern was for her. He knew there was no way he was going to be able to mount his horse again without help. But, it didn't matter. Her life was worth far more than his ever was. Like Jesus, he was willing to make the sacrifice.

He breathed out unsteadily as he watched Vernon gallop away. He did not care for the arrows that whipped the sky past his ears and stabbed the earth in front and behind him. His eyes did not stray from that horse until they were out of the range of the archers. Once he was confident that, for now, Amandine and his child were safe, he felt a strange and out-of-place peace descend upon him. And suddenly he was privy to things he had not been privy to before. He realised that in the moment of his death he had never seen so clearly. He had not understood how dark his days had been until the blinding light of truth chased the darkness away. His eyes widened in wonder, and he found himself smiling despite the circumstances.

The arrows fell around him as if there was some invisible boundary that surrounded him and could not be penetrated. His skin tingled, the sensation not unpleasant, but different. In fact, it was indescribably perfect. His soul — and to his surprise, he realised that he still possessed one — cried out with joy. There was no fear. He wasn't afraid. He had the confidence of a man who had a great and undefeatable army waiting to attack on his command. So this was the feeling Sampson spoke of. No wonder he was so devoted. God really was all-powerful and as it turned out, all-forgiving.

Merton's horse was not so confident in the divine. He pulled the reins from Merton's hand and with his tail held high he bolted. Merton did not blame him. If he were a horse, he would have done the same.

Merton pulled his axe slowly free of his belt and began to walk unsteadily towards the woods. He wasn't used to walking without a stick anymore, but for now, that didn't matter for the hand of God was holding him up, supporting him and keeping him strong. God was everywhere — in the grass at his feet, in the sky above, in the trees. He had been so blind.

With new eyes, Merton looked at the trees. He did not understand what had happened here, or what this show of arms meant. There was nothing in the surrounding area that suggested someone lived here. Tegan guarded her solitude with the same devotion as a knight would guard his king. So either these bastards, whoever they were, had stumbled upon her by chance or they were part of something else. Something bigger. Tegan had been a Knight of Camelot and Cerdic still offered rewards for any man who could bring him the head of one of Arthur's loyal knight's. Riches so easily won could be a very compelling motivation for some. He should know — he was once a mercenary.

"TEGAN," Merton yelled her name as he made haste towards the tree line. Now that Amandine and his son were safe, he could concentrate on the welfare of his druid friend. "TEGAN."

Another arrow flew through the thick foliage, but this arrow fishtailed as if the archer had let loose too soon. A beginners mistake. Or maybe the archer had been interrupted. The arrow fell from the sky with as much menace as a snowflake. And then... Nothing. The only evidence, the only witness, that something of magnitude had happened here was the lifeless shafts of the arrows that now littered the moor.

"Tegan," Merton called her name with more caution as he entered the woods. The earth here was rough and uneven under his feet.

Gnarled tree roots that had knotted together over a century ago were more of a danger to Merton than the arrows had been. Even with God's guidance, Merton felt it prudent to look where he placed his feet.

A horse's shrill whinny echoed through the silent wood and Merton turned to look in the direction the sound had come from, but there was nothing to see, other than the trees. There was a crash of hooves on the forest floor and then once again, nothing. Was this the work of the dark one? A phantom horse? A ghost? Were these the Devil's men?

So this is what it felt like, Merton realised. This is what it felt like for his enemies when he and his men had attacked. The Devil and his demons — how ironic. Was he dead? Had he not noticed his own demise? Was this the Hell that the Church had condemned him to? Was he to relive the fear that he caused in others, over and over again?

A flash of black caught his eyes as it weaved in and out of the tall ferns that also littered the woodland floor in places. A smile pulled at the corner of Merton's mouth as he continued to walk. He wasn't dead. Not yet.

An arrow embedded itself in a tree just to his right. Merton flinched, but that was his only reaction. He wasn't looking for archers anymore.

There it was again, the flash of black and this time Merton caught sight of a pair of seemingly evil yellow eyes. He would recognise those eyes anywhere. Had he not awoken enough times only to be greeted by that very animal's terrifying stare? He did not even hesitate to consider not to follow the cat.

"Lowen," Merton whispered the cat's name. "Where is your mistress?"

But the cat was not giving away any secrets as he led Merton further into the wood. Here, only the wind disturbed the aspens while Tegan's strategically placed wind chimes tolled their sad tunes from the branches of the rowan trees. War was not welcomed here, for this was a sacred place. And as Merton's God and Tegan's Gods collided, Merton felt the presence of his God wax and wane, just as the inconsistent moon does in the darkest of nights. There was no place for his God here. Sampson had known it from the start, and now Merton did as well.

"You think to lead me away from the fight?" Merton stated as he saw Tegan's house in-between the branches of the trees. He felt joy at returning to this place. But also fear that Tegan would not be there to meet him. "Where is she, Lowen?" he asked as he stepped into the clearing. "What is happening here?" The cat did not answer although it would not have surprised Merton if he had. There was something otherworldly about Tegan's cat. Something that wasn't altogether feline.

Nothing had changed, Merton noted as he looked around cautiously. The ancient horse was still stood with her bowed back and tired eyes in the small clearing. The chickens continued to scratch and peck at the dirt. The goat had a new rope tied around her neck. She also had a playful new kid, but apart from that everything else seemed the same. On closer inspection, Merton discovered that the pig was missing, but maybe Tegan had butchered it.

Merton lowered his axe. There was no threat here.

Merton approached the roundhouse, hoping against hope that Tegan would be there. But in his heart, he knew she would not be. Merton pulled aside the curtain that hung limply over the threshold and stepped inside Tegan's roundhouse. A chair had been overturned, and the cauldron had been knocked over, spilling food all over the floor. He stepped further into the room and turned to look at the wall where Tegan kept her weapons. The wall was empty. Every single weapon, including his father's axe, had been taken. But worst of all, there was no sign of Tegan. She would not have gone quietly, Merton knew that. He stepped out of the roundhouse and looked about him one more time, but there was no evidence of a struggle outside. Which meant there were only two possibilities. Either they had killed her, or they had knocked her out. Either way, he would make sure they paid for their crimes. A cripple he may be, but he still knew how to track, and he still knew how to outwit an opponent. He dismissed God, for God was no use here, and allowed the demon back inside. But God was reluctant to let go of him, and that rage, that desire to kill, to seek revenge was not as strong as it should have been.

The cat kept pace as Merton struggled through the overgrown foliage. The ferns clung to his feet as if they were mystical vines intent on tripping him up, or worst still, imprisoning him. *"No, they are protecting you,"* Sampson's voice echoed in his head. *"Go back. Don't get involved."* Merton stopped, and it felt as if the vines were crawling up his legs with a strength that he could never vanquish. Was he losing his mind? Signs from God. Voices in his head. He was Merton du Lac. He was the Devil. Sweat broke out upon his brow, and his back introduced him to a new kind of torment. But with the pain came clarity. Merton had always been the warrior, always the protector. He was always the one who made the sacrifices, regardless of the consequences to himself. God had chosen the wrong moment to show him the light.

The vines loosened their hold on Merton as if they had suddenly remembered some forgotten ancient knowledge. This fight was not theirs to prevent. God, in his great wisdom, had given man free will which meant he could only guide. He could not interfere, as much as he may want to. The path Merton chose to take was his and his alone. God could only sit back, watch, and hope for the best.

The wood was unusually quiet. No birds. No insects. No rodents. When troubles come, the wildlife had the good sense to hide. The hair on the back of Merton's neck rose, and he knew what that meant. He was being watched. And it wasn't by the absent wildlife.

"Show yourself, you cowards," Merton yelled, but he might as well of shouted into a bottomless chasm. There was no way they were going to answer him. Why would they? They had the advantage.

He crept forward, using the trees as living shields. The cat continued to dodge his footsteps, but thankfully the animal kept his mouth shut. If these men, whoever they were, wanted to pretend to be ghosts then so be it. But two could play that game. Merton closed his eyes briefly and listened.

The wood was still silent. It seemed she had inhaled and had forgotten to breathe out again. A twig snapped. Merton opened his eyes and smiled. They may think they had the advantage, but not anymore. The axe felt heavy in his hand, and it hurt to raise the weapon, but raise it he did. He waited, and as he did so, he felt the familiar thrill of the hunt. He had forgotten what it felt like.

Somewhere from behind him, a man screamed in agony, but the sound did not distract Merton from his quarry. The warrior up ahead had turned at the sound of his comrade's cry. Merton watched as the warrior quickly knocked another arrow. If he was going to do it, then now was the time. But something stayed Merton's hand.

"Eldred?" Merton said the name with a dismayed realisation as he stepped out from behind the tree.

The man staggered back as if he had seen a terrifying vision and he dropped his bow. "Merton?" he whispered in fear. "By the gods... This cannot be. You are dead."

Merton lowered his axe just a fraction and stared back. "Eldred?" He said the man's name again in confusion. What was Eldred doing here? The last time he had seen him, they had been in Burgundar.

"You are dead. All of you are dead," Eldred stepped cautiously towards Merton. "I heard that the new King of Brittany tortured you and killed you, along with everyone else. But..."

"You are right," Merton stated, stepping closer. "I was tortured, and I died. But now I am here."

"Then you are a ghost."

"No, Eldred," Merton shook his head ever so slightly. "Look at my face. Can you not see the scars? I took on an army of five thousand. I was set upon, beaten, my sword arm smashed with a mallet, the lash opened up my skin. I died, but then I lived. It is true what they said of me. I am a demon. And, as I discovered, death could not bind me. But I have been told that no mortal man can conquer death," Merton raised his axe with the intent of striking his adversary down. "So if I kill you, then you will die, and you will not live again."

"Wait, wait, wait," Eldred pleaded, holding up his hands as if that in itself would ward off Merton's attack. "Let me explain."

"You and your companions let loose at my woman and child. I do not want to hear your explanations," Merton's voice was soft as he spoke. But so are a cat's movements just before he pounces and rips his prey to shreds.

"That was your woman? Merton..." Eldred began to back away. "I didn't know it was you."

"I guess you did not recognise Vernon either? He is going to be mightily pissed off when he finds out it was you that let loose at us."

"That was Vernon? What? I don't understand any of this. Is he a ghost as well?"

Merton narrowed his eyes as he looked at Eldred. Eldred had been a friend of sorts. Merton never really knew what to make of Eldred. He was nice enough, but Eldred was one of those men who never thought for himself. He never questioned, he just did as he was told. Which was why Eldred never became one of Merton's demons.

Merton favoured men who could take an order and yet also take the initiative. And that was why they had left Eldred behind when they had fled from Wihtgar. Not that Eldred would have come even if they had asked. Eldred had, when it came down to it, when it mattered, always been a coward. He preferred to stand with the many than take his chances with the few. He had stood with Wihtgar.

"Why is Wihtgar here?" Merton asked as he took another menacing step towards Eldred.

"After you left and Stuff arrived a lot of the men deserted, myself included. There was no way we could defeat Clovis, even with the extra warriors that Stuff brought with him. I am here with Daegal."

"Daegal?" Merton spat on the floor after he had said the name. He had never liked Daegal. He was unpredictable, and prone to violent outbursts over the smallest of things. And that was not all. Daegal believed it was his right to have his share of the spoils of war. He was a rapist and a murderer. A man without morals. "What business does Daegal have in my brother's kingdom?"

"We are hunting Arthur's knights. It was that or starve. Merton, you know how it is. We follow the gold."

"Then I suggest you use a different dog, for the scent you are following has run cold. There are no knights of Arthur's in this kingdom. If there were, my brother would know about it."

"You are wrong. There are several. A woman lives here. A druid. She was a knight. We have it on good authority. Cerdic will pay well for her head."

In the distance, there were sounds of weapons clashing — an axe on a sword if Merton wasn't mistaken.

"She is proving a little more troublesome than we anticipated. We have already lost Oswin and Stilwell to her blade. She will pay dearly for their deaths," Eldred stated, clearly agitated by the sound of the fighting. A man cried out in agony and the wood breathed out on a sigh.

"If you don't pay first for your foolishness," Merton warned. "If you have hurt her, I will not be merciful."

"Merton," Eldred's gaze travelled to Merton's axe. "I have no quarrel with you. I do not know what trickery it is that means you are standing before me. But I can see that you are not the man you once were. You have lost your sword arm."

"Yes, I have no idea where I put it," Merton stated coldly.

"I do not want to kill you," Eldred warned as he reached for his axe.

Merton chuckled at that statement. "You cannot kill me, Eldred. I am a demon. Did I not demonstrate that back there? Not one arrow grazed my skin." Merton saw fear enter the other man's eyes. Good. Eldred should be afraid. "This druid that you seek, I know her. I know nothing about what you accuse her of being," Merton lied. "But she is skilled in the art of the old ways. I would advise you to leave her well alone. She is not of this world. You cannot win." Merton heard the softest of sounds coming from the left of him — an indrawn breath, a quiet storm.

"I can kill anything that is mortal," Eldred boasted a little too quickly.

"But what if she is not? Mortal, I mean. What if she is like me? What then?"

Before Eldred could answer, an axe flew through the air and landed in the centre of Eldred's stomach with a sickening thump. Eldred screamed as an ox would do when slaughtered. His skin turned a clammy white and, as his own axe slipped from his fingers, he fell to his knees.

"Begging yer pardon, but I don't have time to stand around here gossiping. Dinner isn't going to prepare itself, is it?" Tegan said, and then this remarkable old woman retrieved her axe from the dying man's stomach with no thought for mercy. Eldred's guts spilt from his body, along with copious amounts of blood and other foul smelling bodily fluids.

Tegan looked once at Merton before she vanished back into the wood. Her face was swollen where she had obviously been hit, and there was blood all over her clothes, although Merton doubted that it was all hers.

"I warned you," Merton stated as he walked towards the dying man. He stopped when he reached Eldred and looked down at him. "You thought Cerdic would pay you so much gold for her head. You thought you would be a rich man. You thought you could go back to Saxony and marry that pretty girl from the village you used to talk about. You thought to raise a family, and you thought how you would boast about how you had caught and killed one of Arthur's knights. You thought you would be celebrated, and stories would be told of your bravery. You did too much thinking my old friend."

"Merton," Eldred gasped in pain as he held his guts in his hands. "Please. Finish it," he begged. "Finish it."

"There will be no gold, no pretty wife from the village, no family, no stories, no more thoughts."

"Wihtgar is going to invade the island off the coast of Hantescire, and then he is to join forces with Cerdic and march on Cerniw. Please, Merton."

"You tell me things I already know," Merton replied. "But unlike you, I know Wihtgar, and he will find the natives of that island no easy win. However, if by luck he does conquer the island, then that is as far as his ambitions will take him. He will not march on Cerniw. His marching days will be done. He will grow fat and thoughts of war will make his mind weary."

"Please. Don't leave me to die like this."

"Do you want to know why I never made you a demon? Even though I knew you wanted to be one. *This.* This is why. My men would never demean themselves by begging for an easy death."

"Please. Please," Eldred began to choke on his own blood.

"Goodbye, Eldred," Merton stated. He walked away, following the path that Tegan had taken.

***

It did not take long to find her. She was locked in combat with a man who was young enough to be her son. Merton did not think to interfere. Instead, he leant back against a tree and watched.

The way Tegan moved, the way she handled her axe was like listening to poetry. It was so controlled, a thing of beauty. Merton had never seen anything like it. It was as if she could predict Daegal's every move before he even knew what he was going to do. Daegal was no youth at his lessons. He was not of the same calibre as Merton's warriors, but he was no easy win. But Tegan... she made it look like she was battling a page. She caught his thigh in an upward slice and then she backed away. She watched him as a falcon does a rock dove. Daegal's hand clasped his leg as if that in itself would stop the bleeding.

Tegan smiled at her prey and beckoned him forward with her hand.

A mixture of rage and fear flickered over Daegal's face as he clumsily thrust his sword towards her. She skipped out of the way and opened up his other leg. The blood pumped from the wound as fast and flowing as a waterfall. She was going to bleed him. Merton could see in Daegal's face the realisation that he was going to be beaten by an old woman. Daegal's thrusts became laboured. He staggered around the small clearing as if he were drunk, while blood continued to pour down his legs and stain the ferns red.

In she swooped again, a cut on the arm this time and then back she went to watch. Daegal fell heavily on his backside amongst the ferns. He tried to raise his sword, but his strength ebbed with every beat of his heart.

"You came to kill me and yet it is you who will die. Pray to your gods and ask them for mercy," Tegan spoke in Cerniw. Daegal did not understand, but his eyes were filled with terror.

"She cursed you," Merton lied in Saxon for he was not feeling generous.

Daegal turned his now failing eyes towards Merton. He held up his hand towards Merton seeking mercy the same way Eldred had done.

"You will find no peace in death."

"Merton…?" Daegal's voice was full of disbelief as well as fear.

"Your Gods are dead. I have come to take you to my Christian Hell."

Tegan, like the falcon she was, went in for the kill. A slash across the neck with her axe and Daegal slumped sideways, flattening the ferns as he did so. And with that, the wood fell silent.

Tegan looked up from her kill and glared at Merton. The rage of war was still in her eyes, and as she took a step towards him, Merton pushed himself from the tree and raised his axe.

"Tegan," he warned quietly. "It is me. Stop—"

Tegan raised her axe and threw it with all her might towards him. The blade skimmed his ear before he had time to react. It smashed harmlessly into the tree behind him.

"Tegan," Merton glowered at her. "For the love of—"

"Did I, or did I not, tell you that if you wanted to come back to me, then we were to meet at the Standing Stones? How dare you disobey me. How do you think it felt having to watch you and your party come under attack knowing that I would not be able to get to you on time? And then, in your idiocy," she stepped closer to him, so close, in fact, that she pushed him back against the tree with her blood-stained hands. "You stayed behind while your friends fled. I watched you walk towards the woods as if you were taking a pleasant afternoon stroll while arrows rained down all around you. Are you completely insane?" she hit him with her fists. "Of all the idiotic things. You are just like your father. Oh, I am so angry with you."

Merton could not help himself — he smiled in the face of her rage.

"Don't you dare smile at me," Tegan exploded. "You stupid ass." She hit him again. "I was so bloody afraid for you. You are the closest thing I have ever had to a son."

"I love you too," Merton stated with a grin. "Come here," he dropped his axe and reached for her.

"No, I'm covered in blood." Her shoulders began to shake and much to his surprise he realised she was crying. Tegan didn't cry. She was always so in control.

"I'm sorry, *Mother*, I truly am," Merton said, hoping to dry her tears with humour.

"Don't you *Mother* me," Tegan's muffled reply made Merton smile. "I'm not your mother."

"Closest thing I have to one," Merton contradicted. "Are you all right? Are you hurt?" He asked with concern.

Tegan shook her head. The tears mingled with the blood on her face, and for a moment she reminded Merton of a child who had sparred with a playmate.

"I have a pounding headache, thanks to one of those bastards who hit me in the back of my head with the hilt of his knife, but I'll live, which is more than I can say for them."

"How many were there?"

"Five. Someone should have told them it would take more than five men to take my head to Cerdic. They are all dead. They can do no more mischief now."

"It looks like they already have done so," Merton stated, as he reached out and touched her bruised and battered face.

"They wanted to enjoy me before they killed me. Their mistake. Do not look so concerned. I'll be fine. Don't fuss. When you get to my age, it always looks worse than it is."

"How did they find you?"

Tegan shrugged. "How do the swallows know when it is time to leave? I do not know how they found me. But tell me, what are you doing here? I wasn't expecting to see you so soon, if at all. The gods said nothing to me about you coming home."

"Perhaps they wanted to surprise you," Merton offered the suggestion and smiled at the look on Tegan's face as she thought on it.

"You are a wild one, Merton du Lac," she chuckled softly. "I think that even the gods cannot keep up with you. Something has happened, hasn't it? You…" she took a step away from him and stared into his eyes. "There is something different about you. You have the same light in your eyes as the righteous Brother Sampson does. And you were reluctant to kill that man back there. I saw you hesitate. You fool. I told you to stay clear of him. Brother Sampson is—"

"Tegan," Merton warned. "Sampson is my friend. I will not hear a word against him. He is a good man."

"Yes, I am sure to you he is. Nevertheless, I will tell you this. I have met many so-called good men who preached on high about the one true God. And not one of them have I ever called a friend. Be careful, men of God are rarely who they pretend to be. But that is not all. There is something else about you that looks different."

"I am sober," Merton jested. "I have been missing your mead."

"I told you, you would. But that is not it either. That woman. The one I saw fall from her horse. What is she to you?"

"My life," Merton returned. "My reason for living."

"Your life?" Tegan looked back at the dead man. "And I thought you were your father's son," there was a disappointment in her voice. "He grieved for Guinevere all of his life, just as I grieved for him. I thought you would do the same for Amandine. But who am I to judge a man's character? I am happy that you have found love again. Who is she then, this new love of yours?"

"The same as the old one. Her name is Amandine," Merton replied softly. "It turns out that I am my father's son after all."

"She isn't dead?" Tegan asked with wide eyes that no longer cried, and a growing grin. "She was alive all along?"

Merton smiled and nodded, but the smile fell from his face as Tegan continued to look at him.

"She has changed," Tegan guessed. "She is not the woman you knew. Something has happened to her. Something bad. And you have brought her to me so that I can help her."

"Yes," Merton always marvelled at Tegan's insight. Sometimes it was as if she could read his mind. "She was tortured because she dared to love me. They were going to burn her at the stake. They accused her of demon worship."

"And you wonder why I do not trust those who preach for your Christian God. She is resentful towards you because of this, isn't she?"

"No," Merton frowned. "Yes. A little maybe. But that is not my concern. She is scared of shadows. She is fearful of everyone, except for me and Tanick. She even struggled to be in Alden's company, and she has known him all her life. I think she is terrified of even the thought of meeting you. God knows what she is feeling right now." He shouldn't be here, wasting time talking to Tegan. Amandine needed him. His son, needed him. "I have to go and find them." Merton did not wait for Tegan to say anymore. Instead, he began to walk back the way he had come, but now that the danger had passed, the pain became so unbearable that he felt a tear slip down his cheek. Damn his useless body. Why could he not be like everybody else?

"The only place you are going to is your bed," Tegan said as she grabbed his arm and placed it over her shoulder.

Merton wanted to protest, but what was the point? Tegan was right. His body was failing him yet again.

"Lean on me, boy. Let me get you home, and then I will go and fetch your Amandine to you. Where did you tell them to go?"

"The Standing Stones. But... You will scare her. She does not know the Cerniw tongue. I have to go."

"I was betrothed to your father," Tegan reminded him. "I have not spoken Breton in a long time, but I am sure I will be able to get by. Let's go home. You can have your tonic. I can change my clothes and then we will see."

"I missed you," Merton stated with a tired sigh. "I missed your kindness and compassion."

"I missed your wit and your nonsense. Now stop all this blabbering. Oh, Lowen, there you are," Tegan stated as she noticed her cat.

Merton raised his head and stared at the feline who was balancing on a tree branch.

"Come down from there and see who I have found. It is your old friend, Galahad." The cat meowed as if replying and leapt from the branch to the woodland floor. He immediately tried to curl himself around Tegan's legs.

"I am Galahad to the cat but Merton to you?" Merton asked with a hint of humour.

"No," Tegan disagreed. "You mean so much more to me than a name. So much more... Shh," Tegan stopped walking and cocked her head to one side, much like a dog does when listening to something important.

"What is it?" Merton asked quietly, for he was used to Tegan's strange ways and he knew she saw things that other people did not. "What do you hear?"

"The winds are stirring over Dozmary Pool," she raised her hand towards the sky with her palm outstretched and caught a solitary raindrop. Tegan lowered her hand and looked down at her palm where the drop of water still lay. "A storm is coming," she muttered. "The Gods have spoken."

"What kind of storm?"

Tegan continued to stare at her hand as if seeing a raindrop was something strange, unique.

"Tegan. What kind of storm? Tegan... Answer me."

"The kind that destroys everything. We must hurry. There isn't much time."

Chapter 25

The Kingdom of Wessex

"So tell me this," David said as he led them into a large lush meadow. Wildflowers stood tall, and their proud heads were turned towards the sun as she warmed the earth with a relentless heat. Butterflies, newly emerged from their cocoons, flitted and floated in the air as they hunted to quench their insatiable thirst, before finding somewhere to mate and lay their eggs. "What happens if you do not find your knights?"

Alan said nothing. Instead, he raised the wineskin to his mouth, quenching his dry throat, before handing the wineskin to Bernice. It was too hot for all this roaming around the countryside, and David's question did nothing to improve his mood. He could feel sweat trickling down his back, which made his tunic sticky and uncomfortable. Alan dreaded to think how Bernice was fairing, as she still hid her features under her hood, just in case someone saw the truth.

Despite David's skeletal appearance that suggested death, there did not seem to be that much wrong with him. Well, nothing that a good bath could not wash away.

"This man you are taking us to see. Who is he?" Alan asked instead.

David seemed unperturbed by the heat and the flies that seemed as attracted to him as they were to a hog sitting in filth. "He is known as Pert. Although, he sometimes forgets to answer to that name, even after all of these years."

"I am not interested in the name he goes by now. What is his real name?"

"You will have to ask him that," David stated. He cleared his throat and spat out some thick green phlegm.

Alan felt his stomach turn. The smell coming from David was hard enough to tolerate let alone his disgusting habits.

"And he was one of Arthur's—"

"Knights?" David chuckled. "Pert, a knight? Whatever next? Pert, a king? No. He was no knight. Nothing that fancy. Kitchen boy, that was what he was."

"Why would a kitchen boy know where *Ochain* sleeps?"

"Strange creatures, kitchen boys, that is all I know. Pert lives on T'other Side Of The Hill. We still got quite a road ahead of us. As luck would have it, I know a short-cut. We should be there by supper."

"Why did you not say it was so far? We hid our horses just outside of Hordon." Alan said, barely containing his rage. They could have been there by now if they had taken the horses.

"I'd forget about them if I were you. You won't be seeing your horses again anytime soon. I don't care how well you hid them — they will be found. Cynric has a nose for horseflesh, and he also likes to hunt. Does it every day when he is home. He is bound to come across them. There's a stream up ahead," David said, changing the subject. "We can rest for a bit if you want. I know I could do with a rest. I am not as young as I once was."

"I am sorry we have put you to so much trouble. If you would rather tell us in which direction to travel and the name of the village that Pert lives in, then I am sure we could find it ourselves," Bernice said, although Alan guessed it wasn't from compassion that Bernice spoke these words, but from a desperate desire to be away from the stench.

"I told you I will take you to Pert and I will. And as for the name of the village, I have already told you. Were you not listening? It is called, T'other Side Of The Hill."

"The village is called T'other Side Of The Hill?" Alan asked, failing to keep the disbelief from his voice.

"Yes, on account of it being on *t'other side* of the hill. We need to travel this way for a little while, and then we come to a rather steep hill. Once we have climbed that, you will be able to see *t'other side*. And then you will understand."

"Surely they could have come up with a better name for their village?" Bernice dared to muse.

"Why? There is nothing wrong with the name? It seems like common sense to me. The village is on *t'other side* of the hill."

***

They stopped to quench their thirst at a small stream. The water here was cold and refreshing. Alan scooped up the water in his palms and splashed it onto his face and the back of his neck. Bernice kicked off her shoes and pulled up her trousers as best she could so she could paddle in the shallows. Alan watched as she limped towards the stream.

"Are you all right?" Alan asked with concern. He mentally kicked himself for not paying closer attention to her needs.

"A couple of blisters," Bernice replied tiredly. "Do not worry. I'll live."

"You will have a few more blisters by the end of the day," David replied cheerfully.

Alan glared at him. He did not like the way David was looking at Bernice. He looked like a predator eyeing an easy meal. He would have to keep a very close eye on this slave of Cerdic's.

They did not stay long at the stream for Alan was keen to press on. He helped Bernice to dress her feet to stop the blisters rubbing even though she protested and said she could do it herself.

"I am fine," Bernice reassured with amusement as Alan helped her to her feet.

"Are you sure?" Alan asked with concern.

She reached up and touched his face. "Yes. Now come on. I am looking forward to seeing this village on *t'other side* of the hill."

Alan was glad she could still jest about such things. He, on the other hand, was finding it difficult to return her smile. He felt uneasy. He feared there was a danger, not yet obvious. Alan could not help but wonder at David's eagerness to help them. But perhaps he was reading too much into it. Alan forced himself to smile, and he held out his hand for Bernice to take.

***

"There," David pointed with triumph as he reached the summit of the steep incline they had been navigating for the last hour. "There she is. T'other Side Of The Hill. I told you."

The sun had begun its evening descent, staining the sky a vivid red, which meant the shepherds would be pleased. But Alan was too tired to marvel at the sun's beauty.

"It is so far," Bernice said with disappointment as she looked to where David pointed. The land dropped away before them, and the long grass bowed to the gentle breeze of the evening sky. "We will not be there before dark."

"If you walk fast, I can't see why you wouldn't be," David replied unhelpfully.

"I cannot see a village," Alan stated as he came to stand next to Bernice.

"It is there," David pointed. "Look. By that little rise, between those trees."

Alan narrowed his eyes as if that would somehow make his eyes see the village. He had never said anything to anyone, but he had always had a little trouble with seeing things in the far distance.

"It is so far away," Bernice said again.

"Then I suggest you best start walking, especially if you want to be there by supper. Unless you would rather linger here and be an easy meal for the wolves."

If Bernice could see the village, then the village was there. Alan shared a look of frustration with Bernice, although there was no way she would understand his meaning.

"Shall we?" Alan asked.

Bernice nodded and together they began to make their way down the hill.

"Are you coming?" Alan turned to look at David when he realised David was not following them.

"I am afraid not. This is as far as I can take you."

"What do you mean?" Alan asked, feeling cold dread travel down his spine. He could not help but wonder if David had betrayed them. Were there soldiers hidden amongst the grass waiting for the signal to slit their throats?

"I am a slave, in case you forgot. I do not have free run of the kingdom. If I am caught any further than here, then I will be beaten. And I would rather die in my bed with a drink in my hand than by a fist in my face."

"You have brought us to the middle of nowhere, and now you intend to leave us? There is no Pert, is there?" Alan made the question sound like a statement. He retraced his steps until he was once again standing in front of their disgusting guide. If they were to die, then he would make sure David did as well. Alan sensed Bernice was close on his heels. Perhaps she was thinking the same thing.

"This is all just a game to you," Alan stated.

"Believe me, it is no game," David replied with a passion that surprised Alan. "You don't understand, do you? You don't get it. The story that one day Arthur and his knights will ride again is the only hope that many of us have. How would you like to be a slave in your own country? How would you like to serve the man whose men raped your mother and murdered your brothers? When Cerdic and his brother came, they burned everything. They took everything. And now here you are, saying that you are the Keeper of the Blade and that all the stories are true. But you are a liar. You deal in false hopes and broken promises.

"Keep walking, and you will eventually come to a village. And that village is called T'other Side Of The Hill. I have not led you astray. From there you must travel south and eventually you will find yourself back in Dumnonia. I suggest you carry on walking and don't stop until your feet are firmly planted in Cerniw soil. We do not want you and your prophecies, here. You are nothing but a torment with your demands," David shook his head in disgust. "Take me to the graveyard, you said. So I did, and it wasn't good enough. And then you demand I take you to Pert. You talk of Percival and the knights, but you have no idea what you are talking about. You do not understand what you ask for because you were not there. I will not help you unite the knights of Arthur," David pulled an ugly-looking knife from his belt. He held it out in front of him with a hand that did not tremble. "Such unity would bring nothing but more blood and more death. You have no idea the destruction such a thing could cause. I will kill you now and throw away your sacred blade," David shook his head as he spoke. "I will not allow you to wake a sleeping dragon."

"Mordred Pendragon is alive," Alan stated, reining in his own temper with the hope that the truth would make David see sense. He looked at the knife in David's hands. It would not take much to disarm him, but he would rather talk his way out of this one, for Alan found no pleasure in killing.

"This is a good thing, and yet you make it sound like I should fear him? Why?" David asked. "Mordred is Arthur's son. His heir."

"Mordred will bring his army over the sea and kill us all. He will not differentiate between who is Saxon and who is Briton. He is a murderer. He is a monster. And he must be stopped."

David began to laugh, the sound not unlike the cackle of the insane. "What do you know of monsters? I had just witnessed my thirteenth summer when the Saxons came. My father was Lancelot du Lac's groom brought over from Brittany. My childhood, until then, had been a happy one. Mordred used to come to the village when he and I were boys, and..." David breathed out unsteadily. "He and I... We were friends. Mordred was my friend. My secret friend, for the King, or my father for that matter, would never have allowed a friendship between us — I was nothing but a groom's son, whereas Mordred was the heir to a vast kingdom. He was also older than me, by almost six years. But we did not allow such trivial things to get in the way of our friendship.

"I know what you think you know about Mordred. But Mordred isn't who you think he is. His reputation was blackened by a Queen who hated him. The Queen, a woman who was supposed to act like his mother, spread terrible rumours about Mordred. She said he was evil," David shook his head in denial. "He was not evil. She lied. She was the evil one. She was a witch. An adulteress. She fooled them all. Including Lancelot. Guinevere," he said her name with disgust, "blackened Mordred's name to such an extent that he ended up being blamed for things he never did. If something went wrong, if something went missing — it was Mordred's fault. She set out to destroy Mordred from the very beginning. From his very first breath, she made Mordred's life a living hell. One terrible day one of Arthur's knights murdered a friend of my father's and raped his daughter. Without any proof, Guinevere cast her evil gaze on Mordred. Arthur had reluctantly asked Mordred where he was when this terrible incident happened. Mordred refused to answer, which Guinevere took as an admission of guilt. But the truth is, Mordred did not tell his father where he was because he was with me. Mordred was convinced that if our friendship were discovered, then I would come upon an unfortunate incident. It had happened to others, you see. Many Lords consider their subjects as nothing better than dogs on a string. We are slaves without the title. Freemen without the freedom. They think we cannot think for ourselves. They think we cannot see how it really is. But we think, and we see, and we know. Arthur, for all his greatness, was the same as all the other Lords of that time. I would not have been a suitable friend for his son, and he would have taken permanent measures to prevent Mordred and me from meeting. Mordred was protecting me. And by doing so, Mordred was condemned for something he did not do. Arthur, thankfully, was not so easily convinced of Mordred's guilt. But Guinevere was nothing if not persistent. In the end, Arthur gave into her demands, and Mordred was sent away to a monastery in Rome. Guinevere ruined Mordred's life. She ruined my life. She ruined Arthur's. And dare I say it — she even ruined Lancelot's. That was the kind of woman she was. Pretty to look at I suppose, but then so is an adder.

"When Mordred returned, many years later, he did not seek me out. I would watch him from afar and wonder if he had forgotten about me. I eventually came to the conclusion that he had. And so life went on — until the day the Saxon's came. While Guinevere ran away to a convent, the rest of us stood and fought for our King, our homes, our supposed freedom, and our very lives. Guinevere will burn in hell, not only for deserting her kingdom in its greatest time of need, but also because of what she did to Mordred. But there is a happy ending to this story. Mordred found her. And he had his revenge. He killed her. Slit her throat from ear to ear. Good riddance — that is what I say," David's voice was full of bitterness and venom.

Beside him, Bernice stiffened, and a small gasp escaped her as they both recalled that terrible day when God had turned a blind eye as the priory burned.

"I thought Guinevere died many years ago," Alan lied. He did not know what to make of David's story. Was this just the ramblings of a drunk? A lie, perhaps, that David had repeated to himself over and over again until he believed it. Or, maybe it wasn't a lie. Maybe David was honest in his recollection. If so, this story made for a very uncomfortable truth. If Mordred wasn't the enemy, then who was?

Could it possibly be Guinevere? No. Alan immediately dismissed the idea. Guinevere was nothing like the monster David had portrayed her to be. She was kind and gentle. Nice.

"That is what you were meant to think. She was very much like Satan — always in the shadows. Always watching. She was evil. The Devil's woman. Mordred found her, hiding in the priory at Holywell. He burned the priory and killed anyone who dared to defend her."

"How do you know this?" Alan asked cautiously as he silently reached for his own knife. No matter what the truth was, he could see the glint of murder in David's eyes, and he realised that David would not be telling them any of this if he did not intend to silence them after.

"It is common knowledge. It is the talk of the barracks," David stated. "Now be on your way, or I will run you through. Don't think that I will not. I have killed many times before."

"I am offering you, and everyone in this kingdom, freedom," Alan tried one more time. "When the knights are reunited, then we will liberate this kingdom. We will liberate Briton."

"Freedom is a very fine idea. But none of us are ever truly free. But let us be honest with each other, to win freedom for the people is not why you want to reunite the knights. You betrayed yourself, Keeper of the Blade. You want to use them to murder Mordred. *That* I will not allow. My father was the groom for Lancelot du Lac's horses, which meant he was under Lancelot's protection. But where was Lancelot when the Saxons came? Where was he when they raped my mother and killed my brothers? Where was he when they tried to kill me?" David snarled. "I will tell you where he was. He was hiding in Brittany, like the coward he was and instead of fighting for our great country he was whoring with his cousin."

"Hold your tongue, or you will lose it," Alan warned. He would not stand here and listen to such lies.

But David ignored the warning. "It was Mordred who saved my life. He killed the bastard who was trying to kill me. And he saved my father. When something like that happens then, loyalties change. My family was always for the du Lacs but not after that. Mordred left Wessex that very night. He could not stay, not if he wanted to live. I thought I would never see him again."

"But he came back," Alan guessed.

"Yes. Mordred returned to Wessex, and he demanded an audience with Cerdic. Mordred conducted himself with honour and humility, but Cerdic threw him into the dungeon as if he were nothing better than a river rat. But Mordred is no river rat. He was a prince and the rightful King of Briton.

"Cerdic planned to do unspeakable things to Mordred. I heard him boasting about it. I would not let that happen. It was so easy. I am no one. I am nothing. A slave, a loyal servant beyond suspicion. I rescued him. Me," David smiled in triumph as he remembered and his eyes lit up with crazed excitement. "And then I stole some money and hid it in the barracks. Cerdic thought that Mordred had bribed the dungeon guards, and he had them executed slowly as punishment," he chuckled softly. "What a boon that was for me. Mordred asked me to come with him. He couldn't bear the thought of me staying here. But my father was very ill. I could not abandon him. I also thought I could better serve Mordred in Wessex. He wanted Cerdic's cooperation. I could help him win that."

Alan could not believe what he was hearing, but at the same time, it made a terrible twisted sort of sense. "How did you help him? What did you do?" Alan asked as he hid his blade behind his back so David would not see.

"I was angry. I wanted Cerdic to suffer. I wanted him to take notice. So, I lit fires. Burnt villages. But that wasn't enough. I had to become something I never planned to be. I had to kill. And to my disgust I discovered that I liked killing. I liked the power. I couldn't stop. Mordred was blamed although no one knew who he was then. But it wasn't him that carried out such atrocities. It was me. It was always me.

"When Mordred found out what I was doing, he beseeched me to stop. He said that wasn't who I was. But I couldn't stop. I wouldn't. Not even for him. I enjoyed it too much," David's eyes were shining with tears at the memory. "Mordred was angry with me for a time, but that did not last. I was useful to him. I slaved my life away in the stables. I knew when Cerdic was going hunting. It was so easy. I handed Cerdic to Mordred on a platter. Mordred ambushed and captured him. He took Cerdic somewhere quiet and convinced him that it would be in his best interest if they worked together. Cerdic agreed. And now we find ourselves here."

"If all that you say is true then you are nothing but a murderer and a traitor," Alan accused.

"A murderer, yes. A traitor, no. I am a loyal subject to the true King of Briton," David spat. "I am not a traitor. But I have not finished my story. Why do you think Cerdic invaded Cerniw?" David asked with a mocking sneer. "The du Lacs and their supporters are so foolish. Mordred told Cerdic to invade. Cerdic protested, he had just signed a treaty of peace with Alden, but he had no choice. I laughed that day. After that, Cerdic was told to march on Sussex. How I hated Gaheris and everything he stood for. Gaheris betrayed Arthur — I bet you didn't know that. He changed sides during the Battle of Benwick. And that is why the du Lacs won. His brother, Gawain, would not have done such a thing. But by then he was also dead, Tristan had murdered him and blamed it on the Saxons. But I, like Mordred, knew the truth. Arthur would have killed Lancelot if it were not for Gaheris. Gaheris changed his name to Natanleod, and then later was crowned King of Sussex, but we all knew who he really was. If you ask me Gaheris deserved everything he got — him, and his five thousand men. He was no match for Mordred and me. I can tell you this for nothing. Revenge has a delightful taste. A little like honey. Mordred was so pleased with me. So gentle." A far away look came into David's eyes. "I do not understand why men seek women for companionship, but then they have not tasted Mordred Pendragon's lips," David said this last sentence as if he were talking to himself. "He, and I, we will be victorious. He will be king. I will be his trusted advisor. His loyal subject. His lover." David smiled to himself.

"You and Mordred are lovers? In your dreams, perhaps," Alan began to laugh, even though he was shocked by such a confession. It seemed so preposterous. So ridiculous. He knew that some men preferred the company of other men and as far as he was concerned that was their business and nothing to do with him. However, the idea that Mordred would share himself with such a disgustingly vile creature as the one that was standing before him... No. Impossible. Not even Mordred would stoop that low.

"He loves me," David stated in the face of Alan's amusement. "Shut up, or I will cut you from your gullet to your groin."

"He doesn't love you," Alan replied, intending to taunt and provoke. He wasn't scared of David. He had met his type before. They preyed on the weak, but Alan was anything but weak. "He has slept with half the servants in Philippe's court. Every night a different woman warms his bed."

"You are lying," David shouted, his spit flying everywhere. "Mordred has no other lover, only me."

"Look at the state of you," Alan continued to mock. "You stink to high heaven. Why would Mordred be interested in someone like you? All I can think was that he was using you. Look at the facts, man. He left you behind. He escaped the Saxons — why did he not take you with him?" As Alan continued to speak, he gently but firmly pushed Bernice behind him while keeping his eyes fixed on David's face. "He does not care for you as you care for him. I doubt he even remembers your name. If he is victorious, I can promise you this... He will not look to you for advice, and he certainly will not allow you to warm his bed."

"You know nothing of our love. It was my choice to stay," David snapped back.

"You betrayed the du Lacs. You betrayed your King. You betrayed your own people, and you betrayed yourself. You disgust me," Alan stated in no uncertain terms.

"The du Lacs betrayed me. Why should I stay loyal to them?" David screamed. His rage burned as brightly as a forest fire. "I watched when Cerdic ordered Alden's skin to be taken from his back. I watched the lashing. And my heart cried with joy at such a sight. So many have died because of the du Lacs. So, so many. More than can be counted. That family is like a plague. They bring death wherever they go."

"You lied to us. You did not drink to drown your sorrows, did you?"

"I drank to celebrate. And then that bastard escaped. And I found him and that bitch in the old tunnel under the stables. I didn't know what to do. I panicked. So I left them there and went and awoke Bors up from his slumber and told him that Alden du Lac was here and we could finally have our revenge. Bors was in on it too you see, a loyal subject of Arthur's and therefore a loyal subject of Mordred's. I had such plans for Alden. I wanted to do to him what his father allowed the Saxons to do to my mother. I was ready to humiliate him. And what better way to do that than through rape. But Bors, he wanted to play the game differently and who was I to argue with someone like him? So I helped Alden escape, and I sat on the knowledge for many days until I could not stand it anymore. I told

Cerdic where Alden and his bitch of a daughter were hiding."

"So you betrayed Bors too?"

"What care I for Bors? He showed his true colours. Anyone who sides with the du Lac's deserves death. But I was too late. Bors helped Alden escape that very day. Cerdic made such a pathetic attempt at hunting them down that it was obvious that he did not want them caught."

"And let me guess, you went running to Mordred and told all."

"I am bored with this conversation now," David stated. "I have told you everything I know. It does not matter if you believe me. I do not care. Take a good long look at the sun, *Keeper of the Blade,* for you will not see her again in this life."

Chapter 26

Alan was ready for this. He had been expecting it. But as David rushed towards him, an arrow came from nowhere. David toppled forward, a shaft with black feathers protruding from his back.

"Get down, get down," Alan yelled with panic as he pulled Bernice down to the ground. He had been right — this was an ambush. There was no shelter here. Nowhere to hide. Alan wrapped his arm around Bernice, using his body as a shield against this unknown enemy.

Alan heard the sound of grass being flattened underfoot as this unknown assailant came ever closer. Alan held tight to the blade in his hand and willed himself not to panic. He wasn't dead yet. He silently vowed he would defend Bernice with his very last breath.

When the footsteps stopped, he risked a glance up as he prepared himself to fight for their lives.

What he saw surprised him. The man in front of him had a youthful face, although at some point his nose had been broken. His hair was long and blonde, and it fell to his shoulders in soft waves. In age, Alan guessed he was in his early thirties. His eyes were of the deepest blue, and they, like Merton du Lac's, saw everything.

"Who are you?" the man asked with a drawn bow as he crept ever closer.

This man was a warrior. Alan could see it in the way he held himself. By the way he held his bow. Cautiously, Alan rose to his feet.

"I do not speak Saxon," Alan replied in Latin.

"The knife," the warrior demanded, switching languages as if it was an everyday occurrence. He glanced briefly at the knife Alan still held.

Alan let the knife slip from his fingers. What use was a knife against an arrow? And at such close range, there was no way the warrior could miss.

"Who are you?" the warrior asked, drawing back on his bow.

"I am the Keeper of the Blade," Alan dared to reply. Such an answer would either spare their lives or end them abruptly.

"Say that again."

"You know Latin?" Alan said instead. "What House are you from?"

"Your name," the warrior demanded.

Alan hesitated.

"Do not try me I have had a very long couple of days."

"My name is Alan, my father was the Keeper of the Blade, but he is dead. Murdered by Mordred Pendragon."

"If you are the Keeper, then show me the blade."

"You told me to drop it."

"Now I am telling you to pick it up."

Alan bent slowly, not taking his eyes off the stranger's face. He picked up Draíocht and held the blade out for the man to see. The warrior took a step closer, glancing only very briefly at the blade before he looked back into Alan's face.

"Who was your father?"

"I knew him only as Kay," Alan stated with caution.

The warrior lowered his bow, and he smiled as if in welcome, but Alan did not feel welcomed.

"My father only knew him as Kay as well," the warrior replied in a very cheerful voice.

David groaned at their feet. Not quite dead.

"Excuse me, while I put a diseased animal out of his misery," the warrior stated as he withdrew his knife. "I have wanted to do this for years. And then you and I, we will talk. For I think we may have a lot to say to each other. Umm…" the warrior turned his attention to Bernice. "You may want to look away."

"Please, I know who this is, do not listen to him. You will regret it if you do," David said through pain-clenched teeth.

"Would you like to lose your tongue before you lose your life?" the warrior asked.

"I am not afraid of you," David spat the words out bravely. "Mordred will find you, and he will kill you."

"Of course he will," the warrior replied, not at all fearful at the mention of Mordred's name. He unsheathed his knife and unmercifully slit David's throat. David's mouth opened as blood pooled from it. His eyes rolled in his head, and he died right there in the long grass with the blood-red sky above him.

"By God's bones. Even his blood stinks. What a vile creature."

Bernice had not risen to her feet, but neither had she looked away. Alan glanced at her only briefly. Her face was as white as death. Her eyes were wide with terror. Alan wanted to hold her, reassure her, but now was not the time.

"You have come directly from Cerniw, right?" the warrior asked as he wiped his blade clean on the grass and returned it to his sheath. This man enjoyed killing, Alan realised. He looked like a fox that had just spent a delightful hour in amongst the chickens.

"Perhaps," Alan replied. This warrior who stood in front of him was unmerciful, which did not bode well. Alan looked about him discreetly, trying to see where the other men were, so that he would know their number.

"Perhaps?" the warrior laughed. "Do not waste your time looking for an army. It is just me. We are quite alone, I can assure you of that."

"What do you want with us?" Alan asked, while thinking *so much for discretion*. This man, whoever he was, was too observant.

"I was hunting late one evening a couple of days ago, and I came across your camp. I heard you talking about the knights and the prophecy. I have been following you ever since."

"Why?" Alan asked.

"Why do you think?"

"I am beyond the age of guessing games. You know who I am, now tell me, who are you?

"Now that depends on who is asking? If you were a Saxon, then I would say my name is Fearghus. But I do not think you are a Saxon. You are too short."

"Do you judge a man by his height?" Alan asked. His dislike for this man was growing stronger by the minute. There was something about him... Something not right.

"I judge a man's worth by many things. I have been watching and judging you."

"And what have you concluded?"

"You are impatient. You are a taker of risks. Some might call it recklessness, but I sense desperation. As to where you are from... Your accent betrays you. You pronounce your words as a Briton would, but your accent has a slight hint of Breton."

"How would you know what those in Breton sound like?"

"I once had the misfortune of knowing a man who hailed from there. I would say that you have lived in Brittany for a long time. Perhaps your father sent you to Lancelot as a page. Or maybe a squire? Yes, a squire is more likely. You favour your left hand, but you have trained yourself to use your right." The warrior glanced at Bernice, "She is your weakness. You cannot say no to her, which is why she is here."

"Enough," Alan demanded. Who was this man and how did he know these things? It was as if he was in his head reading his thoughts. "Answer my question. Who are you?"

"Take a guess."

"I don't have time for this," Alan stated with annoyance. He had had enough of this conversation. "I do not know what grievance you had with David, and quite frankly, I don't care. But you will let us pass. And you will stop following us." Alan reached for Bernice's trembling hand and pulled her to her feet. "If you continue to follow us, I will kill you."

"Such promises so late in the evening... You have wounded me, my Lord," the warrior bowed mockingly.

"Keep away from us," Alan warned. "Do not follow. Come on," he whispered to Bernice.

"I am sorry if I have offended. That was not my intention. Let us start again. My name is Percival. I believe I am the man that you are seeking. Like you, I am a Keeper. The Shield is my cross to bear." Percival bowed again, but this time he bowed as a bard would do when telling a story. It was exaggerated and ridiculous. He straightened with a smile that lit up his eyes. "Nice to meet you. And you, my Lady, it is always an honour to meet a beautiful woman. I must say, what an interesting choice of clothes you are wearing. It must be a Brittany thing." He winked playfully at Bernice although his wink was lost on her for she was in no state to respond to flirtation. "Right, well," Percival cleared his throat — for it was a novelty to be ignored by a Lady. "I suggest we spend the night in T'other Side Of The Hill. It is a humble little hamlet, but it will serve. In the morning we will head back to Cerdic's castle."

"You are not Percival," Alan wished he had kept his mouth shut. He should have played along with whatever fantasy this man was living in. Later he would no doubt blame his tiredness for his poor judgement. "Percival is dead, and even if he were alive, he would be an old man."

"I bathe in the fountain of youth. I can show you where the sacred waters are if you like. But as for you... Is that a hint of the Pendragon around your eyes?"

Beside him, Bernice stiffened, and she looked at Alan with disbelief.

"Oh dear, your woman doesn't know. Do not worry, my dear. I am sure your lover is from the sane side of the family."

"I am not a Pendragon," Alan stated coldly. If he said the lie enough, then one day he would believe it himself. "I am not a Pendragon," Alan said again, but more quietly to the woman by his side.

"Kay, I am told, used to say that as well. But he was never believed either. He and Arthur had the same eyes and the same mannerisms. Or so I am told. Tell me, how did Kay die?"

"As I have already said, he was murdered by Mordred Pendragon. Not that *that* is any of your business."

"But I would wager it wasn't Kay that Mordred was looking for, was it? I am right, aren't I? I will assume, because of the look on your face, that contrary to what this vile creature thought, Guinevere escaped. Where is she now?" Percival raised his eyebrows as he asked this question.

"I have no idea what you are talking about," Alan replied. "Now, if you will excuse us..."

"You call yourself the Keeper of the Blade, and you do not know who Guinevere is?"

"Of course I know who Guinevere is... Was," Alan quickly corrected himself.

"Mordred lived in a world of fancy. He always twisted the truth, no matter how ridiculous it sounded, to make himself the victim. For a weak-minded soul such as David here, he had no chance once Mordred had his claws in him. Mordred, I am told, could be very persuasive. I am Percival, son of Percival, whom you may have heard of. He was known for his wit and his handsome looks, two traits which I am told I have inherited. He was also a Knight of Camelot, and the Keeper of the Shield until his untimely death."

"You are not the Keeper of the Shield. And Percival died when he was four and ten. I have never heard any mention of an heir," Alan scoffed and shook his head.

"He did not die when he was four and ten. He died last year. You know I speak the truth, but you are disappointed that *I* am standing before you instead of my father. Just like I am disappointed that it is not your father who is stood before me. But, we should not think too much on fate and how she wields her sword. In my experience, war is a young man's game. Old men are slow, and they get in the way. It is always best to retire a horse before it stumbles, don't you think?"

"I think you are a fool and a liar. I demand that you leave us alone."

"A fool most definitely but a liar, no. I am who I say I am. I thought you wanted the Shield, or did I mishear you when you and the lovely lady were talking about it?"

"Yes, I want the Shield."

"Excellent. Let me tell you about her. *Ochain* is unremarkable in appearance. Quite heavy. But the stories about her are true. She does cry out in warning when an enemy is near. It is an eerie sound, much like a cat wailing. At first, I hid her in the great northern realm of Bernicia, but there may have been a little misunderstanding between myself and Æthelfrith — a charming man, usually, alas I fell out of favour. He accused me of dishonouring his wife, which I did not do. She was a willing participant in everything I did to her. It was sadly her screams of pleasure that brought the guards running in the first place. The beating I received was worth it though. She was a precious jewel indeed. I fancy I could have fallen in love with her. But now we will never know. Unfortunately, Æthelfrith demanded an apology and money for such dishonour. I had none of the latter, and I would rather have been damned than give him the former. And besides, it wasn't as if he was making love to his wife. The way I saw it…. Someone had to. Æthelfrith should have thanked me. If he had left us to it, I could have filled his Hall with beautiful children. Alas, it wasn't to be. Æthelfrith was enraged when I refused to give him, um… how shall I put it…? *Recompense*, yes, that is the word, for ploughing his wife. So instead he decided he would take my head. But I'm afraid to say I am rather attached to it and did not want to give it up."

"So you walked out of Æthelfrith's court. And brought the Shield here. A likely story," Alan did not believe a word of it. David's story was more convincing than this man's was.

"I wouldn't say walked as such. I was carried out in a coffin. Terrible experience, executions. I wouldn't recommend it as a way to go. It is not something I am planning to do again."

"You are not planning to be executed again, or are you not planning to die again?"

"Neither. Execution is messy. Death is so very tedious. I also discovered that I don't really like tiny spaces."

"So you have decided you are not going to die? You are going to live forever? Are you mad?"

"Undoubtedly so," Percival replied with a lopsided grin. "I thought long and hard about where to take *Ochain*, and I decided that there is no castle more secure than the one in Wessex. It has two moats after all. So I came home and hid *Ochain* right under Cerdic's nose. It has been there for over two years, and as of yet, he has not noticed."

"So let us for a moment pretend that I believe you," Alan said with a frown. "You propose that we walk into Cerdic's castle. Grab the Shield. And walk out again."

"You may have oversimplified it a bit, but yes, you have the right of it. We shall go tomorrow, but for now, I suggest we head to the village. Your good man was right — wolves do roam these hills. It is best not to be out after dark."

"He wasn't my good man," Alan said, casting a scathing look at David's corpse. "He was Mordred's."

"I heard what you said about Mordred. Are you sure he is alive?"

"Alive and well," Alan replied.

"Fantastic. I cannot wait to meet him."

"Mordred is my enemy," Alan stated. "The only place you will meet him is on a battlefield."

"Are you sure you are the Keeper of the Blade?" Percival asked as a guarded look came upon his good-natured face.

"Alan, please. We must get away from him," Bernice whispered desperately under her breath.

"What do you mean by that?" Alan asked, ignoring Bernice's plea.

"Nothing," Percival replied. "I meant nothing by it." He turned his attention to Bernice. "I am sorry you had to witness the death of a monster. But do not waste your time with sympathy for him. I would wager that if his mother were still alive, she would not weep upon hearing of his demise. But come, it is getting dark, and soon the wolves will start their night hunt. We need to get moving."

"We are not going anywhere with you," Alan answered.

"You would be very foolish not to. Come to the village with me and at least spend the night in comfort. If you still doubt me in the morning, then, by all means, be on your way. But I can assure you, I am the Keeper of the Shield, and you will not be united with her unless it is through me."

Chapter 27

Goon Brenn, The Kingdom of Cerniw

He was dead. He was dead. He was dead. Once again he was dead because of her. If only they had stayed at Dor. If only…
 Like a messenger of doom, a chough landed on the standing stone directly opposite the one Amandine was huddled against. The blackness of the bird's feathers was a contrast to the greyness of the stone. His bright red beak looked like he had dipped it in blood. He was a bird from the battleground, a scavenger that picked at the flesh of the dead. The chough opened his beak and called out in his raspy voice. Amandine blindly felt the ground around her for a stone, a clod of earth, anything that she could throw at the bird. She needed not to hear his message. She knew Merton was dead. Finding a small stone she threw it at the bird, but instead of taking flight he merely looked at her. His beady black eyes were all-knowing and seemingly sympathetic. He knew his message was unwanted. He knew, and yet he still delivered it.

When Merton's horse had come galloping towards them, with his head held high and his tail streaming behind him, Amandine had fallen to her knees. She had known then that she had lost him.

All that Merton had left her with was an orphaned child, a frightened horse, and now a bird. It wasn't enough. She couldn't do it. She could not live without him. Not again. The all too familiar pain of despair tore at her heart and made breathing almost impossible.

Why?

Why did he do it?

Why did he stay behind?

Such a ridiculous question, Amandine already knew why. Merton had chosen death so she and the child would live.

And with that knowledge, anger came. *How dare he.* Merton had no right to sacrifice himself without asking for her permission first. She should have known — Merton never did play fair. Amandine dropped her gaze from the chough, but she felt the bird's constant gaze on her as if he was willing her to read his mind. But even if she could, she wasn't sure the bird had anything to say that she would want to hear.

Merton's horse whinnied, the sound shrill, and it made the bird flap his wings in protest. The horse had not stopped whinnying from the moment Vernon had dared to stand in his way. The horse had reared while Vernon had bravely grabbed the reins. The horse's wide eyes and the sheen of perspiration on his coat were a testament to his terror. Vernon had tried to calm the horse, but the horse was in no mind to be soothed. Amandine wondered if the horse felt a sense of shame at leaving Merton behind. If not, then he should.

It is not the horse's fault. It is not the bird's fault. The voice of reason dared to whisper in Amandine's head, but she dismissed it immediately. Amandine knew who was to blame, and it wasn't the horse or the bird. The responsibility for Merton's death lay at her feet. *Oh, God. Oh, God. No. Say it isn't true.* She had only just got him back. This was a nightmare. She would wake up soon. She would...

The clouds overhead darkened and rain fell from the sky, but Amandine paid the weather no heed. What difference would it make to her life if it rained? Her life was over.

Beside Amandine, Tanick began to stir — perhaps because of the rain, perhaps not. The child had fallen into an uneasy sleep. Exhausted by fear and the long day's journey no doubt. Amandine envied him his sleep, and she envied him his youth. Tanick would survive Merton's death. Within months he would forget all about his father, and he would only know him through stories. Amandine, however, knew that she would spend the rest of her life feeling that the better part of her was dead. Why had he stayed behind? Why had he not followed in their wake? Why?

Vernon's dog had deemed it her responsibility to guard Merton's son. The dog whined as Tanick began to wriggle his way out of the blanket Vernon had wrapped him in. Amandine turned her head and looked down at the child through tear-filled eyes. She had to pull herself together. For Tanick's sake, if not for her own. She could not be selfish in her grief. She was a mother now, and that changed everything.

The child opened his eyes and stared at Amandine with those same grey eyes that his father had, and she felt her heart break anew. It would be an agony to watch the child grow up. To see Merton's expression and mannerisms in his son's face every day. Amandine was not sure she was strong enough for that. But what choice did she have? Merton had not left her with a choice.

"Did you have a nice sleep, little man?" Amandine asked in a broken voice as she reached for him. "Come here, my darling."

***

Tanick stared at her with sleepy eyes as she lifted him onto her lap. He reached up and touched her damp cheek with the palm of his tiny hand. He frowned ever so slightly, not understanding the significance of his new mother's tears. But already, in his little life, he understood the significance of a smile. So that is what he did. He used the only weapon at his disposal. He smiled and hoped that his smile would be returned. But when it wasn't, he frowned again. He understood that something had happened, but he didn't understand what. His bottom lip began to tremble because he could feel the sadness, and the grief, and the despair. He just didn't know what it meant.

"Do not cry," Amandine begged softly as she cradled the child to her chest. "Please don't cry."

But Tanick could not help it. His eyes filled with tears and when he dared to look up into his mother's face again, he knew that something was terribly wrong. He wanted his father. His father would know what was wrong. He would make it better. Where was he? Why wasn't he here with them? And where was Emma? He wanted Emma...

***

"We need to leave. We need to tell Alden what has happened here," Vernon spoke in Cerniw as he untethered his horse and brought it to where Amandine and the child sat.

"I don't understand," Amandine replied. She could see the frustration as well as grief in Vernon's face, and she wished she understood Cerniw.

Vernon pointed in the direction of Dor. "We need to go back to Dor. We need to tell Alden that Merton is…" Vernon looked away. He could not bring himself to say that Merton was dead.

"I am not leaving," Amandine stated, for she realised that she did not need to speak the same language as Vernon to understand his intentions. "I am not leaving," Amandine said again, more forcefully this time. "Not without him. Not without Merton. You can go to Dor if you want to, but I will not," she pointed to herself as she spoke and shook her head, hoping that her meaning would be clear even if her words were not.

"No. We cannot stay here. We do not have the provisions to spend the night on the moor. And the weather is turning," he pointed to the ever darkening sky. "You have to think of the child. You have to think of Tanick."

Amandine could read in Vernon's eyes what he wanted to do. But there was no way she was going to leave Merton's body lying on the moor for the birds to peck at and the wolves to fight over. "Here," she handed the sobbing infant to Vernon. "If you will not look for him yourself, then I will find him. Take Tanick to Dor." And with that she stood, brushed the grass from her dress, and began to walk away from him.

Vernon caught hold of her arm in a grip that was as bruising as it was unrelenting.

"No," Vernon growled at her, and he shook his head as he spoke, for he understood her intentions, even if he did not understand what she said. "No. I cannot let you go after him. It is too dangerous. We do not know who let loose at us. Chances are they are still there. Alden will come back here with his army and defeat this foe. We will find Merton. And we will bring his body home, I promise."

"Let me go," Amandine tried to tug her arm free as Vernon led her towards his horse. She knew what he intended. But she wasn't going back to Dor, not without the man she loved.

"Get on," Vernon commanded, his eyes were as cold as steel.

Amandine valiantly tried to pull her arm away from his grasp, but it was to no avail. Vernon's grip was as tight as a vice.

"For Tanick's sake, do not fight me on this." Vernon glanced at the child that he still held in his arms as he spoke. "He has lost his father, would you put him through the grief of losing a mother as well? For Tanick," he pressed. "For Tanick, Amandine. For Tanick."

He was right. What had she been thinking? Amandine's shoulders sagged, and she sighed in defeat as comprehension dawned. Vernon was right. She had to think of Tanick. She was all he had left.

Vernon cautiously let go of her arm, and this time she did not move away. All fight had gone from her now. All she had left was the infinite darkness of grief, and an ache in her heart that cried out with anguish and disbelief.

"Get on the horse," Vernon said again, but this time his voice was filled with sympathy. He was grieving too, she realised.

With arms that felt like lead, Amandine gripped hold of the pommel of the saddle and prepared to mount. But at that moment the chough began to caw. His voice was urgent. Both Vernon and Amandine turned to look at him. They watched as the chough took flight and flew in the direction of the woods.

Vernon swore softly under his breath. He passed Tanick to Amandine while at the same time he reached for his bow.

"Get down," he ordered pointing to the floor.

Amandine was, in that moment, like the standing stone. She was unable to move. All she could do was stand and watch as the bird flew towards the stranger.

Vernon aimed, but as he did so, the bird flew back towards them. The chough's caw was different from before. He wasn't trying to warn them. Not anymore. He was celebrating.

"Vernon," Amandine shouted. "No." Her feet, which only a moment ago were fixed to the earth, moved with a speed that she did not know she possessed. She grabbed hold of Vernon's arm just as he let loose. The arrow thankfully flew wide of its target.

The stranger stopped walking and looked at them. "I am a friend," the stranger called to them twice, once in Cerniw and then the other time in Breton. It was the voice of a woman.

"Tegan?" Vernon yelled back. "Are you Tegan?"

"That I am. You must be Vernon. Galahad warned me about you. He said you would more than likely let loose at me."

"Tegan?" Amandine looked at Vernon and then back at the old woman as she closed the distance between them. Tegan was just as Merton had described her, apart from the large swelling and bruising on her face.

"You must be Amandine," Tegan stated in Breton as she reached the stones. "You are as beautiful as Galahad said. Dry your tears my girl, your betrothed is not dead. I left him back at my house. He is in a lot of pain from his back, but otherwise, he is fine."

"But... But..." Amandine dared not believe it. It was an impossible dream. A conclusion to such awful events that she had never dared imagine.

"He walked through a shower of arrows and came out of it unscathed," Tegan explained. "The Gods favour him. They keep him safe."

"He's not...?" Amandine could not get the words out. Tears of happiness dared to overflow from her eyes. "He's not?"

"No," Tegan, shook her head and her eyes shone with compassion. "He is very much alive. He is worrying himself sick over you and his son," Tegan looked at the child in Amandine's arms and smiled. "But he would not have made the journey here on foot, and my horse is too old to be ridden."

"He is not dead?" Amandine had to ask again. She looked at Vernon in disbelief.

"Is Merton alive?" Vernon asked in Cerniw.

"Very much so," Tegan replied in the same language before switching back to Breton. "Now, are we going to stand here talking or would you like to be reunited with him?"

"He isn't dead?" Amandine asked again, just to make sure.

"Oh my dear child," Tegan walked right up to her and reached out and touched her face with her calloused fingers. "It would take more than a few arrows to kill Merton du Lac."

Chapter 28

The light in the roundhouse was fading as the storm began to lose a hold of its temper. Merton rose to his feet, grimacing in pain as he did so, and poked at the fire with a stick. Tegan had insisted on cleaning up the mess and preparing a stew rich with cabbage, turnips, various herbs, and several handfuls of oats, before she left to fetch Amandine and his son. Merton had never felt so frustrated in his life. But the more he tried to hurry her along, the slower her every action became. So, in the end, he had sat down in what he considered to be his chair and glowered at her.

The interior of the roundhouse momentarily shone brightly as a flash of lightning lit up the sky outside. A peal of thunder followed. With an unsteady hand, Merton lit several rushlights, and prepared himself for the smell of animal fat to fill the room. Tegan had no need for expensive beeswax candles or even tallow candles for that matter. When it was too dark to see, Tegan went to bed, and when the sun rose, she got up. Tegan was in tune with the seasons and the days. Living out here on her own meant that she did not have to comply with complicated court conventions. She lived a simple life, and it was one Merton was willing to embrace. But he wished she would bloody hurry up. The longer he was away from Amandine and Tanick the more anxious he became. He did not like to think of them out there on the moor in this weather. He wanted them here, where he could see them. Where he could hold them.

For want of something to do, he picked up the wooden ladle and stirred the stew. The oats had thickened up nicely, and the turnips were beginning to soften. He would have to keep his eye on it. The last thing he needed was a reprimand for letting the pottage burn. He banged the ladle on the edge of the cauldron to dislodge the oats that had clung to it and then put it back on the table.

Another flash of lightning lit up the house. The bright light reflected off the cauldron for just an instant, but it was enough for Merton to see the secret that it had hidden for so long. There was an engraving, it was very small, but it was there. Before Merton thought better of it, he grabbed a cloth and carefully lifted the cauldron off the hook. Doing his best not to drop the cauldron, he placed it on the nearby table. Such a simple task cost him dearly. He breathed out slowly, the way Tegan had once shown him, and waited for the pain to pass. Once the pain was again tolerable, Merton reached for a rushlight so he could take a closer look at the engraving. There were several images — an ear of corn, a harp, and a staff. Whoever had made this cauldron had left their stamp upon it. Underneath the images was an even smaller script. So small, in fact, that Merton could barely read it. He could just make out the first two words in Latin — *Be loyal*. He did not need to see the rest to know what it said. Merton scoffed softly to himself. Of course. He should have guessed.

Merton grimaced as he picked the cauldron back up. It took all of his strength to lift the cauldron back onto the hook. Once the cauldron was safely back in its proper place, Merton reached blindly for a chair. He sat down timidly and groaned softly in pain. *"It will pass,"* he whispered to himself. But in the midst of such pain such knowledge brought him only a little comfort.

The wind picked up and blew at the curtain that Tegan had hung instead of a door. The curtain had been woven with the thickest wool, but the pounding rain soon saturated it and the smell of damp sheep as well as animal fat mingled with the smell of the cabbage. It wasn't the most pleasant of combinations.

Merton reached for the mead with a hand that shook. He had not taken the tonic that Tegan had thrust into his hand before she left; it was still sat there untouched on the table. He knew what Tegan was like for adding valerian to her potions. He did not want to be asleep when Amandine arrived. He drank deep of his cup and waited for the numbing sensation in his head that would make him care a little less about the pain in his back, arm, and legs.

Lightning once again lit up the room, and seven peals of thunder rang out loud and clear across Alden's kingdom. Merton closed his eyes and breathed in deeply. He had never been the most patient of men, and he had still not got used to the idea of staying at home when there was work to be done. The bodies of the dead needed burying — they would only attract the wolves if they were left. The animals needed feeding. Wood no doubt, needed chopping. An endless list of chores and he couldn't help with any of them. Just look at what lifting a cauldron had done to him.

He opened his eyes and looked at the empty wall where Tegan's collection of weapons once hung. The wall looked like a barren landscape without the weapons. Tegan had mumbled something about their whereabouts while she chopped up the vegetables. She did not seem to be overly concerned about them.

Merton put down his cup and prepared to stand. He sat on the edge of the chair for a long moment as he called on his courage. It was not a battle with an enemy he feared anymore. It was the battle with himself that took the most out of him. Holding his breath, he made his reluctant body stand. He wobbled on his feet and if it were not for his grim determination, as well as the support of the table, he would have probably collapsed back onto the chair. Using the furniture to help him walk across the room, he made it to the doorway and drew back the curtain. The rain was easing up, and the dark clouds were moving away. The worst was over. For now, at least.

How did it come to this? Merton sighed as he pondered upon his past. He was four and twenty and yet some days he felt as if he were a hundred. With a regrettable sigh, he leant his head upon the frame where a door should have hung. If someone had told him just two years ago that this was what his life would be like he would not have believed them. He had always thought that he would die on a battlefield. He had never imagined that, instead, he would be crippled and unable to fight. He felt like a bird that had once flown to the very height of Heaven. And then one tragic day a scratchy sack had been thrown over his head. The next time he saw daylight he found himself in a golden cage. Now all he could do was look up at the sky through the gilded bars and remember. A fitting torment one might say for the Devil. Heaven would be forever out of reach now that he was in Hell. But he wasn't in Hell, he reminded himself. Not anymore.

The lamp of God burnt brightly, so his feet could see which path he should take. He smiled at the thought. God's presence may not feel as strong in Tegan's domain, but he was still here.

Merton's time as the Devil now felt as if it had happened to someone else. Tegan had once said that in one lifetime you live many lives. She was right. He was different to the man he had been and not just because of the physical. It wasn't just for Amandine's sake that he had chosen to come here. Merton did not want to go to war. He did not want to see a war. He did not want to be part of it. Was he selfish? Probably. He felt guilt at leaving Alden to face their enemies alone, but at the same time he felt relief that he would not have to deal with it. Merton glanced back at the cauldron and sighed. It seemed that trouble followed him wherever he went. Now he knew what he knew, Merton could not help but wonder if Daegel and his men had sought something far more valuable than the few coins that a head of a knight could bring them.

A horse whinnied. Tegan's old mare pricked up her ears and looked towards the direction of the call, as did Merton. He sighed with relief, and for a moment he sagged against the doorframe. He thought about going out to meet them, but then thought better of it. The rain would make the going slippery and he had no desire to fall.

"Thank you, God," he whispered as Tegan rode into the clearing on his horse. Vernon followed closely behind her with Tanick in his arms, and Amandine sat behind him.

"Merton," Amandine called his name when she saw him. She almost fell off the horse as she tried to dismount. "Merton," she called his name again and then she was running across the muddy ground that separated them. Amandine threw herself at him, her hands wrapping around his neck. He stumbled back several steps before he found his balance again, but right now he wouldn't have cared if they had tumbled to the floor. She was safe. Tanick was safe. That was all that mattered.

"Thank you, God," he whispered under his breath again. And he meant it. He meant every word. It wasn't just something to say in the heat of the moment. The words had a meaning he had never before explored. God was here. God was protecting them.

"I thought you were dead," Amandine gasped, tears spilling down her cheeks as she said the words.

"I thought I was dead too," Merton jested, pulling back a little so he could look into her face. "Are you hurt at all? Is Tanick?" he looked towards his son who Vernon was in the process of passing to Tegan. The child seemed to find something incredibly amusing about Tegan's face for his laughter rang out like a celebration in this sacred part of the woods.

"No. No, we are both fine. Shaken and a little wet, but…" and then she was kissing him. She was kissing him as if this kiss would be their last and although he shared her desperation, he did not like the image that her frantic kiss portrayed. This wasn't their last kiss. It was the first of many. He clung to that thought as he closed his eyes and for a brief moment lost himself in her.

***

As gently as he could, he rolled Amandine over so her head lay on her pillow instead of his shoulder. The soft glow of the fire was the only light in the house. He could not see her clearly, but he could hear her quiet breathing and inhale her unique scent. Merton smiled into the darkness. He gently smoothed back a wayward strand of hair from her cheek and replaced it with his kiss. His touch did nothing to rouse her. He immediately suspected Tegan had put something in Amandine's drink so that the terrors of the day would not disturb her sleep. He was thankful to Tegan for that. Amandine needed her sleep. Unfortunately, Merton had not taken his tonic, so those same terrors disturbed his. *If she had died. If an arrow had…* No. He would not think of it. *What ifs* had no place in God's Kingdom.

Merton moved back the furs, trying not to make a sound as the ever-present pain burned his muscles and pulled at his skin. He had a persistent pain in his chest ever since the first arrow had struck the earth in front of his horse. He had not said anything to anyone — he figured that if the pain was anything to worry about he would be dead by now. Why worry the people he loved unnecessarily?

Merton closed his eyes briefly as he prepared to stand. When he did so, the pain became almost unbearable. He needed to take Tegan's tonic. His body craved it. But he wanted to wait just a little longer.

Tegan had made a bed up for Tanick out of some rolled up blankets and a sheepskin rug. Vernon's dog was curled up next to him, with one ear cocked as if listening for trouble. The child was safe, no mice or rats would come near him while the dog stood guard. Lowen was sat on the table, glaring at the dog with a look of utter contempt. His tail flicked from side to side, and his eyes did not waver from the dog. Lowen was not so welcoming of his mistresses latest houseguest.

Stepping around Vernon, who was sprawled by the fire, Merton used the furniture to keep his balance. Thankfully, Tegan had placed his walking stick on the table. Merton picked it up and leant heavily upon it. He pushed the curtain aside with his stick and ventured outside.

There was a chill in the air, but at least the summer rain had stopped. The orange glow of the fire drew his attention. Tegan was sat with her shoulders slumped as she looked into the flames. Merton was concerned for her. She had said very little in the past few hours. Merton had thought that it was merely exhaustion that was curbing her tongue. But if that were so then why was she out here? Why wasn't she asleep?

He walked unsteadily towards her. Even with the stick he was not so sure on his feet. Tegan did not look up as he approached although he knew she felt his presence.

"Are you all right?" Merton asked cautiously as he sat down next to her on the plank of wood that she had placed across two tree stumps to make a poor man's bench.

In answer, she reached across and placed her hand on his knee. They stayed like that while the moon rose ever higher in the sky. Merton understood the need for solitude and silence after a battle. But he also understood the need to be close to another. As he stared into the flames, he could not help but wonder what Tegan was thinking. She had been through a great ordeal today, and even though she once was a knight, it did not take anything away from the fact that Tegan was an old woman. She should not have to face such things at her age.

Tegan pulled her shawl more tightly around her shoulders and turned to look at him.

"You are in pain," she stated softly.

"I welcome it," Merton replied. He stared at the fire as it spat sparks of gold and white smoke up into the night air.

"You are such a liar," Tegan chuckled softly into the night. "Take your tonic, boy, and I will heat up some rocks. Then I command you to go to sleep. We have a lot to plan in the morning. I was thinking we could clear the trees from over there," she pointed into the darkness, "and build you and your family a house. It might not be as grand as your rooms at Dor, but I think it will serve."

"Thank you," Merton took her hand in his and squeezed gently. "I know how much you value your solitude."

"I do not mind sharing it with you and besides, you are family. I understand why you fell in love with her. Amandine has a good heart, I could see it as soon as I looked into her eyes."

"She does," Merton agreed. "I am afraid for her though—"

"It will take time," Tegan reassured. "She has you and Tanick," Tegan smiled when she said the child's name. "I think she will be all right. I am not saying it is going to be easy. There will be good days and bad days. I fear the bad days will be terrible. But we will face each one together, and we will help her overcome her fears. She will not be like this forever. I am sure that Amandine's confidence will one day come back, but in the meantime, I will help you look after her."

"I knew I could count on you," Merton replied. "Thank you, Tegan, for everything you have done for me and for everything you will do for her."

"Don't be daft, my boy. There is no need to thank me. And besides, when you left, it wasn't the same. I've grown used to you. I like having you around. And now I can be a grandmother to your son. He is a beautiful child, Merton. The absolute image of you."

Merton smiled as any father would when his child was complemented. "Tanick will be lucky to have a grandmother like you. And I know my father is looking down on us right now. He brought us together —"

"I do not know about that. But it is a nice thought," she glanced up through the tree canopy at the sky. "It is a cloudy night. I was hoping the stars would reveal what the future would hold…" she sighed. "It seems they are not sharing their secrets tonight."

Merton looked up at the sky. It hurt his neck to do so, but he ignored the pain. "What do you think is up there?"

"The future. The past. Everything."

"Do you think your gods know our fate?"

"Of course they know. I knew a man once who understood the

secret language of the stars. He was not one for talking though. I was quite disappointed when I met him. I thought I would learn many wonderful things from him, but alas, he liked to keep such things to himself. Some people are like that — they do not like to share."

"What happened to him?"

"He left this world for the Otherworld."

"Willingly?"

"We are all willing. The Otherworld is a better place."

"So why fight? Why defend yourself? If the Otherworld is so great—"

"Because despite the promise of the Otherworld, the people we love are in this one. This is our home. Why would we want to leave it?"

"It is the same for us Christians, but the promise of a perfect afterlife has been overshadowed by the certainty that most of us will never see it. But I have a thought that maybe Hell isn't that much different to here. Maybe *this* is Hell."

"Don't tell Brother Sampson, the shock might kill him," Tegan said with a chuckle. "On the other hand, it would be one less Christian priest."

"He is a good man, Tegan. I convinced him to disguise himself as a nun. It was his deception that meant that the woman I love is still alive."

"A nun? You got that monk to dress up as a nun?" Tegan laughed. "Only you could convince such a moral man to do something so against his nature. I wish I had been a fly on the wall when you had that conversation."

"I had a little help. The Abbot of Brittany happened to agree with me."

"You do have friends in high places, don't you?"

"I have friends in low ones too," Merton replied.

"And where do I fit in?"

"You have a place in my heart—"

"Oh, stop it," Tegan squeezed his fingers again. "I am too old to tease."

"You are never too old to be teased," Merton contradicted.

"Not by you, it seems. Do you want some mead?" Tegan asked, letting go of Merton's hand and rising abruptly. "I'll be right back."

Merton watched her leave until she was swallowed up by the

darkness. He turned back to look at the flames, and for a moment he allowed his mind to drift. His thoughts took him back to Dor and the brother he had abandoned. He prayed to God to keep Alden safe. His fingers tingled with a strange warmth as if God were listening and had heard his request.

"Here," Tegan emerged from the darkness carrying a jug of mead, two clay cups and an axe. She handed the axe to Merton and placed the cups and jug down on the woodland floor.

"My father's axe," Merton stated. The wood of the handle felt warm in his grip, and he fancied he could feel his father's hand on his own. Guiding him.

"It saved my life today, as it has done in the past. It is yours now," Tegan replied.

"Are you sure? I know what you went through to get it."

Tegan laughed at the reminder. "Lancelot would want you to have it. Take it. And may it serve you as well as it served me."

"Thank you," Merton said as he looked back down at the axe. He did not own anything that once belonged to his father. He wondered if Tegan knew how very precious such a gift was. When he looked into her face, he saw that she did.

"Tegan, I have been meaning to ask you…" he hesitated, wondering if he should bring up the cauldron. What would she say if he said he knew who she really was? Would she be angry? Would she rage? Perhaps some questions were best left unasked. "What happened to the pig?"

Tegan was busy pouring the mead. She handed him a cup and then filled her own. "He died. No idea why. But that is pigs for you. Sometimes they just do that."

"How inconsiderate," Merton replied, trying his hardest to conceal his grin.

"I was not best pleased with him. But these things happen." She took a sip of the mead. "This is just what I needed. By the gods, Merton, I ache. I may have to borrow my stick back. I forget sometimes how old I am."

"Your age does not stop you from doing what you needed to do," Merton observed. "Whereas it is not my age but my body that stops me from doing the things I want to."

"You sound bitter. I have told you before. You must not think about what you cannot do. Bitterness and regret are not good company to keep. You have so much. You should be counting your blessings not dwelling on your curses."

"Wise words, from the Keeper of the Cauldron."

Tegan stilled at his words as if he had unwittingly cast a spell to render movements impossible. Merton placed his cup down on the ground and reached for hers. She did not resist. Her fingers gave up her cup, and he placed it next to his. Merton then took her hand in his and turned her to look at him. When he looked into her eyes, he knew he had made a terrible mistake. He should have kept his peace.

It took several long moments for Tegan to come out of her self-imposed trance.

"What gave it away?" she whispered.

"I saw the inscription, and I have recently been in the company of the Keeper of the Blade."

"Do not trust a word he says. He was always a sly one." Tegan said the words with so much venom that Merton was momentarily taken back.

"Not the original Keeper, I meant his son. Kay, I believe that was the name he went by, is dead. Mordred killed him. His son, Alan, is a good man. I like him. He is searching for the knights. He means to unite them and find the ancient relics. He believes that the people will fight for us if the relics and the knights are on Alden's side."

"Do not think to bring this Alan here. He would kill me, and there would be nothing I could do to stop him."

Merton frowned at her words. "I don't understand. Why would you have to die? You are a knight chosen by Arthur to protect the ancient relic…" Merton's frown deepened when Tegan reached for her cup and downed the contents in one go. She quickly refilled her cup and would have lifted that to her mouth as well, but Merton caught her wrist. "You are the Keeper of the Cauldron, aren't you?"

"Well…"

"Tegan," Merton sighed her name when he recognised the look in her eyes. "What have you done?"

"It is a long story…"

"It always is with you. Come on," Merton encourage. "Out with it. Why is Dagda's Cauldron hanging over your hearth?"

"It began with a challenge—"

"Not another wrestling match, I hope," Merton teased.

Tegan chuckled at the reminder. "No, No. This time it was

supposed to be a fight to the death," she laughed softly. "But when I discovered my opponent was death, what hope did I have? And yet, I could not let him have it. I am sorry, Merton, but I am suddenly feeling quite fatigued. I think I will go to bed now." Without another word, Tegan rose and slowly made her way back to the house.

Merton remained where he was. Tegan had piqued his curiosity, but she was right. The hour was late, and tomorrow would be a busy day, for they would begin work on his family's new home. Tegan would no doubt elaborate on her tale in her own good time.

Chapter 29

Trevena. The Kingdom of Cerniw

In his heart, he knew he should stay. It was what God wanted. Brother Sampson was sure of that if nothing else. But he also felt obliged to return to the monastery. Although he dreaded what would greet him when he returned. Pride, greed, lust, envy, gluttony, wrath, and sloth — all were resident evils at Caldey.

It had not always been this way. As a child, the monastery had been Sampson's home, his place of sanctuary. But questionable leadership meant that the reputation of the monastery had taken a decidedly downhill turn.

Sampson had tried his best to make a difference. He had tried to reason with the monks, but they refused to listen. They had mocked him for his piety and jeered him when he had attempted to bring order to the chaos. It had been very frustrating.

Sampson understood that the problem with sin was that it was more tempting than virtue. The monks could not see the error of their ways because they did not think what they did was wrong. Sampson did not know how to reason with such men.

Temptation was everywhere, and the Devil preyed on weak minds. Unfortunately, there was more than one weak mind at Caldey. Sampson sometimes wondered what would happen if Jesus miraculously presented himself to the monks. Would they hide in terror? Fall on their knees in worship? Probably not. They would more than likely put a goblet of mead in the Son of God's hand and beckon him to make merry. Oh, the shame. Was it any wonder that he had no desire to return?

Sampson's horse rudely pulled the reins out of his hands and stretched out his long neck so he could graze on the cliff top grass. Instead of reprimanding the horse, Sampson leant forward and gave him an absentminded pat. The horse, feeling encouraged, took a few steps forward and continued to graze. Sampson let go of the reins altogether and rubbed his hands over his eyes. As he did so, a cold sensation travel down his spine. The Devil was close. Sampson could feel his menace in the air. Sampson's horse must have felt it too, for he snorted and began to paw at the dry earth with his front hoof. Sampson took up the reins and looked behind him, but there was no one there. No one from this realm, anyway.

Sampson muttered a prayer for protection under his breath, and he nudged his horse on with his heels. The horse's ears flicked forward and backwards, for he heard more than the wind and the birds above and around them.

"Courage," Sampson whispered to his mount. But the horse knew nothing of courage, and he shied at the flowers while he chomped nervously on his bit.

"Be calm, my friend. I am here. I will protect you," Sampson spoke quietly as he placed a calming hand on the horse's neck. The horse was instantly soothed, and he stood still and placid while waiting Sampson's next command.

An arrow whizzed unexpectedly overhead. Sampson was startled although the horse was not. To Sampson's amazement, the arrow vanished into thin air, much like a ghost. The arrow had come from Sampson's left, but he did not understand how it could have. Left would have placed the bowman at the edge of the cliff, but there was no one there. This was a vision, Sampson was sure of it. It was a sign from God. But what did this sign mean? What was God trying to tell him?

"Galahad," Sampson muttered the name with an edge of fear as he interpreted the vision. Had something happened to his dear friend? He closed his eyes and prayed, for what else could he do? He prayed to God to keep Galahad safe. Oh, how he prayed. Galahad was the only real friend outside of the Church that Sampson had ever had. He might not always agree with him. But he loved him.

Sampson muttered a pleading "Amen" and opened his eyes. He

would trust God to keep Galahad safe. He had no reason to doubt God because something had happened on the journey back from Brittany. It was like a burning fire inside of him. God was sharing things with him. Showing him things that most men never dreamed of. He could see Satan's army. He could see God's angels. He could see it all.

Sampson waited for the warmth that often accompanied such prayers. He did not have to wait very long. Holy peace fell upon him. Such peace banished all fear. For fear did not have a place in God's kingdom. Whatever trial Galahad faced today, he would be victorious. For God would protect him, Sampson was sure of that.

Sampson cast his worries to God and looked at the road he had still yet to travel.

"No one who puts a hand to the plough and looks back is fit for service in the kingdom of God," he stated with a frown on his brow. If that were true, then why was he going back to Caldey? His future was here, in Cerniw. Elisha slaughtered his oxen and never looked back, so why should he? Sampson wanted to go out into the world and bring the gospel to all of God's children. How could he do that if he were stuck in a monastery for the rest of his life? Jesus did not sit in a temple and wait for the believers to come to him. Jesus went out into the world and found the lost sheep. Sampson wanted to be like Jesus more than anything else. He wanted to bring hope to the hopeless. Freedom to those whose freedom had been oppressed. Justice to those who had been wrongly accused. Salvation to those who needed it the most. He wanted to show the world God's power, his beauty, and his mercy.

With a heavy heart, Sampson nudged his horse on with his heels. He was duty bound to the monastery, at least until a new Abbot had been appointed. Patience was what he needed. A farmer did not harry his crop along. He did not berate the seedlings for not growing fast enough. The farmer had to wait for the early, and the late rains — every man who tilled the soil knew this. The crops were ready when they were ready. And it wasn't as if God's children were going anywhere. They would still be waiting for God's truth in the days that followed this one. God had patience and so must he. And besides, it was a long way to Caldey. Anything could happen between here and there.

The first drops of rain fell from a darkening sky. Sampson hastily pulled up the hood of his cloak and nudged his horse into a trot, for he had no desire to be caught in the rain. But with each step the horse took, Sampson felt his soul weigh down with a duty he did not ask for or want.

***

As daylight gave way to evening, the harbour of Trevena came into view. Sampson had made good time. He had come prepared to spend the night under a hedge, but he had the coins for a room at a tavern — for Alden had made sure of it.

As the hour was not late, Sampson decided to turn his horse in the direction of the town. There was someone here that he had not so long ago treated with an edge of contempt. He owed her an apology.

***

The Bors Tavern was a filthy pit of immorality. It was not the kind of place one would expect to find a monk. But as Sampson dismounted and handed the reins of his tired horse to a disgruntled stable boy, he knew that there was a great deal of good that he could do here. This may not be his sermon on the mount, but it was a good place to start.

With determination, he pushed the door open. The smell of heat, alcohol, and human sweat filled his nostrils. He screwed up his nose in disgust. Just for a moment his resolve floundered. The last time he had been here he had Garren, Yrre, Eadger, and Josephine by his side, now he was alone. Although God was forever near. He prayed silently to God to give him the courage of Daniel so he could go into the Lion's Den and come out not only unscathed but successful.

With a deep breath, which he immediately regretted for the smell was truly repugnant, Sampson took that first sacred step on the path to becoming a disciple.

"Do not look for the lost sheep in the church, for you will not find them there. Go to the fields, the towns, the taverns," Abbot Daniel's wise words came back to haunt. Abbot Daniel was right, as always. Without a doubt, Daniel was one of the wisest men Sampson had ever met.

Sampson breathed out, and with his head held high, he stepped into the crowded room. He took a moment to get used to the smell while averting his eyes from a woman who was proudly flaunting all that she owned. Whores and thieves, he would turn none away, all were worthy, all deserved a chance to change their ways and live life as God intended. Sampson raised his eyes and looked into the woman's face. No condemnation shone in his eyes, for condemnation was not the way of a good shepherd. The sheep had to feel safe. They had to come willingly. There was no point beating them over the head with a stick, for all that taught them was how to avoid the stick and also how to hate. The woman's easy smile fell from her face, and she quickly reached for her clothes, while slapping away the hands of those who had thought to have their way with her. And that was when everyone else noticed him. The room fell quiet with the kind of silence that was never comfortable.

"Oh, by God, not again…" A man shoved a woman roughly from his lap and stood up. "Now I told ee before, I don't need your sort in me 'ouse. Yer bad for business. No," the innkeeper raised his hands in mute appeal. "Don't go." He watched as his patrons quickly put down their pitchers before making a hasty retreat for the door.

Sampson suppressed a smile. They may flee from him now, but later they would flock towards him. They would listen to what he had to say. They would turn their faces to the light and welcome God into their lives with open arms and, more importantly, an open heart.

"Now look what ee done," the innkeeper chastised, he looked thoroughly fed up. "What do ee want? I thought we'd seen the back of ee."

"A room, if you please," Sampson stated as he pulled out a few coins from his purse. "You do have one, don't you?" he asked when he saw the innkeeper's frown.

"I kent 'member."

"This is a tavern?" Sampson asked as he placed the coins on a table. The innkeeper's eyes lit up when he saw the coins worth.

"I 'ave a stable. And that were good 'nough fer Jesus, weren't it?" the innkeeper laughed at his own quick wit, but when he turned around to share his jest with his patrons, he remembered that everyone had left and his laughter died away. "Will that serve ee?"

"Does it have a bed?" Sampson asked. Instead of feeling offended he felt highly amused by this confrontation.

"A bed that is good 'nough fer 'orses."

"I will take it, but I do not think such a humble room is worth so much silver," Sampson said as he slowly and purposefully put the coins back into his purse.

"Yer wanna proper bed, with a mattress and blankets?" the innkeeper asked, his attention fully focused on Sampson's purse.

"I would very much like a proper bed, with a mattress and blankets. Thank you," Sampson said, and he retrieved one of the coins from his purse and placed it on his palm.

The innkeeper licked his lips as if in anticipation of a great feast.

"Water ter wash in? I reckon yer be wanting that too."

"A little water does wash away the dirt from the road," Sampson agreed, trying his hardest not to laugh as he reached for another coin.

"I s'ppose yer be wanting food as well."

Sampson took out another coin. "Your wife is a very good cook."

"Aye, that she is. CHESTEN," the innkeeper yelled his wife's name from the corner of his mouth. "Chesten, that monk of yours is back. CHESTEN? Are yer deaf?" The innkeeper picked up a tankard of ale as he made his way towards the staircase. "Chesten, what the 'ell are yer doing?" his question was met with only the creaking of the banister rail that he leant against.

"I'm sorry 'bout this," the innkeeper stated as he looked back at the monk. "I upset 'er this morning. I commented on how old she looked, and now she's as testy as an adder. It ain't my fault she's going grey, tis it?

"What yer doing back this way, anyway? I thought yer were heading on ter Dor. But yer look like a man who be thinkin' of heading back up north."

Sampson smiled at the innkeeper's words. The populous of Cerniw considered anything on the other side of the Tamar River to be north. If only they knew how big this island really was.

"I have been called back to my monastery at Caldey. There has been a death."

"Oh, 'ave there? Sorry 'bout that then. Someone close?"

"The Abbot."

"Oh... That's a right shame. I am sure he were very godly an' all."

He was more like you than you could possibly imagine, Sampson thought grimly.

"So what 'appens when one of yer lot die?"

"Same as anyone else," Sampson replied with a slightly confused expression.

"So yer don't jump the queue then? I'd of thought that being all godly, God would 'ave welcomed yer into Heaven—"

"I don't think it quite works like—"

"CHESTEN," the innkeeper bellowed again.

There was a rattling of a door and then footsteps pounding on the floorboards above.

"If that's the healer send 'im up," Chesten called.

"What der ee want a bloody healer for?" the innkeeper called up the stairs.

"I told ee..." Chesten said as she ran down the stairs, her gaunt face flushed with rage. "I told ee to send for the healer. Do ee never listen yer great..." Chesten's eyes widened when she saw Brother Sampson. "I were praying for a miracle. I never expected my prayers to be answered. Come quickly, Brother Sampson. I 'ave need of ee."

Sampson did not think to ask what Chesten's need was. Her face portrayed her concern. He immediately made to follow her.

"Hang on a minute. Yer forgot to pay," the innkeeper said, holding out his dirty palm.

Sampson slapped the coins in his hand and ran up the stairs.

Chesten opened a door that creaked on its hinges and walked into a dimly lit room that smelt of sickness and death.

"I were out at the market when his boat came in ter harbour. Ee looked so lost, I'll never forget his face. I went up to 'im, I did. And I asked 'im if ee were in need of a room. The poor man, ee started sobbing like a baby. Well, I couldn't leave 'im in such a state, so I brought 'im back here. Me husband weren't very impressed. Ee said we ran a tavern not a refuge for the poor. So I reminded 'im about the Good Samaritan, and that is how I left it. I tried to get the poor man to eat, but ee wouldn't take nourishment, although I have managed to get some water into 'im. I am mighty worried about 'im, Brother Sampson, that I am. You don't think it's the plague do yer? Me husband will never forgive me if it is."

Sampson picked up a candle and walked over to the bed. The man who lay on it was impoverished. His stick-thin fingers clasped desperately at the threadbare blanket that covered him. His eyes were sunken, and the surrounding skin was black with fatigue. His cheekbones protruded from a gaunt face, and his beard and hair were matted with filth. He was close to death. Sampson reached down and touched the man's forehead with the back of his hand. His skin was cold and clammy. Death was but a breath away. There was nothing Sampson could do for him. He raised his right hand from the dead man's face. He felt the presence of Chesten by his side, but he ignored her as he began to mutter in Latin, *"deus, Pater misericordiárum, qui per mortem et resurrectiónem Fílii sui mundum sibi reconciliávit et Spíritum Sanctum—"*

The dying man opened his eyes and looked into Sampson's face.

Sampson's eyes widened with recognition, and he snatched his hand back.

"Brother Jagu?" Sampson whispered the name as he looked into the face of a friend.

"Yer know 'im?" Chesten asked.

"Yes, he is from the monastery in Brittany."

"A monk? Are you sure? Ee ain't dressed like one? And ee don't look like one."

"In my saddlebag are my herbs. Go, fetch them. Quickly."

"Right away. Right away," Chesten said, racing from the room.

"Brother Jagu," Sampson spoke his name as he sat cautiously on the edge of the bed. He took Brother Jagu's frail hand into his own. "It is I, Brother Sampson. You are safe now. Can you hear me?"

"Brother Sampson? God has delivered me to you." Brother Jagu smiled. He clung to Sampson's hand with a considerable strength for one who looked so frail.

"I have a message for…" Brother Jagu looked at the rafters for a moment as he tried to catch his breath. "For Alden."

Sampson noted that Brother Jagu's eyes had lost none of their kindness despite his current circumstance. He wondered what terrible plight had befallen his dear friend. His mind ran over a dozen possible scenarios, none of them good. What had happened after they had left Brittany? Who had taken the blame for Amandine's escape?

"From…" Brother Jagu's lips trembled with every word he spoke.

Sampson leant in closer to listen, for Brother Jagu's voice was failing him.

"Bastian… From Bastian. He says… To tell Alden that he was wrong and that he is sorry. He said to tell Alden to bring his army to Brittany for Mordred… Mordred… He killed them. He killed them all." Brother Jagu's eyes were filled with grief.

"Who did he kill?" Sampson whispered as a cold fear wrapped

itself around his heart. "Brother Jagu, who did he kill?"

"Mordred and Archbishop Verus... Daniel. Daniel is dead."

"Our Daniel?" Sampson dared to ask. Abbot Daniel had been his mentor. His teacher. His friend.

Brother Jagu nodded weakly while tears gathered in his eyes. "Daniel was accused of high treason. He was guilty. I know he was. Daniel was not the type of person to let her burn. He rescued her and condemned himself. It was so like him to stand up for the innocent. I tried to hate her, for her life meant his was sacrificed. But I cannot hate someone who Daniel was so willing to risk everything for. Mordred tortured him. Tied him to a chariot. He died in the Great Hall surrounded by his enemies. I was not allowed to stay with him. None of us were. And then they took his body and threw it on the pyre that had been meant for her."

"What have I done?" Sampson muttered to himself as he looked down on Brother Jagu with despair. He had feared this would happen. He had feared that there would be consequences. He had tried to warn Daniel. He should have tried harder. *"Dear God, what have I done?"*

"There is more. Archbishop Verus is evil. He and Mordred are as thick as thieves. Archbishop Verus ordered us to congregate in the Chapter House. He said we were in need of religious instruction. He said that Abbot Daniel had led us astray. But I... A voice spoke to me, Brother Sampson," he held even tighter to Sampson's hand. "It was God. He told me not to go. God spoke to me," Brother Jagu smiled, and his eyes lit up with a terrible joy. But the joy was only fleeting, and the light in his eyes soon died. "Archbishop Verus told Mordred to barricade the doors, and then he had Mordred set fire to the monastery. I heard them screaming. I tried to save them... I tried. They are all dead, Brother Sampson. You and I, we are the last. We are the last..."

Sampson looked down with disbelieving eyes. It hurt his ears and broke his heart to hear such a confession. *Why had God not told him? Why had he been kept in such ignorance?*

"Everyone is dead?" Sampson asked, praying with all his might that Brother Jagu would take back his words.

"Iscariot, that is Archbishop Verus' real name. He has been consumed by a demon — that is the only explanation I can come up with. Brittany needs you, Brother Sampson. You must expel the demon and chase away the darkness before it is too late."

"They are dead? Abbot Daniel is dead?" Sampson's eyes filled with tears. "He is dead?"

"My comfort in all this suffering is this... God has not left my side. He never leaves us, Sampson. He never leaves..."

Brother Jagu's head fell slowly to one side, his grip on Sampson's hand slackened. Sampson watched through his tears as Brother Jagu exhaled for the last time.

Sampson sat there in silence. Such a brief conversation, and yet it was the most significantly upsetting one Sampson had ever participated in. They were dead. They were all dead. Sampson shook his head in despair. He could not go to Caldey now. He would not be part of a church that sanctioned murder. He would write to the Pope immediately and tell him of the terrible events in Brittany. But he doubted very much that the Pope would listen to anything he had to say, for everyone knew that Archbishop Verus was a favourite.

Alden needed to hear this. Everyone did. He would set out for Cerniw at the break of dawn. But first, Sampson had to do what was right by Brother Jagu. He raised his trembling hand and cried his way through the sacraments.

Chapter 30

T'other Side Of The Hill. The Kingdom of Wessex.

To kill a wolf is no small thing, but to catch a fox — now that takes cunning. Despite grave misgivings, Alan and Bernice followed Percival to the village. It was the howl of a wolf that had been the deciding factor in their decision.

When they had set out with David, they had not known how far away this so-called Pert lived. They had not thought to bring supplies. If they had, then they would have rather braved the wolves than trust in the fox.

They arrived in the village just as the moon was rising high in the sky. The village, like any other, had a large wattle wall around its perimeter. A deterrent to any wildlife that thought to snatch an easy meal of sheep or sow. Or worse still, a child. But Alan did not doubt that if a fox were to jump on the wall, then the whole thing would come tumbling down.

Percival knocked on a roughly sawn door, which immediately set a dog barking. Somewhere in the night, a pack of wolves called to each other as they planned their hunt. Alan had fought in many battles, but the sound of those wolves sent shivers down his spine and chilled his heart.

A flash of torchlight reflected through the high wall, and a man's hacking cough drowned out the sound of the night. An unsure voice asked, "What do you want?" in Saxon.

Percival replied. Alan did not know what he said, but within moments the door had been opened, allowing admittance.

The village elder mumbled something and started to cough again. Whilst coughing he bowed as if he were in the presence of a king. Alan turned to Bernice for a translation, but her eyes were fixed on the elder, so Alan turned back to look at the peasant before him. The torchlight reflected the fear and sickness in the village elder's eyes, and Alan's misgiving grew with each breath he took.

"Don't you ever keep me waiting again," Percival snapped.

Bernice winced at his words, but Alan was like a deaf man. He wished he understood this short and sharp exchange, but he did not.

"I am sorry, my Lord," the elder grovelled, trying to catch his breath as he did so. "We were not expecting you."

"More fool you," Percival stated as he brushed past the elder. "We seek food and shelter for the night."

"Shelter we can do," the man replied meekly, lowering his eyes. "Please… I will be but a moment." The village elder handed Alan the torch and disappeared into the night.

By the light of the torch, Alan could see that the village was indeed a small settlement. But Alan had not expected it to be so old. There were just a handful of weatherworn roundhouses that must have been built decades previously. There were a couple of animal pens, but when he held the torch towards them, he noticed that they housed no animals. He saw that wood had been stacked up high against one wall and opposite that was a granary. However, someone had torn off the door of the granary, and although Alan could not see inside of the building, he guessed that grain was no longer stored there. Alan also noted that there was only one entrance in and out of the village. That was foolish. It was always a good idea to have a back door.

No one else was curious enough to see who had arrived so late in the evening. Or maybe they were just afraid. Alan feared it was the latter. He watched with a growing sense of anger as a pregnant woman, her five small children and a man were harried out of their roundhouse. All the children were sobbing, having been awoken and told not only to give up their beds but also their home.

"I am sure we can make a camp—"

"Don't be ridiculous," Percival snapped back in Latin. "They are peasants. We are their betters. It is right that they give up their house for us."

"Even still…"

"You worry too much, Keeper of the Blade."

Alan wasn't worried. He just felt that it was common decency to let a child sleep in his own bed.

The village elder came back, his face a sickly grey. "This way…"

The village elder pushed back the wattle door of the roundhouse that the family had been forced to flee from. The room was bare of any furnishing. Skins and furs had been thrown on the floor and dried herbs hung from the rafters. A small fire battled to stay alive in the centre of the room. This was a house of a family who had nothing.

Alan, who still felt guilty at evicting the family, saw that Percival was less than impressed with the house. It was in no way suitable for a fox of his stature.

"This will not do," Percival yelled, his eyes flashing with anger. "Your pigs are better housed than this."

"We don't have any pigs," the village elder daringly pointed out.

Percival raised his hand as if to strike. The village elder closed his eyes and waited for the blow.

"Bernice," Alan whispered quickly. "Translate."

But Bernice seemed to be transfixed by what she was witnessing. Her lips moved, but no words came forth.

"You will pay for your insolence," Percival hissed, dropping his hand for he had thought of a much better way to punish this disobedient serf. "By the gods, you will pay. But in the meantime, get us some food."

"What food?" The village elder asked with desperation. "The soldiers came a sennight ago, and they took everything. They even took the goat. We lost a babe yesterday because he did not have anything to drink, the goat was all that was keeping him alive."

"Why would I want to know this? As far as I am concerned it is one less Briton to have to deal with. Bring us some food now, or suffer the consequence. Do you need a reminder of what happens to those who disobey me?"

"I cannot give you what I do not have," the village elder wheezed.

"Food. Now," Percival demanded. He took a menacing step towards the village elder. "I do not want to hear any more of your excuses."

The village elder looked at Percival with defeat in his eyes. But he bowed respectfully all the same as if Percival were a king and he the fool.

"Sit yourself down then. You might as well make yourself at home," Percival said, switching back to Latin.

But like the unwelcomed guests that they were, Bernice and Alan remained standing.

"I do not understand how people live like this," Percival continued. "Filthy pigs. I would not touch the furs," he warned, looking at Bernice as he did so. "They are crawling with fleas and goodness knows what else. It is no wonder so many of them die. They have no idea how to take care of themselves."

Alan narrowed his eyes, but he did not comment. Those born to wealth often failed to see the struggles of the poor. They thought that the poor were poor because they were lazy. Or because they were stupid. But unbeknown to the wealthy it wasn't the poor who lived in poverty, not in the true sense of the word. Alan had noted that it was the poorest who were the first to share what little they had with a neighbour. Whereas the wealthy hoarded their treasure. Locked it away in case anyone should think to steal it. Those with wealth held their poverty within them, and that was far more disgusting than a roundhouse without furniture and a fur full of fleas.

The village elder returned moments later. In his hands he carried a wooden tray. Upon it were two very small loaves of bread.

"What do you call this?" Percival asked, switching back to Saxon. He picked up one of the small loaves and smelled it. "This is fit only for the pigs. What is it made of? Peas? Beans? Acorns? Are you trying to poison us?"

"We don't have anything else," the village elder mumbled in his defence. "We cannot afford wheat, and as for our crops... You ordered your men to burn the grain—"

"They are such liars, these people," Percival said, talking over the village elder in Latin. "They pretend they have nothing, but I know they have plenty. They eat like kings, I tell you."

"You are a liar," Percival repeated the words in Saxon. "You live like kings."

"My Lord, you know that is not true. If we—"

"Are you calling me a liar?"

The village elder looked at Percival with disbelieving eyes.

"Well?" Percival demanded.

"No. Of course not," the village elder stated, knowing he was beaten. "I would never—"

"One more word from you and I will cut out your tongue and feed it to your dog," Percival stated. To make good on his threat, he unsheathed a vicious blade.

"Do what you have to do, my Lord. Without food, we will all be dead by summers end."

Alan guessed where the conversation was going, and he was about to step in, but Bernice was quicker. She took the tray from the village elder's trembling hands and smiled at him. "Thank you, Sir," she stated kindly. "You have been most hospitable. Now please, go back to your bed. We are more than capable of looking after ourselves."

The village elder looked decidedly unsure as to what to do.

"May God bless you for your kindness," Bernice added.

"And may he bless you," the village elder replied, despite knowing what such recognition of the Christian God would mean for him and his family. But in truth, what more could their lords and masters do to them? They had taken everything else. Why not their lives?

"Go," Bernice tilted her head in the direction of the door. The village elder did not have to be told thrice. Keeping his eyes on the blade that Percival still held in his hand, he quickly backed his way out of the roundhouse.

"So you speak Saxon," Percival asked, with a hint of hatred in his eyes. "Did you understand everything that was said?"

"I do and I did," Bernice admitted nervously as she turned to look at him. "It is a wise man who teaches his children the language of his enemies."

"The Saxons are your enemies?"

"They are everyone's enemies."

"Is that a fact?" Percival asked as he took a menacing step towards her.

"That's far enough," Alan warned. "Let's break the bread and eat in friendship."

"I am not eating that, and neither are you," Percival stated, snatching the other loaf from the tray and throwing it out of the door. The bread was snapped up by the starving dog, who took it to his hiding place in the shadows so he could eat in peace.

"That bread was probably all the village had left," Bernice berated.

"How dare you throw it to a dog when there are children in this village that are starving."

Percival smirked in the face of Bernice's reprimand. "I can see why you are taken with her. She has quite a temper. I like that in a woman. How about we share her?" Percival took another step towards Bernice. "I am sure she is quite the wildcat in bed."

"How about we don't," Alan replied, stepping in front of Bernice.

Percival laughed and sheathed his knife. "I was only jesting. I expect she is full of the pox, anyway. Right… I am going to find myself some real food and a real woman, not one that dresses up in men's clothes. Don't wait up for me. But I permit you to dream of me," he said looking at Bernice.

"I do not need your permission. For I have no intention of dreaming of you."

"One day I will torment your dreams. I can promise you that. If you change your mind," Percival looked at Alan, "let me know. You would be surprised how good sharing a woman can feel," he smirked at them both and then with another one of his mocking bows, he stormed out of the roundhouse in search of easier prey

"We cannot stay with him. I do not think he is who he says he is. The villager addressed him as my Lord. Why would he do that?"

"The Knights of Camelot were, on the whole, noblemen."

"Perhaps. But I don't like him. And I don't trust him."

"Neither do I. But he knows where the Shield is. And I have to find it, Bernice."

"He says he knows," Bernice replied guardedly.

***

Neither of them slept. Not that they could have if they had wanted to. Percival was in no mood to let the villagers pass an easy night. When one woman finished screaming, it wasn't long before another one started.

"He is the Devil," Bernice whispered in the dark. "I don't care who he says he is. We have to stop him."

"Shh," Alan warned quietly. He hated himself for even thinking this, but it was better the village women suffered at Percival's hand than Bernice. As they stood in that roundhouse, holding hands, Alan wished he had never heard of the Keeper of the Blade or the prophecy.

The screaming continued. As did the sound of triumphant laughter. Alan was spared the misery of knowing what was being said, but Bernice understood every word.

"Not all men rape," Alan stated, as he drew her into his arms. "I would never hurt you."

"I know," Bernice replied. "I know you would never—"

The sound of footsteps approaching their roundhouse silenced them both.

"Get behind me," Alan commanded. Bernice immediately did as he instructed. Alan raised Draíocht and waited. But no one came. A mouse ran over Bernice's foot, and she squealed in terror. Alan turned to look at her. And then, like a shadow or an unexpected plague, their assailant attacked.

"Drop the knife," a man whispered in his ear in the language of the Britons. The point of the man's blade pushed into the exposed skin of Alan's neck.

"Who are you? What do you want?" Alan demanded to know as he looked into Bernice's eyes. If this were to be his last moment, then at least he would die looking into the face of the woman he loved. It was a small consolation.

"I said drop the blade."

"You will have to kill me first," Alan replied.

"Alan," Bernice's voice trembled as she said his name.

"That bastard out there who, along with his friend, is currently raping his way through the village said you are the Keeper of the Blade, is that true?"

"Yes," Alan answered. He flinched as the knife dug deeper and he felt the warmth of blood as it trickled down his skin. "And Percival is the Keeper of the Shield. That is the only reason we are with him. I do not condone his actions this night."

"*Percival?* Is that what he told you his name was? He lied. He is not the Keeper of the Shield."

"And how would you know that?" Alan asked.

"Because I am the Keeper of the Shield."

The man removed the knife from Alan's throat, and Alan turned around to face his assailant. The man before him was old and haggard to the point of starvation. His greasy grey hair hung lankly down his back, and his white beard did nothing to hide the silver scar than ran down his left cheek. His eyes looked like the sea when the sun shone upon it. He had the type of gaze that was hard to look away from. And yet, his clothes were little better than rags.

"You are Percival?" Alan asked with disbelief as he touched the scratch on his neck.

"No," the man shook his head with a frown. "They call me Pert. My real name I dare not mention. It is not safe for you here. We need to move quickly because as soon as Wihtgar realises you are gone all hell is going to break loose."

"Wihtgar?" Alan asked with disbelief. "Wihtgar is here?"

"The man who brought you here is Cerdic's nephew. You are not the only one who seeks the Keepers of the Relics. Quickly. Time is of the essence."

***

The fox was occupied. If he had not been, then they would never have escaped. They walked in silence and stuck to the shadows. There was no rest, no stopping to catch one's breath as they retraced their steps up the steep hill. They dared not light a torch but instead relied upon the moon that hung in the sky like a candle sent from Heaven.

Alan kept Bernice's hand firmly in his as they desperately tried to put as much distance between the village and themselves.

Alan still could not believe that they had been in the company of Wihtgar. Alan had heard the stories of Wihtgar and his brutality. It was said that even Merton, who used to ride with Wihtgar, could not stomach the man for very long. Alan cursed himself for being a fool. He should have seen it. He should have known.

Alan wondered if his desperation to unite the knights would get himself and Bernice killed. He didn't even know if he believed that Pert was the man he sought. Pert did not look anything like a knight, but neither did he look like a kitchen boy. He was a serf. A no one.

A soft wind blew. With it came the smell of blood and the sound of animals gorging themselves on a kill.

"We will go around," Pert whispered, breaking the silence for the first time since they had fled.

"What are they eating?" Bernice asked, her voice trembling with terror.

Alan did not answer. He didn't need to.

They did not stop walking until they reached the river, but even then Pert gave them time only to cup their hands, drink a little, and splash water on their face.

"Where are we going?" Alan dared to ask.

"I need to retrieve the Shield and after that… I think you are the one with the answer to that question."

"How do I know you are who you say you are?"

"You don't," Pert replied. "You will have to trust me. Come on. We have spent enough time here already."

The day was growing lighter, and Alan could see the tracks the tears had made on Bernice's face. She was also limping dreadfully now.

"How much further?" Alan asked, looking back at Pert.

Pert sighed and looked at Bernice. "I know a place where we can rest for a while. We have a long way to go, my Lady. But if you could put up with the pain a while longer, I believe we will find temporary sanctuary at the Abbey in Glastingberie."

"There is a Christian Abbey in Wessex?" Alan asked sceptically.

"When I say Abbey, it is more of a wattle hut with a cross made out of wood. They do not have a congregation… No one would dare praise God openly. Cerdic tolerates the Abbey only because the monks who live there are exceptionally good at making mead."

"How far away is this Abbey?"

"It is left of the Tor." Pert replied.

"We passed the Tor on our way here. We saw no Abbey."

"Were you looking for one?" Pert asked. When Alan remained silent, Pert continued. "Please be reassured that it is there. Now, I fear that Wihtgar will have realised that you have flown. Come. We need to hurry."

Chapter 31

The Abbey at Glastingberie. The Kingdom of Wessex.

"Sometime between the death of Jesus and Paul's desperate appeal to Caesar, Joseph of Arimathea came to Briton to trade. But such a long journey had taken a toll on Joseph's body and his spirit was low. He and his twelve companions climbed *We Are Weary All Hill.* And there, he thrust his staff into the ground and promptly went to sleep. When he and his companions awoke in the morning, his staff had taken root."

"It turned into a thorn tree," Bernice stated as she sat down on a stool in the Abbot of Glastingberie's private chamber. A monk put a bowl on the ground and filled it with warm water. The monk then bade Bernice to soak her feet in the bowl. "I know the story," Bernice winced slightly when her burst blisters met the warm water. "Joseph and his companions established the first Christian Church in Briton, here, in Glastingberie." She breathed out unsteadily and did her best to let the water ease her aching feet.

"It isn't much. Not compared to the glory of the churches in Rome," the Abbott, a timeworn old man who had witnessed much and had an agonising ache and evil in his hands, hips and knees, admitted with a sad smile. "However, this Abbey was here long before the Romans thought to convert. But as they do in everything, the Romans had to outdo the ones who came before them. I often wonder what Jesus would make of their gilded buildings while the poor sit outside and starve. And I wish someone would explain to me what kind of God they think they are praising. Would God be happy to see the priests swing their thuribles and fill the church with expensive incense, while at the same time these same priests allow the cries of the hopeless to go unanswered? Forgive me, it is not my place to be judgmental, but we live amongst such poverty here. We have sold what little the Abbey had to help the people survive, but now we have nothing, and there are so many in need. When I think of how much the Church of Rome has and how she keeps asking for more… It reminds me of Judas. And how he complained when Mary poured that expensive perfume on our Lord Jesus' feet. Judas said the perfume should not have been wasted in such a way, but it should have been sold, for it was worth a year's wages. He said it could have helped so many. A plausible argument, one would think. But nothing was as it seemed when it came to Judas. Judas was the keeper of the moneybag. He did not complain about the perfume because he wanted to give the money to the poor. He complained because he wanted the coins for himself. Judas was a thief hiding behind a mask of good intentions. His life was a lie. And his greed eventually destroyed him."

"You sound like Brother Sampson," Bernice replied solemnly. "He despises hypocrisy as well. He says the Church of Rome has lost her way."

"He is brave to say such things, but I fear that he is right. *They have sunk deep into corruption, as in the days of Gibeah.*" The Abbot smiled again, but it was a smile like that of the disciples who had been forced to witness their saviour and beloved friend die on the cross. The Abbot's smile was filled with sorrow, and nothing would ever change that. "I look forward to meeting Brother Sampson one day. I have heard so many wondrous things about him. He has come far for one so young. I do not doubt that he is destined to become a fine Abbot."

"I do not think he wants to be confined between four walls, no matter how sacred they are. He wants to deliver the message of God to all who can hear it. He has also become a good friend to the Prioress. A great comfort."

"What happened at Holywell…" the Abbot shook his head. He breathed in loudly and then sighed his distress. "Trust in the Lord to avenge that wrong."

"That is what Brother Sampson says as well. But I fear the Prioress does not hear him, which is unusual. When Brother Sampson speaks, I have noticed that people listen."

"Brother Sampson sounds much like Bishop Patrick then," the Abbot mused as he reached for a drying cloth.

"Did you ever meet him?"

"Bishop Patrick? Yes, I did. I was a young man of ten and seven when he came to visit us at Glastingberie," a faraway look came into the Abbot's eyes as he remembered.

"What was he like?" Bernice asked, full of curiosity.

"Everything I expected him to be and then more. The light of God burnt brightly inside of him. He could make the most ardent disbeliever, believe."

"Did he really drive all the snakes from Eire into the sea?"

The Abbot laughed. "I don't know about that, and I was certainly too shy to ask him."

"It wasn't the snakes he drove out of Eire, it was the Druids," Pert stated as he sat himself down on the clay floor.

"Snakes and Druids. One and the same, are they not?" the Abbot asked, glaring at the man who dared to interrupt their conversation. "The only thing worse than a Saxon is a Druid. They are children of the Devil."

"If you say so," Pert replied under his breath.

"Is it true Bishop Patrick died here?" Bernice asked, drawing the attention of the Abbot back to her.

"Yes, unfortunately, it is true. Once there was talk of Patrick becoming the Abbot of Glastingberie, but I think his heart was always in Eire. Although he visited us often. Alas, it was during such a visit that an ill wind blew over the Abbey. Many of the brothers succumbed to it. Bishop Patrick burned with fever for four days. Despite my efforts, his fever never broke. He died here. We buried him under the altar."

"I thought his body was taken back to Eire?"

"No," the Abbot replied. "One day, perhaps."

"This is the holiest place in all of Briton," Pert stated, his voice heavy with sarcasm. "What can Eire offer that Glastingberie cannot?"

"When things are more settled, we will make sure he is returned to his beloved Eire," the Abbot continued, ignoring Pert's comments. "We dare not leave the Abbey at this time. Tensions are high since

Holywell."

Alan leant against the wall of this humble room and listened to the easy conversation between the woman he loved and the Abbot of Glastingberie. There was a strange sense of peace in the grounds of this holy church. It was a place for reflection and prayers. The Abbey offered salvation. Peace. But Alan knew this peace would not last. The fox knew where they were. Alan was sure of that. How long would Wihtgar wait before he attacked? How long did they have before what happened at Holywell would be repeated at Glastingberie?

Another monk entered the Abbot's chamber with a tray filled with fresh wheaten bread and some hard-boiled eggs. He set about passing the food around.

Alan picked up one of the eggs and bit into it. He had not felt hungry until now, and he happily accepted the small loaf of bread that the monk offered him. Between mouthfuls, he mumbled his thanks.

"So what do you plan to do now?" the Abbot asked as he, with difficulty, knelt on the floor and gently lifted Bernice's feet out of the water. Then with great care, and much pain on his part, he patted her feet dry

"Please," Bernice begged with a look of mortification on her face. "You don't have to—"

"First and foremost, I am a healer," the Abbot reminded Bernice gently. "Now let me tend you."

Bernice smiled and her eyes filled with tears. "You are surely sent from God."

"We are all sent from God. It is just that some of us have forgotten that fact," he turned and looked briefly at Pert when he spoke.

When her feet were dry, the Abbot put a poultice of calendula over the wound. "There," he smiled. "Keep applying the calendula, and the blisters will soon heal."

"Thank you," Bernice replied with humility.

The Abbot patted her on the knee. "Now I am down here, I am not too sure if I can get back up," he chuckled humorously.

Alan immediately offered his assistance, but Pert did not move from where he was sitting.

The Abbot gladly clasped Alan's offered hand. With the support of Alan and another monk, they managed to pull the Abbot back to his feet.

"Do not cast me away when I am old; do not forsake me when my strength is gone," the Abbot said. "Thank you, my son. Now answer my question. What are your plans?"

"We need to retrieve the Shield," Pert replied before Alan could.

"And then?" the Abbot asked, still looking at Alan.

"Look for the next knight," Alan answered honestly. "Wherever he may be."

"You do not know where the knights are?" The Abbot asked. He did nothing to hide the surprise in his voice

"I know that they are in hiding somewhere in Briton."

"Somewhere in Briton?" the Abbot chuckled softly. "You could be looking for years and never find them."

"I do not have years. I have a few months at best. War is coming."

"War is always coming. There will always be men who breathe threats and murder the innocent. It is a dark time we live in. But then I think perhaps it is no darker than it has ever been. Man has always had a thirst for war. I am sure that is not what our Lord intended when he created us. He must be breaking his heart as he looks down from Heaven and sees what has become of his children."

"Yes, he must weep," Alan replied. "But his tears do nothing but fill the seas and the rivers. And although I do not want to see another battle let alone another war, I think it would be foolish if we ignored the threat. Ignoring it will not make it go away. We must be prepared."

"Do you truly believe that the knights of old and the pagan relics will somehow help you to win this so-called coming war?" the Abbot asked.

"I would not be here if I did not think that," Alan replied.

"I think you are wasting your time. There is no need for relics and ancient weapons. We have God."

"Well then the next time you are speaking to God could you ask him to send us an army of angels and several legions of knights on horseback," Pert replied.

Everyone turned to look at Pert for his words were bordering on blasphemy and his tone was disrespectful.

Pert tore at the bread he had been given with his teeth and began to chew slowly.

"Your tongue is as sharp as the serpents," the Abbot stated with contempt. "With the passing of the years and the hardships you have faced I would have thought you would have learnt by now when to keep your opinions to yourself."

Pert scoffed and carried on eating.

"He and I never did see eye to eye," the Abbot explained to Alan and Bernice. "Even as a young knight, he was always opinionated."

"Pert was a knight?" Alan asked, but the Abbot ignored him.

"Arthur never complained that I was opinionated," Pert replied.

"No, I don't suppose he did."

Pert scoffed again, but the Abbot ignored him.

"Were you there when Arthur died?" Bernice asked.

Alan stood up straighter. He was interested in the Abbot's answer. Even Pert, he noticed, had stopped chewing and was looking at the Abbot.

"Yes. Bedwyr brought him here. I tried my very best, but the wound was fatal. There was nothing I could do but make his last moments as comfortable as I could. He didn't want to die. He said there was too much still to do. He breathed his last in this very room."

"Where is he buried?" Alan asked.

"I am afraid that is a secret," the Abbot replied. "There are those who would desecrate his grave and steal his body away. Only myself and one other knows where Arthur rests.

"When will you retrieve the Shield?" The Abbot turned to Pert when he asked this question.

"Tonight, after the castle has fallen asleep."

"The castle?" Alan asked.

"That is where the Shield is," Pert stated.

"That is where Percival... I mean that is where Wihtgar said it was as well."

"Everyone in Wessex knows it is there. They just don't know where it is," Pert said matter-of-factly. "Believe me, they have looked. They would kick themselves if they knew where it really was."

"The best hiding places are the ones in plain view," the Abbot replied thoughtfully.

"Well you should know, my Lord," Pert said, rising to his feet and brushing the breadcrumbs from his clothes. "You buried Arthur after all."

***

As night fell, the crickets sang a midnight psalm to God in Heaven. Alan kissed Bernice softly on the cheek and stared into her face for a moment longer.

"Come back to me," she whispered with tears in her eyes. "Don't do anything foolish."

"We need to get going," Pert replied with an edge of impatience as he kicked at the dusty earth with the toe of his shoe.

"Stay with the Abbot," Alan ordered as he touched her cheek softly with the back of his fingers. He did not want to leave her here, but she was in no fit state to go where they were going. "And if the worst happens, then you must return to Cerniw and tell Alden that I have failed. Please, do not cry for me. Take up the life that you were—"

"No," Bernice shook her head. "I love God, but I can never be again what I once was. I will wait here for you. I will wait for you forever."

"I will come back," Alan solemnly promised as he pulled her into his embrace and kissed her softly on the forehead.

"You should not venture out tonight, there is an evil moon," the Abbot warned, and they all looked up at the sky. The moon had turned a blood red. *"The sun will be turned to darkness and the moon to blood..."*

"He is right," Bernice stated, grabbing hold of Alan's tunic. "Do not go. Not tonight."

"I must," Alan replied gently. "You know I have to. This cannot wait. If the Shield were to fall into the wrong hands—"

"Exactly. You do not know this Pert," Bernice whispered, "any more than you knew Wihtgar. He could be delivering you into the hands of—"

"No," the Abbot spoke up. "Pert and I do not always see eye to eye, but he is the Keeper of the Shield. He is the knight you seek. He knows the castle. He knows it well," the Abbot sighed sharply. "If anyone can get you in and out, then it is he. But I implore you once again, do not venture out tonight."

"Listen to him, Alan."

"There may not be another chance," Alan reasoned.

"Alan is right," Pert said as he walked towards them. "This may well be the only chance of retrieving the Shield. Don't worry, my Lady. I will bring your knight back to you. Alan, we need to go."

Alan gently uncurled Bernice's fingers from his tunic. He raised her hands to his mouth and kissed her knuckles. "I love you. And when I come back, the Abbot will marry us."

"Just make sure you do come back," Bernice pleaded. "I cannot bear the thought of..."

Alan pulled her close one more time and inhaled her earthy fragrance of rain and sunshine. "I will."

This time when he pulled away, she let him. "Look after her," he glanced at the Abbot as he spoke. "Please. She is my reason for living."

"As God is my witness, I will," the Abbot replied. "Come, my child," the Abbot gently drew Bernice away from Alan, but her steps were reluctant, and she kept looking back as the Abbot led her away.

It was a cruel torment, love. Alan had known there was a reason he had avoided it all these years. Alan allowed himself one last loving look into Bernice's face, and then he reluctantly turned away and followed Pert out into the night.

A fox cried out in anguish as one of the monks opened the large oak door that would take them out of the protection of the Abbey grounds. Wihtgar could be out there, hiding under the cover of night and waiting for his opportunity to attack. Alan glanced back at the Abbey as the oak door was pulled shut and locked from the inside. There was no going back.

"Are you coming or not?" Pert asked from the shadows. "If we are to do this, then we must do it tonight."

"Why the urgency?" Alan asked with a sudden touch of suspicion.

"Because the longer you are in Wessex, the greater the danger to us all."

"I came here to liberate—"

"You came here to liberate? And what do you mean by that?"

"I mean—"

"Do not beguile me with fancy words and insincere promises. You have no intention of liberating anyone and even if you did, how would you enforce this liberation? Would you keep a standing army in Wessex, just in case the Saxons returned? Would you one day think that it would be in Wessex's best interest if you were king?"

"Absolutely not," Alan interrupted with indignation. "I have no interest in wearing a crown."

"So you say now. But I think if you were offered the kingship of Wessex, you would have a hard time saying no."

"You do not know me, so do not judge me by your own standards."

"And whose standards should I judge you by if not my own?" Pert asked.

"I ask you not to judge me at all. I have done nothing wrong. I am not on trial."

"We are all on trial. We will all one day be judged. I always thought it better to be judged by your peers than by an omnipotent God, who would never understand."

"I will take my chances with God," Alan replied. "All you need to know about me is that I truly believe that the relics will help us defeat the Saxons and anyone else who dares threaten the security of our island."

"They haven't done a very good job so far. And I suspect that this isn't about the Saxons at all. We have been under their rule for a long time. Why now? What has happened that makes you spring into action like a newborn lamb? You are completely unaware of the dangers your actions could cause, aren't you?"

Alan breathed out unsteadily as Pert walked away from him, and he recalled David's words, for he had said the same as Pert. Why was it dangerous to unite the knights? Why was it dangerous to unite the relics? The prophecy said…

Alan glanced up at the red moon. Perhaps the Abbot was right. This moon… It was a bad omen, but for who? It was then that Alan realised that Pert had not answered his question. Why the urgency? Why tonight?

Pert led the way through the long windswept grass. The crickets chirp, like that of an ancient people welcoming Caesar back from conquest, followed them as they made their way across the vast plains of Avalon. An owl hooted, and both Alan and Pert ducked as a colony of bats came from nowhere and flew all around them like a swarm of angry bees. Darting and soaring. Swarming and diving. The sounds of their wings flapping drowned out the song of the crickets. Alan fell to his knees and covered his head with his hands. Time seemed to slow while the bats tormented them. There was so much against them this night. The moon. The bats. What was next? Wihtgar and a thousand men? Mordred and a Roman Legion? Eventually, the bats flew off across the summer land where the hunting was better and the company less judgemental.

The crickets, through such revelries, continued to chirp, for their song would not be silenced, even in the midst of death. Alan slowly rose back to his feet. He was glad to see that Pert had also fallen to his knees and that he too now was rising. He did not want the Keeper of the Shield to think that the Keeper of the Blade was a coward.

"Are you all right?" Alan dared to ask.

"Airy mouse, airy mouse! fly over my head…" Pert sang the children's rhyme with amusement. "It is the witches' hour. Are you scared, Alan?"

"Are you, Pert?" Alan asked in return.

"No," Pert replied. "The natives of this kingdom do not scare me. I fear neither wolf, nor bat, nor witch."

"And what about the foreign invaders?"

"I do not fear thieves. For that is all the Saxons are."

"They are more than thieves. They killed your King and slaughtered your kinsmen."

"That does not mean I have to fear them," Pert replied. "I belong to this land. They do not, and that is why tonight we will not be caught. I know the castle better than the back of my hand. I know all her secrets and believe me, she has many."

"How long were you a Knight of Camelot?" Alan asked as they began to walk through the high grass again.

"I was there at the very beginning," Pert replied with an air of caution. "I saw the rise and fall of the greatest King that ever lived."

"What did they used to call you?"

Pert chuckled in the darkness. "Gawain," he answered.

Alan stopped walking. He reached out and grabbed Pert's arm, bringing him to a stop as well. "Gawain is dead." Alan was sure of it. Just as he had been sure that Percival was dead. It was only those who had thought to deceive him that had said otherwise. His father was included in that number although Alan had yet to figure out why he would lie about something like that.

"I must be a ghost then," Pert stated, ripping his arm free of Alan's grasp.

"You are not Gawain," Alan raised his voice above the noise of the crickets. "But you are someone of importance. I will find out who you really are Keeper of the Shield."

"You make it sound like a threat," Pert spoke with amusement.

"It is not a threat. It is a promise."

"I would not make such promises if I were you. Sometimes the truth isn't what you want to hear. Sometimes the truth can destroy you. I know for a fact that it very nearly destroyed me. Now, are you coming or not?"

"Not until you tell me who you are."

"Have I asked you who you are?" Pert queried, turning to look at Alan in the glow of the red moon. "They said you were the Keeper of the Blade. But you are not the man Arthur chose. I should know for I was there. And yet, I trusted you enough to save your life."

"Why? Why do you trust me?"

"Because you have the look of your father."

Alan breathed out unsteadily. "My father is dead."

"I figured as much. He was always a sickly man. He never recovered from—"

"He was murdered by Mordred Pendragon," Alan stated coldly. "I saw Mordred slit my father's throat from ear to ear."

Such words silenced Pert, and even the insects fell quiet for a time as if they too were grieved to hear such a fate of a man who once walked amongst them.

"We should get on," Pert finally broke the silence with a voice that seemed to Alan to be thick with unshed tears. "I am sorry for your loss. I truly am. Your father was a brave man — even if it didn't always seem that way. I, for one, have never forgotten him."

Chapter 32

"*There is nothing concealed that will not be disclosed, or hidden that will not be made known...*"

Pert laughed softly into the night. "You are quoting scriptures at me now? If I wanted religious counsel, I would have stayed in the Abbey."

"I don't understand why you want to keep your true self a secret from me. I am going to find out, eventually. I assume the other knights will know who you are?"

"They will know," Pert replied before lapsing back into a sort of mournful silence.

"How well did you know my father?" Alan asked, hoping that the answer would give him a hint as to who Pert really was.

"Well enough," Pert replied, giving nothing away.

"You and he were friends?"

Pert scoffed and shook his head as he did so.

"You are not going to answer any of my questions, are you?"

Instead of replying, Pert continued to walk through the long grass. The blood-red moon lit the way for them, and the crickets continued to chirp their night-time hymn.

"What were the differences between the Keepers of the Relics and the Knights of Camelot? What made you so important—"

"Make no mistake, we were all important to Arthur," Pert interrupted. "Be it, peasant or knight. That was what made him such an extraordinary king. You see, it is one thing to have loyal subjects but quite another to be loyal back. Arthur saw his kingship as a privilege, not a right. He did not think he was more than any other man. We were all equals in his eyes. He just got to wear the crown."

"He sounds a lot like Lancelot."

"He was nothing like Lancelot," Pert replied with anger. "You cannot compare the two."

Alan frowned in the darkness. He had feared this, and he had been right to fear it. He now had the confirmation that his allegiance to the du Lacs was going to be a problem.

"Is that why you stayed in Wessex?" Alan asked cautiously. "Out of loyalty to a dead King?"

"I could not live a life in exile. This is my home. My," he cleared his throat. "Arthur's people... They loved me. They took me in. They hid me from the Saxons. They kept me safe. Just like they had always done. My father, he was a powerful man. A warrior. If I said his name you would recognise it. He had two sons. My elder brother was a sickly child but my father doted on him. Whereas I was the illegitimate bastard. The dirty secret. Sometimes I wondered why he did not drown me at birth. It would have been the merciful thing to have done. Instead, I was forced to live a life of fear and ridicule. Every day I begged for scraps. Every day I feared a beating."

"Some men do not deserve children," Alan replied, genuinely appalled by Pert's story. Although he was confused as to why Pert was telling it.

"I agree. Some men do not. When I was eight, my father sent me away to learn the ways of a knight. He said he did not think I would amount to much, but he could not bear to look into my face for a moment longer. I fell on my knees in front of him and begged him to change his mind. I had no love for him, but I feared what he would do to my mother. His control over her was almost absolute. She was courageous, in her own way. She used to steal food from the kitchen and give it to me in secret. She would tend my cuts and bruises. Once she even took a beating for me."

"Why did she not take you and go home to her family?"

"What family? My father had murdered them all. She had nowhere to go, and my father's influence was considerable. Everyone feared him. But no one more than I. The day of my departure, my father ripped me from my mother's arms and flung me into a cart. He broke my arm, but the only pain I can remember is the one in my heart as the cart took me away from my mother's love. I never saw my mother again. I was told she died of a fever not long after, but the healer who had tended her during those final moments told a different story.

"When I was five and ten, I had a summons from my father to come home. I wanted to ignore it, but there are some things you cannot ignore. To this day, I do not know why he sent for me. He beat me black and blue for no reason other than that he could. He treated me like a dog. It was his right to hit me. I was not allowed to defend myself. Although I once dared to fight back. One small moment of defiance. But he was far stronger than I. Needless to say; I never fought back again. In the end, I could not take any more. I ran to the gorge, determined to throw myself off the cliff. But a woodsman saw me, and he dared to speak to me. He told me that death was not the answer and that I would bring shame upon my mother's name. I knew he was right and yet, I could not go back to my father. The woodsman took me back to where he lived. His family treated me with kindness. His wife tended my wounds. The woodsman had two children. I grew particularly found of his daughter. She was beautiful. I could not help but fall in love with her. I wanted to marry her but... we could not."

"Because she was a peasant?" Alan guessed.

"No. Not because of that. It was because she was... It doesn't matter. It was a long time ago. And she has been dead for many years.

"I stayed with the woodsman, in his little house in the woods, for half a year. Not once did my father look for me. Not once.

"It was a risk though. If it had been discovered that the woodsman and his family were hiding me from the... From my father, then they would have paid with their lives. So I left early one morning and walked back to... To where my swordmaster lived. And there I stayed with my swordmaster's family until I had learnt everything a young knight needed to know."

"Why did you come back?" Alan asked as he tried to make sense of the story. There was something about it... Something that bothered him. But he could not fathom what that was.

"The Saxons came to Wessex. My father was caught up in the massacre of the royal household. My brother was as well. A generation of men... gone. I came back because it was safe for me to do so. And Arthur was looking for loyal men to replace those who had perished in his father's court. Arthur was a good king, far better than his predecessor. There will never be another one like him."

Alan agreed for he knew not what else to say. But with such loyalty to a king long dead, how could he expect Pert to change allegiance and fight on the side of the du Lacs?

"We are almost at Hordon," Pert lowered his voice to a whisper. "If this night is going to bring us any surprises, it will be here."

"Then we should avoid the village," Alan stated, for it seemed like the obvious thing to do.

"If only it were that simple," Pert sighed and withdrew his knife. "Be vigilant."

***

The village of Hordon was shrouded in darkness. No torchlights flickered. No dogs barked. It was eerily quiet. Not even the gentle snores of the inhabitants broke the silence of the night. Here no crickets chirped. No foxes barked. No sheep bleated. And no wolves howled. Only the ghosts stalked the shadows.

The hair on the back of Alan's neck rose, warning him of a danger as yet unseen.

Pert grabbed his arm all of a sudden and pulled him into the shadow of the roundhouse they were passing.

"Shh," Pert warned softly. "I knew it. Look."

Alan turned his head and saw what should have been the shimmering silver of an axe's blade, but because of the reflection of the moon, it appeared a blood red. Here was the ambush Alan had been waiting for.

"How many?" Alan whispered.

"Eleven, twelve maybe. I knew Wihtgar would not want to get Cynric involved. Saxon pride. It makes them almost predictable. They are not Cerdic's men. They are mercenaries."

"So Wihtgar is here."

"More than likely." Pert grinned in the darkness. "Want to have some fun?"

"I would rather just grab the Shield and get the hell out of here. I have not come here to start a war. And besides, we are outnumbered."

"We are already at war. And the numbers will never be in our favour. Wait here," Pert ordered, and before Alan could mutter a protest, Pert had stepped away from the protection that the roundhouse offered them.

"Pert," Alan whispered his name as loudly as he dared, but Pert was unperturbed and carried on walking.

"My Lords," Pert spoke loudly and clearly in Saxon. "I have some information about the man you seek."

"By God," Alan whispered under his breath. Although he did not understand anything that Pert had just said, it wasn't difficult to imagine. He should have trusted his instincts. He knew that bastard could not be trusted.

"And who are you?" Wihtgar's all too familiar voice seemed conspicuously loud in the silence of the night.

"They call me Pert. I am, but a humble peasant, my Lord," Pert bowed with respect when Wihtgar stepped forward.

"You said you saw the man I seek. How do you know of him?"

"I am from *T'other Side Of The Hill,* my Lord. You were there last night. I was hoping that the information I had for you would mean that you would leave us in peace."

Wihtgar laughed. "You are brave, old man, to come to me alone and demand such consideration. Tell me what you know."

"I was coming back from the market in Meare. I go there every other sennight to trade. I saw a man and a woman. And I saw something very strange."

"Strange?"

"I swear, my Lord, that the shield the man was carrying began to speak. It warned them of my presence."

"A talking shield?" Wihtgar asked.

"Dark magic has been used on that shield. I dared not follow any further, but I returned home with all haste. I was going to the castle to see if my Lord Cynric—"

"Do not bother your Lord. My men and I can deal with this man and his talking shield. Tell me, where were they heading and you will be rewarded."

"I was coming back from Meare. They were going towards it."

"Here," Wihtgar tossed Pert a coin.

"Oh, thank you, my Lord. Thank you ever so much. But instead of a coin I was hoping you would leave us in peace."

"How dare you demand such a price." Wihtgar spat in Pert's face. "Be thankful for what I have given you. Now get out of my sight."

Alan watched in disbelief as Wihtgar shouted an order and his mercenaries came out of hiding. They were a hard-looking group indeed. Alan prayed that he would never have to face them in battle. Wihtgar's men mounted their horses and rode with all haste out of the village.

Pert wiped the spit from his face with his sleeve as he watched them leave. "Bastard," Pert whispered under his breath.

Alan deemed it safe to step out from his hiding place.

"Here," Pert said, tossing the coin to Alan. "I have no use for it. I have bought us some time. Let us not waste it. Follow me."

"What did you say to him?"

"I said I passed you on the way to Meare. I said you had a magical shield."

"And he believed you?" Alan asked.

"Of course he did. I am but a poor peasant. And peasants don't lie. We can't afford to because the consequences do not bear thinking about."

***

Pert led the way out of the village without any further incidents. Alan followed Pert into a small coppice. Here, they both crouched down and watched the flickering torches as they cast shadows on the castle walls.

"She is beautiful, isn't she?" Pert mumbled under his breath as they looked upon what was once King Arthur's stronghold. "I knew she would be. I knew it as soon as I saw the drawings. Arthur, Lancelot and the builder spent many long hours going over and over the drawings. Sometimes they even forgot to eat, so engrossed were they," Pert laughed softly at the memory. "I never thought Camelot would fall into Saxon hands," laughter gave way to despair. "Cerdic does not deserve this castle. He defiles it with his very presence."

"Where is the Shield?" Alan asked. He did not want a history lesson. He wanted to grab the Shield and leave before Wihtgar realised that peasants do indeed lie.

Pert smiled in the darkness. "Do you want to see something remarkable?" he asked with humour in his voice again.

"I just want the Shield," Alan replied, trying his best not to show his frustration with the suggestion of a further delay.

"I will show you, anyway. It is on the way. Come on. We have time."

Alan began to protest, but little good that did.

***

"I thought all the tunnels had been destroyed?" Alan asked several minutes later as Pert pulled open a trapdoor that was covered in moss and grass. How Pert found the entrance to this tunnel in the dark, Alan did not know. And that coldness of doubt made a shiver run down Alan's spine. What if the Abbot had been wrong? What if Pert wasn't the Keeper of the Shield? What if this tunnel led only to death?

"Have you ever seen a rabbit?" Pert asked.

"Of course. Until recently I lived in Brittany," Alan said before he had time to think of the consequences of such an answer.

"Brittany?" The way Pert repeated the kingdom's name gave Alan more cause to doubt. Pert said it as if it was a curse.

"Who was your swordmaster?"

Alan thought it in his best interest not to answer.

"Your silence is condemning. I will ask again, who was your swordmaster? Give me a name. I demand a name."

"You can demand all you want," Alan replied. "I am the Keeper of the Blade, that is all you need to know."

"You do not need to say a name, I can guess. What was your father thinking to send you to him? How could he betray me like that? After everything..."

"My father did not betray anyone. He wanted what was best for me."

Pert shook his head. "So it is a du Lac who thinks to unite Arthur's knights? I must admit, I didn't see that one coming," Pert snorted in disdain.

"I am not a du Lac," Alan contradicted.

Pert snorted again. "If your swordmaster was who I think he was, then you most certainly are a du Lac in everything but blood."

"My swordmaster was a good man, that is all you need to know of him," Alan replied.

"I will have to disagree with you on that one."

"It wasn't his fault that Camelot fell," Alan should have changed the subject, but he felt a compelling need to defend Lancelot's honour.

Pert scoffed. "Lancelot could always weave a compelling argument. No doubt he made himself look like the victim. But remember, there are always two sides to every story. It would be wrong to judge Arthur by the words of Lancelot. As it would be wrong to judge Lancelot by the words of Arthur."

"Lancelot never spoke of Arthur. Never. He did not condemn, nor did he condone."

"And yet his silence said it all," Pert replied.

"You condemn him no matter what—"

"Because of him, I watched my friends die. I watched the people I loved die. And everything I knew was destroyed before my very eyes. If Lancelot had been with us then the Saxons... They would not have stood a chance. We would have won."

"Lancelot was just one man. Don't you dare blame him for Arthur's failures. And I doubt very much that Lancelot could have done anything to change the outcome of the war."

"You didn't know him very well then," Pert replied with a terrible seething anger.

This is what Alan had feared. Lancelot was hated and therefore so was anyone who had ever associated with him. How would he convince these loyal knights of Arthur to fight for Alden? There was no point in finding the knights or the relics if they refused to cooperate.

"Before you judge Lancelot. Before you condemn him, maybe you should look to yourself. I do not hold with people who blame others for their own mistakes."

"Spoken like a true du Lac," Pert scoffed. "It is as if *he* were standing in front of me with his holier-than-thou attitude. If I had known who you were—"

"Let me guess... You would not have saved us from Wihtgar's treachery. You would rather the relics were forever lost than come under the control of a man who wants to use them to unite the people and bring a peace to this island that would last for generations."

"I used to think like you. I used to think I could change the way things were for the better. But let me spare you the agony of finding out the hard way. Even with the relics, what you speak of is nothing but a dream. I am an old man, and I have seen much. I do not believe there is such a thing as peace."

"Then let me convince you. Help me. Help me unite the knights and the relics, and I will give you and Briton the peace that you both crave."

Pert shook his head and turned back to look at the castle.

Alan breathed out unsteadily and rose to his feet. There was no point continuing. He knew when he was beaten.

"Rabbits," Pert blurted the word out, and Alan was taken by surprise.

"What about them?" Alan asked nervously.

"They are not like hares, they live in warrens. Think of Camelot as a huge warren. There is more than one entrance, and there are ever so many tunnels. This one will lead us to where we want to go. But we must be careful. For we will be walking right under Cerdic's Great Hall."

***

The tunnel was dark and cold and narrow. But to Alan's surprise, the air did not smell of mustiness or mice. Instead, it smelled of a church. Of incense burning. Alan closed his eyes, for they were of no use anyway, and touched the wall on either side of him. The walls were rough and surprisingly made of stone.

"We are about to walk under the Great Hall," Pert whispered in the darkness. "Tread carefully, Keeper of the Blade."

Alan opened his eyes. A strange light came down from the cracks in the floor above their heads, and it made seeing where to place his feet easier. Above them, men snored. Pert looked over his shoulder and grinned. Pert was enjoying this, Alan realised. He relished the challenge and the adventure.

Pert put his finger to his lips, reminding Alan to be silent, but Alan needed no reminder. This was madness.

Above them, a dog began to whine and scratch at the Hall floor. Alan feared the worst when the dog began to bark excitedly. Angry footsteps pounded on the floorboards above, and then the dog cried out as a hand connected with his back. The Saxon hissed something in his language and hit the dog again.

"Let's go," Pert mouthed the words as he looked back over his shoulder.

"This is suicide," Alan mumbled under his breath.

The further they walked the stronger the smell of incense became. It was so overwhelming that it was becoming difficult to breathe. Sweat broke out upon Alan's brow, and he found himself gasping for breath, he could not help it. But he wasn't the only one. Ahead of him, Pert was also struggling to breathe.

They came to a sort of cross-roads. Pert was right when he said there were many tunnels. Alan wondered how many of these tunnels Cerdic was aware of.

"This way," Pert stated.

The tunnel led to a small room, and it was here that the incense burned. The air was so thick with the smell of Frankincense that Alan's eyes stung and he felt nauseous. A lit torch was attached to the wall, and Pert reached up and took it down.

"We were expected?" Alan coughed, clearing his throat of the burning taste of incense. "What is this game that you are playing with me?"

"It is no game," Pert replied. "Follow me."

"I am not taking one more step until you tell me who you really are and what this is all about," Alan stated with a growing sense of anger.

"My name is unimportant. Arthur may be dead and the knights scattered, but their memories live on. They live on here."

"So what is this, some sort of shrine?" Alan spoke with ridicule as he looked around the tiny room.

"Not quite," Pert replied. "We need to go up those steps and through that door," Pert moved his torch, so the steps and the door were illuminated.

"And what is on the other side of the door?"

"You will have to open it to find out. Trust me, Alan. You will want to see this."

"I want the Shield. You are wasting my time," Alan turned to leave, he had had enough of Pert's games.

"Behind that door is Arthur's Round Table. For us… For those who are left… It is as sacred as the cross that Jesus died on."

Alan paused, although he did not turn around.

"Do you not want to see it?"

"You lie. Behind that door is Wihtgar and his mercenaries," Alan stated over his shoulder, for he was sure that Pert was leading him straight into a trap.

"If that were so it would indeed be a sacrilege. You wanted the Shield. I'm taking you to the Shield. The Shield is in that room, along with a million memories and a hundred ghosts. You can stay here if you want and I will retrieve the Shield. I just thought you might like to see…"

Alan heard Pert's footsteps as he slowly climbed the stairs, and he heard the creak of the door as it swung open on rusty hinges. Like a stubborn donkey, Alan was determined not to turn around. If Wihtgar wanted to stab him in the back, it would be no different to what Pert had just done. But nothing happened. The silence stretched on as surely as the incense continued to burn. In the end, curiosity got the better of him, and Alan turned around.

Pert had left the door open, and without conscious thought, Alan walked up the steps. He paused in the doorway, for there was a wall directly in front of him, but to the side of the wall, a light beckoned. Alan followed the light, and before he knew it, he was in a room that was larger than any Great Hall he had ever been in. And there, as if in a dream, was Arthur's famous table. It was large and round, just like in the stories. The wood was highly polished, and it reflected the light of the many torches that hung on sconces around the chamber. The empty chairs had been pushed in, waiting patiently for the knights to take their place once again.

"This is our church," Pert stated. He was holding onto the back of a chair and staring across the length of the wide table. His eyes were resting on the chair directly opposite. "But the congregation are dead. Or hiding, much like the disciples after Jesus died," Pert breathed in unsteadily. "Cerdic blocked up the door," Pert nodded towards a large archway where two huge oak doors still hung. "The only way into this room is through the tunnel. Cerdic does not even know there is a door there. A clever trick. A wall that hides a door, but at the same time blends with the rest of the room. One of Lancelot's better ideas." Pert sighed and looked down at the table. "Every day the table is polished. Our one small act of defiance. It is a shame that Cerdic will never know."

Alan stepped further into the room, his hand reaching out to touch the back of the chair that Pert was staring at. He then touched the table itself. The wood was warm and smooth under his fingertips. The table looked as if it had just come from the carpenter. There were no rings from wine goblets scarring the wood. No scratches of any kind. Alan shook his head in wonder. Here the knights had gathered. Here they had debated.

"This is where Arthur sat," Pert stated. "And where you are, that is where Lancelot sat."

"This was Lancelot's chair?" Alan asked, touching the chair again.

"Yes," Pert replied. "And that was Gawain's," Pert pointed. "Tristan sat there. Bedwyr there. Bors, Gareth, Leodgrance…" Pert's words faded to nothing. There were so many chairs belonging to so many knights. It would have taken an age to name them all. Pert's eyes flicked back not to Alan, but to the chair Alan was holding.

"Where did you sit?" Alan asked.

Pert gripped Arthur's chair so tight that his knuckles showed white. "Over there, next to Leodgrance. *This* is what Lancelot abandoned. This empty table is his legacy."

"I did not come here to talk of Lancelot," Alan stated, letting go of Lancelot's chair and taking a step back. "I came here for the Shield and…for you."

"I am old. I am no use to you. But tell me, what will you do with *Ochain* when you possess her? Will you use her to fight the Saxons? Or will you use her for some other purpose? Will you use her for revenge? Will you use her to help kill Mordred?"

"Where is it?"

Pert looked at the centre of the table where a Christian cross had been carved into the smooth woodwork. "The Shield is underneath the cross, but to retrieve it, you will have to break the table."

Alan looked at the carving and then back into Pert's face in disbelief. "The Shield is in the table? How did it get there?"

"*Ochain* is part of the table. And how she got there is of no importance."

"You want me to break the table? Surely there is another way?"

"This table was not designed to be empty. What point is a table if no one sits around it?" Pert spoke with much bitterness. "It is like a bell without a hammer. A knight without a king. The days of the Round Table are over. It should be destroyed, like the knights who sat around it were. By God, I hate him," Pert looked back at

Lancelot's chair. "And I will never forgive him for what he did to us."

"You had better fetch me an axe then," Alan replied, he had had enough of Pert and his accusations. And dawn was just on the horizon. They were running out of time. "I will not leave without the Shield."

"And so like Lancelot, you would desecrate something that was holy. Something that was precious. Shame on you, Keeper of the Blade. Shame on you. And shame on Lancelot. I hope he is roasting in Hell for all the pain and heartache he has caused."

Chapter 33

The Kingdom of Cerniw.

"*Do not let your hearts be troubled. Do not let your hearts be troubled. Do not let your hearts be troubled and do not be afraid...*"

Sampson closed his eyes as he choked back on yet another sob. Abbot Daniel was dead. He was dead. All the monks. All his friends. They were all dead.

The guilt that came from surviving when everyone else had died was a heavy burden to bear. Sampson knew he could give up his suffering to God, and he knew God would take up the yolk. But this was *his* punishment. *His* burden. *His* yolk to carry. It wasn't God's.

"Oh, Daniel..." Sampson sniffed back his tears. What good would come of the world now that Satan was in charge?

Sampson had left Trevena at first light. Chesten had wrapped up a small freshly baked loaf and had handed it to him.

"Thank you," he had said, looking down at her small offering. Chesten was not like her husband. She did not look for profit in everything. She gave freely, and she felt deeply. When first they had met, Sampson had misjudged her. He had judged her by her husband's actions. He would not make that mistake again.

"Do not worry about Brother Jagu, may God rest 'is soul," Chesten had said, as she placed her work-worn hand on top of his for a moment. "I will make sure ee has a proper burial. A proper

Christian burial. The poor, poor man."

"If it were not for the heat, I would take his body back to Dor," Sampson had stated. Brother Jagu had sacrificed so much so that his message could get through. He deserved a eulogy, and a Requiem delivered by a Bishop and witnessed by a king. But the heat brought the flies, and everyone knows that the flies have no respect for the dead. And besides, Sampson did not have the time or the coins to hire a cart and horse.

"I know ee would. But do not fret. Brother Jagu will be safe enough in Trevena. This soil is as good as any other. And I will tend to 'is grave and pray for 'is soul every day so that ee finds peace in 'is death."

"Thank you, Chesten, for everything you did for Brother Jagu. If it were not for you, he would have died in the street. Instead…"

"God was guiding me hands," Chesten had replied. "I know you do not think much of me, Brother Sampson," she glanced back at the tavern before turning back to look at him. "And I know you think me lowly and… Well, I wanted yer to know… I…I…think a lot of ee. Brother Sampson, when yer speak people do listen to ee. Aye, they might curse yer to start with…"

Sampson laughed softly at her words, although his laughter was thick with grief.

"But I think they cursed Jesus as well, didn't they?"

"They still do," Sampson replied mournfully.

"Well, folk do curse what they don't understand. And I think for some, Jesus' teachings are beyond them. Ee told us to love our neighbour, but how do we do that when we don't know how to love ourselves?"

Such wise words from someone so humbly born. Sampson had not known what to say. He had never thought about it like that before.

"We need saving, Brother Sampson, from ourselves if nothing else. Never give up on us. We need God, and Jesus, and you."

"You are a good Christian woman, Chesten. I will pray for you."

She smiled at his words. "And I you. God go with you, Brother Sampson. God go with you."

***

The flies were gathering and tormenting his horse. The horse shook his head to dislodge the flies, but they just came back again. There was no getting away from them.

Sampson allowed his horse to come to a stop. He needed a moment to gather his emotions. What good would it do if he were to enter Dor and not be able to speak a word of what had happened?

Sampson wondered what Alden would do when he learnt the truth? But more importantly, what could he do? What did Bastian expect Alden to do? The Breton army outnumbered the Cerniw one. They had more men, more arms, more horses, more everything. And of course, they had Mordred and the backing of the Church of Rome. What hope could the army of Cerniw have against such numbers?

Sampson sighed as he nudged his horse on again. It all seemed so hopeless.

As Dor came into view, Sampson's horse picked up the pace. For the animal was glad to be home. And yet, Sampson felt no pleasure in his return. For his news was too grave and the consequences too far-reaching. He was a man of peace. He did not sanction war. But what other option was there? The monks were dead. The monastery destroyed. Someone had to stand up and say something. Do something. Their deaths could not be forgotten. They had to be avenged. But Sampson felt conflicted. Daniel would not have wanted bloodshed in his name. Perhaps this was the time to be cautious. It was not the time for rash decisions that would later be regretted.

Sampson looked up at the archers that patrolled the battlements.

"God will shoot them with his arrows; they will suddenly be struck down..." Sampson mumbled the Psalm under his breath. *"The righteous will rejoice in the Lord..."* he sighed unsteadily. *"Their day of disaster is near, and their doom rushes upon them."* As he said the words, he felt a terrible sense of foreboding. Would he one day see the high walls of Dor come tumbling down? Would he see a beach full of bodies?

Sampson felt a hand on his shoulder — the weight was heavy yet calming to his troubled and fearful mind. He did not turn around to look. He knew that if he did, there would be nothing to see. God's presence was like a warm southerly wind upon his face. God was a reassuring strength that he could not see. That he could not touch. But God was there, all the same, giving guidance, giving hope.

"Let us settle this matter," Sampson said aloud. His voice was stronger. More confident. More sure. Sampson was fed up with imagining the worst. He would face whatever was to come, head on. He felt the hand of God grip his shoulder more forcefully, and then God's hand let go. But Sampson knew that God would always be near. God would be there for him in times of grief and in times of joy. And with that in mind, Sampson nudged his horse on.

***

They said that death was the wages of sin. They also said that eternal life was a gift from God. You die, but once. And then you live forever.

Sampson leant back against the far wall of Alden's Great Hall. The day had been long and strenuous. Alden had seemed happily surprised at his return, but the smile of welcome had soon left his face when Sampson had explained why he had abandoned his journey. Alden had immediately summoned the war council.

The Bishop of Cerniw had sat with his head in his hands as Sampson told them of Brother Jagu's final words.

"So brave," the Bishop had said over and over again. "A Mass will be said. We must pray for his soul. We must pray for them all." Tears had gathered in the Bishop's eyes. "I cannot believe that Archbishop Verus would do such a thing. I met him once when I was in Rome. I can't say I was particularly taken with him, but he is a man of God. He is meant to condone evil, drive it out, not embrace it. I will write to the Bishop of Rome immediately. I will make my voice heard. Even if I have to go to Rome myself. This will not go unpunished. Archbishop Verus must be stripped of his position, and he must pay for this crime with his life."

"The Bishop of Rome will not listen," Sampson had argued. "Archbishop Verus has the Pope's ear."

"I will send some men, disguised as merchants, to Brittany," Alden had stated. "Although I do not doubt your words, Brother Sampson, I need confirmation. Philippe is not above deception."

"Brother Jagu would not lie," Sampson had argued. "And he would not be hoodwinked."

"I am not casting doubt on Brother Jagu's integrity or his bravery at bringing me this message."

"Then why send men to Brittany?"

"This is the first message we have received from Brittany since Galahad brought Amandine home. We have dallied long enough. We need to know what is going on and then we will have a better idea of what we are up against."

"We could get a message to Bastian. Brother Jagu said—"

"I do not trust Bastian. He was the one who betrayed us in the first place."

"He helped you escape."

"And yet, many times I have wondered why he did," Alden had replied.

"What of Philippe?" Yrre had asked, and all eyes turned to him. "Do you think he knows that the monks were murdered?"

"If he does not, then his hold on the throne is not as strong as he thinks," Alden had replied with a frown.

"You think Mordred seeks the throne?" Sampson had asked, looking at Alden as he did so.

"If Mordred becomes the King of Brittany, then heaven help the rest of us," the Bishop had stated. His words had not been met with any disagreement, and that was the most disturbing thing of all.

The meeting had been interrupted by a discreet knock on the door.

"Come," Alden had stated.

A travel-weary knight had entered, and he had bowed humbly.

"Sir Casworon, what news of my brother?" Alden had asked, and all eyes turned to look at the knight.

"Grave news, Sire," Sir Casworon had stated.

"Tell me."

"I followed Garren to Wessex. There he met with Cerdic—"

"Cerdic of Wessex?" Alden had spat the words out, rising to his feet in anger.

"Yes, Sire. From there, the two of them rode to Winchester, where they met up with another man that I did not recognise. From there they headed to Sussex, gathering men as they did so. For what purpose I do not know. They chartered a boat to Brittany."

Alden had sat back down heavily in his chair. "Garren has betrayed me. I knew he wanted my throne. I knew it. But I never expected him to seek an alliance with Wessex. And why… Why would he go to Brittany?"

"Your enemies are gathering, Sire," the Bishop had stated. "It will be a war on all fronts."

"A war that we must win," Alden had replied gravely. "If we do not, the consequences for Cerniw will be dire."

***

The servants brought in the evening meal to the approval of all that was there. And although the worry of what was happening in Brittany was in everyone's mind, for now, such things could be pushed aside for the evening was to be enjoyed. Alden had already sent a merchant boat, laden with cargo, to Brittany. The men on board were some of Alden's finest and most trusted knights. They would discover the truth about the monastery and the truth about Garren. However, it would be many days before they returned. *If*, they returned.

War was inevitable. It was just a question of when and where. And when that war came, many would die. So tonight may well be the last chance to feast and be merry.

Despite his own heartache, Sampson could understand why Alden had ordered such a feast. It was what any good king would do. For it reminded his men what they were fighting for.

Alden had ordered a barrel of his finest wine to be served to his knights and guests. For what was the point in keeping it for a special occasion that might never happen?

As with tradition the King and the Queen were served first. And that was when Sampson saw it. A dark but beautiful shadow. Most people, when they thought of demons, thought of monsters, but this demon was different. He was breathtakingly beautiful, although his eyes were hard, like granite. The demon moved gracefully, and Sampson followed the demon with his eyes. The demon, aware that he was being watched, grinned at the young monk and then purposely came to stand behind Alden's throne.

Sampson pushed himself off the wall of the Hall and began to walk towards the demon, chanting a prayer for protection under his breath as he did so. Sampson knew not to take his eyes away from the demon's face. The demon could do nothing when Sampson looked upon him. But then Josephine bumped into Sampson, and for a moment he looked away. When he looked back, the demon was gone.

Alden said something, which Sampson did not catch. Everyone

raised their goblets in the air and then to their mouths. It was then that the demon reappeared and Sampson realised the truth. Poison. The wine had been poisoned.

"ALDEN," Sampson screamed the King's name as he pushed and shoved his way to the throne. "NO."

Alden frowned as he lowered his goblet and looked at Sampson with confusion as he came running up to the high table.

"Poison," Sampson gasped. "The wine has been poisoned."

"Alden," Annis rose to her feet, her eyes wide with fear and panic.

Alden looked at Sampson with horror, and then he turned to his wife. The goblet fell from his fingers. The deep red wine spilt from the goblet and congealed on the table like the blood of a sacrifice. Alden reached out with his hand and lovingly touched the Queen's cheek. He whispered her name softly, and then he gasped in pain. He bent over double, crying out in agony.

"Sire," Sampson said, clambering over the table to reach the King.

"Send for Galahad," Alden cried as he put one hand on the table to balance himself. "Send for him."

"Sit down," Annis insisted, helping Alden retake his seat.

"Please, send for him. Annis…" He moaned in pain and his breathing became laboured.

"Alden look at me. Stay with me," Annis sobbed. "You are going to be fine. Sampson for the love of God, do something."

"He needs charcoal," Sampson stated. "Did you drink any of it, your Majesty? ANNIS, LOOK AT ME," Sampson yelled. "Did you drink any of it?"

"No. No, I did not," Annis reassured. "Please help him, Sampson. Don't let him die. I can't…"

"I'll be right back," Sampson promised. He pushed his way back through the crowd. Time was of the essence. Alden needed that charcoal, and he needed it now. "Get out of the bloody way," Sampson yelled, and as the Red Sea did for Moses, the crowed parted, and it was then he saw not one demon but many. The Bishop cried out in pain, and he fell to the floor. Several of Alden's knights began to clutch their stomachs. All around him, people were falling. People were dying.

War had come to Cerniw, and it had been served in a goblet of wine.

Epilogue

Benwick Castle. The Kingdom of Brittany.

God had forsaken him. God had forsaken them all. Only the Ankou stalked this kingdom now, looking for his next victim.

Philippe could no longer distinguish what was night and what was day. How long had it been? How long had he been here? He closed his eyes against this eternal night and leant back against the cold, damp wall. There was no rest for him. No sleep. No escape. No peace. His mouth was so dry that his lips had cracked. Initially, he had tried to quench his thirst by licking the moisture on the dungeon wall, but there was only so much, as Ankou knew, that a soul could bear. It was better to die in this lonely room than fight to live, just to be cut down at a later date by Mordred in some disgustingly vile manner. It was better to die alone than for the entertainment of a crowd. He would not die as Abbot Daniel had.

When Mordred had declared himself king, no one had disputed his claim. There was no outcry. Just acceptance. Bastian, that traitorous bastard, had fallen on his knees in front of Mordred and pledged fealty. Mordred had made Philippe watch all of this and more. So much more...

The child was dead.

The little girl, whose name he did not know, but whom he had vowed to protect was dead. She had been brave. So very brave. She had not cried out as Mordred put a rope around her neck. She had not made a sound. But she had looked at Philippe in confusion. He was meant to be her saviour. She had trusted him. Philippe had closed his eyes as Mordred hoisted her into the air, so he did not see the dolly fall from her hand. It was only later that he saw it discarded on the floor.

They had cheered.

The nobles had cheered while the little girl dangled from the end of a rope. What kind of men had made up his court? No, they were not men. They had never been men. They were monsters. He had not known. He had not seen their wickedness. He had been fooled, and he had played the fool.

A sob escaped Philippe's mouth, but there was no one here to hear it. He could scream, and no one would come running, not that he wanted them to. He had seen the evils of man and, if by some miracle he ever got out of here, he wanted nothing more to do with them ever again.

Philippe's teeth began to chatter as a sweeping coldness passed close to him. He had never believed in ghosts, but this cell was full of them. Voices whispered in the dark — begging for mercy, pleading their innocence, weeping in despair. But there was no mercy and no salvation. There was no one to wipe away the tears, not here. For this is where the forgotten dwelled.

Philippe's ankles were swollen, and they throbbed with every beat of his heart. The soldiers in red had shackled him, and then they had passed the chain through an iron ring on the dungeon wall. They had unmercifully pulled his arms above his head until they had almost dislocated them. The pain that had instantly travelled down Philippe's back was like nothing he had ever experienced before. But then Mordred used his fists and the pain…it travelled everywhere. Until all he knew was pain. And then Mordred had… No. He would not think of what Mordred had done next. It was better that way. But needless to say, there wasn't a place that didn't hurt. There wasn't a muscle that didn't burn. Mordred had beaten him until his legs no longer supported him. And now it was the chain that did what his legs should do. But as it did so, the shackles cut into his wrists and blood dripped down his arms.

There was no dignity in the dungeons of Benwick Castle. Philippe had no choice but to soil himself, and yet the smell and the humiliation were inconsequential. It didn't matter. Nothing mattered. Not anymore. He was dead to the world. Dead and forgotten.

He would die on his feet. Philippe had no choice or say on that matter. Mordred had not given him a choice. Philippe remembered when they had pulled, what they had thought was, Merton's body from the dungeons. The corpse had stunk and was crawling with maggots. No one had wanted to go near it. Would that be his fate too?

Philippe's head lolled forward as he struggled to hold on to consciousness. A rat ran over his foot, but what did it matter? Soon he would be dead, and the rats would feed their young on the rotting flesh of his body. The flies would lay their eggs. But at least then, he would be free. Philippe took comfort in that.

As he drifted in and out of consciousness, he became aware of a flickering light. A flame of hope that burnt so brightly he could not look at it. He could not comprehend the sound of the chain as it clanged against the ring. The chain had been what was keeping him on his feet. And now that it was gone, he fell. However, he did not reach the ground. Instead, he felt the bony part of someone's shoulder in his chest and a dizzy sensation as he was tipped upside down. And then he was being carried up the flight of steps. Voices were speaking in urgent whispers. Not that he understood what they were saying. Perhaps this was part of death. Perhaps Ankou had come for him.

He breathed in the fresh night air. The air was so crisp, so clean, that he willed his eyes to open. But he could see nothing. Nothing. He could hear whispered orders and the pounding of many feet. But he could not comprehend what he heard, and he could not fathom a guess as to what was going on.

He felt himself being lowered and the night air was replaced with the smell of hay and horses. The cart jolted under him, and he knew it was Ankou, taking him to the afterlife. He was thankful. Glad. His suffering had come to an end. No longer did he need to concern himself with Mordred Pendragon. Sleep claimed him the same way as an executioner claimed his next victim. There was nothing he could do. His fate had been sealed. Death was here.

***

"Philippe."

Someone raised his head. He wanted to protest. He wanted to shout out. But then he felt the coolness of water against his lips. Life had a taste — he had not realised before. Never had he drank something that tasted so pure, so very good. He drank and drank. He couldn't get enough of this life-giving liquid, but then someone took it away, and he cried out in protest. The words that left his mouth were so incomprehensible that even he could not understand them. He was weaker than a baby. He could do nothing but hope he would be cared for.

He must have slept, for how long he didn't know. He dared not open his eyes, for he could hear some strange sounds. No rats. No ghosts. Just the gentle crackling of a fire and a woman who was singing softly to herself. Had he made it to Heaven, despite his sins?

The singing stopped, and he wanted to complain, he wanted to listen some more. But then someone lifted his head again. This time instead of water, he was offered broth. The broth tasted of paradise, and he swallowed every spoon full with a greed that would not be satisfied. With determination, he opened his eyes.

"Welcome back," the woman smiled sadly down at him, although she did not look him in the eyes.

It was Alwena. He tried to say her name, but it came out as a groan of undistinguishable syllables. He wanted to ask her if she was dead too?

"Shh," Alwena reached up and brushed his hair from his forehead. "You are burning with fever, but for now you are safe. Go back to sleep. Go back to sleep, Philippe."

He didn't want to sleep. He wanted answers, but he did not have the strength to ask any questions.

"Sleep," she urged again. "Sleep," she continued to stroke his hair as she spoke, which brought back memories of his mother. Philippe tried to stay awake but his eyes were heavy, and it was all too much effort.

***

He dreamt of demons. He dreamt of Merton. He dreamt of Mordred. He dreamt of a kingdom on fire. In the flames, he could see grotesque faces that were laughing at him. Taunting him. He tried to turn and run away from them. But the faces, they were everywhere. He couldn't get away. There was no escape. He had made a mistake. He wasn't in Heaven. He was in Hell.

He awoke again, but this time there was no warmth, no comfort, no broth. A bucket of freezing water was unexpectedly poured over his body, and he cried out with the shock of it. But he didn't have the strength to move. He did not have the strength to defend himself. Another bucket was thrown over him and then another and another. It was like an incoming tide. It wouldn't stop.

"You are killing him," he heard Alwena's cry of distress as if from a great distance.

"The fever is killing him. We have tried your way. It isn't working."

Philippe recognised that man's voice, he did. But he could not place it. His head felt like it had been stuffed with wool.

Another bucket of cold water was thrown over him, and all thoughts left him. He cried out in agony, but the torment didn't stop.

"That's enough. THAT'S ENOUGH," Alwena cried. "For the love of God, you must stop."

But the torture didn't stop. The water kept on coming until he couldn't take it anymore. He closed his eyes and prepared to die.

***

When next he awoke he was wrapped in furs, but still, he shivered. He was so cold. He had never been so cold in his life. He needed more furs. He needed the fire to be stoked. He tried to speak, but it came out as a groan.

"You have done everything you can, Alwena. It is up to him now."

"Alwena," Philippe whispered her name and almost immediately she was by his side. Like before, she lifted his head and began to spoon broth into his mouth.

"You should starve a fever," that elusive man stated.

"Go away," was Alwena's reply. "You have done enough damage already. If he dies, it will be because of you."

"The child..." Philippe began to speak.

"Shh. Do not think of her. Drink."

***

Philippe awoke to the sound of a gull as it flew overhead. The unmistakable roar of the sea as it pounded the surf made Philippe reconsider where he was. There was no sea in Hell. At least he didn't think there was. He opened his eyes and stared at the damp stone wall in front of him. It had all been a dream. He was still in the dungeon. But his arms — they were free of the shackles, and they were part of his body once again. He could feel them. He stretched out his fingers; they were stiff, but he had control of his hands. And he was lying down. He wasn't standing up. And best of all, he was warm.

As well as the smell of the sea, there was an overwhelming smell of garlic. He had never liked garlic that much, it always gave him a headache. He felt an intense heat on his chest, not quite burning, but warm enough to warrant concern. His questioning hands reached up to push this warm nuisance away.

"Shh," Alwena stilled his restless hands. "Leave it alone. The poultice is good at drawing out fevers." She then placed her hand upon his brow, and he looked up at her in confusion. She looked back at him. "Your fever has broken, thank God."

"Fever?" Philippe had memories of demons and monsters, and the occasional memory of his mother as she brushed his hair from his eyes. He did not know he had a fever. "Where am I?" Philippe asked, trying to sit up despite his weakness.

"Somewhere safe," Alwena reassured.

"I can hear the sea," Philippe said as he closed his eyes and yawned tiredly.

"Yes," Alwena replied. "We are by the sea. I have made some more broth. No. Don't try to sit up. You are not strong enough yet."

Philippe watched her as she spooned the broth into his mouth. Alwena looked like she had aged ten years. Her face was grubby and her hair a tangle. There was a bruise on her cheek, and there were the red bruising marks left by fingers around her neck.

"They hurt you," Philippe stated as he reached up weakly and brushed her cheek with the back of his hand. She flinched away from his touch, and his hand dropped back to his side.

"There is nothing wrong with me. Now eat your broth."

He frowned at her, but he swallowed another spoonful of the broth when she held the spoon to his mouth. She fed him in silence. She did not look into his eyes again, not once.

"I couldn't save the child," Philippe said when he had eaten it all.

"I do not want to speak of her. Do you want some more?" Alwena asked, but still, she would not look at him.

He studied her for a moment. "Yes. Thank you."

She nodded her head and stood. Philippe watched as she struggled to walk toward the fire and he became suspicious. She had the walk of a woman who had just given birth, or... Philippe had seen it many times when he was growing up. The nobles, his father in particular, could do anything they wanted to the slaves and the servants. Their nobility meant they were beyond reproach.

"What did they do to you?" Philippe asked as she struggled back to where he lay.

"What do they always do to women?" Alwena answered with tears in her eyes. "They shared me amongst themselves. But Lord Josse, he stopped it."

"Lord Josse, who is he?" Philippe asked with confusion. He could not recall anyone with that name in his court.

Instead of answering, Alwena sat down carefully on the sand and began to feed him again. But he turned his head — his hunger had disappeared in the face of her torment.

"You need to eat," Alwena stated, swiping at her tears with the back of her hand. "You need to regain your strength."

"I am sorry," Philippe said the words quietly as he stared into her face.

"What do you have to be sorry for? You did not rape me," she mixed the broth with the spoon.

"Look at me," he ordered softly.

She did so reluctantly, but she couldn't hold his gaze.

"I am sorry," he said again. "No woman should suffer such a thing. I am sorry for your pain and your humiliation."

"I know," Alwena touched his arm briefly with her hand. "Eat."

"I have questions," Philippe stated. "Where are we? How did I get here?"

"Eat first. Questions later."

***

"Is he awake?"

Philippe dreamt he was on a moor. A great fog had descended around him, and he could not see his way. All was lost. He was lost.

"He is still very weak. Please, I beg you. Let him go. He can do no harm to you or your family now. He has suffered enough—"

"*He* has suffered? Tell that to my brother. Tell that to my wife.

Wake him."

"My Lord, you spared his life. Have mercy, I beg you. Please…"

"Wake him."

The colour of the mist stung Philippe's eyes until he could no longer see anything but pure, innocent white. There were no other colours here. There was nothing here. Only him.

"Philippe."

A woman called his name, but Philippe did not feel compelled to answer. He fell to his knees and closed his eyes. Here, on this moor, there was no past and no future. Nothing was expected of him. No one could hurt him.

"Philippe."

Why was his tormenter forever whispering in his ear? Did she not understand he wanted to be alone?

"Philippe. It is time to wake up. Philippe."

With reluctance, Philippe opened his eyes and the peace he had so relished in, vanished like the mist on a hot summers day.

"Alwena," he whispered her name and looked into her face. She had tears in her eyes.

"I am sorry. I am so sorry," she whispered.

Philippe frowned, for he had no idea what she could be alluding to.

"Leave us," a man ordered from behind her.

"No. I am not going anywhere," Alwena defiantly answered. "Hit me if you will, but my place is with him."

"He is not worthy of your love or your sacrifice. Josse, if you would."

"No," Alwena cried as Josse grabbed her arm and dragged her away. "No. Let me go. LET ME GO."

Philippe tried to rise, but he was still so frail and his eyesight was not as clear as it once was. Had the beating he had endured from Mordred's hands damaged his eyes? "Who are you? What do you want?"

"What do I want?" the man laughed. "I should think that was obvious. I want my kingdom back."

"Budic," Philippe cowered, wishing he had more than a few furs to protect him.

"I doubt Budic would have rescued you from the dungeons," the man stated. "Are you thirsty? Can I get you a drink, *Sire?*" the man mocked. The man turned then, and Philippe could just make out his face in the shadows of the cave.

"Alden?" Philippe whispered the name with pure fear. Better Budic than Alden. "Alden, I am sorry. I went too far. I never meant…"

"Not Alden," the man said, stepping closer. "Try again."

"You are not Merton…"

"Not quite."

Philippe looked into the face of a ghost. This wasn't real. This wasn't happening. There was only one other son of Lancelot. Only one other heir. But he was dead. He had been dead for years.

"Garren?" Philippe shook his head. His eyes must be deceiving him. "Stay away from me. Stay away. Alwena," he cried her name in desperation as tears poured down his cheeks. "Leave me alone. Please. Leave me alone. Please, God…save me. Save me."

"There is no point praying to God. He does not listen. And anyway, it isn't me you should fear. Calm down. I am not going to hurt you, Philippe. I had every intention to, but…Mordred beat me to it. And I believe in a fair fight, although I have heard that you do not."

Garren wasn't real. He couldn't be real. "Away from me phantom. Away. Leave me alone. Get away from me. GET AWAY."

"I am not a ghost. I am very much alive. Philippe, you and I are long overdue a conversation. I know you had a terrible childhood and an awful father, but really, Philippe, to turn on your own family," Garren tutted as he shook his head.

"You have come to kill me," Philippe stated, he was shivering uncontrollably now. He was as scared as when Mordred had… When Mordred had… Oh God, it wasn't only Alwena who had been… He remembered now.

"I should," Garren agreed. "I heard what you did to my wife, Philippe. How you allowed the Church to abuse her. And I heard how you locked her in a room and kept her prisoner."

"I left her in the care of the Church," Philippe stated, and as he did so he realised that there was nothing that Garren could do to him that Mordred had not already done. He felt shame and disgust. Anger and fear. Guilt and shame. And shame. So much shame. Death would be a sweet mercy now. "I thought she would be safe," Philippe whispered. "I didn't know they would… I didn't know."

"And now I have heard that you signed her death warrant. And that she was to die on a pyre. You sentenced my wife to death."

"She didn't die. Merton came for her. I helped her escape. I helped—"

"You dare mention my brother's name? You tortured him. Beat him. And then threw him into the dungeons to die."

"Merton wasn't meant to be there. If he had stayed away—"

"Oh, I see. It was his fault for coming home. Philippe, Philippe, Philippe, what am I going to do with you?"

"You can do anything you like," Philippe whispered.

"If that were not bad enough, you lost my father's kingdom, *my kingdom,* to a Pendragon of all people." Garren scoffed.

"Please don't send me back to Mordred," Philippe looked back into Garren's face. Please, he… He—"

"I know what he did to you," Garren stated, but there was no sympathy in his words. "Have no fear, Philippe. I did not save you from Mordred so that I could give you back again. You are coming with me."

"Where are we going?" Philippe asked as tears continued to slip down his cheeks. He would have preferred death over having to live with what Mordred had done.

"You do not need to concern yourself with such unimportant matters. You see, dear Cousin, you have brought shame on the du Lac name. You have lost my kingdom. I think I deserve some recompense."

Shame, there was that word again. "I have no money," Philippe whispered. "Mordred has taken everything from me. I have nothing. I…I have nothing. I am nothing."

"Then I shall take your life as mine was taken. You are mine now Philippe, and you will obey me in all things. If you do not, then I will hand you over to my brother. If you think what Mordred did to you was terrible, I can promise you, what Merton will do will be ten times worse."

"Merton wouldn't do what Mordred did," Philippe replied with tears in his eyes. "He wouldn't," Philippe cried out in pain, and he reached up to his own head with trembling hands and began to pull at his hair.

"Let me go," Alwena continued to cry from outside of the cave.

"Let her go, Josse," Garren commanded, and he took a step back away from Philippe's trembling, tortured body.

Alwena came running, as best she could, back into the cave and regardless of her own welfare, she pushed herself between Garren and Philippe.

"Get away from him," Alwena cried, slapping Garren in the chest with the palm of her hands. "Get away."

Garren grabbed her wrists and held them in a bruising grip. "Your loyalty would be commendable if Philippe were not who he was. We will be sailing on the evening tide. Make him ready." He let go of her hands so violently that she fell forward one step.

"He isn't strong enough. He isn't…"

Garren raised his hand as if to hit her.

"No," Philippe cried, trying desperately to rise. "If you want to hit someone, then hit me. Hit me. She has done nothing to deserve it—"

"My brother did nothing to deserve it," Garren raged. "And yet you took his arm and the skin from his body. My wife did nothing to deserve it, but you signed her death warrant," Garren turned to look back at Alwena. "Do as you are told and make him ready. Or I will string you up. Do not make the mistake of doubting my words. If I give the order for your death, you will die. There will be no waiting for your execution. No reprieve. Just death."

"Garren," Josse entered the cave. "There is an army approaching."

"Mordred?" Garren asked with a frown.

"Mordred," Josse confirmed.

"He took his time. Let him come. He will find one or two surprises waiting for him. But make sure he does not see you. He must not know that you are with me, Josse. And tell Cerdic to gather the men and meet me at the beach. We sail within the hour. You," he looked back at Alwena, "make sure he is ready. No excuses or I will kill you both where you stand. And you," he looked down at Philippe. "You better start praying to God that my brother will be merciful."

Author's Notes

The Dark Ages: Where history and legend collides.

The Dark Ages is, I think, one of the most fascinating eras in history. However, it does not come without challenges. This was an era where very little was recorded in Britain. There are only a handful of primary written sources. Unfortunately, these sources are not very reliable. They talk of great kings and terrible battles, but something is missing from them. Something important. And that something is authenticity. The Dark Ages is the time of the bards. It is the time of myths and legends. It is a period like no other. If the Dark Ages had a welcoming sign it would say this:

"Welcome to the land of folklore. Welcome to the land of King Arthur."

Throughout the years there have been many arguments put forward as to who King Arthur was, what he did, and how he died. England, Scotland, Wales, Brittany and France claim Arthur as their own. Even The Roman Empire had a famous military commander who went by the name of Lucius Artorius Castus. There are so many possibilities. There are so many Arthurs. Over time, these different Arthurs became one. The Roman Artorious gave us the knights. The other countries who have claimed Arthur as their own, gave us the legend. It is up to us as to what we make of it.

Folklore and time made Arthur a Christian King and gave him a castle full of noble knights. We are told that Arthur and his knights cared, for the most part, about the people they represented. Arthur was a good king, the like of which has never been seen before or after. He was the perfect tool for spreading a type of patriotic propaganda and was used to great effect in the centuries that were to follow. Arthur was someone you would want to fight by your side. However, he also gave ordinary people a sense of belonging and hope. He is, after all, as T.H. White so elegantly put it, *The Once and Future King*. If we believe in the legend, then we are assured that if Britain's sovereignty is ever threatened, Arthur and his knights will ride again. A wonderful and heartfelt promise. A beautiful prophecy. However, there is another side to these heroic stories. A darker side. Some stories paint Arthur in an altogether different light. Arthur is no hero. He is no friend of the Church. He is no friend to anyone apart from himself. He is arrogant and cruel. Likewise, history tells us that the Roman military commander, Lucius Artorius Castus, chose Rome over his Sarmatian Knights. He betrayed them and watched as Rome slaughtered them all. It is not quite the picture one has in mind when we think of Arthur, is it? It is an interesting paradox and one I find incredibly fascinating.

Mixing fact with legend is always a challenging task, and when dealing with the sources that are available during this time, it is difficult to distinguish what is real and what is fictitious. The names that come out from this period are usually somehow connected with Arthurian Legend. In the earlier books of The Du Lac Chronicles series, we met Anna, Budic's Queen and Garren's lover. Budic and Anna are based on 'historical' figures of the time, but even they are associated with King Arthur. Anna, it is said, was Arthur's niece. She, like Mordred, was a Pendragon. The story states that Anna died and, not long after, Budic was usurped by his cousin. Budic fled to Dyfed and the court of King Aergol Lawhir. Here Budic stayed and here he plotted to win his kingdom back. It is also said that a ferocious dragon plagued Brittany and her people during this period. I have taken this legend and given the dragon a name — Mordred Pendragon. It seemed fitting.

Britain was slowly becoming a Christian country, but her people still clung on to some of their old beliefs and traditions. The Ankou that Philippe fears has come to take his life can be found in Breton, Cornish and Irish mythology. The Ankou is the personification of death itself. The Ankou collects the souls of the departed and takes them out of the house and places them in a cart. The Ankou then takes them to the land of the dead.

Even the Church has its fair share of legends and myths during this era. One Abbey, in particular, plays a crucial role in the Arthurian story. Glastonbury Abbey, in Somerset, England, is one of the few abbeys in Britain that can boast of being associated with two of the most endearing legends of all time. These legends have not only shaped Britain, but they have influenced her Kings and Queens.

Sometime in the 12th Century, a great and terrible fire had spread through Glastonbury Abbey, and unfortunately for the monks, they did not have the coffers to pay for the repairs. If only they could encourage more pilgrims to come to the Abbey. What could they do? Pray to God and hope all would be well…?

Thanks to Geoffrey of Monmouth's book, *The History of the Kings of Britain,* the nation had been gripped by 'Arthur fever.' This was particularly true of the Welsh who were threatening to revolt… Again. *"Britain would rise again,"* the Welsh said, and what they meant by that was that *Arthur* would rise again. He was the champion of the Welsh. So Arthur's body was needed, and it was needed in a hurry. Not only would the discovery of his grave bring in the pilgrims and the coffers but it would also silent the Welsh — Arthur could not rise again if he were dead. The monks of Glastonbury, with more than just a little encouragement from the establishment, 'discovered' Arthur's grave, and then they announced it to the world. This was Arthur's final resting place. Glastonbury was the Isle of Avalon. The pilgrims came and so with them, came the money to make the repairs. It was a win, win situation. At least that is what Henry II, had hoped it would be. However, for the Welsh, just because there was a body, that didn't mean Arthur was dead.

Alongside this story came an older tale about Joseph of Arimathea. In the Bible, it is said that Joseph was a respected member of the Jewish council and, more importantly, he was a secret disciple and follower of Jesus. When he heard of Jesus' death, Joseph went to Pilate and asked if he could have Jesus' body for burial. Pilate agreed. So Joseph took Jesus down from the cross, and according to the Gospel of Matthew, he buried Jesus in his own tomb.

By profession, Joseph was a merchant, and he traded in tin. It is of little wonder that at some point he travelled to Cornwall. Back then,

Cornwall was known as *The Island of Tin,* and for a good reason. During his travels, Joseph found himself in Glastonbury. It was in Glastonbury that Joseph introduced the natives to Christianity and he oversaw the building of the first Christian church. Many poets, such as Robert de Boron, wove Joseph's story into Arthurian Legend. This idea was cemented further when John of Glastonbury (c. 1340) — a Benedictine monk and chronicler — assembled the history of Glastonbury Abbey. Unsurprisingly, the Chronicles refer to Arthurian Legend on several occasions. John stated that when Joseph came to Britain, he brought with him two vessels. One of these vessels contained the blood of Jesus and the other his sweat. From this, the French poet, *Chrétien de Troyes,* wrote a story about Sir Percival and his quest for the cup of Jesus. It was de Troyes that gave us the Quest for the Holy Grail. The idea of a magic cup — cauldron — was a prevalent theme in Celtic myths, not so much the Bible. It was, in short, a pagan tale that was rewritten by the French poet, with a socially acceptable Christian theme. However, it captured the imagination of the country, and it has been associated with Arthur and his knights ever since. Joseph and Jesus' blood drew the pilgrims to Glastonbury Abbey and with the discovery of the grave, so did Arthur. It is said that Joseph hid this Grail in Glastonbury's well, and that is why the water in the well, to this day, has a reddish hue to it, and some say, tastes of blood. This version of events was believed — there was no reason not to believe it. Indeed Elizabeth I told the Roman Catholic Bishops that the Church of England pre-dated the Roman Church in England because of Joseph's missionary work. This, if nothing else, shows the power of folklore. **It never ceases to amaze me how influential stories can be.**

If you would like to read more about Arthurian legends, myths, folklore, as well as world history, and to keep up to date with my latest news, then please pop over to my blog — Myths, Legends, Books & Coffee Pots — and say hello!

https://maryanneyarde.blogspot.com/

I hope you enjoyed reading The Du Lac Prophecy. Please consider writing a short review on the site from which you purchased my novel. It would mean a great deal to me. Thank you.

Bibliography

(Author Unknown) — *The Anglo-Saxon Chronicles* (J. M. Dent, New edition, 1972)
Bede — *Ecclesiastical History of the English People* (Bloomsbury Publishing Plc, 2012)
Berresford Elllis, Peter — *Celt and Saxon (The struggle for Britain AD 410-937)* (Constable and Company Ltd , 1994)
Berresford Elllis, Peter — *Celtic Women (Women in Celtic Society and Literature)* (Constable and Company Ltd , 1995)
Berresford Elllis, Peter — *The Mammoth Book of Celtic Myths and Legends* (Robinsons, 2002)
Berresford Elllis, Peter — *The Druids* (Constable and Robins Ltd, 2002)
Bottrell, William —*Traditions and Hearthside Stories of West Cornwall* (1870)
Christie, Neil — *The Fall of the Western Roman Empire: An Archaeological and Historical Perspective* (Bloomsbury Academic, 2011)
Delaney, Frank — *Legends of the Celts* (HarperCollins, 1994)
Dillon, Charles Raymond — *Superstitions and Folk Remedy* (iUniverse, 2001)
Geoffrey of Monmouth — *The History of the Kings of Britain* (Penguin Books Ltd, 1966)
Gildas — *On the Ruin and Conquest of Britain* (Serenity Publishers, LLC, 2009)
Gwynn, David M — *Christianity in the Later Roman Empire: A*

Sourcebook (Bloomsbury Academic, 2014)
Hutton, Ronald — *Pagan Britain* (Yale University Press, 2014)
Malory, Thomas (Sir) — *Le Morte d'Arthur* (Penguin Classics, 2004)
Matthews, John, Caitlín — *The Complete King Arthur: Many Faces, One Hero* (Inner Traditions, 2017)
Matthews, John, Stead Michael J. — *King Arthur's Britain: A Photography Odyssey* (Blandford, 1995)
Mewes, Wendy — *Discovering the History of Brittany* (Red Dog Books, 2006)
Nennius — *The History of the Britons* (Dodo Press, July 2007)
Oliver, Neil — *A History of Ancient Britain* (Orion Publishing Group, 2009)
Pryor, Francis — *Britain AD: A Quest for Arthur, England and the Anglo-Saxons* (HarperCollins Publisher, 2005)
Roberts, Alice — *The Celts* (Heron Books, 2015)
Rolleston, T.W. — *Myths and Legends of the Celtic Race* (Waking Lion Press, 2008)
Sjoestedt, Marie-Louise — *Celtic Gods and Heroes* (Dover Publications, 2000)
Taylors, Thomas — *The Life of Saint Sampson of Dol* (Kessinger Publishing 1925)
Troyes, Chrétien — *Lancelot, le Chevalier de la Charrette* (Yale University Press, 1997)
Troyes, Chrétien — *Arthurian Romances* (Penguin Classics, 1991)
Wood, Michael — *In Search of the Dark Ages* (BBC Books, 2005)
Wood, Michael — *In Search of England* (Penguin Books, 1999)
Wood, Thomas E — *How the Catholic Church Built Western Civilization* (Regnery History, 2005)

References

Scripture quotations taken from:

The Holy Bible, New International Version (Anglicised edition) Copyright © 1979, 1984, 2011 by Biblica (formally International Bible Society).
Used by permission of Hodder & Stoughton Publishers, an Hachette UK company
All rights reserved
'NIV' is a registered trademark of Biblica (formally International Bible Society)
UK trademark number 1448790

Quotes in order of appearance:

"Do not suppose that I have come to bring peace to the earth. I did not come to bring peace, but a sword." Matthew 10:34
"For it is better, if it is God's will, to suffer for doing good than for doing evil." 1 Peter 3:17
"A false witness will not go unpunished, and whoever pours out lies will not go free." Proverbs 19:5
"You shall not give false testimony against your neighbour." Exodus 20:16
"With their mouths the godless destroy their neighbours." Proverbs 11:19
"Those who are kind benefit themselves but the cruel bring ruin on themselves." Proverbs 12:2

"If they persecute me, they will persecute you also." John 15:20

"Some trust in chariots and some in horses, but we trust in the name of Lord our God." Psalm 20:7

"It is finished." John 19:30

"Though he slay me, yet I will hope in him." Job 13:15

"Fear and trembling have beset me; horror has overwhelmed me." Psalm 55:5

"Do not be afraid; do not feel discouraged, for the Lord your God will be with you wherever you go." Joshua 1:9

"Outside is the sword; inside are plague and famine." Ezekiel 7:15

"The sun rises and the sun sets, and hurries back to where it rises…" Ecclesiastes 1:5

"All streams flow into the sea, yet the sea is never full. To the place the stream comes from, there they return again…" Ecclesiastes 1:7

"Is there anything of which one can say 'Look! This is something new?' It was here already, long ago. It was here before our time. No one remembers the former generations, and even those yet to come will not be remembered by those who follow them…" Ecclesiastes 1:10-11

"I am the resurrection and the life." John 11:25

"In this world we will face many troubles. But take heart! I have overcome the world." John 16:33

"Hear the word of the LORD, you kings of Judah and people of Jerusalem. This is what the LORD Almighty, the God of Israel, says: Listen! I am going to bring a disaster on this place that will make the ears of everyone who hears of it tingle…" Jeremiah 19:3

"Praise be to the LORD my Rock, who trains my hands for war and my fingers for battle." Psalm 144:1

"All who draw the sword will die by the sword…" Matthew 26:52

"Nation will rise against nation, and kingdom against kingdom…" Mark 13:8

"Why, you do not even know what will happen tomorrow. What is your life? You are a mist that appears for a little while and then vanishes." James 4:14

"Truly, I tell you, if you have faith as small as a mustard seed, you can say to this mountain, 'Move from here to there,' and it will move. Nothing will be impossible for you…" Matthew 17:20

"No one who puts a hand to the plough and looks back is fit for service in the kingdom of God…" Luke 9:62

"They have sunk deep into corruption, as in the days of Gibeah." Hosea 9:9

"Do not cast me away when I am old; do not forsake me when my strength is gone…" Psalm 71:9

"The sun will be turned to darkness and the moon to blood…" Act 2:20

"There is nothing concealed that will not be disclosed, or hidden that will not be made known..." Luke 12:2

"Do not let your hearts be troubled and do not be afraid..." John 14:27

"But God will shoot them with his arrows; they will suddenly be struck down..." Psalm 64:7

"The righteous will rejoice in the Lord..." Psalm 64:10

"Their day of disaster is near, and their doom rushes upon them." Deuteronomy 32:35

The Du Lac Prophecy

Printed in Great Britain
by Amazon